Published by WillowOrchard Publishing

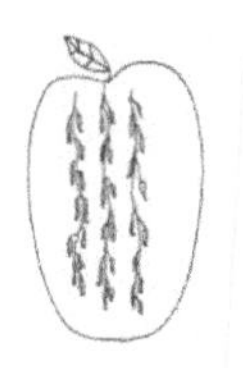

www.lakent.co.uk

Sad Pelican

First published in Great Britain in 2021 by WillowOrchard Publishing

Published by WillowOrchard Publishing.

978-0-9575109-7-5

A CIP catalogue record for this book is available from the British Library

Information about the DI Treloar series, its characters and the authors, and stunning photographs of Cornwall settings found in the series can be found at www.lakent.co.uk

Contact the publisher at info@willoworchardpublishing.co.uk

To the Mevagissey Volunteer Team,
who kept us fed during lockdown.
Thank you.

The river Camel Estuary that summer

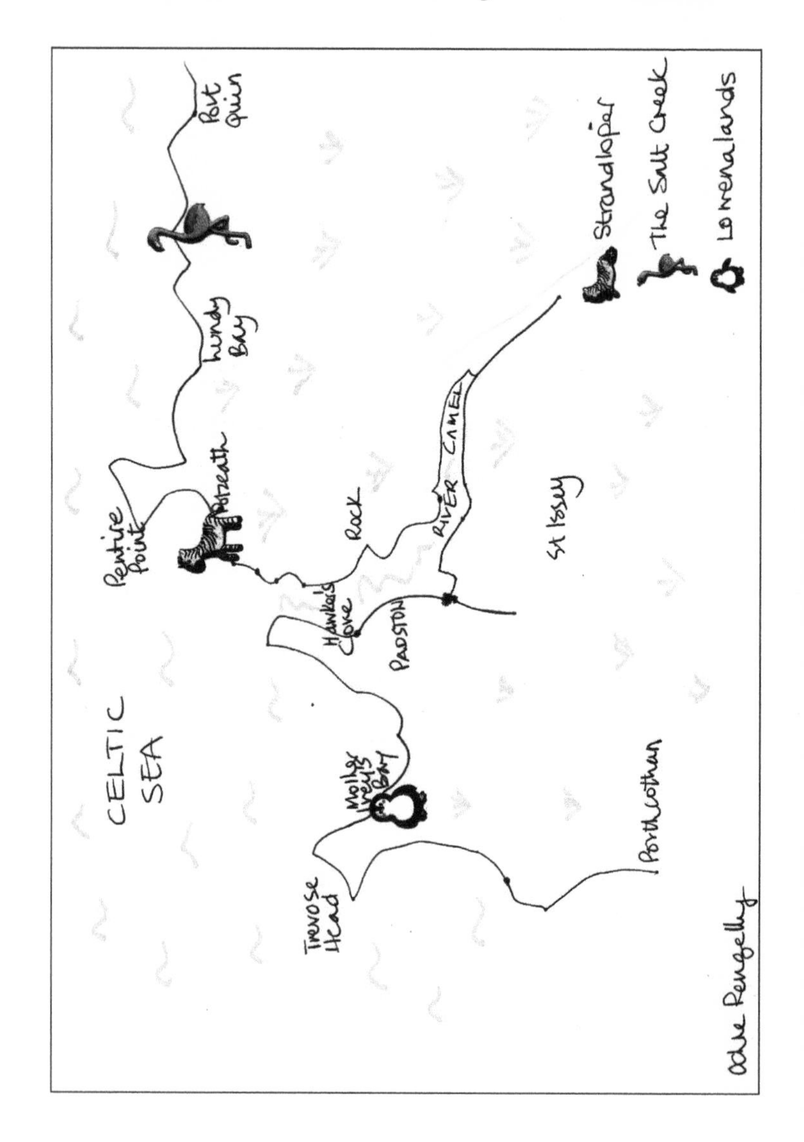

Chapter One

They had arrived on Midsummer's Day. Since retirement, they came every summer on that day, travelling down from their home in Wallingford near Oxford. This year Myles and Francesca Westgarth were staying at one of the Pilots' Cottages in Hawker's Cove which overlooked the Camel estuary north west of Padstow.

They always stayed somewhere on the north coast. Francesca's maternal grandparents had been Chenoweths, tenant farmers from Holywell just along the coast towards Newquay, and she had spent every childhood summer holiday at their farm cottage. It had been a magical idyllic time, not just the usual story of fond memories through rose tinted lenses, but truly glorious summer days of blue skies, flower-strewn meadows and warm azure seas; wild open spaces, golden beaches, ozone scented clifftops, rocky coves and endless horizons. A time of boundless possibilities. So now, freed from the tyranny of the nine to five, she was back again, revisiting.

Early summer in Cornwall, before the school holidays, before the hordes of visitors, when everything was clean and new, freshly refurbished for the long high season. It was the time for young families with pre-school children, retired couples, older caravanners and northern Europeans seeking the Cornwall of their television screens.

That morning promised warmth and cloudless skies. The faintest soft breeze caressed her face as she carried a tray of tea out to the terrace overlooking the Old Lifeboat Station across the small bay. At five o'clock the world was quiet and calm; it was her favourite time of day, even in the deepest of winters. Myles came out to join her at the table bringing Banjo, their five year old Airdale terrier, at his master's heel as ever. After tea they were off along the coastal path to walk the mile and a half into Padstow for the morning papers and fresh bread. It was a morning full of childlike hope.

The path ran beside the estuary passing Harbour Cove and St George's Cove. Normally they would walk along the sand as far as St George's Cove, the nearest beach to Padstow where the 'No Dogs on Beach' ban applied between Easter and October and Banjo would be dutifully leashed, but that morning the tide was in. It was a perfect morning. Across the water the east facing walls of the white-washed houses above Daymer Bay and St Endoc were glowing soft gold in the reflected light of the rising sun.

It was Banjo who made the discovery. As usual he was running on ahead and out of sight as they approached St George's Well. But far from usual, when Myles made his customary short whistle nothing happened, no dog appeared.

'Goddamit, what's wrong with that dog. BANJO!' Myles was annoyed. He was proud of the dog's obedience and his ability to control him. He hated to be obliged to shout, especially so early in the day.

'I expect he's over-excited. It must be the sea air,' said Francesca in a mollifying tone.

But then a thought crossed her mind. Banjo was a keen hunter, true to his breed originally created in the Aire Valley of Yorkshire to catch otters and rats between the Aire and Wharfe rivers. Had he come across something dead?

The first member of the serious crime team to arrive was Detective Inspector Samantha Scott. This was hardly surprising since she was living just outside Porthcothan only five miles away. Sam had been back in the UK for three weeks. Although an established member of the major incident team she had just returned from an extended secondment to Interpol in Lyon in the south of France. During her absence she had sold her house in Truro and had taken an extended let on a privately owned holiday cottage on the north coast whilst she considered her options.

'My first thought was it was like the opening of an episode of *Midsomer Murders*. If we were at home in Oxfordshire I'd be looking for the camera crew. They were always in Wallingford filming the town centre,' said Francesca Westgarth. She was talking very quickly, probably in shock Sam thought.

'Well I suppose it must be a coincidence with it being six months exactly from 23rd December, but it struck me at once,' said Myles.

Met with enquiring faces he continued, 'You know, Tom Bawcock's Eve? Mousehole? During a lull in the storms - which were so bad the boats hadn't been able to go out – fisherman, Tom Bawcock caught enough fish to stop Mousehole starving. It was 23 June yesterday that's six months from Tom Bawcock's Eve. Though I thought the tradition was specific to Mousehole.' The others continued to stare at him.

'Look,' Westgarth pointed towards the sand. 'Look from this standpoint. That unfortunate fellow has his feet sticking out of the sand sculpture like a pilchard.

Sam turned and looked at the scene again. The sand was indeed shaped into a huge pie with crimped pastry. The pie dish formed from a circle of slatted wooden fencing.

'Of course, Stargazy pie!'

The next arrivals on the scene were from the local policing team, Sergeant Diggory Keast and Police Community Support Officer (PCSO) Christopher "Kitto" Betties.

'How the hell could you build something like that overnight in the dark?' It must have taken a crew of people. What the hell are we dealing with here, some kind of murder club?' asked Keast.

'Maybe it's a new kind of activity holiday: Estuary exterminations? Camel carnage?' said Betties with a grin.

'Seaside slaughter?' said Keast joining in.

'Enough already!' barked Sam. 'We need to get it covered over better than this or it'll be all over the Internet by lunchtime.'

'They're bringing up a small marquee from Wadebridge. It should be here any minute,' said Keast. The Royal Cornwall Show had taken place earlier in the month and there were some tents still left at the showground on the A39 some eight miles from where they stood.

'Good initiative Sergeant,' said Sam with a smile. She needed these guys onboard. Local support was critical.

'And the doctor's been called. He's a local GP, Dr Zac

Jordan. He's on his way,' said Betties.

'Excellent,' said Sam meaning it. These guys were no slouches.

With the Westgarths having cancelled their plans for Padstow and returned to Hawker's Cove, Sam and the two local policemen had taken a closer look at the strange construction on the high water mark in St George's Cove. A sand embankment some four metres long and a metre high had been surrounded by the slatted fence to form a giant pie. The sand had been crimped like pastry crust around the edges and half buried in it, poking out from the crust, were four surfboards and one body, presumed male from the size of the feet, to represent the pilchards.

'Could it be just a coincidence? The killer comes across the sand sculpture and sees a convenient disposal site?' asked Betties.

'Nah,' said Keast,' well I suppose it's just possible but highly unlikely. There's been no competition along here. This has been built around him. You couldn't just force a body in without destroying the sculpture.'

'I agree,' said Sam, 'and it's a strange subject matter for a sand sculpture: wrong coast, wrong time of year.'

'That Westgarth knew about it though didn't he? Worth a look?'

'Yes Sergeant. Definitely. Unlikely I think, but we need to eliminate the Westgarths. I don't suppose there's any CCTV coverage of this beach, no handy webcams?'

'I'll ask over in Daymer Bay, but I doubt there's anything pointing over this way. Long time since we kept a watch for Vikings around these parts.'

As they stood gazing over the Camel towards the white buildings across the water they heard voices approaching and tuned back to greet the newcomers. A dark-haired man of about thirty five dressed in cut-off Levis, a washed out pink T-shirt and boat shoes, carrying a medical bag was heading towards them from St Saviour's Point. Loping along beside him was a taller man, forty something, with thick blonde hair, dressed in khaki Chinos and a plain white shirt, sleeves rolled to the elbow. He carried a small rucksack slung over one shoulder. Sam Scott felt her heart lurch and her pulse quicken despite herself. It was her boss and the unrequited love of her life: Detective Chief Inspector Félipe Treloar.

What's he doing here? Sam thought Treloar was still on holiday and anyway, she was a DI now and quite capable of handling this. She had heard good things about Chief Superintendent Nicky Chamberlain. He was supposed to be a giant leap forward from his predecessor, Suzanne 'Frosty' Winters who had been obsessed with the media and fixated on the appearance of her teams' performance in the public perception. Plus ça change.

Despite more than a year living in Lyon, a sophisticated southern French city, surrounded by intelligent, cultured, attractive men, here, on this deserted beach in north Cornwall the mere approach of the bastard could reduce her to silly schoolgirl status. Would she never be over him, or at least beyond him?

Since her return they had not crossed paths as he had been on leave. She steeled herself, determined to be aloof and professional. She had changed; he would see.

Treloar smiled warmly, tilting his head in that familiar, almost intimate way. Sam melted. *Merde! Merde! Merde!*

'I could have coped,' Sam said tetchily.

'There's this ugly vandalism/burglary business over in Polzeath and Rock as well Sam. Apparently, it is not "politically acceptable" to leave that to the rank of sergeant. So far there's just been property damage and petty theft but it is escalating and it could turn nasty.'

'So you're here to deal with that, not for this,' she pointed towards the body being slowly pulled from the crumbling sand of the Stargazy pie.

'Jesus Sam, when did you get so territorial? You used to be a team player. What's this . . . power grab? Is this the way they operate at Interpol, politicking? Treloar was angry and as ever, not afraid to show it.

Sam flustered, 'no, no of course not. It's just that this was to be my first murder as Senior Investigating Officer.'

'Well it's not, so get over it. I've never rated that

ranking hierarchy crap, you know that.'

Sam stood hands on hips.

'Are we going to be OK with this?' Treloar asked with a sad smile.

Sam shook her head as if dispelling spider webs and smiled back. 'Of course, of course. Just like old times.'

'Over here Sir!' came a shout, 'He's out!'

'After you Sir,' said Sam with a grin extending an ushering arm.

'Why thank you Inspector,' Treloar nodded and led the way. Truce in place, they walked up the beach to join the group gathered around the sandy remains.

'Any ideas on an ID?' asked Sam looking down at the face of a pale fair-haired man in his mid to late thirties dressed in jeans, Reebok trainers and a navy blue polo shirt.

'Sandy?' said Betties. Treloar fixed him with a stare and the young officer took a step back, head bowed.

Keast was studying the face intently. 'It's Jolyon Ellis, local . . . well businessman I s'pose you'd say. He's some sort of financial advisor accountant type. Married to a lovely local girl, Tipsy.'

'Tipsy?' Treloar queried.

'That's what they call her. Theresa, Theresa Soames as was, Theresa Soames-Ellis now.'

'Live locally?' asked Sam.

'Mmm . . . Wadebridge way as I recall.'

'Any issues, stories, history, gossip?' asked Treloar.

'Not a one on her,' Keast said, 'not married long. Don't know much about him, London I think, somewhere up there.'

'So how come you recognise him?' asked Treloar.

'I've known her all her life. She introduced me to him at a do not two months since.'

As Sam organised the removal of the body and the search of the immediate vicinity, and a police photographer was recording the scene, Treloar was standing on the coastal path above the beach waiting to speak with Doctor Zachary Jordan. He surveyed the scene in front of him. The Camel estuary was unusual for the north Cornwall coast, wide and flat, lined with sandy bays; very different from the rocky headlands of his homelands west of St Ives. But he was distracted, struggling to take it all in, because he was thinking about DI Scott. Sam had changed. Over a year at Interpol in Lyon had left its mark. Her carefree freshness had been replaced by a calmer more measured air. She was thinner, her hair cut artfully and highlighted subtly. Her clothing was more stylish, more expensive. As his old family friend, Dr Tremayne, the former police surgeon, had warned him on the phone: 'We've lost our fresh young girl Phil. She's been tamed and civilized by our friends across the sea.'

'I know you can't say anything definite, but any thoughts Dr Jordan?'

'Zac please.'

'Phil.'

'Well Phil, there are no obvious external injuries, no blood or bruising. He hasn't been shot, stabbed or strangled and I don't think he's been smothered. Some kind of toxin would be my best bet. You'll need to wait for John Forbes. I'd say he's been dead about ten hours.'

John Forbes was the Home Office pathologist in Truro.

'OK. Thanks Zac.'

'Do you need me for anything else?'

'No.'

'I'll be off then.' The men were shaking hands as Sam approached. Dr Jordan beamed at her and stuck out his hand. 'Dr Zachary Jordan, Zac.'

'DI Scott, Sam.' They shook and Treloar noticed that the doctor held her hand a little longer than was strictly necessary whilst he unashamedly ran his eyes over her.

'Right Sam,' he said, 'the doctor was just leaving and we need to get on.'

'Oh right,' said Jordan turning to walk up the beach. As he reached the edge of the sand he glanced back grinning and waved, specifically at Sam Treloar thought.

'Let's track down the wife, Tipsy Soames-Ellis,' he said moving to follow in the doctor's footsteps. 'Friends?'

'Always,' Sam replied softly with a smile. It was 11.30.

BBC @bbcsouthwestnewstoday 32m
The BBC understands that a body has been found on a beach near Padstow. Foul play is suspected and the site where the body was found is understood to be "strange". News is still coming in so we will provide updates as and when we know more. If you have information do please let us know. #padstow

Billyboy W@surfingpadstowbeaches 30m
@bbcsouthwestnewstoday Early on water this am @stgeorgesbeach, just in. On board saw police + fuss. Wondered wtf going on. Cdnt get near, kept away by bys in blu. Thru gap saw surfboards, heap of sand + black plastic sheet. On path heard dog involved. Crazy?! #padstowdogbody

Andy Sykes@dogwalkingpadstow23 26m
Mornin Bill Was walking Skipper on beach this am, told by another D walker an emmet's dog found a body?! Couldn't get near either. Through gap saw head, looked like someone asleep in sand. @surfingpadstowbeaches @bbcsouthwestnewstoday #padstowdogbody #beachbody

Joy D@loveDwalkingpadstow 25m
Mornin Andy. Me n woof saw buzz (ha!) on beach as walked past. Didn't see much. Police keeping people away. Further along beach oheard police guy + girl by land rover talking about stargazy pie & laughing? Whats that about??!! @bbcsouthwestnewstoday @dogwalkingpadsow #beachbody

Andy Sykes replied
John Billing@SolihullBillingDwalker 21m
Just back from Dwalk with Rusty. Interesting stuff down there! Googled stargazy pie, it's a sardine pie! Christonabike!! Sounds terrible. @loveDwalkingpadstow @dogwalkingpadstow23 #dwalkerssolihul #wmidsdwalkersl

John Billings and 103 others follow, @loveDwalkingpadstowreplied
Andy Sykes@dogwalkingpadstow23 18m
Hi John. Yep, V unusual Dwalk this am, Skipper V excited with all the people!! Bizarre, getting weirder. Stargazy Pies a #cornish treat. Only had twice. Its Sardines in pie, or Pilchards. Heads & tails out, better than sounds. @SolihullBillingDwalker @loveDwalkingpadstow #beachbody

Joy D@loveDwalkingpadstow 16m
Andy, just shows. Lived here years, never heard of it, will look it up. Not sounding great so far!! @dogwalkingpadstow23 #beachbody

BBC @bbcsouthwestnewstoday 15m
Sources tell BBC that scene where body was found on Padstow beach could have been arranged to resemble a stargazy pie. Our local reporter is researching. BBC will issue further bulletins as more information becomes available. #beachbody

. . . .

thechef@thecornishchef&artist 2m
Sorry to hear about body, hope it's mistake. Stargazy pie? Read our blog later; pic, history, recipe. www@thecornishchef&artist. Tell friends. bbcsouthwestnewstoday @loveDwalkingpadstow @SolihullBillingDwalker @dogwalkingpadstow23 #beachbody #cornishfood #padstow

Chapter Two

Jolyon Ellis and wife Theresa did indeed live in Wadebridge but that morning there was no reply from their home when Sam called from the South West Coastal Path which ran along the top of the beach.

'OK. So where's Theresa?' mused Treloar.

'Well, Keast says she mainly works with local businesses in Padstow as some sort of troubleshooting administrator, a Girl Friday type. He suggested we try a man called Pasco Trefry. He's organising a festival at the end of the season and apparently Theresa is heavily involved.'

'Right, so if she's not with him he'll probably know how to locate her. What do we know about him?'

They had reached the end of the coastal path at the top of St Saviour's Lane in Padstow where Treloar had parked his venerable Land Rover. Sam smiled at the sight of the vehicle. 'Well for one thing we won't need to trouble your trusty old vehicle. He works from home, and he lives just there,' she pointed at a large white house just down the lane. 'It's called Rum House, something to do with smuggling spirits in the nineteenth century.'

'Mmm. Very handy for the body deposition site Inspector,' Treloar said.

Pasco Trefry had taken early retirement from his position in Whitehall as a senior civil servant in the Home Office when his wife had died of breast cancer three years previously. He had wanted to get away from the life they had shared, finding the reminders overpoweringly paralyzing and he wanted his young teenage daughters, Keren and Elowen, to grow up in the Cornwall for which they were named, the land of his childhood. So they had relocated from Chelsea to Padstow, and Rum House in St Saviour's Lane.

Pasco's latest project, in his campaign to bring traditional Cornish heritage to a wider audience, was his boldest to date: The Ally Ally Oh Festival. To be held at the end of September, beyond the accepted summer season, it was a risky proposition both financially and personally; a failure would severely damage his reputation and standing in the local community. But since his wife's death he had found himself prone to taking risks bordering on recklessness, and he found this new approach to life exhilarating and liberating.

Pasco Trefry was highly principled and adhered rigidly to his ethos. His festival committee would only allow members whose businesses offered a service throughout the year, not those who closed and abandoned the town from October to Easter with the relaxation of the parking restrictions and the dogs on the beach ban. He remembered growing up in the town when the businesses served the local population and he despised "Fair Weather Traders."

He was a great administrator and organiser, famed for his memory and his recall of detail, and his fondness for bow ties. That morning he was sporting a particular favourite, in Cornish Modern Hunting tartan, and as Sam was arriving at St George's Cove, the festival committee members were gathering at Pasco Trefry's house for their weekly meeting.

'Jeannie? Why such a bad mood?' asked Tipsy.

'Have you not heard about these bloody vandals hitting holiday properties?' snarled Jeannie Hicks who was representing her boss, Cecily Farrant, the owner of a holiday property management company.

'Oh yes . . . somebody said something just now . . . No! Was that you?'

'Too bloody right, little shits! If ever Cecily caught hold of one of them . . .'

'Jeannie! You mustn't talk like that and you must be careful. Who knows what might happen if you . . . disturbed them whilst they were . . . doing whatever they do.'

'I'll tell you what they bloody well do, filthy little bastards,' snarled Jeannie, thinking back to the start of the vandalism.

It is June 16th, the first busy changeover day of the season. Cecily Farrant is in the offices of CHILL – Cornish Holidays In Ledya Locations - which she owns and manages, signing people in, handing over keys, answering questions about rubbish collection, best places to eat, ferry times, boat hire, the usual. Across the room her assistant Jeannie is waving frantically to attract her attention whilst obviously trying to placate somebody on the telephone.

'No! How awful! We'll get someone over there right away. What? Well yes . . . No, no don't you worry we'll call them and I'll call you back within fifteen minutes with an alternative. Now, why don't you go to the St Enodoc Hotel and have tea? We'll pick up the tab. Yes I absolutely promise, fifteen minutes.'

'Issue?' Cecily asked as Jeannie ended the call with a deep sigh.

'Issue? I should say so. That was Mr Hanson.'

'Waterside?'

'Yes Waterside. They just arrived, took the keys from the wall safe to let themselves in. Everything was normal and then . . . well . . . the place has been totally trashed.'

'Trashed?'

'Yes. Broken crockery and glassware all over the kitchen floor, something unspeakable stinking out the fridge; sodden towels in the bath and toilets, slashed curtains and fish guts, heads, prawn shells in the beds. Oh and FUCK OFF BACK TO ENGLAND sprayed on the living room wall. All in all, I'd say trashed was an accurate description.'

'You call the police, I'll find the Hansons somewhere else. Shit we're really full . . . It will need to be an upgrade . . What about The Tower?'

'Well yes, they'd love that, anyone would.'

'OK. Offer him The Tower and get me the cleaning crew on the line NOW. I'll call the police.'

Pasco Trefry stood to address the group gathered in the conservatory of his house in St Saviour's Lane.

'Ladies and gentlemen, I'd like you to join me in welcoming a new member to our team. She joins us as a new business venturer who has childhood associations with our community. May I introduce Coco Holding, owner of The Salt Creek hotel?'

There was a round of applause and a cry of "hear, hear"

as Coco stood to acknowledge the group, but her reception was not one of unanimous unalloyed joy. Somebody was not delighted, not in the slightest.

'I thought we were going with The Festival of the Brine?' said Jeannie huffily.

'Yes well, as Coco pointed out – too many culinary connotations: bottled capers, tinned tuna - so much fresher and modern The Ally Ally Oh, don't you agree?' said Trefry

'And more in keeping with Obby Oss. I think it's perfect, just perfect,' gushed Tipsy Soames-Ellis.

Obby Oss was the name of the May Day celebrations in Padstow, dating back more than two hundred years. People dressed as hobby horses are lead through the town. The Old Obby Oss, the original, and the Blue Ribbon Oss, which was introduced in 1919 by the temperance movement, in an attempt to discourage drunkenness associated with the event.

'What the hell does Ally Ally Oh mean anyway?' asked Jeannie

Tipsy took up the challenge. 'It's from the nursery rhyme:

"Oh the big ship sailed on the Ally Ally Oh, the Ally Ally Oh, the Ally Ally Oh,

Oh the big ship sailed on the Ally Ally Oh, On the last day of September!"

Don't you see? It even fits in with the timing: the festival is at the end of September and the Ally Oh is the Atlantic Ocean. How marvellous!'

'Yes. How clever of precious Coco,' Jeannie muttered as Trefry wandered off to join Coco in the garden leaving Jeannie with Tipsy.

'She can bring us a lot of useful contacts,' Tipsy pointed out, placating as ever.

'Scarcely her. More so her husband wouldn't you say?' Coco's husband, Tommy Holding, was a world renowned rock impresario.

'Let's not be churlish Jeannie. I think she'll be a brilliant addition to the team and don't forget she is opening The Salt Creek to coincide with the festival. I think she should be on the committee. Come on,' pleaded Tipsy, 'she'll be really useful, get us some great press coverage. And she seems full of terrific ideas; I've seen some of the plans for The Salt Creek; just gorgeous.'

'Oh I'm sure she'll contribute endlessly.' *And Cecily is really, really going to loathe her*, she thought.

Chapter Three

Cecily looked up from the eyepiece without moving the telescope at all when the door bell chimed, then raised her hand and looked again at her phone; it had made a whooshing sound as it alerted her to an incoming text message. She was puzzled. "I know for Christ's sake! . . . Which one?" She had muttered under her breath as she slid the phone into her pocket and walked towards the front door.

'Hi, great, you made it,' she had enthusiastically said and moved to one side to let them through the door, 'welcome to Halwyn, come in, come on in Jeffrey, Karen, go on through and up the stairs and make yourselves at home. Start without me, do,' she said with a smile. 'I'll be up in a few minutes, I was just making sure that I was ready for you. Go on up, go on, get stuck in, make yourselves at home. Isn't it great, did you find us OK? How was the lunch?'

'Oh hi Cecily, yes, all good, great. HE had the Fruits de Mer, the big one! No problems at all, the directions were perfect,' replied Karen, heels clicking on the polished wooden floor as she brushed past so close that her elbow pushed the right side of Cecily's jacket back and across the arm. 'Love the feather, wow,' she said and with her right forefinger she had stroked the red feather, flecked with golden dust and encased in something crystal clear that was barely thicker than the feather itself. It was pinned to the right breast of Cecily's dress. Cecily smiled and looked down at the feather before pulling the front of her jacket back into place.

Karen followed Jeffrey towards the stairs. 'Do go on Jeffrey,' Karen said and nudged Jeffrey in the back to encourage him up the stairs before turning back towards the door. 'See you in a minute,' Karen had said as she raised her left hand, smiled, and waggled two deep red finger nails before turning away and following Jeffrey up the stairs.

She glanced outside and could see that they had arrived

in a big shiny grey Beemer, an X5. It was reversed up to the still bare earth of the flower beds to be, parked on the newly raked and still clean looking gravel covering the turning circle; new and very smart, dwarfing her own new red Zed, a sporty BMW. Over the Zed's roof she saw the fluffy white chickens at the side of the drive, pecking at the ground around the pink, yellow and blue chicken sheds that had been another of her great ideas, before gently swinging the heavy door closed, shutting it with a quiet but satisfying and solid click.

She had paused before the hall mirror to check that she was still looking good. It was full-length and edged with oak that had been stylishly washed with something clever to leave luminescent light grey highlights bringing out the wood grain. It was very old, and had been a door frame, and rescued from the barn from which the splendid and reassuringly expensive Halwyn Barn holiday let had been converted.

Even in the early afternoon and after her six a.m. start, she saw that she was still looking great, glad that she had decided on her favourite red dress. It fitted well, wasn't too strappy, and it showed off her curves on demand and revealed just the right amount of flesh for the occasion. And she loved the skirt to bits. It could be business-like, flouncy, look demure, or show off her legs . . . whatever; and the jacket, mid-grey, tightly tailored, soft leather with a V-neck, went with it perfectly. "Flexible", she thought as she smiled at herself in the mirror, "you can never be too sure what you might need to do next."

The See by Cloé lace-up ankle boots were a must, she had three pairs, pricey but well worth it - black, navy, and today's maroon. They were stylish but practical and worked well and looked good for anything; around the offices or at a business lunch, greeting the mostly wealthy people who were her customers, or touring buildings in all states of renovation with developers or owners, and even the occasional council planner or fire inspector.

"Not half bad for a girl from the Crumbles end of Eastbourne," she had thought, and drifted off for a moment remembering a giddy half hour on a sunny afternoon on the beach with her first. She shivered, remembering the chill and the bite of the pebbles, and moved her hand under her jacket and touched the feather, smiling.

Then she had bent to unfasten the bottom three white buttons of the dress, it finished three inches above the knee, straightened and pushed her right leg forward revealing the silky hint of a flesh-coloured stocking, and smiled at herself again in the mirror.

She ran her tongue over her still red lips, saw that her dark eyes needed no more of the touch of eye shadow that was also lasting well, and unfastened the top button of the dress. She flicked the ends of the black shiny hair that she had inherited from her Greek mother back over her shoulders, smiled at herself again and walked down the hall.

She paused at the foot of the stairs to listen out for Karen and Jeffrey, who had indeed started without her and very enthusiastically, and went through the white door at the end of the hall, closing it behind her.

The telescope was mounted on a brass tripod to the right of a glass-topped coffee table standing a metre from the full width expanse of glass that hid absolutely nothing. The view was still breath-taking even though it was by now an old friend, especially today with the blue sky and a few cartoon-fluffy clouds being the icing on the cake.

The Camel River was down below, around half a mile away; the tide was in and the river was flowing slowly leftwards, through the green hills that rolled down the sides of the valley to her right, past Cant Hill across the estuary, directly opposite, with its odd-looking mounds which were all that was left of the old copper workings, black and white cows in groups dotting the slope.

With the tide in and on the ebb, the river was meandering slowly past the legendary village of Rock to her left - on the other side of the estuary from the hidden-from-view Padstow that was on her side of the river but out of her sight behind Halwyn Hill - and on out to sea. She could see Pinkson Creek down to her right, and she knew that if she went out onto the deck she would see her own 'place in the country', with its own marvellous decks, just half a mile away set into the hill on the other side of the creek. She smiled as she looked at her favourite stone at the bottom of the rock face just above the full creek, and as she thought about the hidden door in the crevice behind it.

She walked straight to the telescope, it was a Nikon Prostaff, “a brand that will impress,” she had told the owner when they were discussing décor and fixtures and fittings, and she bent slightly to look though the viewer mounted on the angled body of the telescope to refresh her memory. There were better views she could have had than from here, but this view did help, nothing that she could see had changed.

At the bottom of the hill the blue and white ice-cream van was still on the Rock foreshore; she had been surprised at the memories that it had brought when she first saw it, that it had reminded her of Eastbourne and Billy, and of the sound of the closed fist, the solid slap as it had backhanded against the girl’s pudgy cheek, after she had at first refused to hand over the ice-cream cone. At his wide smile as he had walked with the stolen ice cream held out towards her so proudly.

With a very slight downward movement, seesawing the seeing end upwards, and an even slighter twist of the eye-piece to re-focus, she could also see that nothing had changed at the top of the hill. Behind and way up from the Rock golf course, the scaffolding around the chimney of the renovated house high above Polzeath, which also had views right across the estuary to Padstow, was definitely being taken down.

Great, she had thought and then she had swung the telescope to the right and tilted it and then first slowly found, and then refocused on, the small faux spires at the corners, the battlements of the St Endellion church tower and the Cornish flag that flew there.

She straightened and looked up, and with her naked eye St Endellion was barely a grey smudge on the horizon, to the right and up and beyond the top of the green slope of Cant Hill.

Brilliant, she had thought, *they couldn’t have chosen a better day . . . love it . . . great way to get ahead of the plan, let’s go and see how they are getting on.*

Chapter Four

On a hot noon, at the end of a frustrating, tedious morning Tommy Holding walked into a crowded Strandloper for a cold beer. Coco was hard to like and impossible to love and over the years Tommy had found himself wishing she would just go away. When they had met, she had been beautiful and funny and infuriating, now she was just infuriating. Their inability to have children had left her endlessly throwing herself into grand schemes, the latest of which was The Salt Creek, a boutique hotel makeover on the cliffs above Lundy Bay. Makeover? More like rebuild. And then she'd dashed off to some committee meeting leaving him to deal with the bloody contractors and some tiresome jobsworth from Cornwall Council. Jesus.

Tommy had grown up under the grey blanket, dripping skies of Surrey, and then he had started to travel. He'd flown into LAX at night where the lights of Los Angeles went on forever. He'd seen the cleanly order of Toronto with its immaculate subway, the wondrously shabby glamour of New Orleans. Seen Sydney Opera House and thought it small and grubby.

And then he'd arrived in Africa. South Africa.

Cape Town. The immensity and distance of endless blue skies; the majesty of the mountains butting up against the coldest of blue seas. Africa wasn't just another country, it was another world; God's first best work like a triumphant first album, never to be repeated. It was big, untamed, uncivilised and glorious. It was awesome.

So when he had first driven across the Tamar Bridge on an early blue-skied summer's day, heading west along the A38, he had heard a distant much-loved chord sound in his memory; something reminiscent of something good. Cornwall? Maybe God had made this place too.

Strandloper was his sort of place. Built of planks of weather-washed greyed wood like an old waterside warehouse it stood at the top of Polzeath beach. Outside on the decking, small wooden candy-striped beach huts housing extra folding wooden chairs and parasol umbrellas. Inside it was casual but not scruffy: no empty barrels, unopened boxes, parcels awaiting shipment. No clutter on the bar like barricades: piles of dirty trays, piles of plates, stacked glasses, cocktail shakers, cake stands, racks of brochures, Tupperware containers of God knows what. No tubs of straws, in fact no straws, never an abandoned, un-cleared table.

Everything was refurbished or replaced every year: no split or broken chairs spilling stuffing, no grubby stained cushions, no chipped or cracked crockery or glasses, tarnished cutlery, dead light bulbs or dying plants. No mismatched wall coverings or colours; no blinking neon signs, no dust and grease-trapping fancy light fittings. No churning vats of Day-Glo gloopy slime for children. No dusty bowls of age-old lemons. No grizzling sandy-footed children, tired and bored, a long way from home, missing their friends. It was a magical place and its magic rubbed off on the clientèle; everyone was smiling.

As Tommy approached the bar his focus zoomed in upon a young man behind the counter like the famous camera shot in the film *Jaws*. He was pouring a pint of Cornish Rattler from a hand-pump but Tommy was back in 1996, aged 21, about to stage his first triumphant rock tour. Everything faded around him and he felt his knees buckle. Someone was in his face, concerned, grabbing his arm, speaking slowly, but Tommy was oblivious, transfixed, hurtling down a tunnel back in time. Tommy was staring at himself. Not just a physical resemblance, it was the image in a time-warping mirror; the way he smiled with his head tilted to the left, his posture, his gestures, a sudden deep timbred laugh. It was him at 21. 'Flesh of my flesh,' he mumbled.

'You alright mate?'

'Get him a chair, quick!'

As he became aware of his surroundings again, brushing his helpers aside with thank yous and a broad smile, another bolt struck. On the far wall were a series of blown-up photographs of seascapes on giglé. He stumbled up to the bar for a closer look. They were in black and white, but he recognised the locations. He had been there. They were images from his own memory: exact. He had been there, seen that very view on that very day the photos were taken. A hot flame ran through his body from his toes to the tips of his hair: Ruby Tuesday. And he was back in South Africa. Some twenty years ago. The happiest week of his life.

It is a glorious blue African-skyed day. Tommy Holding is sitting at a window table in the first floor Blues restaurant in Camps Bay just over Table Mountain from Cape Town, gazing at the Atlantic Ocean, overhearing a conversation in English at a nearby table. A softly spoken female, placeless, unplaceable British, and a male, obviously South African.

'Lit's git art off here.'

'But I haven't finished.'

'Shame.'

'Really Piet I don't want to leave.'

'Now now I say,' towering over the girl he grabbed her wrist roughly.

'Is there a problem Miss?' Tommy stood and faced the couple.

'Ha! Miss!' the man snorted. 'Arm out off here,' and throwing a bunch of Rand notes on the table, knocking a glass of red wine spilling across the white table linen, he stormed out of the restaurant.

'I'm so sorry about that, I'm Ruby.'

'Tommy.'

And so began the most memorable, glorious week of his life.

She moved in with him to the Presidential Suite at the Cape Sun in Cape Town, a huge bed, a fitted kitchen and a bath you could swim across, literally. She showed him her favourite restaurants and bars: Cantina Tequila at the Victoria & Alfred Waterfront, Renaissance in Hout Bay. A tiny Mexican, just down from the salt and pepperpot buildings, and the Wild Fig. They drove up the west coast to the tidal lagoon at Langebaan and stayed at The Farmhouse. Of course! Strandloper! Strandloper was the beach bar at Langebaan!

He had taken her to the Michael Jackson concert with backstage access. When he had meetings in the suite she had made herself scarce, strolling around the stalls at Greenmarket Square, returning with recycled glassware and hand-painted plates. And forever taking photographs.

That last Sunday they had driven to Noordhoek and walked the length of the beach, 8 kilometres, then eaten pizza at the Red Herring. They'd driven back along Chapman's Peak Drive through Hout Bay past the Sentinel rock that looked like a giant's head. She'd called it Gulliver. They'd stopped at Llandudno and then on through Camp's Bay and up the mountain over Kloofnek and back into Cape Town. The best day of his life. No question. And here it was, that day, captured in black and white on the walls of a Cornish beach bar.

And then it was over. He came back from Greenmarket Square and she was gone. Just a note.

"I'm sorry. I can't. Your wife rang. I said I was an associate. I just can't. Call it Catholic guilt. Go well. R."

The business deal was never sealed. His heart wasn't in it. With Ruby gone. Go well. Well in some ways he had, gone exceedingly well: fabulously successful, fulfilling career with the concomitant fame and fortune. But in comparison with that week, the sheer vividness, the utter joy and fullness of it, the intervening years had been hollow and monotone.

And now this. Ruby Russell. He had a son, and he had a son with Ruby Russell. Ruby Tuesday. Still I'm gonna miss you.

''Scuse me mate. You waiting to be served?'

A sun-reddened, beer-gutted bald Mancunian was glaring up at him, a tear and sand-streaked faced child clinging to his muscular hairy leg.

How long had he been standing here? What if she were here? What if she were to see him? Had seen him? He was filthy, sweaty, salty and sandy from the sea, his hair plastered to his head, his T shirt old and ripped. His feet were bare and gnarled. Christ, he was old. Ignoring the grumpy man he turned and fled. There on the wall above the entrance was all the proof he needed. "Licensed to sell . . . . . . Ruby Russell."

Chapter Five

Sam and Treloar had called into The Old Ship Hotel in Mill Square in Padstow for coffee. Set back from the street, the hotel's front courtyard was lined with picnic tables, where people sat with late breakfasts and drinks. Inside, it was quiet at that time of day and they felt comfortable to sit and talk without being overheard.

'Any word on Col?' asked Sam.

'Nada.'

Col was DS Colin Matthews. Whilst Sam had been on secondment with Interpol in Lyon, Treloar had been embroiled in a nasty people trafficking case involving the Cornish Spargo clan. Matthews had been exposed as having been corrupted into aiding and abetting the Spargos and, before he could be brought to book, an accomplished sailor and David Bowie fan, he had departed the UK on a large yacht, The *Serious Moonlight,* not to be seen again. Many in the team still harboured sympathy for Matthews who had been bullied and coerced by their former boss, Detective Superintendent Suzanne Winters, who had mysteriously got off with a transfer to Lincolnshire.

'I should have sensed something was wrong.'

'Christ Sam, you weren't even here, you were in France. Nobody saw it, nobody. Not 'til it was too late. You only see something like that coming in hindsight.'

'Mmm. Even so . . .' she carried on perusing the menu then slammed it shut. 'Right. If we're coming back here for lunch, fish and chips for me.'

'Christ I don't believe it. Eighteen months in Lyon, a culinary Mecca and you're *still* choosing fish and chips! Didn't the French do anything to educate your palate?'

'Eighteen months without fish and chips means so many portions to catch up on! Anyway you're one to talk. I bet you're still going to have the goats' cheese bruschetta.'

'Don't be absurd it's June. I'm having the goats' cheese rocket and spinach salad.'

As it transpired, they ended up with takeaway pasties: Cornish for her, cheese and onion for him, which suited Sam a great deal more than it did Treloar.

'Christ Sam, did you chew any of that?'

Sam and Treloar were sitting in his Land Rover eating their pasties. Despite her new svelte groomed image and cool demeanour Sam Scott still ate as if expecting someone to wrench the food from her grasp at any moment.

'How you don't get indigestion is beyond me.'

Sam grinned, wiping her hands on a paper napkin. 'I've been waiting almost two years for one of those. Don't get me wrong. French food is marvellous but there's nothing quite like a warm well-made Cornish pasty.'

Treloar peered warily at his half-eaten cheese and onion offering. The son of a Spanish mother, a brilliant cook, who had brought up her four children as vegetarians, he did not share Sam's love of the pasty. Or for that matter fish and chips, burgers and, heaven forfend, kebabs. Pizza, good thin crusted pizza, was tolerable but this stodgy, greasy creation was beyond edible.

Seeing his distaste Sam grabbed the pasty from him. 'Give it here,' and finished it in four mouthfuls like a starving dog. 'Mmm. Not as good as the meat one but not too shabby.'

'How can you possibly tell? It didn't touch the sides.'

Christ, he thought, I sound like a maiden aunt. What is wrong with me? But Sam didn't react at all which actually made him feel worse. This new Sam was unsettling.

'It's strange that they didn't seem remotely upset,' she said, 'not one of them. Not even particularly shocked.' When they had arrived at Rum House earlier that morning they had found an Ally Ally Oh festival committee in full swing. The news of Ellis' unfortunate demise, broadcast to all present by the widow herself, had caused uproar, and Treloar had suggested to take Theresa home to talk. But she was adamant she wanted to stay, she had work she wanted to finish before she spoke to them, and so to humour her they had agreed to come back after lunch.

'Yeah. Not even the wife.'

'Tipsy.'

'What? You think she'd been drinking?'

Sam snorted. 'No! That's her name. One of the others actually called her that: Theresa AKA Tipsy. Childhood nickname that stuck apparently.'

'Well it does beg the question, who was this bloke that nobody seems bothered by his unexplained suspicious death?'

'Indeed. Jolyon Ellis qui ệtes-vous?'

'Shouldn't that be qui étiez-vous?'

'OK clever-dick.'

'OK clever-dick, Sir.'

Sam flashed him a brilliant smile. Weren't her teeth whiter, straighter? She had changed. But why? Was there someone? She'd always been so girly, like a pretty head-girl, athletic and wholesome. Now she was slimmer, smarter, more polished.

'So,' she said, 'I spoke to Francesca Westgarth and arranged to see them this evening.'

'And they're visitors, not locals?'

'Yes, from Wallingford in Oxfordshire. They're staying at Hawker's Cove near the old lifeboat station.'

'Well I would like to talk to them myself as they're not resident here. First to find the body . . .'

'Last to see the victim alive. Well it's not them. Their dog's too sweet. Anyway we can drive: up to the Padstow Farm Shop, turn off to Crugmeer and on to Lellizzick, then down the No Through Road to Hawker's Cove.'

'Or we can take the coastal path?'

'Exactly.'

'No contest. We walk.'

'Right. Now the festival meeting's over, shall we go and actually talk to Mrs Soames-Ellis and find out what she really thought of her husband given she didn't seem shocked to learn that he was dead?'

Chapter Six

'. . . . and with the speakers, look!' Cecily heard Jeffrey saying from outside as she reached the top of the stairs, 'Great, and it looks as though we can control it all from this . . . wow, these seats are really comfortable . . . you wouldn't think it given they're all wood. Look, just push there and the leg support just slides out.' Jeffrey was on the deck, exploring.

'Wow, this al fresco kitchen's brilliant,' she heard Karen say, 'what a neat idea, and you can still see everything even when you're prepping and cooking, Jeff you're going to love it. Maybe we could get one at home, is it gas or are these real coals?' Karen was asking, looking at the grill. She heard a door open, 'Wow, brilliant, Jeff look at this,' Karen said with her head inside the larder cupboard that also opened at the back, into the kitchen inside, with a sliding door.

Cecily had looked quietly on from just outside the patio door at Karen exploring the outdoor barbeque kitchen. Karen closed the larder cupboard and opened the fridge side of the massive fridge / freezer that had been her idea but to which the owner had instantly agreed. 'What's this?' muttered Karen, 'Tarquin's Gin . . . Cornish . . . not had that before . . . tonic too . . . right, priorities, there must be some glasses somewhere out here.'

She had stepped forward, 'knock knock,' she announced as she walked fully out onto the deck and sat on a tall stool that she had earlier placed next to the blonde-wood topped glass balustrade that ran the length of the deck. She draped her arms along the top of the balustrade, her dress slipped to the sides of her legs as she crossed them, placing her right foot on the bottom stool rung. 'Er Jeffrey, she had said, 'you might find it even more comfortable with one of those,' she said and pointed at the lounger cushions leaning up against a natural wooden cupboard door behind him.

'Idiot,' said Karen.

'The glasses are in that cupboard to your left,' she said pointing, 'do you like ice?'

'Oh, yeah, great, thanks.'

'With a bit of luck it'll be ready by now, I topped up the ice-maker with water as soon as I arrived. Just put a glass under there for now,' she said pointing at a recess in one of the fridge / freezer doors, 'and press that lever. 'And if it should happen to rain while you're out here cooking just press that button there,' she said pointing at a large round plastic button. The left half was green and the right half white. 'Do you want to try it?' and Karen did. A green and white canopy whirred quietly out from the wall until it completely covered the cooking area and two metres either side and out to the edge of the deck.

'Wow,' Jeffrey said, 'it was lucky you were there when we dropped in. We could have been really stuck.'

'No, Jeannie would have been able to help if I hadn't been there. She keeps the place running and always knows what to do. Anyway, she can usually get hold of me if I'm out or at one of the other offices.'

'Oh, right,' Karen said as she opened the Tarquin's and began pouring, 'I thought there was only the one CHILL in Padstow.'

'No. Not now, well yes, but no. That's the main office, where I set up really. So yes, there is only one CHILL in Padstow, but you can also CHILL in Port Isaac, Porthtowan, St Ives . . . No, we've got nine now, mostly small, nothing too grand. It's good to have a base where keys can be picked up and dropped off when needs be, where guests can call in and ask for help or information, whatever. And the cleaners and greeters can work from, and for people like you of course that just happen to turn up! It does happen occasionally, and today the timing couldn't have been better!'

'Well, you're not wrong, it couldn't have been,' Jeffrey volunteered, struggling a little to raise his ample body from the lounger to its feet. He walked across to the balustrade and stood next to her, and she soon noticed him finding it hard not to glance down at her legs, and her breasts. 'When we walked round the harbour and saw your office we thought it was a B & B at first! We're so glad this place was finished early and there was still a couple of weeks to go before the first booked guests turn up. Don't worry we'll be sure to give it a proper launch! Cheers,' He said, holding up the large and heavy glass that Karen had just passed him, and laughing.

Karen returned with her own glass, which was almost full, slid over another stool from next to the balustrade and sat on it facing Cecily and Jeffrey and crossed her own legs. She wore mid-blue leg-tight jeans with ripped knees, and Cecily saw that the red high heeled pumps matched Karen's lipstick as well as her nails. 'Cheers,' Karen said, 'Oh bugger, here's me being bloody rude isn't it? Cecily, sorry darling, have a sip of mine,' and the ice in the glass tinkled and a little of the gin and tonic splashed over the top as she passed the glass.'

Cecily took a sip and a few drops dripped from the glass onto her right breast, and Karen watched the drink trickling slowly down and underneath the dress towards the nipple, the dampness darkening the dress as it rolled, and the cold liquid making the nipple swell as it arrived.

'Well,' Jeffrey exclaimed, 'if I was a gent I'd offer to dry that for you . . . but . . . here Karen,' he said, passing her a white handkerchief, 'you can dry,' and choked back a laugh.

'You mean you're not a gent?' Cecily questioned, reaching for the handkerchief before Karen could take it and she gently dabbed at the long dark patch on her breast and the dark swell of her nipple. She turned to look at Karen and raised her eyebrows.

Jeffrey was still looking at Cecily's breast when he said 'Cecily, remind me, what does CHILL stand for?' this time giving vent to the full laugh, and before long Karen was laughing and giggling and couldn't stop, and Cecily smiled and politely chuckled and shook her head.

'Well', she said when they had finally calmed down and Jeffrey had stopped snorting, 'to make the sales pitch, here we go . . . you can tell your friends how you coaxed it out of me,' she smiled and raised her right eyebrow at him . . . 'The key is the Ledya! Cornwall Holidays In Ledya Locations'.

'Ah, yes, they're like that. I know that they would all like to know . . . well maybe some of them,' he said and looked at Karen and winked, 'and . . . Ledya?'

'Easy too, it's Cornish for 'leading'. What do you think?' She said as she uncrossed and recrossed her legs the opposite way around.

'Spot on, brilliant, clever,' he said as he glanced at her legs, 'just look at that,' he said looking up and sweeping his hand across the landscape from right to left, eh Karen.'

'I was,' said Karen quietly.

'So, tell your friends all about us. Maybe they can make it for the festival, the Ally Ally Oh, in September, near the end. Maybe you can find the time to come back too, it'll be a lot of fun. I should know, I'm organising it!'

Her phone rang and she slipped it out of her jacket pocket and looked at the caller ID, 'talking of which I'd better take this, sorry,' she said, 'Darling, Freddie, hi, I was just talking about you, well us,' she said and winked at Karen, then listened, then said, 'well bloody hell, hardly any warning, can't be as bad as his Bar bloody View I suppose, I hate that place, why can't he just . . . ? Oh God. Creep.' She sighed and then said, 'Not your fault Freddie, OK, see you there then darling. Soon as I can.'

'Well, that's great, anyway I've got to dash now, thanks for giving me a bit of time to get you sorted while you enjoyed the Seafood Restaurant, glad we managed to get you in there. I picked up a few microwave meals and bits and pieces from the butcher and fishmonger down on the quayside, not much, it's in the fridge. Milk, tea, coffee, should keep you going for a couple of days until you get yourselves a bit more organised . . and to the supermarket. I'm sure you'll find it, a couple more gins, whiskeys, beers, just help yourselves.

Call the office if you need anything. Someone will drop off information packs tomorrow, they haven't been made up yet. One with everything about the area and one about all the kit, appliances, how they work . . . the ovens, the grill, the washing machine, the home cinema, you know the sort of thing . . . the Wi-Fi, the ice machine, TVs, music system.' She said smiling and handed a set of keys with a large Maroon and white CHILL key tag to Karen. 'Enjoy!' she shouted as she walked down the stairs, 'What did you think of the chickens? Yours are in the blue. Do you like fresh eggs?'

@thecornishchef&artist

The Cornish chef & the artist

After all the interest in Stargazy Pie this morning (hoping they're wrong about the body BTW!) thought it might be interesting to bring together a few pieces from the archives to tell you all about the fabulous Stargazy - history and all.

Stargazy pie made by yours truly, shot by the artist

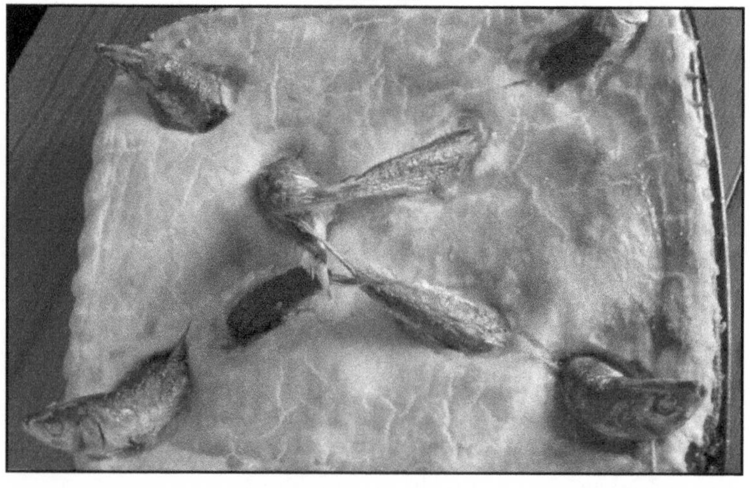

Mousehole (pronounced Mowzzle), a fishing village on the south coast of Cornwall near Newlyn, 3 miles from Penzance was where the Stargazy pie was first made. Ages ago, in the 16th century! In those days the good folk of Mousehole lived mostly on fish, but one winter it had been too stormy for the fishermen to venture out for weeks and the villagers were starving. Just before Christmas an extremely brave fisherman, Tom Bawcock, went out fishing, braving the fierce seas and not only did he make it back, he caught enough fish to feed the whole village for some time!

A huge pie was made, using seven types of fish, with their heads sticking out through the pie crust so that everyone could see what was inside. The villagers did not go hungry any longer, and Tom Bawcock's Eve has been celebrated in Mousehole ever since, on 23 December!

It's because the fish in the pie were looking upwards, and that first pie was served at night, that the dish is called stargazy pie!!

The Stargazy pie is well tasty and not too hard to make, with sardines (when was the pilchard rechristened as the sardine and why? Answers on a postcard please . . .), potatoes, eggs, bacon, onions, and parsley. Prep time around 30 mins, cook time 35 - 40 mins. Here's how I do it.

I use: Puff pastry 300gm, rolled out to fit top of pie dish. Sardines, 8, bones out, keep heads & tails. Chunky fish like Hake or Monkfish, 250gm, no bones or skin, small diced. Smoked streaky bacon, 4 rashers, de-rinded, chopped. Onion, 1 large, peeled, halved, sliced. Eggs, hardboiled, 2, diced. Fish stock, 250 ml. Cider vinegar, 2 tbspn. Plain Flour, 2 tbspn. Fresh parsley, chopped, 3 tbspn. Butter, 1 v good knob. S & P to taste. Egg beaten for brushing.

Here's how: Pre-heat oven to 200°C. Melt butter in pan over medium heat, add bacon, fry 5 minutes, stir twice, add onions & fry 5 more minutes, stir twice. Add flour, stir in. Add fish stock slowly, stirring hard. If lumpy, mash with back of a fork & stir again. Simmer until thickens into sauce.

Rub dish with butter. Add sauce mix to dish, stir in diced egg & parsley, then diced fish & cider vinegar. Add S & P to taste, stir. Lay sardine fillets over top. Lay pastry over & brush with egg, crimp to dish lip with fork, place in oven for 35 mins. Remove pie, use knife to make 6 holes in pastry top for 3 sardine heads (eyes out!) & 3 tails, push them down gently but firmly into the holes until they're supported but still sticking well-out from the pastry.

Return dish to oven for 5-10 minutes depending how you like your pastry. Remove and take to table & impress your guests my 'ansome!!

(Putting in the heads and tails near the end stops them burning & looking too frazzled - you're not going to eat them anyway).

Chapter Seven

"Effective, efficient, capable, competent." These were the adjectives most often used to describe Theresa Soames-Ellis, much to her chagrin. She would have preferred "erratic, whimsical, mercurial, scatty even, "effective" was just so not sexy. Known as "Tipsy" since childhood, she hated being the one singled out to "get things done", organise, administer and record. She wanted to be the one who was forgetful, creative, magical but as her father always said: 'you can't change how you're made Tipsy, my angel'.

So that day she was back at her desk at Rum House being effective. Upstairs, Pasco Trefry was also at his desk. He stroked his hand slowly across the surface of the A4 sheet Tipsy had brought up to him. It was just a print out of an email attachment but still. It was from Ochre Pengelly.

Cambridge – some twenty five years in the past

It is Michaelmas term. A bitterly cold November day brings snow swirling in the air. Pasco Trefry is sitting at a table by the front window of the Eagle pub looking out onto Bene't Street. There is a crackling fire in the grate. His friend from Christ's, Orlando Pengelly, is returning from the bar with two pints of Greene King Abbot.

The door blows open and Pasco sees his friend smile broadly at a tall girl in a scarlet duffle coat, her masses of blonde hair piled and secured on top of her head defying gravity and the fierce easterly wind. She raises a hand to Orlando and he nods his head towards the table. She turns and crosses to join the two young men.

'You found it,' says Orlando.

'Of course,' the girl replies in a deep, mellifluous voice.

'Pasco, this is my sister Loveda..'

'Ochre!!' she interrupts.

'Sorry, sorry not Loveday. Let me start again.'

He places the pint glasses on the table and raises his hands as if in surrender.

'This is my sister Ochre. Ochre, this is my dear friend and fellow Cornishman, Pasco Trefry.

She removes her coat to reveal that she is clad in a baggy wide-sleeved shirt topped with an ornate beaded waistcoat in jewel colours and soft leather knee-high cuffed boots over midnight blue velvet trousers.

'My, you look just like a pirate,' Trefry exclaims.

'Thank you!' she beams in response.

Orlando smiles, 'don't encourage her. She's writing a story about a pirate, Captain Perish Penhaligon and his boat.'

'It is not a boat, it's a brig, and it's named the Torment.'

The girl turns to Pasco extending her hand and his heart is stolen.

But it wasn't to be.

She had remained, famously, celibate whilst he had married Fleur and they had enjoyed a happy, quiet marriage producing two beautiful daughters before breast cancer had killed her. But he had never forgotten that cold Cambridge November day.

Smiling softly he pulled open a small drawer in his antique desk and extracted a well-thumbed manilla envelope. Gently, he opened the flap and tipped out a tatty square of soft cardboard. It is an old beermat. On one side is an advertisement for Green King IPA. On the other, the print has been peeled away and on the bare card is a faint ink drawing of The Bridge of Sighs at St John's College, from the River Cam beneath. It has faded over time but there, in the left hand bottom corner is the signature, Ochre P.

When the door bell rang at Rum House, it was Tipsy, secretary and general factotum to the Ally Ally Oh Festival committee, who ran to answer. She pulled the heavy wooden door open to reveal a familiar handsome couple, a tall blonde man and an effortlessly stylish woman, both in their thirties, both looking deadly serious. The man held out a wallet towards her showing his photograph.

'Detective Chief Inspector Treloar and Detective Inspector Scott of the Devon & Cornwall Police for Pasco Trefry. May we come in?'

There was a soft knocking on the door and Trefry rose and crossed the room to open it.

'Good afternoon Chief Inspector, do come in.'

'Thank you Mr Trefry.'

Treloar entered the first floor room which was clearly a study: books lined all the walls and an old desk sat in the bay window with views over the Camel. There was a pair of battered leather sofas, one facing the window, one the Dutch-tiled fireplace, with a heavy, low wooden table between.

'Do take a seat. May I offer you coffee or tea?'

'Thank you but no,' Treloar replied.

The two men sat, Treloar facing the window with sight of the door. Force of habit.

'Dreadful news about Soames-Ellis,' Trefry said softly. 'Surely you cannot suspect Theresa? She is in no way malicious and whilst formidably efficient, in no way . . . imaginative.'

'No. We are satisfied that Mrs Soames-Ellis was in St Ives at the relevant time. I understand she had visited the Tate to discuss sponsorship of the festival and stayed overnight with her parents before returning to Padstow. We are merely seeking background information on Jolyon Soames-Ellis. Did you have any dealings with him?'

'Lord no! I'm very fond of Theresa but Jolyon . . . well not to speak ill of the dead, but the man was a charlatan and we, the festival committee would have no truck with him.'

'Would he have known your opinion?'

'Probably. It was scarcely a secret, but to be fair, I do not know of many local businesses or organisations that would have contemplated any dealings with the man. Too many burned by his dubious practices; too much money . . . "misappropriated". Nothing proven but still. He had a bad reputation.'

'Can you think of anyone who was particularly "burned"?'

'No. But I am the wrong person to ask; I am not close to the business community, not on a day to day basis My involvement is only through the festival. Otherwise, I have little interaction.'

'Whose idea was the festival?'

'Mine. I wanted something for the local people, the community here in Padstow and its hinterland. Something not aimed at the summer season visitors, not engineered to line the pockets of the fair weather traders with their pop-up shops selling tat made in China. Something to promote the real Padstow, the real Cornwall and the precious marine environment we are charged to husband, not the Padstow of half a million annual visitors and 60% second homes and holiday rentals.'

'A noble cause,' said Treloar with conviction, 'though I sometimes fear a lost one.' He had formerly worked in Marine Conservation.'

'Let us hope not Chief Inspector, let us trust in good sense and good will.'

Downstairs. in a less prestigious, makeshift office in a room overlooking the rear garden Sam and Tipsy Soames-Ellis were seated at a pine kitchen table strewn with paperwork.

TIpsy's ChecKLisT

- Cornwall Council licenses – liquour, music, entertainment

- Sponsors (Cecily+)

- Refuse collection
- temporary events' notices
- temporary road closures
    - Signage

- Liaise – Pasco?
- Police
- RNLI
- Harbourmaster
- Town council
    - Rock / St Minver councils

- Closing Dinner Invitations
    - Closing Dinner

- Kernow Showtime – marquees, smaller tents, ropes with stands, seating, tables, umbrellas, lighting, gates, bunting
    - Park & ride, & park & float license, schedules & signage

- Advertising / tourist info centre
- Social media – website, facebook, instagram, twitter
- TV / radio, BBC Spotlight, Pirate FM, Visit Cornwall – Cecily
- Posters / flyers
- tickets
- programmes
    - Raffle prizes – Cecily etc

DAILY RAFFLE PRIZE Blank = nice to have

☐ = committed

♥ = **SECURED!!**

♥ ~~Salt Creek lunch~~

Strandloper beach towels

cookery course

♥ ~~sailing lesson~~

♥ ~~limited edition Ochre Pengelly print~~

☐ kitchen linens

seafood hampers

palm/fern

placemats and coasters
cushions
♥ ~~picnic blankets~~
wetsuit
body board
♥ ~~Zennor Aromatics seaweed candles~~
driftwood sculpture
seaglass plaques
♥ ~~cookery books~~
seagrass baskets
☐ Dr Roz The Rolling Deep signed script
♥ ~~Cornish still white wine~~
♥ ~~Cornish sparkling white wine~~
☐ Cornish chocolate truffles
☐ Cornish pasties
☐ Cornish clotted cream tea hampers

'I am so very sorry about your husband Mrs Soames-Ellis,' said Sam. 'I was surprised to find you here today under the circumstances.

'Really? Best to keep busy. Best not to dwell.'

Sam was genuinely shocked that this woman could be so unaffected by the violent death of her husband. Perhaps she was one of those dim, jolly hockey sticks types, sent off to boarding school at the age of four to learn how to curtsey and keep a stiff upper lip.

'How long were you married?'

'Oh. Let me think. Just over a year. It was a lovely wedding. Here at St Petroc's. We had seven bridesmaids, all in mother-of-pearl satin with palest pink rosebud posies. And we had a lovely marquee in Mummy and Daddy's garden. That was before they moved to St Ives of course.'

'Right,' said Sam bemused.

'No. Best to keep busy. Just like when Noah died.'

Sam knew that Tipsy was an only child so was Noah a friend? Sam had lost her best friend to the notorious Down's Devil serial killer in Brighton when they were at primary school. She knew how devastating and formative such a loss could be.'

'Was Noah your friend?' she asked gently.

'My best friend,' Tipsy replied sadly. 'my first pony.'

Sam was speechless.

'But Daddy said "Tipsy, best to keep busy poppet. Best not to think about it." And then of course we went off to get Daisy, who was a bay and much prettier than Noah. So here I am! Pasco would be lost without me. There's loads to do and the others on the committee are really hopeless. Well except for Cecily of course. She's a force of nature; unstoppable. She's raised loads of money; people just can't say no to Cecily. But even she says I'm "indispensable". And the festival is just going to be epic! There'll be loads of scientific marine stuff of course, but there's going to be dragon-boat racing and fireworks! Oh and lots of yummy fishy food stalls. And, you'll never guess who Pasco has got for the opening. Oh bother, I can't tell you, it's a secret, but you'll be blown away! Pasco is so clever.'

'Right. And what about Jolyon, your husband? Do you know who might want to harm him?'

'Apart from Daddy you mean?' she snorted a laugh and then blushed deeply. 'Gosh I'm joking, really I am. Daddy didn't like Joly but he wouldn't . . . anyway he was with me in St Ives so that's OK. No. Joly was a bit naughty, with money I mean, but no. It was only money after all. He never hurt anybody. Just skimming.'

Sam had researched Jolyon Ellis and knew he had allegedly misappropriated many thousands of pounds from funds.

'Not so much skimming as dredging, the huge amounts of money we're talking here.' Sam commented.

'But from any individual company it really didn't amount to a great deal. They never complained about the service they were getting, not one single, solitary one of them. This is such an enormous . . . overreaction. It's overkill.' She clasped her hand across her mouth as she realised what she had just said. 'Sorry, sorry, it's just so silly that's all.'

'And it wasn't wrong to steal all that money?'

'It wasn't really anyone's money. It wasn't *real* money. Nobody was out of pocket. It's EU funding after all. There's been millions sloshing around, millions. OK, Joly took some, well diverted it really, but he did a fantastic job for these people. All those awards he won for them; best this that and the other. He always said he'd have been forced to charge them loads more without the sidelined monies. I really don't understand what their gripe is if you think about it. It's only money. Is it really worth killing over?'

'Sidelined? Don't you mean misappropriated?

Theresa looked at her blankly.

'Perhaps it was just a passing lunatic? That's what Mummy thinks. She says they are so much happier to be in St Ives. Once the festival is over I'm moving down there. It's not as tacky as Padstow. Padstow has really gone downhill over the past few years. That's what Mummy says.'

Leaving the office, Sam found Treloar waiting in the hallway by the front door.

'Well,' he asked, 'anything?'

'. . . She loved her first pony?'

Chapter Eight

Tommy Holding crossed Polzeath beach in a daze. He headed off the sand at New Polzeath, joining the coastal path and drifting back up onto Pentire Headland. Cutting inland he reached the narrow road which ran past the entrance to The Salt Creek, stepping quickly onto the grass verge to make way for a fast-moving TVR sports-car. Arsehole. Reaching The Salt Creek he turned in.

The drive leading up to the main house was lined with banks of agapanthus in glorious bluebell-blue bloom. It was the only thing he had demanded of Coco in the redevelopment. The majestic flowers reminded him of that magical trip to South Africa where they had grown wild along the N2 roadside from the airport into Cape Town. They made him smile to this day.

After South Africa Tommy had thrived, his triumphs and tribulations followed avidly by the world's media. His wife Coco had been very open about their sorrow at their inability to have children. People had lauded her candour and courage; the attention she had brought to the issue; the donations flooding in to her charity. But she needed something more, once her minor acting career had started to fade, and so she had taken up interior design. The latest and grandest project was The Salt Creek.

Ruby Russell was in a foul mood. She needed to get back to Strandloper. Somebody, one of her employees, one of the worthless locals she had given a chance, was ripping her off. Money and stock were disappearing from Strandloper, and she was so going to find the culprit. She was driving too fast in her beloved Formula Red TVR Chimera 500, forcing some arsehole walker off the road as she sped past. Some bloody middle-aged early season emmet no doubt or another bloody incomer with a pet project like that new 'bijou' hotel. Still, an upmarket hotel and spa catering to Londonistas and media darlings was no threat to her.

Driving the lanes between the dense hedgerows she was assaulted by the pungent vegetal smell, forcing her to hold her breath at times. The oppressive stench was not helping. She needed to calm down. Dodging the staycationers in their sleek black 4x4s, petrified and panicking in the narrow lane, she arrived in New Polzeath only to be engulfed by the yummy mummies in their top-end hatchbacks and perfect pastel outfits with their foul-mouthed, foul-tempered offspring.

Finally she parked and crossed the road onto the beach. It never ceased to amaze her how people, who would recoil from close proximity to others in a restaurant or a park, would abandon all inhibition and reserve to strip virtually naked and pack themselves together on the smallest strip of sand at the first glimpse of the sun. Roll on September. But a full beach meant a full bar so she would comfort herself with watching the cash roll in whilst she wished the days would roll on to blessed autumn.

Strandloper was heaving which cheered Ruby immensely. She nodded to Josh behind the bar and pointed to the small office beside the kitchen. She was going to review the CCTV coverage and find the thief.

Settling in the office chair she switched on the screens. She scrolled to the coverage of that morning as business began to pick up. Most of the cameras covered the bar area and she followed the routine of money changing hands, orders being entered onto consoles, drinks being served. Nothing dodgy. People were smiling, asking questions, looking up at the bottles and optics, down at menus; chatting to fellow customers and the staff. Nothing unusual, nothing of concern.

Then her eye was drawn to something odd.

A man, stock still, frozen staring to his left at something behind the bar. At what? A movement brought an arm, then a head into view. A smiling handsome face. This was the focus of the man's attention and this was her Josh. Now the man turned and the camera caught him face on. The resemblance was extraordinary and unmistakeable. Shit. Shit. Shit.

Josh had never shown the slightest interest in his father, his identity, his name, his location or his story. To be fair, Ruby had never proffered any of this information but she had always been relieved and thankful that he had never pressed her. Josh had grown up with a succession of nannies, au pairs, house guests and club and bar staff, but his mother had always been around, always in the background, rarely absent for any length of time and never neglectful. Josh was her life. Well, and her businesses of course.

Russell Enterprises owned two successful clubs in Newquay and one in Falmouth, but Ruby's latest venture and most cherished project was Strandloper, bought, designed and built for Josh. It was to be her finest achievement and her gift to her precious boy. If people didn't like it they could go elsewhere. She didn't need the money. Strandloper wasn't for the money, the clubs made money, lots of it. This was her perfect place; this was for her and Josh; this was her pride and glory for her pride and joy.

And now this. Shit. Shit. What to do? Tommy Holding may have fled, she had seen him run from the bar, but he would be back. Ruby knew that his wife Coco was creating The Salt Creek, hell, everyone in Cornwall knew that, but he had famously and repeatedly called it her project, her business, her mission and nothing to do with him. Now this. Of all the beaches in Cornwall, of all the bars, why hers? This was going to end badly for someone, but whatever it took, that was not going to be Josh.

Chapter Nine

The early evening light was thick with the yellow glow of an imminent thunderstorm. It had followed a fat late summer afternoon, the air bright and thick as clotted cream. In London it was raining. Tommy didn't get Cornwall. It was fine in the winter when you could get around but the summer sucked. Too many bloody people just drifting about in cars, on foot, in boats and on surf boards they didn't know how to handle. Just making fools of themselves. Ghastly.

Tommy missed London. He had chosen the multi-million pound house in Primrose Hill. He missed the gym and the indoor pool. He missed Regent's Park, the canal, even the zoo. Well maybe not the zoo. He missed being able to walk down the road to a great pub or restaurant, Christ a choice of great pubs and restaurants! Cinemas, theatre, shops. Enough already of the great views and the clean air. Where was the entertainment? Where was the culture? What did Ruby Tuesday see in this place? His boy must be bored out of his mind. His boy. Christ.

Coco had wanted a project house, something to renovate and make her own, but Tommy had put his foot down. The hotel was a large enough "doll's house", his home was to be different: calm and quiet; no building, no remodelling. So they had bought a converted engine house near Port Isaac, altered before the planning restrictions on the domestication of Cornwall's industrial heritage. The house was adequate, spacious and isolated, but for Tommy the phenomenal secluded rose garden had swung it. He had to admit grudgingly that the quiet held a certain appeal. Occasionally. He did like to sit out amongst the wonderful colour and scent in the evening air. It soothed him. He needed soothing. His boy. Christ almighty.

What to do?

Did the boy know he even existed?

What had she told him?

He seemed happy. He looked healthy. What could he, Tommy Holding, offer him now? But this was his son, his flesh and blood. But he had obviously managed twenty years without him, would his appearance now in the boy's life cause distress, horror, anger?

Why had Ruby said nothing?

And what would this do to Coco?

Christ he should have just kept walking past that damned bar.

But whatever, whatever happened now; if he said nothing, did nothing, let it go, at least now he would know. But he wanted more, he needed more. He wanted to know the boy, help him, mean something to him.

Was that selfish?

Could he really put his own happiness above that of all those people this knowledge would impact: the boy, Ruby . . . Coco. But then again perhaps the boy would want to know, would want to know him.

Ruby would just have to accept it. And Coco . . ?

No. This would destroy Coco. If only he'd just kept walking. No. The genie was out of the bottle. He could not unknow this.

A son, he had a son!

Break it down. Break it down into manageable pieces; you don't eat an elephant in one bite.

The boy. The boy needed to know. Would he be angry, hostile, indifferent, welcoming?

Ruby. Would she feel threatened, ashamed, regret?

Coco. Did Coco actually need to know anything about the boy, about Ruby, about the affair?

No. No better for everyone if Coco knew nothing.

But how likely was that?

So of the four individuals here; two were totally innocent, and one of them was certainly oblivious to the situation, and now one of the other two knew and the other had known all along. Ruby Russell. He needed to talk to Ruby Russell. And even twenty years too late she would talk to him one way or another.

Chapter Ten

When it came to fear or anger, fight or flight, Ruby's first instinct had always been flight. As she'd grown older and increasingly successful, the switch to fight had started to come sooner but always, initially, flight prevailed. And flight was home: Solitaire.

The Russells lived in an isolated secluded property in a wooded valley between Porthcothan and Penrose. The house had originally been an artist's studio but Ruby had extended, adding wings leading from the original building. Her latest addition was a living space built on stilts out across the shelving grounds. It ended with a deck overlooking a stream which rose near St Eval and ran down to the sea at Porthcothan.

The house was located off a No Through Road at the end of a long winding drive. Solitaire was surrounded by mature trees, shrubbery and high hedges. From the front facing windows only greenery could be seen, from the rear more greenery with the occasional glimpse of sky. 'Like living underwater', as Josh would say. Ruby, who had grown up on the twelfth floor of a Plymouth tower block, loved it. Total privacy: heaven.

The stilted extension built out over the stream was entirely made of reinforced glass, walls, floor, and ceiling, like an enclosed jungle walkway. Sycamore, weeping willow, holly and rhododendron dominated the rear of the property, whilst the front was a riot of colour with pelargonium, fuschia, nasturtium and cosmos in Cornish hedges and a rambling of terracotta pots and troughs.

Ruby stormed through the house discarding clothes, shoes, bag and keys. Barefoot, in just shorts and camisole she burst into her 'jungle tunnel' and slumped into an oversized wicker chair positioned on the reinforced glass floor above the stream. Here, watching the water trickle or gush beneath her - depending on the weather - was where she thought, plotted and created. This was her 'mind zone' and she needed it now more than ever. What to do?

When she had fled Cape Town, awash with fear and guilt at the pregnancy she had wanted space. So, she had travelled to Namibia. Crossing the desert she had stopped at a tiny service area in a place called Solitaire. It had been spotlessly clean and surrounded by nothing, the inspiration for her home.

From here she had travelled on to drive the Skeleton Coast up past Walvis Bay and Swakopmund almost into Angola. On Swakopmund seafront she had watched the pelicans from the restaurant at the end of the jetty and had marvelled at the huge carved wooden animals along the seafront, inspiration for the large driftwood pelicans now perched on the far bank of her stream. 'Sad Pelican' as Josh had named the original on his third birthday. Why sad she had asked? Because he's all alone, had come the serious reply. That night she had tracked down the supplier and ordered a second pelican. Once it was installed next to the original she had called Josh and pointed across the bank.

'Look Josh, look who flew in overnight!'

She would never forget the joy on Josh's face.

So it was in Namibia that she had decided to keep her baby and to face the consequences of that decision. Her parents had been appalled and she had left home to stay with her estranged grandfather. He had turned out to be something of an eccentric and a great supporter. He had encouraged her in every endeavour and when he died, much to the amazement of her parents and the world in general he had left her a substantial sum of money which funded her first club in Newquay. She had bought a derelict seafront hotel and turned it into the town's most successful nightclub: GRAMPS. *What should I do Gramps,* she asked now?

Her musings were interrupted by the ringing bell tone of her mobile. She let it go to voicemail.

'Ruby Russell,' her greeting announced.

'Ruby Tuesday,' came the reply in a voice from the past.

So here it was. No chance of mistake, no chance of escape.

Chapter Eleven

Whilst Ruby was brooding at Solitaire, Josh was enjoying the lull after the storm as the lunchtime crowds had faded away back to the beach, sitting at the bar with his friend Ross Chamberlain. Sharing a relaxed easy charm, the two had struck up an immediate connection when the new lifeguard had appeared the previous summer. The two young men had met through a Strandloper sponsored project to raise money for the RNLI to fund special equipment giving disabled children access to the sea.

It was Josh who had coined the nickname 'Poldark' and Ross took it in good spirit. Born in Cheshire, Nicholas, his father, then rising through the ranks of the Greater Manchester Police had given no thought to the fictional character when naming his baby son. The Chamberlains had not envisaged living in Cornwall. Given the recent television incarnation of the eponymous hero was a national heartthrob, Ross could have few objections.

Josh yawned. He had been in at six that morning to make a batch of sausages.

'You look tired mate.'

'Yeeaahh. Busy day. Need to get on though. Got to get through Ma's "Clear the Decks" routine before the evening swell.'

'What's that?'

'Here. See for yourself,' Josh leant over the bar and pulled out a laminated card.

☺ CLEAR THE DECKS ☺

- **PUT ON YOUR FAVOURITE MUSIC**
- **OPEN ALL THE DOORS & WINDOWS**

- **CLEAR & CLEAN ALL THE TABLES, SHELVING & BAR COUNTERS & OUTSIDE TABLES**
- **CHECK PLANTS & POTS FOR CIGARETTE BUTTS & DISCARDED RUBBISH**
- **SWEEP & MOP ALL FLOORS & DECK AREAS**
- **CHECK & CLEAN TOILETS – HANDWASH, LOO ROLLS, DISPENSERS – WIPE THE MIRRORS, TAPS & SINKS, EMPTY BINS**
- **PLUMP CUSHIONS, CHECK BLINDS**
- **CHECK MENUS & UPDATE MENU BOARDS**
- **CHECK FRESHNESS OF FLOWERS ON BAR**
- **STRAIGHTEN BOTTLES & BEHIND-BAR AREA**
- **WASH GLASSES & EMPTY BOTTLE BINS**
- **REFILL PAPER NAPKINS, CRISPS, NUTS, CHOCOLATES**
- **GET A DRINK ON STRANDLOPER ☺ ☺ ☺**

'Shit! How often do you have to do this lot?'

Josh raised his hands to indicate inverted commas. '"First thing, after lunch, as needed, keep checking", Ma's mantra. You know she loves South Africa. Always on about how professional the bars and restaurants are, how everything is "clean and quality". That's where the name of this place comes from. Strandloper. Beachwalker. A tribe that wandered the coast of Namibia and The Cape.'

'Well she has a point. Nobody wants to drink or eat in a tip.'

'Yeah. It's not so bad when we all lend a hand.'

'So who chose this shit music?'

'Oy! That's classic music numbnuts. That is Domenico Scarlatti's *Harpsichord Sonatas*. Thank your own personal gods Ma's not here or it'd be The Doors.'

'Hey! I like The Doors. Anyway this sounds a bit like *Riders on the Storm*.'

Josh looked at his friend aghast, then grinned and handed him a bucket, 'you can start outside.' But before they could leave the bar a wiry boy in his late teens with bleach streaked hair and baggy board shorts carrying a Seasalt hemp carrier bag came up to them grinning.

'Where's the MILF then?' he drawled

Josh said nothing just stared at him, unsmiling.

'Don't worry Mummy's Boy I'm not stopping. Just brought these flyers for the Ally Ally Oh festival. Give 'em to the luscious Ruby,' He licked his lips, snorted a laugh and turned on his heel.

'Who was that?' Josh asked.

'Nasty little shit. Ma's banned him. Nasty little rich boy whose mummy and daddy have a second home in Rock and keep bailing him out when he gets into trouble. Name of Siegfried Carew, goes by "Salty".

'Well it's better than Siegfried I suppose,' said Ross.

The phone rang and Josh answered.

'Afternoon, Strandloper.' He listened then frowned and spoke curtly. 'No she's not here. Try her mobile. Bye.'

Ross looked at him quizzically.

'Spencer.'

'Ah, the Idris Elba lookalike who carries a torch for your mother.'

'Torch? More like a fucking lighthouse.'

'Well mate, you've just got to accept that your mother is one hot babe.'

'Fuck off Poldark!' Josh grinned and slapped his friend on the back. 'He's had some bloke on looking for Ma. Tommy Holding. Why does a grown man call himself Tommy? Well soft.'

'Tommy Holding. *The* Tommy Holding?

'So?'

'Tommy Holding's mega. He's like Lloyd-Webber and that Harvey Goldsmith guy; big promoter and producer, but mostly he does bands. Seriously all the big festivals, all the big tours. Wonder what he wants with your Ma?'

'Fuck knows. Boardmasters maybe? She does get involved with that, what with the Newquay clubs.

'Possibly. Bit small fry for Tommy Holding though. Could be a family thing'.

'He's not family, not that I know of.'

'No, dickhead. The Tommy thing; Tommy, not Tom or Thomas. Think Mikey Holding! Not Mick or Mike!!'

'Who the fuck's Mikey Holding?'

'Jeez Josh you are so dumb. Michael "Mikey Holding": great West Indian fast bowler; commentates on Sky Cricket with Bumble and Nas. Perhaps Tommy Holding has Jamaican ancestry?

'Who's Bumble and Nas?'

Spencer Gabriel did not have Jamaican ancestry; his family was from Trinidad and Tobago. Captain Gabriel, formerly of 3 Commando Brigade, had been medically discharged from the Royal Marines after a boating accident whilst on R&R in Cyprus had severed his left arm just below the shoulder. He now had an Ottobock muscle-powered upper limb prosthesis with optional hand or hook. Gabriel often wore the latter, hence the inevitable moniker of "Captain Hook".

A powerfully built six foot five man he acted as Ruby's minder and club security manager and his menacing presence had diffused many an aggressive situation. He was devoted to Ruby, fiercely loyal and protective and so when an insistent, angry Tommy Holding had rung GRAMPS, Ruby's original club on the seafront in Newquay, Gabriel had given him short shrift and made a note of his name. An avid rock fan, he knew who Holding was, and he too was curious as to what the man would want with the boss and why he was so agitated.

Chapter Twelve

Viola Lawrence and Leah Kidd had nothing in common. Strictly speaking, they were of a similar age, attended the same school in Norwich where they had just finished A Levels and were both female, but that was the end of the similarity. They were poles apart. With one exception; they were both gifted tennis players and as a doubles pairing, they excelled. Viola was a great athlete, accomplished gymnast and superb swimmer. Leah just liked tennis. And it was their doubles pairing in that game that had afforded Viola her chance of freedom.

Dreams of Wimbledon had convinced Viola's mother to set aside her fears of stalkers, rapists, drug addicted housemates and predatory tutors, arsonist neighbours, floods, terrorists and general maniacs and allow Viola to apply to the University of York with Leah, rather than UEA – The University of East Anglia - in their home city. On a roll following this unimaginable victory, Viola had also wangled a post exam jolly – three weeks in Cornwall. She would have to go back before Leah for the family holiday – three weeks at the villa in Sardinia – but for now . . . Released from the shackles of a smothering upbringing, free at last, she was going to make the most of it in case it was all snatched away. Things were looking up for Viola Lawrence.

Only Leah, wise beyond her years, felt a troubling sense of foreboding.

Mrs Lawrence suffered from GAD (Generalised Anxiety Disorder) and was constantly "catastrophising". People late home were dead. Heavy rain presaged floods. An unexpected knock at the door was a harbinger of doom. It was a cruel affliction. She had wanted the girls to stay in a summer letting, a secure house, preferably with an alarm system and CCTV, but Leah's mother, a lone global backpacker in her youth, had prevailed, so it was a camp-site, but with the concession of a 1950s' vintage caravan, rather than a tent, that had been booked for the girls.

Viola and Leah had met the others at Crab & Kipper, the fish café stall beside the camp site. Of similar age and history, they had been drawn together like magnetised iron filings. And several of them shared a passion for the Captain Perish novels of local author Ochre Pengelly. That afternoon they were sitting at the top of the beach just down from the neat beach bar Strandloper.

'It's like spring break at Myrtle Beach. Cool. Love the campervans,' said Joel, who was from New York.

'Wasn't *The Smuggler Horde* set here?' asked Ravi.

'No that's further down the coast near St Ives. But the Camel estuary is in *The Doom Maiden*,' said Viola, the voice of authority.

'Please don't tell me you're into those awful Ochre Pengelly sagas?' said Leah shaking her head. The others stared at her in horror. Even Joel looked aghast.

'Of course they are!' cried Viola. 'You know she lives there, down near St Ives, in some massive granite mansion set all alone on top of a hill.'

'Really?' asked Ravi.

'It would be über cool to meet her,' said Joel.

'I don't imagine you can just pitch up and knock on the door,' said Leah.

'No . . . s'pose not . . . but still?' said Viola, her eyes shining in anticipation.

'Which is your favourite?' asked Joel.

'I love *The Mermaid Bride*. It's so sad,' said Viola.

'I thought they were all called Captain Perish and something?' asked Leah.

'Well of course. But Perishers use just the last bit of the title. Like a shortcut,' said Viola.

'Right,' said Leah, not really getting it at all.

'Yeah well, my fave's *The Bloody Wreckers*. It's got the best baddies,' said Joel.

'And it's the most violent,' Viola shuddered.

'And it has the most sex,' Joel grinned.

'I love them all, and of course with *The Doom Maiden*

being set around here. We should do some sort of treasure hunt trail sort of thing,' Viola said.

'That would be neat,' Joel agreed.

'*The Bloody Wreckers* has the smuggler pirates who get turned into vampires. They make the mistake of wrecking this ship that's carrying a French vampire baron bloke and his acolytes,' Viola was explaining at length to Leah.

'His what?' asked Joel.

'Acolytes. It's like followers, servants.'

'What like roadies?' Joel was teasing her now. 'Yeah, roadies crossed with groupies.'

'Doesn't Jackson Power, the Hollywood megastar, live around here too?' asked Joel.

'Yeah. And his son Hitchcock is so hunky,' said Viola.

Viola's phone buzzed with an incoming text.

'It's just a reminder from my mother. My phone has the GPS switched on,' said Viola, 'she says that if I'm abducted it will help the police trace me. That reminds me, I need to call in.' Viola's mother was paranoid. Diagnosed.

'Somebody better hide that thing then if we're gonna have fun,' Joel grinned at Viola who threw back her head in laughter and caught a sun-bleached, tanned young man staring. She smiled.

Siegfried Carew hated Strandloper. He hated Polzeath, Rock, Padstow, Cornwall in general. And he hated those two smug bastards: Russell and Chamberlain. Russell, with mummy's beach bar and clubs, set up for fucking life and Chamberlain, with a top cop daddy and a lush babe magnet job as a lifeguard. Bastards. Salty could not understand why his parents had to have a holiday home here.

Why not in The Lakes? There he could hike and climb and hang-glide. Salty didn't want to be by the sea, on the beach, surfing and sailing. He didn't care about "right breaks off Pentire Point and intermediate-friendly walls". Salty liked the air, he hated the water; Salty couldn't swim. All there was here for him were the Crazy Golf and the trampolines. And he could always take the ferry to Padstow and ride The Camel Cycle Trail to Wadebridge.

And that was at the heart of his anger and resentment.

Russell and Chamberlain were lucky; their parents appreciated them. Salty's parents knew he hated the water, but they persisted with that hateful fucking nickname: Salty, and year on year his mother dragged him down here for the summer. Russell and Chamberlain had parents who loved and valued them. Salty did not.

On the sand at the edge of the boardwalk sat a group about his own age. He knew the type: school-leavers let loose after their exams. Too much sun, too much booze, too much sex. Sex? One of the two girls laughed loudly and in throwing back her head caught him looking. Expecting a glare, a total blanking or a finger, he was stunned when she smiled straight at him, before turning back to her companions. She was lovely. He must find out her name and where she was staying.

Unconsciously, he raised his hand to touch the tattoo on his left shoulder blade. It was an automatic gesture now, unplanned, unintentional. This one word was the chorus of his life. From his father's mouth, referring to him, Salty had heard it whispered, shouted, shared with teachers with friends, with colleagues; at open days, sports' days, dinner parties, weddings, barbecues, carol concerts. It was drilled into his soul and branded on his body: DISAPPOINTMENT. It was his curse, but now he was going to fight back.

Chapter Thirteen

Fran Westgarth was in a bad mood after finding a body on the beach that morning, having her planned time in Padstow ruined and having to put up with Myles under her feet all day. Padstow had changed. She remembered visiting The Seafood Restaurant in the 80s – no Oyster Bar nonsense, fewer tables, more space between them; enormous servings of fish soup in a tureen 'Où sont les neiges d'antan?' Where are the snows of yesteryear anyway? And the blue-sky days? All getting warmer, warmer and greyer, greyer and duller, endlessly worse.

A life subsumed. She had been brilliant. She had been lauded. What had happened? Life, academe, society had all been stacked in favour of Myles. That's just the way it was. And of course there were the children. No, no, don't mistake this; she loved her boys. Maybe because they were boys. Her flesh made male and therefore open to all the advantages life has to offer. Nothing, nothing beyond their grasp whereas always, everything, just beyond her reach.

She had bought cornflowers from the farm shop to add to the poppies from the garden and field edges. She had put them in an empty Polish gherkin jar. She had bought pork to make rillettes to go with the sourdough bread they had eventually bought. Out on the terrace she was rereading the Aurelio Zen novels of Michael Dibdin for the umpteenth time and they still made her smile. The police were coming to interview them again. Some man in charge, of course, telling the story of their morning's discovery to a mere woman would never have sufficed.

Treloar and Sam walked along the coastal path, tempted by the soft golden sands of the estuary, but mindful of their appearance; it would not be professional to traipse sand through the Westgarth's holiday let. The old lifeboat slipway came into view and beyond, across Hawker's Cove beach, the terrace of pilot cottages facing back upriver and across to Rock. They had made good time. With the path still sealed off from St George's Cove to Hawker's Cove they had not been impeded by tourists laden with beach paraphernalia, strolling walkers and intransigent, obstructive photographers bent on the perfect shot. Indeed. They had passed nobody.

'Here, follow me,' said Sam leading the way across to the rear of the terrace and up the path to an open door.

'Hello! Mrs Westgarth!'

A middle-aged woman in a loose-fitting lavender shift dress approached them through the kitchen bringing a gentle through breeze and a soft smile.

'Actually, it's Dr Westgarth, strictly speaking. I'm not one to stand on ceremony, and I didn't mention it earlier, but under the circumstances, I think it best to be accurate.'

'Absolutely. Essential in fact,' said Treloar extending his hand and offering her his finest Treloar smile, 'Chief Inspector Félipe Treloar.'

Dr Westgarth visibly preened, 'Félipe? Unusual.'

'My mother is Spanish.'

'Of course. Do please call me Fran, everyone does, and please, please come through. We're on the terrace. It is so lovely outside this evening.'

'Thank you Fran,' said Treloar, ushering the two women ahead of him, ignoring Sam's rolling eyes.

They passed through a kitchen and sitting room decorated in the ubiquitous blues, creams and yellows and back out into the warm daylight on the terrace where Dr Westgarth (male) was seated at a weathered wooden table, a tan and black bearded dog at his feet. He rose as they emerged and the dog stood with him.

'Ah, Inspector Scott, good evening.'

'Dr Westgarth, Chief Inspector Treloar.'

The men shook hands and the dog approached Treloar growling softly. He recognized a cat man when he smelled one, and Treloar shared his home with three cats.

'Banjo! Enough! Apologies Chief Inspector, he's been overly excited since his discovery this morning. Banjo! Basket!'

At which, the dog surveyed the humans on the terrace and turned with contempt to trot inside passing Fran Westgarth who was emerging with a tray of coffee. Treloar rose to take the tray from her and place it on the table. Sam smothered a snort with a cough. Fran Westgarth smiled sweetly.

'Treloar pulled a Moleskine notebook from his jacket pocket. 'We have your contact details; Doctors Francesca and Myles Westgarth of Ferry Lane, Moulsford in Oxfordshire.' Myles bristled at not hearing his name placed first. 'And your work?'

Myles spoke quickly as Francesca opened her mouth then clamped it shut. 'Fran was a chemist, before the boys of course, and I am an atmospheric physicist.'

'Ah of course, Wallingford,' Treloar interjected, 'the world-famous Centre for Ecology and Hydrology.'

'Indeed,' Myles beamed. 'I am impressed.'

'Well before joining the police I worked in marine conservation.'

'Ah . . .'

Francesca interrupted, earning a glare from her husband. 'Strange career move Chief Inspector.'

'Not enough powers to stop the baddies Fran,' he whispered conspiratorially.

She actually giggled.

'Now I understand that you have already spoken with Inspector Scott, but I just wanted to garner your impressions from this morning for myself.'

'Garner?' Sam whispered under her breath.

'Rightly so Chief Inspector,' Myles blustered, 'I completely understand. Well, we left here at half past five . . .'

'Ten to six,' Francesca interrupted, 'you were dragging your heels, as usual.'

'As you wish Francesca,' Myles spoke through gritted teeth. 'We always take the same route into Padstow, either across the beaches, tides permitting, or along the coastal path. This morning we took the path.'

'You say "always",' Treloar enquired, 'but I understand you arrived on Midsummer's?'

'Ah yes,' Myles smiled, 'but we come every year. Not to

this property, but to the locality.'

'Thank you, just clarifying, please continue.' Treloar made a note in his Moleskine.

'Rightly so, clarity is everything,' Myles nodded. 'So Banjo, the Airedale, was running ahead - we leash him just before St George's Cove, mindful of the dogs on the beach ban – and he suddenly disappeared from the path and we heard him barking furiously from the beach.'

'So you tracked him down.'

'Yes, and there, at the top of the beach, was the unfortunate fellow in the pie.'

'By the way,' Treloar said, 'was that the first thing that sprang to mind; the pie?'

'Well no, the man, but he was clearly dead.'

'I took his pulse Chief Inspector,' said Francesca, 'the posterior tibial artery behind the ankle. Buried headfirst in sand and cold to the touch it seemed hopeless, but I did check.'

'You did well Fran, 'Treloar smiled at her, 'it must have been a tremendous shock.'

Myles huffed. 'As I was saying, the man was dead and obviously the circumstances were bizarre. It was clear to me that the scene had been staged as a parody of the stargazy pie. As I have explained, we summer in Cornwall every year and I have studied matters Cornish and of course my wife . . .'

'My family is Cornish on my mother's side, Chenoweths, farmers from Holywell just down the coast. I spent every childhood summer there,' Francesca spoke wistfully.

'As I was saying,' Myles continued, 'we immediately called the police and your chaps arrived promptly. Then Inspector Scott came along and, having spoken to her we were dismissed. Is there any news on the cause of the fellow's demise?'

'Early days Dr Westgarth as I'm sure you will appreciate,' Treloar answered in a sombre tone. 'I understand you saw nobody on your way out, and on your return journey, you came back the same way?'

'Not a soul. We did come back along the path, arriving as your men were sealing the path,' Myles stated categorically.

Treloar continued, 'and on the beaches, on the estuary, no boats, nobody in the fields?'

'Nobody, nothing moving.'

'Fran?' Treloar turned to her with a smile.

'Not a person nor a creature. We came straight back here and then later, we headed out to the farm shop for supplies. I couldn't face Padstow somehow. Perhaps tomorrow?'

'Will the path be open in the morning?' Myles asked.

'Our forensics people should be finished by then. I'll ask someone to contact you to confirm the reopening,' Sam spoke for the first time.

'Oh Myles I don't want to go that way tomorrow,' Francesca pleaded.

'For Christ's sake woman you were a scientist!'

'I'm still a scientist!'

Glares were exchanged, and at the raised voices, Banjo reappeared, barking. Sam and Treloar exchanged "time to go" looks and rose to their feet. Treloar extended his hand.

'Well thank you for your time Doctors Westgarth. We have your contact details. I hope you will be able to enjoy some of your remaining stay. When do you leave?'

'In twelve days,' Francesca said sadly, 'I only have twelve more days.'

They walked back along the path in a washed golden light and soft caressing breeze.

'Garner? Seriously? The world-famous Centre for Ecology and what?'

Treloar grinned. 'The Centre for Ecology and Hydrology.'

'How the hell?'

'I looked him up. From what I heard of his initial statement, he's clearly a pompous know-all, and like all self-important men he would respond to flattery. You catch more flies with honey.'

'Smart-arse.'

'Smart-arse, Sir.'

Chapter Fourteen

'They should be there by now, wonder what they'll manage tonight . . .' Cecily Farrant was on the deck . . .

She'd thought they'd be interested, and she wasn't wrong. Had had an eye on them since they first appeared back in January. Just after the Christmas lights in the harbour had been taken down. Locking the office after working late she'd heard laughing and conversation off to the right and saw them. In the Mill Square shelter, three boys, two sitting on the wall on one side and one on the other, and two girls sitting on the slatted wooden bench running along the back. It had rained earlier and the grey slate roof reflected the streetlights. Under the shelter cigarettes glowed and cans were swigged. Four bikes leant against one of the walls and a skateboard rested on the slate finished top of the other.

She watched until after ten, looking through the kitchen window of her flat above the CHILL office, no light on. Not long after she had poured a wine and sat at the breakfast bar two of the boys sauntered down the lane away from the harbour and reappeared a few minutes later carrying six packs, from the Old Boat pub presumably.

They were there three or four nights a week. Occasionally an old Ford Fiesta would cruise up to the gap between the walls of the shelter, music thumping, it got louder if the window came down. They would wander over, one of the boys would listen at the window. Sometimes the car would rev before turning sharp left up past the Old Boat and out of sight, and they would saunter back into the shelter. More often it would drive off and along North Quay Parade past the CHILL office and shops on the left and the straight drop down to the water on the right before turning right into the car park at the front of the harbour. Which was virtually deserted. Just a couple of fishing boats moored up on the far side, and a few winterised yachts.

There would be a short conference and one or two of them would go back into the shelter as the others sauntered along North Quay Parade and round to the car where they gathered, dug into pockets, and things were exchanged through the driver's window. The car would turn and drive back up the parade and round the harbour, before disappearing from view and they would saunter back to the shelter, underneath her window. If it was open she sometimes thought she caught one of the sweet smells of her own youth.

Seemed like good kids, kept themselves to themselves, surly. Nodded in passing if she caught an eye. An occasional nod back.

One night, early in mid-April she had been locking up the office, about to go round the back and upstairs to the flat and saw one of the girls, long dark hair, beautiful, bobble hat, walking out of the shelter pushing her bike, turning towards her and about to walk up the Mill Square lane towards the pub. 'On your own tonight?' she asked the girl.

'Dunno yet. Looks like it . . . have they been here, you seen the others?'

'No not tonight, bit late isn't it? Glad I saw you though, want to ask you something. Fancy coming up for a drink?' She shook her flat keys and jerked her thumb up towards the flat. 'I'm Cecily,' she said holding out her hand. 'Got red or white wine but I guess you're a beer or lager gal, got them too . . . only bottles though, no cans.' She smiled and raised her eyebrows.

'So, I'm Demmy,' said the girl looking surprised as she shook Cecily's hand. Cecily didn't know if Demmy had been surprised that she had been offered a handshake, or that she herself had taken the offer and shaken Cecily's hand. 'I'll try the red wine please, not had much before, thanks.'

'Well Demi, nice to meet you, come on up'.

Cecily led the way up the two flights of stairs to the kitchen. Like many holiday properties the living quarters of the flat were on the upper floors, located above the bedrooms to make the most of the views. She had poured herself a Pinot Grigio and a Tempranillo for Demmy and they had sat at the breakfast bar.

'Well I can see how you knew it was getting late for them,' said Demmy. 'Quite the view, good job we behave ourselves over here,' she said, smiling. She took a sip of wine, 'not bad, I reckon I could get used to this.' Demmy stood up, took off her bobble hat and put it in a pocket, shook off her grey fleece jacket and hung it on the breakfast bar stool and sat back down. She crossed her legs, exposing a knee through a rip in her skinny blue jeans. One of her black plimsols quietly tapped the crossbar at the base of the stool.

'Love that,' she said, pointing at the feather pinned to the collar of Cecily's jacket, 'so, how can I help you?'

'Well, it's about help with the business. CHILL. Business development. Do you go very far on your bike? What about the others?'

'I'm cool, what do you mean?'

'CHILL, it's the business, my business, I run it. The main office is downstairs. We let properties, around Cornwall, to people on holiday. I wonder if you, and maybe your friends, would be interested in helping me with development, business support, that's a bit like promotion and advertising. How far can you go on the bike?'

They both looked up as a bright light suddenly switched on across the harbour. A trawler was running slowly on the high tide alongside the South Jetty, its spotlight on to pick out the winch they would use to offload the catch. There was a white-sided lorry, looking light grey in the few low lights, waiting in the distance at the end of the jetty. The spotlight also picked out a yellow forklift truck that was waiting by the winch. They lifted their glasses and took a sip of wine.

'Bike?'

'You'd have to do a bit of travelling, not too far, carrying a few bits and pieces. Can you get up to Wadebridge, over to say . . . Port Isaac? I'd be paying you. What about carrying things?'

'How much? What for? Never been as far as Wadebridge by bike, shouldn't be a problem though by the

river on the trail. Don't know about Port Isaac . . . there's hills, big ones. Could probably get Aleksy to borrow a car, so yeah . . . if I could go in a car, yeah. Carrying what?'

'Well Demi, what I've got in mind is confidential, you couldn't tell anyone else about it, except the others if they decide to help. They couldn't tell anyone . . . anyone! Can they keep things to themselves? Who is Aleksy? Tell me a bit about yourself. How old are you, why do you hang around in the shelter?'

'There's f all else to do. Don't like the youth club, home's a drag, the crew's fine and we don't upset anyone down there in the shelter. We just hang out. I'm mates with Carla from school. She lives down the road from me, she might look like she's eleven 'cos she's so small but she's fourteen. You should see her on a skateboard, wicked. I'm fifteen. Carla is John's sister, he's the ginger one. Their dad was a fisherman till he couldn't catch enough fish. Fu.. bloody Frenchies' fault they reckon. Had to sell the boat. Now he does odd jobs around the town, works on farms when he can.

Aleksy's sixteen and Tomasz is fifteen. They're Polish, came here with their mums and dads. Aleksy's mum and dad pick flowers and vegetables, on the farms, when they can, Tomasz's mum and dad make candles in a place over near the old airport. Aleksy Laska and Tomasz Krakowski. No-one at school likes them 'cos they're foreign, think they should go back home, idiots. They're OK. They do alright at school, good at languages, German and French, how weird is that! Aleksy's brother's got a car, he . . . er . . . doesn't do much. A Fiesta. A bit crappy but it goes. Aleksy drives it sometimes. We can keep secrets. Carrying what?'

'Demi, I'd like you to . . . ' she stopped when a dark coloured estate car pulled up suddenly next to the shelter and a woman jumped out leaving the door open and ran into the shelter looking frantically around.

'Demelza! Demelza!' the woman shouted.

'Oh crap . . . that's mum, it's not that late is it, I've not got my watch on,' said Demmy.

'Ah, Demmy . . . not Demi,' Cecily said.

'What?'

'What's your surname?'

'Gellis, why.'

She went to window and opened it, shouted. 'Mrs Gellis. Mrs Gellis, Demmy's up here, she's fine, hang on we'll come straight down.' Cecily and Demmy hurried down the stairs and out to the shelter.

'Sorry mum, sorry, didn't see the time.'

'God Demmy, we expected you hours ago, Aunt Abbie came over to talk to you about the French tutorials. We were worried and . . . you know . . .' Her black boots and the bottoms of her baggy blue jeans were muddy. So were the cuffs of her dark check white shirt. She had mousey shoulder length hair.

'Sorry, it's my fault,' Cecily interrupted. 'I was talking to Demmy about a job, a part-time job helping me out at work. At CHILL. That's my office,' she said pointing back at the office. 'I own it. We're a holiday letting agency, renting places to holiday makers, and I need some part-time help. Demmy came in for an interview, I think she would be great.' She was glad she'd been wearing a dark blue trouser suit and mid heels. Smart, classy without being showy.

'Well . . . you should have remembered,' Mrs Gellis spluttered at Demmy. "Come on back, Abbie's waiting. Now, put your bike in the back," she said to Demmy before walking to the back of the Audi A3 estate and opening the rear hatch.

"See what I mean," Demmy said, "Sorry. I think yes, sounds interesting. Still want to know what and how much though, I'll see what she says. I'll still be around, whatever . . see you." Demmy held out her hand and Cecily shook it, looking more surprised than Demmy had. Her mother just stared and Demmy wheeled her bike towards the car.

She had slowly reached up and touched the feather pinned to her collar with the fingertips of her right hand. Remembered the Red Indian that had started it.

Staring towards and through the Audi as it drove off and round the harbour before disappearing, she thought about Billy, her first. She was thirteen, he was fourteen, At Debenhams, outside, trying to understand the window display showing off the new fancy dress department. Cowboys, indians, nurses, doctors, Frankenstein, Dracula, pirates, mermaids ...... amazing.

They'd gone in, up to the second floor. They were all there, more, the indian was mesmerising, with an incredible head-dress of red feathers. She was staring at it, Billy looked at her, she nodded. He reached up and slipped it off the mannequin, the black wig came with it and he slid them, carefully, into his duffel bag, and they had just walked out. No shouting, no sound of running feet, great. Later she gave Billy one of the red feathers, after he had handed her the stolen ice cream at the beach, on the stones.

It was still warm on the deck. She raised her glass to her lips for an absent-minded sip. Nothing doing, it was empty. It brought her back, to Demmy, Aleksy and the others. She smiled. 'So, what are they doing tonight?'

Chapter Fifteen

The B3276 road from Padstow to Newquay cuts across the headland to rejoin the coast at Porthcothan then skirts the sea through Morgan Porth and on down to Newquay. Porthcothan beach is smaller and quieter than many of its neighbours, with a stream rolling out across the sand and jagged rock outcrops like broken teeth flanking the bay.

When John Forbes the Home Office pathologist had called from Truro, Treloar had arranged a conference call from Sam's place. The nearest decent sized station was too far away and with no temporary incident room yet established they needed privacy. Sam's holiday place was only a few miles away. They headed west in convoy turning off the road just before it sloped down into Porthcothan and up a lane across the headland towards the sea.

When Sam pulled off the road onto a short gravel drive and stopped outside a terraced barn conversion Treloar could not help but notice that she had chosen somewhere so reminiscent of his own Lost Farm Barn home high on the moors between St Ives and Penzance. Inside all was white walls and wood, exposed beams and what Treloar family friend, the artist and author Ochre Pengelly, would call 'Kernow kitsch': furnishings in blue and yellow, seascape prints and giant metal fish, starfish ceramic bowl sets, driftwood sculptures and blue and white striped blinds. But it was light, airy and clean. Has she chosen this with me in mind he thought?

'Nice place.'

'Yeah, suits me and it's a friend's so it's not costing me much.'

So much for that theory Treloar he thought. Sam crossed the open-plan kitchen to the fridge.

'What did you make of the Westgarths' Stargazy Pie idea?'

'Well, I can see their point but it seems a little far-fetched. Would you have thought of it if they hadn't mentioned it?

'You're right. If someone was making a statement of some kind it is a little obscure, hardly an OMG moment.' She opened the fridge and peered inside, 'beer, wine, coffee?'

'Beer would be good.'

'Beer it is,' Sam said, pulling two bottles from the fridge door and opening a drawer. 'Let's sit outside,' she gestured to a sliding door.

Treloar pulled the door open and stepped out onto a paved terrace. Wooden fencing and stone walls provided privacy from the neighbouring accommodation. The terrace was east facing, and since the sun had moved over the barn's roof, the area was largely in shadow and pleasantly cool. Treloar selected an Adirondack chair and dragged it to the wooden table. As he sat, a beautiful large grey cat strode purposefully across the lawn to join him, settling at his feet. Treloar liked cats and recognising that, they liked him.

Sam emerged barefoot, carrying two bottles of San Miguel and a bowl of mixed nuts.

'This is well done,' Treloar gestured around him. 'Cheers' he took a bottle an raised it.

'Well, coming from you that's praise indeed,' Sam grinned, lifting her own bottle in return. Treloar had spent over a year on the conversion of the two barns that formed his home doing most of the work himself.

'I see you've met Sorrel,' Sam tilted her bottle towards the cat.

They sat in companionable silence for a while drinking their beer.

'It was great news about your father,' Sam said softly, 'it must have been . . .'

'Mind-blowing?'

'Well . . . yes . . . I mean, obviously. I spoke to Lucia and she was ecstatic. But then, as I remember, she never believed your father had died, just like your mother.'

Some ten years earlier, Treloar's father Jago had disappeared whilst swimming in the sea below the family farm. Late in the previous year he had been revealed to be alive and had returned to Cove Farm. He had been forced from his home under threat to his family from Gideon Spargo, chief of the criminal Spargo clan. His reception upon his reappearance had been mixed. Treloar's mother and second sister Lucia, had indeed been overjoyed; Beatriz, the youngest sister and most devastated by Jago's apparent loss had been at first furious, but her anger had quickly turned to rapture. But it was Eva, the eldest sister, quiet, stoic, unassuming Eva who had turned to stone at their father's reappearance.

'Has Eva mellowed at all towards your father?'

'Well as you probably know from Lucia,' his tone revealed that he was disgruntled by how much family business had been shared with Sam, 'my parents are over in Spain and Eva's busy with the farm. I did sense a . . . softening when I saw her last. Hard for her to forgive unconditionally, but she's a good Catholic; she'll get there.'

'It must have been a tremendous shock . . . for all of you obviously.' Sam was faltering. She had picked up on Treloar's tone and was regretting raising the subject. But hell, it was a huge event, an elephant in the room, was she supposed to ignore it? She knew that when Jago had disappeared it was Eva who had stayed at home with their mother Inès to work the farm. Now she must be feeling cut loose, up-anchored, redundant. She, Sam, would have been seething with resentment.

'. . . everyone tells me. But still . . .'

Sam had not been following and was relieved when Treloar's mobile rang. He put it on speaker and placed it on the table and Sam sensed that they were both grateful for the reprieve.

'John. Hi. I'm here with Sam.'

'Sam! Welcome back and congratulations on the promotion. In at the deep end with a strange one though.'

'Indeed doctor,' Sam acknowledged, 'and thank you.'

'Yes it is very strange,' John Forbes continued. 'I can't tell you much yet. No obvious physical signs of violence. Nothing natural; he was fit, in good shape, no health conditions, and obviously not his age. I can confirm that he was dead when he went into the sand. There are tiny amounts of sand, a few grains, between his lips and in his nostrils but nothing in his mouth or nasal passages or lungs; little enough to surmise that he wasn't pushed down into the sand – which would have taken extreme effort – but rather placed in a hole and sand piled around him. I think cause of death will prove to be a toxin of some sort and no puncture sites, so not injected. So, something he ingested. We're running the tests.'

'OK John,' said Treloar,' but if it is something he's taken, you're saying he took it voluntarily, it wasn't forced down his throat.'

'Well I suppose he could have been held at gunpoint, but no, most likely I'd say it's something he's taken unwittingly.'

'Unless it was an assisted suicide?' Sam said. Looking at Treloar's face, which was showing the equivalent of "you are joking, I presume", she continued, 'well obviously that's unlikely but it is . . . yes, well alright, that would be extremely . . .'

'So John; we wait on the test results. How long?'

'I'm pushing Phil, so as soon as I know, you'll know. I hear he was "posed". Stargazy pie of all things. Someone local then, or someone who knows Cornwall well.'

'Not necessarily,' Sam piped up. 'It was on a Rick Stein programme.'

'Ah indeed', said Forbes, 'well that widens your suspect pool to . . . well, anybody really. I should stick to my own knitting and leave you guys to the hard work.'

'All suggestions welcome John,' said Treloar warmly, 'you know me.'

'Good to hear Phil. I'll get back to you soonest.' And with that he was gone.

Treloar ended the call and pocketed his phone.

'Poison eh? A woman's weapon,' said Sam dramatically.'

'Christ Sam, if I'd said that you'd be throwing that bottle at me. Anyway, lots of poisons leave physical traces, burning of the mouth and throat, and John found none.'

'Drug then?'

'Possibly. Or snake venom.'

'Snake venom??' cried Sam, then seeing Treloar's grin, 'Hah bloody hah.'

'Well it's more likely than assisted suicide.'

'Well my money's still on wifey. Any grown woman who puts up with a stupid name like "Tipsy" is clearly deranged.'

A piercing, grating whine struck up beyond the rear hedge: strimmer. The cat shot off around the side of the barn.

'Well that's one thing I didn't miss in downtown Lyon; the British garden tool at the slightest glimpse of the sun. Shall we?' and with that she picked up her beer and the bowl of nuts and headed indoors.

Chapter Sixteen

As Treloar joined the A30 at the Chiverton Cross roundabout, heading west, the vista opened up and with it, his heart. He was heading home to the high windswept moorlands, the granite headlands of Zennor and Gurnard's, the boundless horizons. There he could breathe.

Sam. He knew he should "put her out of her misery" as people kept telling him, but how? He did nothing to encourage her. When he had first spoken to her on the beach in Padstow that morning he knew nothing had changed. He had briefly thought about saying something there and then, but it was so difficult; he valued her as a colleague, hugely. He just did not want her, and he never would. Surely she must realize by now that it was never going to happen between them? She was far from stupid.

It was an issue. It had gone away, well she had gone away, but now she was back and so was the issue. The elephant in the room. Fuck. He so did not need this.

Everybody was telling him this should work, "they" should work, from his mother to his friend Fitzroy. Though no actually, thinking about it, that wasn't true. One person had remained strangely quiet on the subject: Lucia. Lucia, his second, closest sister who, from her home in Barcelona, had formed a friendship with Sam during her secondment in Lyon. He needed someone to cut him some slack, loosen the hawsers. Lucia?

Looking at it objectively Sam was eminently suitable: clever, attractive, funny. OK, she was his colleague and subordinate but that was not insurmountable. No, he couldn't use that as an excuse. The problem was that he felt absolutely no spark, nothing; certainly no obsessive gut-churning yearning and he needed that. Amy, his ex-wife, had been very beautiful, very silly, totally infuriating, and totally without commitment, but despite it all, despite his sisters' united dislike, despite his friends' dismay, despite their hopeless incompatibility, he had burned for her, always. With Sam there wasn't a flicker.

At the end of the Hayle by-pass he turned off the A30 heading towards Lelant before bearing left up Mill Hill through the dappled shade of the tree tunnels, up, up to meet the B3311 which runs between St Ives on the north coast and Penzance on the south. Turning left towards Cripplesease, Nancledra and Gulval he was almost home.

At the crest of a hill he turned right off the road onto a narrow lane by a brick and slate sign for "Lost Barn Farm Shop". On his left he passed Lower Farm then a few minutes later the rough track on his right to Lost Farm and Higher Farm. The lane petered out into a track heading onwards and upwards until he reached a gap in the hedge, the unmarked entrance to Lost Farm Barn, home.

Treloar had purchased two derelict barns, a stable block and sheds together with twelve acres of woodland, moorland and sloping pasture from family friend, now neighbour, Edmund Maddox who owned the Lost Farm Estate. Over two years he had worked to convert the two barns into a substantial house doing most of the work himself. He parked at the rear of the stable block, grabbed his phone and jacket and headed off, not into the courtyard which would take him to the kitchen door, but round the side of the further shed and off across a scrubby field towards the small wood which bordered the moor. He needed air.

Apart from the issue with Sam, and the not inconsequential matter of a suspicious death, there was still the unresolved problem of his father's return, to be specific, Eva's reaction.

Treloar loved his three sisters fiercely. Beatriz, 'Bee', was the baby, eighteen years' his junior but closest to him in appearance with her golden hair and bright blue eyes. She was bright and trusting, quick to laugh and shout, cheerful, funny and smart. She was an upcoming chef in a St Ives restaurant owned and run by Jowan Nancarrow, happily living with his son Jory, and playing jazz piano and double bass in a local R&B club. Beatriz was sorted.

Lucia was the middle sister some eleven years older than Bee. If Bee was closest to Treloar in appearance, Lucia was closest in spirit. She was brilliant and beautiful, creative, clever and charismatic. Amicably separated from her Italian husband, Luca lo Verde, she lived in Barcelona with her two sons, working as an internationally renowned photographer. Lucia was magnanimous, big-hearted, brave, and eternally optimistic.

Eva. Eva was closest to Treloar in age, just two years younger, but oceans apart in both appearance and temperament. Dark-eyed and once raven-haired like Lucia her hair was now steel grey and close-cropped. Where her siblings were all lean and long-limbed, Eva was thin and small. She was often mistaken for their mother, or when the two were together, for their mother's sister. She was serious, soft-spoken and quiet, brooding and thoughtful. As Doctor Anthony Tremayne, family friend, once described her to perfection: still waters running deep. Eva had had never moved away from the family home Cove Farm. She worked with their mother cultivating fruit, vegetables, herbs and salads and sold them locally and online. Eva had always been there at their mother's side, occupying, if not filling, the void left by their father's disappearance. And now he was back.

Treloar loved all his sisters and they returned that love; they were all fiercely loyal and protective of their big brother. But Lucia was his soul mate. It was to Lucia he had always turned in times of trouble. Lucia would know what to do about Eva. And Sam?

He had been so deep in thought that he had not noticed the path he had taken, but now he found himself at The Dancers, a ring of standing stones high on the carn. He smiled at the thought that this was the place where he came to reflect, to remember, where he often found himself, unwilled. From here the sea was visible on both north and south coasts. Here he felt the most free. To the west he could see Radgell, Ochre and Orlando Pengelly's house standing solitary even higher on the carn. Back behind him to the east was his own home with the small, wooded valley below running down to the sea at Mount's Bay. To the north, he could not see, but could picture, Cove Farm his childhood home standing at the cliff edge, at the end of his boyhood's world.

A sudden gust of wind sent a soft moaning through the nearby wood. Then, directly above him he saw a single raptor hovering: kestrel. After what seemed an age the bird swooped down to land on the furthest stone and fixed him with a cold eye. Treloar shivered and checked the time. He had been home for nearly two hours.

Back at Lost Farm Barn he entered the garden through the wooden gate and crossed to the rear door to the kitchen. As he lifted the latch a small tortoiseshell cat dashed across from under a hedge to wrap herself around his legs, purring and nudging.

'Hola Lola,' he said softly, opening the door to let them in.

'Pronto?'

'Lucia, you're in Milan?'

'It is not for your good looks that they make you Chief Inspector Flip.' Lucia regularly took the boys to Milan to see their father.

'I was up at the stones. I was watching a kestrel.'

"My heart in hiding stirred for the bird, the achieve of, the mastery of the thing"

'Oh yes,' Treloar cried in delight, 'I remember that from primary school.'

'Indeed it was a favourite: *The Windhover*.'

'"The mastery of the thing", that is so perfect.'

'And "the heart in hiding", querido, that too,' Lucia replied sadly, pausing. 'Up at the stones? What is it Flip?'

'Nothing really; just work.'

'And Sam?'

Treloar sighed. In the background in Milan he could hear his nephews laughing.

'A tavola, tutti, a tavola. Mangiamo,' Lucia called out. Then turning back to him, 'Just tell her Flip. She's a big girl. I must feed the boys'

'I know, I know but this murder needs my full attention it's . . . weird.'

'Oh yes, I forget, I know and such a coincidence.'

'What do you mean you know and what coincidence?'

'Bee called. This Ellis man who was killed, cabrón, he cheated Jowan. Whoooah Césare! Basta, basta! Flip, un verdadero caos. I must go. Speak later. Ciao.'

Looking back he would remember how incredible it was that such a throwaway comment, a postscript to a truncated telephone conversation, should prove to be the first distant rumbling of a brewing storm.

Chapter Seventeen

Polzeath is on the north coast of Cornwall just east of the mouth of the Camel estuary in the lee of Pentire headland. It is popular for surfing and that evening, among the usual campers and caravanners and visiting groups of year-end students and school-leavers, was a young man on a mission: Siegfried Carew. He was hunting for the girl from the beach outside Strandloper earlier. He didn't know it yet but her name was Viola Lawrence. He didn't know where she was staying but he was going to find her. And he had.

'In the words of M R James: if you dig you may find that what you seek to uncover was buried for a reason.'

Leah was holding court around the mock campfire. As open fires were banned on the site, the students had cobbled together a couple of disposable barbeques and some citronella outdoor candles in hurricane lamps. They were cooking sausages and baked potatoes in foil.

Leah was regaling the others with tales from M R James, one of her favourite ghost story writers. She had started with *A Warning to the Curious*, where an ancient buried crown is dug up by a man doomed by its discovery, moved on to *A View from A Hill* where a pair of old binoculars give worrying glimpses of the past, and now as night had fallen, she was concluding with her favourite, *Lost Hearts*:

> *"Whilst the girl stood still, half smiling, with her hands clasped over her heart, the boy, a thin shape, with black hair and ragged clothing, raised his arms in the air with an appearance of menace and of unappeasable hunger and longing."*

Whilst Ravi and Joel had scoffed at the start, it was secretly very pleasing to Leah that they had not wandered off, and in fact, were sitting quietly, listening as avidly as the rest of the group. Viola's eyes were like saucers.

As she drew towards the end of the tale, Leah noticed a small, lone figure sitting cross-legged at a distance from the edge of the group at the head of the path leading down to the beach. Suddenly there was a whoosh and a lone firework burst overhead as if scripted, illuminating the shining eyes of a night creature; a cat, a fox . . . something feral. Surely it couldn't hear her from there? She glanced around the faces lit by the candlelight, wrapt, waiting for the end of the story then back to the solitary listener . . . they were gone. She shuddered. She was starting to fall for her own magic.

With the final story finished, the group started to clear away the debris of the feast from the mock campfire with reassuring laughter and nervous chatter, trying to break the spell Leah had cast. Everyone was smiling and congratulating her; it had been a really good night. Well done Leah! Only Viola was nowhere to be seen.

Troubled by the Leah's stories, unable to sleep, Viola was brooding on the past.

It's Halloween and she is having a party. The basement kitchen is filled with fairy lights shaped like pumpkins and witches and moon and star clusters and the large trees in the rear garden are draped in black and lurid green netting strewn with more tiny pumpkin fairy lights.

The theme is Viola's obsession: the Captain Perish books of Ochre Pengelly and people are dressed as vampire pirates, mermaids, smugglers and dead brides. Viola is ecstatic.

As Viola's mother is paranoid there are absolutely no naked flames, no candles or tea-lights, but to compensate for this blatant disregard for Viola's theme there is a wealth of hideous looking food including Viola's younger brother Ferdie's favourite, Blood and Pus, a mixture of fruit jellies taken from Nigella Lawson's book Feast.

Everything is totally cool until she hears her mother screaming from the garden. She rushes out Somebody has lit a Sparkler.

Well that had been another ruined party and another embarrassment to get over with apologies to her friends. This break in Polzeath was not going to be ruined by her mother. Her mother was not here and she was going to make the most of that for sure. And she had seen that guy again. He had been at the campfire listening to Leah. He had not joined them exactly, but he had been there, and she had deliberately left before the end of the stories and come back to the caravan named Marilyn Monroe. Yes she had come back alone and very slowly. But she was sure he had followed. Now he knew where she was staying she felt sure she would see him again. He looked fit and . . . forbidden. Feeling much happier, she went back to her bunk.

They were working a number of holiday homes which were on changeover that Friday. They were all with local holiday letting agencies where Salty had contacts and he had schedules of the changeover days that summer. This would be his second raid of the season. The first had been a total blast.

Chapter Eighteen

Cecily was still on the deck, fresh glass of wine in hand, leaning against the balustrade. It was a warm night. She was propped up by her forearms resting on the stainless steel capping, ankles crossed, wearing an old long T-shirt, originally black but now faded to grey; one of her favourites for relaxing at home when she had no visitors. Jeffrey and Karen's lights were still out. 'Probably needed an early night,' she said to the river, before her eyes glazed and she remembered the meeting earlier in the day.

'Freddie . . . darling . . . hi,' she said in greeting to Pasco Trefry and pecked him gently on his right cheek after levering herself up to his height using his shoulders. 'Well I see I'm not the only one a bit late, what happened?' She had said looking across the room at the earlier arrivals. 'I see Hansel and Gristle have made it, and the Good and the Ugly . . . where's Bad? What's that smell?'

'Cecily!' Pasco whispered loudly, 'Well, not great is it? No, sorry about that. We'll have to wait a while longer for a few more to arrive. I decided to move the venue because Titus has just agreed a six-month let on this place and he wanted the committee to see it first hand - he's keen for us to adopt it as the 'M & M' centre for the festival. Well, you've . .'

'M & M?' interrupted Cecily.

'God, he's got me at it already, sorry, yes, Map and Merchandise, and the festival information and commercial centre. Somewhere to promote it, and from which to run it when it's all happening. You've got to admit, it's in the right place and there's plenty of room.'

'Well, Bad by name, bad by nature . . . what's in it for him? There must be something,' she had asked, not particularly quietly.

'Not quite sure yet,' replied Pasco, 'but I'm certain we'll find out in due course. Speaking of the devil,' Pasco said when he saw Titus Hicks walking towards them from a now

open door at the back of the room.

'Welcome to the Padstow Hub, what do you think?' asked Hicks and extended his arm and turned full circle. 'We've got the office out back,' he pointed to the door from where he had just emerged, 'and of course the café upstairs. Not sure how we'll be using the balcony yet but hey, it's still early days.'

'You're telling me. How long this time Titus for your latest pop-up?' asked Cecily coldly, 'Early June now, so . . . what . . . October, November . . . ? What IS that bloody smell, is there a dead horse somewhere?' She turned and whispered to Pasco, nudging his elbow gently with her own, 'what do you think Freddie?'

'Well hello Cecily, nice to see you too,' said Hicks, 'and how are WE today? Do give me a bit of credit darling. No I've got it for six months with an option, and I reckon if people get behind the Christmas Festival it'll be worth hanging on until the end of the year . . . I was wondering about a November book fair, now that 'you know who' has moved into books . . . what do you think?'

'Well Titus,' interrupted Pasco,' I'm sure you'll tell us more when we get the meeting going, talking of which we really ought to get it moving, come on.' Pasco picked a discarded shelf bracket off a nearby shelf, walked over to the green baize covered tables and rapped hard with the bracket. Then said, when the hubbub had begun quietening 'OK, ladies and gentlemen . . . people please, ah yes, over there is the tea and coffee, please help yourselves if you wish and take a seat so that we can begin. We're already running a little late but we need to crack on, the stragglers will have to catch up when they arrive I'm afraid.'

Three square tables had been pushed together into a rectangle and covered with green baize that overflowed the edges, providing either a modesty panel or an awkward piece of fabric hanging on your knee depending on your point of view. Pasco, as Chair of the committee, stood at the end of the rectangle that allowed him a good view of the harbour whose western wall was just the other side of the road outside.

Titus sat at one of two seats at the other end, next to "Ugly", Jean, a chunky and well wrinkled fifty something with a single bushy caterpillar eyebrow and sideburns. She was the matron at the Camel Bar View Rest Home that Hicks owned. She wore a dark pink matronly dress and red plimsoles. "Good", Barbara, an attractive twenty-year-old blonde who was Titus's Personal Assistant, wearing a white blouse and shortish navy-blue skirt and high-heeled black shoes, sat next to him at right angles.

Cecily sat at the Chair end, and smiled at "Hansel" and "Gristle" as they took the two remaining seats on her side of the table. Hans was German, second generation, and "Gristle", Graza, was Polish. They ran an amazing delicatessen in Padstow that specialised in the sausages which Hans smoked in a large garden shed behind the shop. He had learned how from his father who had been a prisoner of war at a camp on Bodmin Moor and had never returned home. He chose instead to smoke and sell sausages made from the pork and beef he reared, on land rented from local farmers, to shops and then supermarkets across Cornwall. He had married one of the farmers, whose husband had surprisingly chosen to join up, and did not make it back after helping to liberate France.

Graza was thin, gaunt, and bony, even though everyone knew she ate like a horse, and made amazing cakes and sauerkraut for the shop. They wore their shop clothes - blue denim overalls, a salami draped with colourful green sauerkraut embroidered onto the chest pocket below LOCAL DELI, over red and white checked shirts, red Crocs and pink socks. Both had shoulder-length black hair.

"Good" and "Ugly" shouldn't have been there, so if the five people who should have been there but weren't yet turned up, three of them would have to stand. "Nice one Titus, why are they here?" She thought to herself.

When everyone had sat down and quietened, and was looking at him, Pasco said, 'We'll need to agree it formally of course, but we changed the meeting venue so that Titus could show us his latest venture which he has also suggested we adopt as the Ally Ally Oh communication and promotion centre. Or as Titus prefers to call it - the Ally Ally Oh M and M Centre; the Map and Merchandise centre!

Titus has some great ideas and I thought it would be helpful for us all to see the venue before agreeing to use it . . . if we do . . . and er . . . at the same time as discussing what it could be used for . . . to help us . . . . Well, I know it wasn't on the agenda . . . we may need an extra meeting to make up lost time . . . and I'm sorry again for the last-minute venue switch, but off you go Titus.'

'Welcome to the Hub everyone! Sorry about the pong. I think you'll all know that the Cornish pasty company that was here folded when their franchise plan didn't work out, something about volumes and distribution I'm told and not being able to call pasties Cornish if they're not actually made in the county. Anyway, the banker's bad luck was my good luck and here we all are! I'm afraid the whiff is what's left of the boxes of vegetables and a meat freezer that had been turned off without being emptied. Sorry about that . . . not quite as bad now as . . . '

'Titus please, get to the point . . . we've got a lot to cover,' interrupted Pasco.

'Right, sorry Pasco. Yes, I just wanted . . . right . . . well. This is going to be The Padstow Hub. We're opening the ground floor next week, and the upstairs in around three weeks. The Hub will be an interactive social and entertainment centre - a combined licensed internet café, mini-cine, book exchange, and boat trip and B & B booking centre. It's got great footfall as you all know, this close to the harbour, and we'll be bringing a lot of it inside.

I thought it would be ideal for the Ally Ally Oh committee to take a few feet of shelf space and a desk, maybe two, and a couple of phones to promote the festival and run it, take bookings, provide visitor information! And counter space, for a till, for the promotional goods for the venues with festival merchandise and prepaid bookings, or maybe we could use one of mine, but then you wouldn't have a dedicated festival salesperson.'

'Thing is, I need to know now because I need to know how much space to allocate for everything to make sure it all looks good and works together. Pasco thought it sounded like a good plan and, well, here we are. What do you think?'

Stunned silence. Everyone looked at one another, then at Pasco.

'Well . . . merchandise was on the agenda, and promotion, so I thought . . . '

'Yes, Pasco,' Cecily said, 'it was, and great ideas they are too, but . . .' and she ostentatiously picked her copy of the agenda off the table, noisily scrunched it up and rolled it

between her hands into a small ball and threw it across the room. Directly into a square office rubbish bin, just inside the main door, almost ten metres away. "Hansel" and "Gristle" applauded. Cecily bent her head and bent her arm in a mock bow.

'Well Titus, I can see that you've done yourself proud and managed to get yourself a great place here, I wish you well with the venture. Don't know how you do it, so many things on the go, especially with the Camel Bar View Rest Home to run. I have to say though that I do agree with Pasco that it would be useful to have somewhere central and permanent to promote the festival and run it from,' she looked round the table and saw most of the others nodding.

'So, what's the bad news Mr Hicks?' Cecily smiled at him, 'or are you proposing to provide this wonderful facility out of the goodness of your heart? How much, and when?'

Raising the wine glass to her lips she was surprised to find it empty again and started toward the fridge for a refill. Stopping for a second she looked across Pinkson Creek at Halwyn Hill, and smiled, thinking of Jeffrey and Karen again. She gazed at the yellow and white haze of the Padstow harbour lights reflecting off the river beyond the crest of Halwyn Hill, the blue, white and yellow lights opposite along the Rock waterside and the yellow lights at the hilltop above the golf course.

On her way to the kitchen she caught her reflection in the mirror in the hall and paused. Her breasts were still firm, looking great, even if she said so herself. She knew lots of others thought so too, including Pasco Trefry. Her legs were long and looked great below the T-shirt. It was an old replacement for one of four that she and her friend Cindy had bought at the Knebworth '86 concert. *QUEEN* could still be seen in white below the once bright gold coat of arms, one of the iconic emblems of the band.

Chapter Nineteen

'Well my word there is a God,' mumbled Pasco Trefry placing the telephone handset down on its base station.

'What's that Daddy?' asked his daughter Keren.

'Titus Hicks is dead.'

'Who?'

'Titus Hicks. I've known him since we were boys. A nasty, brutish bully then, and a nasty, brutish businessman now.'

'Oh him. I know. Chief fair-weather trader.'

Trefry smiled, 'That's him Peasie.'

'What happened to him?'

'I don't know, just that his body was found early this morning in his garden.'

Josie Franklin, recently retired from the Royal Horticultural Society's gardens in Wisley, had arrived at the garden in question behind a huge ugly brick-built bungalow near St Issey at 08.30 that morning for her weekly visit. She liked to keep her hand in and whilst she found Titus Hicks to be a deeply unpleasant man, their paths rarely crossed and he did have a glorious flower garden. Josie was free to do as she pleased effectively and that was design, planting, dead-heading and a little light weeding. The heavy work, lawn mowing, hedge and tree work was all down to a pair of 'lovely young men'. She walked up the path with her Dalmatian Toby at her heel to pass behind the garage to the gate.

'Hideous house, hideous owner eh Tobes?'

Crossing the lawn to collect a trug from the shed she had noticed that the doors to the large solardome greenhouse were open, which was unusual and unhelpful, as she had left some newly planted seed trays in there and the doors should have been closed overnight. When she reached the shed she noticed that Toby was no longer behind her. Turning, she saw him standing at the open greenhouse door.

'Toby!' she called. The dog ignored her which was unheard of.

'Toby!!' she called more loudly but the dog stood his ground and began to bark.

'For God's sake what's the matter boy?' she called hurrying across to the troubled dog. She reached the trembling dog and followed his fixed stare through the greenhouse door. Inside, staked out on the ground with twine and pegs like a parody of Swift's Gulliver was Titus Hicks, dead.

At 10.30 DI Sam Scott was waiting for Dr Zac Jordan to conclude his examination of the body and talking to Treloar on her mobile.

'Where are you Phil?'

'Just turning off the A389. What have we got?'

'Well, as you're so close, let's wait for your first impressions,' and with that she rang off.

Born and bred in Cornwall, Félipe Treloar loved his homelands with a passion, rejecting an offer of promotion to move to London to join the Met, but the summer roads were like Danté's circles of hell, growing in horror as the season deepened. This morning he had been at a standstill on the A30 Hayle bypass for fifteen minutes for no apparent reason. If this case dragged on, getting home would become a nightmare lottery and he would have to find somewhere closer to Padstow. Once the school holidays started, the random nature of the traffic tailbacks would make the journey home untenable. And those days were fast approaching. When the schools let out and all hell lets loose. Hordes with their noise, pollution and litter; breathing his air, clogging his roads, dirtying his beaches, spoiling his life. July and August; the nightmare weeks. Perhaps he could stay with Sam? Maybe not. Not funny, not even a little bit funny. Sam. He couldn't think about that now.

In stark contrast to his plain utilitarian property, Hicks' garden was a revelation. Terraced banks stretched to the distant rear hedge with bed after bed of flowers in shades of blue, white and purple. Treloar recognised some of them from his mother's walled garden at Cove Farm: cornflower, campanula, nigella and swathes of lavender. To the side of the garden stood a large, solardome greenhouse full of lush green plants.

Treloar walked down the granite chippings' path towards a group of people standing by the open doors to the dome. He could see Sam in conversation with the doctor from the Ellis body deposition site at St George's Cove. He was touching her arm and leaning in to speak; Christ, he practically had his tongue in her ear. Tosser. This shitty day was heading downhill at speed.

'Dr Jackson,' Treloar smiled, extending his hand.

'Dr Jordan,' Sam corrected with a frown. Treloar never got names wrong, never.

'So what have we here doctor?' he continued.

'Can't tell you much except he's dead obviously. Could be natural causes, could be something else. No obvious external violence though and he was bound either after death or whilst unconscious; there are no signs of a struggle; no chafing or marks of any kind.'

'Could he have been complicit, some sex game gone wrong?'

The doctor frowned, 'well that is possible I suppose.'

'For fuck's sake Phil, he's fully dressed. And look at the setting!' Sam spat.

'Please excuse my colleague's language doctor,' Treloar smirked.

Sam glared at him, but Zac Jordan turned to her with a smile, 'Not at all. I find such words very sexy coming from a beautiful woman.' Sam was aghast and Treloar snorted his derision but the doctor was oblivious to both.

'Yes Inspector, I have noticed the setting and I assume you are alluding to the resemblance to the Eden Project biodomes.' Christ why was he sounding so pompous he asked himself? This poxy little doctor was getting to him. Basta. Enough.

Zac Jordan turned to Sam. 'Well, I must get on, busy day. I'll email my report unless you'd like to discuss my findings over dinner Inspector?'

Sam was speechless. 'Very like that other chap though, the staged body I mean. Still, that's your domain Inspectors,' and with a nod he hitched up his cargo shorts, picked up his bag and sauntered up the path towards the bungalow, pausing to smell a bank of lavender.

'Christ,' said Treloar, 'I thought he was going to pick you a bunch of flowers!'

'Not quite Doc Tremayne,' said Sam wistfully, referring to the former police surgeon.

'Fuck me no,' Treloar snorted.

'Language, Chief Inspector.'

'Not sexy?' Treloar grinned.

'Perleeese,' Sam huffed.

The two inspectors walked back through the garden towards the house. They could not help but admire the wondrous array of flowers. Sam chuckled softly.

'What?' asked Treloar.

'Keast was here before you arrived, first on the scene. He was telling me that word has it he grows, grew, all these so that he didn't have to shell out on florists when his care home residents died.'

'Well with his rate of attrition that would be a key financial consideration.

'Doesn't make the flowers any less beautiful though.'

'No Sergeant.'

'Inspector.'

'Sorry, old habits . . .'

'Well all this beauty is not down to Hicks. The gardener who found him, Josie Franklin is responsible for the glory.'

'Where is she now?'

'Oh I sent her home. She had a dog who was very distressed. I think the dog was upsetting her more than the dead man. He surely was not liked.'

'Could she tell us anything useful?'

'No not really. She saw nobody, heard nothing until the dog started barking. The only thing out of place was that the solardome door was open. I took her details and let her leave.'

'Fine. What does this remind you of?'

'The Eden Project. We've already agreed that.'

‘No, I was thinking more about the staging of the body, the contrivance.’

‘Well obviously it’s the same as Jolyon Ellis. Well, not the same, but another Cornish theme to the body deposition site.’

‘But why the Gulliver twist?’

‘Well, I suppose without that, the death might have looked like natural causes and we wouldn’t have made the connection to the Eden Project and the link to Ellis and the Cornish theme.’

‘And the same type of victim.’

‘How so?’

‘Well both local businessmen with dubious reputations. These local business groups can get very heated: battles over the Christmas lights, late night opening, parking, advertising and media promotion, you name it, they fight over it.’

‘But this is taking the usual petty power struggles to the extreme isn’t it?’

‘Yeah. There’s something else going on here. It’s too . . . weird.’

‘Holy shit! Porthaven. Oliver Osborne. You’re right. How did I miss that?’

‘A while back now Sam. Coincidence perhaps?’

‘Really?’

‘Well I can’t see a link between a wealthy London QC found staked out, drowned on a beach and two dodgy Cornish businessmen, and besides, we know why Osborne was killed and who did it. And there was no Cornish theme there. Maybe this is that exception that proves the rule: pure coincidence.’

‘Or copycat? It was a well-known story.’

‘Indeed it was.’

As Treloar drove up the hill out of Padstow along the narrow hedged lanes which resembled bobsleigh chutes, heading for the A30, what he could not know was that a solution to the Sam problem was just over the horizon.

Jean Post@dogwalkingpadstow13   45m
Cming bk frm creek walk, JimtheDog said polis fnd + body, in Eden like Gulliver. Jeepes! Bys in blu on Trevorrick Rd wont let thru. Got to use fpath! Wots goinon? #padstowdogbody @dogwalkingpadstow23

Andy Sykes@dogwalkingpadstow23   42m
Mornin Jean. Was Toby, Josie Fs Dal found Titus Hicks dead in his greenhse! Tied dn like Gulliver. Any #dogwalkingpadstows know more? Are we safe? @dogwalkingpadstow13 @SolihullBillingDwalker #padstowdogbody @bbcsouthwestnewstoday

Joy D@loveDwalkingpadstow   39m
Mornin Andy. Down by Camel. Seen O. Heard Eden setting & tied like Gulliver. Sounds mad. Why the dogs? Are we safe? @dogwalkingpadstow23 #padstowdogbody

BBC @bbcsouthwestnewstoday   36m
The BBC has learned that a body has been found in a garden in St Issey in an unusual theatrical setting. Suspicious death thought likely. News still coming in, will update as we learn more. If you have info let us know. #suspiciousdeathscornwall

Andy Sykes replied
John Billing@SolihullBillingDwalker   31m
V quiet again for Rusty & me on canal Dwalk. Not like down there! Careful Dwalkers. Whats Eden? Who's Gulliver? After sardine pie! Nuts!!!!!!! @loveDwalkingpadstow @dogwalkingpadstow23 #dwalkerssolihul #wmidsdwalkersl

Andy Sykes@dogwalkingpadstow23   27m
Hey John. Worryin times. Loads bys in blu about, don't know whats hapenin esp re Dwalkers. 2 murders now. Eden = big Cornwall

indoor gardens place. Gulliver??!! You're kidding right!!! @SolhullBillingDWalker @padstowdogbody @loveDwalkingpadstow #suspiciousdeathscornwall #padstowdogbody

Gillian Trebarry@gillianDwalkerpadstow 23m
Out early this am. Was guy on stepladder with camera by Titus wall. George barked hard so crossed rd. Heard Josie Fs Toby going mad b4. B4 lots bys in blu here, only 2 then. None came to me @bbcsouthwestnewstoday #suspiciousdeathscornwall #padstowdogsbody @dogwalkingpadstow23

Police@DevonandCornwallPolice 17m
If you have information about the suspicious death being reported in St Issy this morning please make yourself known to local police and pass on what you know.

Andy Sykes replied
Barry C@IslingtonDwlkers35 13m
Hey Padstow Dwalkers. Be careful down there! Maybe pair up so u rnt finding stuff on your own (well, your pals and you). @dogwalkingpadstow23 #padstowdogsbody #islingtondwalkers

John Billings Barry C and 234 others follow, @gillianDwalkerpadstow replied
Andy Sykes@dogwalkingpadstow23 11m
Hey Islington bloke. Tks. Maybe not a bad plan @SolhullBillingDWalker #padstowdogbody @loveDwalkingpadstow #suspiciousdeathscornwall #padstowdogbody #padstownews

Gillian Trebarry@gillianDwalkerpadstow 10m
Good idea Barry, scary stuff. Just call your Dwalker pals & sort. PLEASE RETWEET. @dogwalkingpadstow23 @loveDwalkingpadstow #padstowdogsbody #padstownews

Chapter Twenty

Viola came rushing across the grass. 'Guys! Guys! she's coming here! Ochre's coming here! Can you believe it?'

'No,' said Leah flatly. She was totally unimpressed by Polzeath and couldn't imagine why any self-respecting, successful person with a choice would want to come to the place.

'Here? Why?' asked Joel.

'Here? Polzeath?' asked Ravi simultaneously.

'Well . . . no. Not *here*, here. Not to Polzeath actually, not to this camp-site obviously.'

'Not here at all then,' Leah teased.

Viola glared at her, hands on hips. 'She is coming to Padstow. She is coming to film a piece to camera for the preview for some festival thing happening in the autumn. And guess who else is coming?'

'Prince William?' asked Leah with feigned innocence.

'Of course not. Dr Roz!'

'Whoah . . .' said Joel, 'sex on legs.'

'You heard she's getting married?' said Ravi sadly.

'So?' said Joel, 'I don't want to marry her, I just want to fu . .'

'Enough already!' shouted Viola cutting him off.

The boys exchanged grins as she stomped off towards the beach path.

'I'll go after her,' said Ravi getting to his feet. He had a secret crush on Viola which everyone knew about. Leah watched as he caught her up and they crossed the beach together heading for Strandloper.

Fifty miles to the west and a cultural world away, Ochre Pengelly was talking with her brother Orlando at their ancestral home Radgell, high on the carn above Zennor.

'God almighty. Why am I doing this? It's bad enough

having to do the artwork, but to turn up for some promotional jamboree? Really?'

'Because, sister dear, it's in a very good cause and one dear to the heart of your precious readers, so your adoring Perishers will love you afresh and be falling over themselves to buy more books and merchandize.'

'Brother, thou art a cynic.'

'Realist, realist, please. I think it's a splendid idea. Just think what we could do around here with the extra funds; we could finally do something about the tower. The western side is falling down.'

'God how I suffer for my art and your home.'

'Your art? Scarcely. Your painting, your sculpture, that is your art. These juvenile fantasy sagas are . . . well, your whoring.'

'Hah! You don't object to the money.'

'Absolutely not. You earn it, I'll spend it.'

'Do you have to be so judgemental?'

'No, but I do so enjoy it.'

'Anyway. I've told Hermione no more merchandize.'

'Oh why?' whined Orlando. 'I loved those miniature pirates. They reminded me of our childhood and those plastic figurines that would land in your cereal bowl from the Rice Krispies packet.'

'You never ate Rice Krispies. In fact, you never ate breakfast. You fabricate the past Orlando.'

'Better than remembering it,' he said softly, and they exchanged a wistful look and changed the subject in mutual unspoken agreement. 'Shall we eat out tonight?'

'Yes! Let's go to Bee's.'

'Marvellous thought.'

'Bee's' was *Seafood on Stilts*, a popular restaurant on the harbour in St Ives where Bee – Beatriz – Treloar's youngest sister, was the rising star chef.

Chapter Twenty-One

The grey sky was low that morning, clouds touching her face like moist cobwebs as Ruby walked along Padstow quayside. The weather had changed. It would be quieter in Strandloper with fewer visitors to the beach, so she had decided, against her better judgement, to attend a presentation on the Ally Ally Oh festival. Ruby was not a joiner; not of clubs, committees, parties; there were no like-minded people in her world. In her view, at the extreme, if you put a person in a uniform they join a different reality, creating bullies and bullied, from the Brownies to the SS. She did not get involved in the local tourism promotion scene, but Josh had persuaded her that the festival was a good thing that she should sponsor and so she had received an invitation to that morning's event. Anyway, with Tommy Holding's reappearance in her life she needed the distraction.

'Hey! Hey! Ruby! Hang on!' came a voice behind her. She turned to see a small dark-haired woman dashing along the pavement towards her.

'Hello Tulip. What brings you here?' Ruby greeted her with a smile. Tulip Khan was a freelance journalist who had featured Strandloper in a piece for a national that Easter. She and Ruby had hit it off and the review had been extremely positive.

'This Ally Ally Oh thing,' Tulip replied, struggling with a laptop bag, a huge tote, and a takeaway coffee.

'Here. Give me one of those,' Ruby held out her hand.

'Thanks you're a star,' said Ruby offloading the tote.

'What the hell have you got in here, bricks?' Ruby swung the bag's strap over her head and settled it on her shoulder.

'Oh you know just . . . stuff. I have to carry so much shit around and I'm paranoid about leaving anything in the car. You know how cutthroat my business is. What are you up to, scouting out a new venue for the Russell empire?'

'Hah! Never in Padstow. Wrong crowd. No, like you, for my sins, I'm off to this festival 'thing'. Josh suckered me in.'

'Oh come on. It's in a good cause, not just a pocket-liner for the shoulder months.' In the course of research for her article Tulip had picked up the jargon; the shoulder months referred to May and June, September and October, sitting at either end of the main summer season.

'Good cause? Yeah well, we'll see. We're heading for the Padstow Hub, Titus Hicks' new headlining project and if he's involved, well I wouldn't be so sure myself.'

'Shit. Haven't you heard?'

'What?'

'He's dead.'

The Padstow Hub was a 'new concept'. A redeveloped failed Cornish pasty franchise and the rooms above it, had been converted into a series of meeting rooms and a large open space where the upper floor had been stripped, its partition walls demolished. This space, incongruously titled 'the heart of the hub', overlooked the inner harbour and out across the Camel estuary to Rock. The irony, that this was the last project to be undertaken by Titus Hicks, was not lost on most of those assembled that morning. The crowd had divided into whispering clusters and there was little doubt over the subject of their hushed conversations.

The room was unfurnished apart from a raised dias against one wall where a small group were locked in intense discussion. A distinguished middle-aged man was surrounded by four women vying for his attention.

'There he is, our leader. Pasco Trefry and his hareem,' Ruby whispered to Tulip. She scanned the room, nodding and occasionally smiling as she recognised people. Then her gaze settled on a couple standing alone and silent by the window. The woman, in her thirties, was dressed smartly and stylishly in a navy blue linen suit which stood out amongst the casually attired crowd. But it was the man who drew Ruby's fascinated attention. He was tall and lean but fit-looking with tousled blonde hair. Dressed in stone chinos and a pale blue cotton shirt, sleeves rolled to the elbow, he too was scanning the room whilst speaking to his companion without ever looking at her. Suddenly his lighthouse gaze landed on her and Tulip and his face broke into a deeply attractive broad grin as he raised a hand.

'Hey!' called Tulip beside her, smiling and returning

the man's gesture.

'Who in the name of God is that?' purred Ruby.

Treloar and Sam had arrived before the crowd. This was to be a chance for them to observe a large part of the community in which both Jolyon Ellis and Titus Hicks operated. From what they had overheard so far neither man would be much missed. The overriding mood was one of muted excitement. People were intrigued, but not overly concerned, at the recent deaths of two of their neighbours

'Well our victims don't seem to have had many friends here, and this must have been their milieu, the business and commercial community,' said Sam quietly.

'No. There's hardly glee but there's sure as hell no grief,' Treloar was scanning the room when he smiled and raised a hand in greeting. Sam followed his gaze across the room to locate the object of his attention.

'Friend of yours?' she asked.

'That, Inspector, is a very rare creature indeed.'

'Really?' Sam felt her hackles rising. She needed to get a grip on this adolescent jealousy.

'That is a member of the press with a conscience and a moral compass: Tulip Khan.'

'Ah yes. I've heard Fitz say good things about her.'

"Fitz' is it?' Treloar smiled, referring to a mutual colleague who had helped them both in dire times. A former Metropolitan Police Chief Inspector, Fitzroy's current role, indeed his entire agency, was now more sinister, more covert and more powerful than the Met. Fitzroy was some kind of spook.

'Benedict Fitzroy, in my not inconsiderable experience of the man, has no bad things to say about any female of any age or appearance, Treloar continued.'

'Yes you're right. He's another rare creature: a man who actually likes women for themselves, and we recognise that in a man and value it.'

'That's me told.'

'But seriously, I understand she was very helpful with the situation with Col and the Spargos.'

'Indeed she was. I like her.'

'And who's that with her?'

'Mmm?'

'With Tulip Khan. Small dark woman just by her shoulder. She's very . . .'

Looking back on that moment, Treloar would remember it as like an Alfred Hitchcock dolly shot. Everything emptied from his mind, and his vision, the surrounding noise, the assembled people, Sam and Tulip Khan, as he stared at this woman.

'Don't you recognise him? Surely you've seen him in the papers or on the television, he's often in the media. That, my sweet, is Detective Chief Inspector Félipe Treloar of the Devon and Cornwall Police. He's lush isn't he?' Tulip grinned. Ruby was silent, transfixed, but before Tulip could notice, the sound of clapping hands and a raised voice echoed through the room.

'Ladies and gentlemen! Ladies and gentlemen please!' Pasco Trefry called out and the murmurings subsided and all eyes face front.

'As I'm sure most, if not all, of you will know, Titus Hicks was found dead yesterday.'

A few gasps and murmurings ensued but Trefry continued.

'Whilst Titus was not directly involved with the festival, the committee believes that it is only fitting that this gathering be cancelled as a mark of respect.'

There were further mutterings and a couple of snorts from the room.

'I trust that you will all concur and appreciate the spirit in which this decision has been taken. I hope we may rearrange for a not too distant occasion. Thank you.'

And with that, he walked down the steps from the dias and left the room.

As Trefry was speaking, a couple slipped in at the back. They would have gone unnoticed but for the fact that Ochre Pengelly was impossible to miss: a tall statuesque woman with a mass of blonde hair piled seemingly precariously on her head, dressed in a shocking pink shirt-dress and lime green trainers. Beside her, in black, brother Orlando was a wraithlike shadow.

'Well now what?' asked Ochre grumpily.

People seemed reluctant to leave as if they might miss

something and small groupings reformed. The committee party had descended from the dias in Trefry's wake and were circulating amongst the crowd. One individual caught Ochre's eye. Watching this woman as she worked the room was like watching a beautiful fragile vase revolving on a turntable. Perfect. But at closer inspection, occasionally the light would catch a tiny flaw, a weakness that could cause the vessel to shatter at the slightest touch. And Ochre watched closely. It was there in the woman's eyes, caught briefly at a certain angle. Ochre knew it for what it was. She recognised it from her childhood: madness. Some people are too far out to rescue.

It is a glorious late summer's afternoon and two children are sitting on the lawn of a walled garden scenting of roses. The boy is reading aloud from Treasure Island*:*

'He was plainly blind, for he tapped before him with a stick, and wore a great green shade over his nose and eyes . . .'

From an open window of the looming granite house behind them come raised voices and the sound of glass smashing. Neither child reacts. It is just their parents: normalcy. Time passes slowly in the languorous buzzing heat. Then a new sound does disturb the world of Robert Louis Stevenson and the boy, Orlando Pengelly, falters and falls silent. A strange wail, perhaps a distant seabird, but growing louder and louder. Instinctively both children turn toward the source.

Blocking the sun, growing larger and larger, crying louder and louder a dark shape is tumbling down the side of the house's south western tower.

With a splintering thud, it hits the tall garden wall and disappears beyond onto the moor.

Later that evening the brother and sister will be told that their mother, Orla Pengelly, is dead and the pirate Captain Perish Penhaligon will be conceived in the mind of the eight year old Loveday (Ochre) Pengelly. It would be a decade before Perish Penhaligon would set sail beyond her imagination with the launch of Captain Perish and the Doom Maiden, *but he was formed that day.*

Ochre and her brother Orlando were standing by the window

avoiding everyone.

'Tell me again, brother dearest, why am I doing this?'

'Because it is a good cause; because it will be good for your profile and your precious Perishers will love it; and, above all, because Pasco is our friend.'

'Pasco is your friend.'

'Now sister dear you know that's unfair. I may have met him at school but he has been our guest, and we his, on many occasions, and, as you are well aware, he has been in love with you for thirty years.'

'Orlando you talk such nonsense. Pasco was totally devoted to his late wife and you know it.'

'That is irrelevant. One never gets over one's first love.'

'Really. You don't talk nonsense; you talk utter bollocks.'

Ruby Russell and Tulip Khan had been forced into a corner by the crowds surging towards the buffet table in the spirit of what a pity it would be to waste good food at an ecological event. Ruby had lost sight of Treloar in the melée following Trefry's announcement.

'Are you OK Ruby, you seem distracted? Were you a friend of Titus Hicks?'

Ruby spluttered. 'Hicks? Christ No.'

'Yes, I heard he could be a pain in the arse.'

'Titus Hicks was not a pain in the arse; he was an arsehole. A pain in the arse is temporary but an arsehole is forever.'

'Or not, as in his case,' Tulip said.

'Mmm?'

'But seriously Ruby are you OK? You seem . . . troubled.'

'What? No, I'm fine. Now fill me in on these people. Who is the woman in the very red dress who has just dragged poor Pasco Trefry back into the room by the arm? He looks terrified.'

'That is Cecily Farrant. She runs CHILL, the holiday letting agency. Very ambitious, very successful, apparently ruthless. I wouldn't trust her as far as your bodyguard Spence could throw her.'

'Ah, quite some way then. The name does ring a bell now I think about it; I've heard her described as driven.'

'Yeah, driven right round the bend; she's fucking nuts if you ask me. Too . . . too just too.'

'And the girl scurrying around like a mouse?'

That's Teresa Soames-Ellis, Trefry's general factotum and recent widow.'

'*That* Ellis?'

'Indeed.'

'Christ what's she doing here? She doesn't look grief-stricken to me.'

'I know, interesting isn't it? Still I've heard he was another arsehole. Very dodgy.'

Pasco Trefry and Cecily Farrant were joined by another woman, a willowy flame haired beauty in a green shift dress and scarlet stilettos. Very chic, not very Cornwall.

'Who's that? She looks out of place in this mob?' asked Ruby.

Tulip looked across, 'Oh well now, that is the new rising star of the business community. She's doing that new hotel just along from you towards St Agnes, you know The Salt Creek. Very plush, very expensive, very London. I'm surprised you don't know her: Coco Holding. She's married to Tommy Holding, the rock impresario. You must have heard of him.'

Ruby visibly paled and took a step backwards.

'Shit girl, you really are not OK are you?' asked Tulip concerned.

'No, no, I'm fine. Let's get out of here. Drink?'

'Fine by me. I thought you'd never ask.'

As Ruby and Tulip slipped out of the room by a side door, a sudden burst of laughter drew the attention of the remaining audience to the main entrance where a tall woman in a Panama hat swept into the room with a trailing entourage.

'I am soooo sorry. Are we werry late?' she gushed.

Pasco Trefry turned aghast to the new arrival. 'Christ, nobody told her we've cancelled. That should have been Tipsy but under the circumstances . . . excuse me.'

He strode across the room arm extended to greet the latecomers. Watching the commotion, Orlando Pengelly turned to his sister.

'My, my. Well that's a coup for Pasco. He's kept that under his hat: Dr. Roz no less.'

Dr Rosamond Lacey had read Natural Sciences at Christ's College Cambridge specialising in Earth Sciences, Climate, Science and Oceanography in her third year before taking her doctorate at Imperial College London. In 2013 she had appeared as a guest expert on a BBC documentary on the islands of Britain and had never looked back. Now she was the nation's favourite documentary presenter with a stable of highly successful 'science for the masses' programmes and a celebrated appearance on a dance show. 'Dr Roz' was flying high.

She was instantly recognisable for her quirky 1950s fashion style; a fondness for Capri pants and Peter Pan collars, pencil skirts and flared dresses; kitten heels, ponytails and scarlet lipstick, and her trademark Panama hat. Her delivery was intimate and chatty, gossipy and conspiratorial, and highly animated with much gesticulation and waving of hands. She was loved by grandmothers and teenage boys alike. But earlier in the year she had broken the hearts of thousands of the latter when she had announced her engagement to twenty one year old Internet wunderkind Badge (Bajinder) Wood.

That summer had brought her to Cornwall with a dual purpose. She was preparing to cover the *Ally Ally Oh* festival on her new autumn series: *The Rolling Deep*, and she was planning her wedding, to be celebrated at The Salt Creek hotel which would open temporarily, especially for the occasion, before its formal opening to coincide with the start of the festival. Her production team was staying in a large rental property in the centre of Padstow, while Dr Roz was at Rick Stein's St Edmunds House, for now.

Chapter Twenty-Two

After the aborted Ally Ally Oh festival gathering Treloar walked through the Padstow streets to the property which Diggory Keast had secured as a temporary incident room for the team. The Count House was new to CHILL, recently wrested from a rival letting agent by Cecily Farrant, and yet to be listed. The ground floor had been completely refurbished in preparation for the first letting with wooden floors throughout, wooden blinds, wooden fish murals and wood-burning stoves. God help the forests. Upstairs, one ensuite bedroom was ready for occupation and this was to be Treloar's temporary home when required.

Keast had arranged a two month initial rental with CHILL, guaranteeing total privacy. This seemed very generous giving the income the company was foregoing, but Cecily Farrant was adamant that helping the police was good for the company's profile, especially with the local population who could be hard to keep 'onside', and as the property would not have been ready for occupancy that summer the delay was 'no great shakes'.

From the police's perspective, The Count House was in central Padstow and offered ample parking, privacy and a pleasant working environment. It also provided a fully equipped kitchen, superfast Broadband and overnight accommodation. With the installation of some secure cabinets and the temporary changing of the locks, which did discomfort Ms Farrant, the deal was done.

The properties that CHILL managed were at the higher end of the market: nothing that would cost less than three quarters of a million pounds to buy. As Diggory Keast was wont to say 'Christ, where are we supposed to live?' Many locals felt that, like Venetians, they were being forced out by tourists, driven inland from the coast, albeit not by giant cruise ships.

Not for the first time, finding himself in front of a temporary incident room housed in holiday accommodation, Treloar was struck by how the places lent themselves to the purpose. There were always plentiful furnishings: multiple seating areas, a large dining table, more crockery, hell more everything than you would expect to find when you considered that a house that would normally home a family of four or five was stretched to sleep eight or ten and fitted out accordingly.

As he neared the arched entrance into the former courtyard his mobile rang.

'Treloar.'

'Phil it's Tulip Khan.'

'Hi Tulip,' he said with a smile in his voice, 'sorry I didn't get a chance to speak with you at the meeting. What can I do for you?'

'Yes well, it's rather what I can do for you.' Tulip was normally very upbeat and the flat serious tone of her voice troubled Treloar. 'I'm sorry,' she continued, 'it's not good but I thought you'd want to know soonest.'

'What is it?'

'There's a story popping up on the feeds. It's not our there yet, not widely, but it will be soon. It's about you.'

'Me?'

'Yes. It's linking you with the murders.'

'Me?'

'Yes Phil you! It says you knew both Jolyon Ellis and Titus Hicks, that you resented them, and it implies that you had motive to kill them.'

'Me?'

'God stop saying that!'

'Sorry, but it's ridiculous.'

'Look I'll text you what I can'

'Where's it going to appear, and who wrote it?'

'I don't know . . . well . . . not in print, not yet but . . . it's out there. Oh, I forgot, you don't do much social media do you? But there's already some of the TV and papers kicking it about on the feeds and online news. People are picking it up and it's starting to circulate. Tap the links I send and you'll see. It all depends who picks it up and runs with it. But be prepared, I haven't told you the worst of it yet.'

'Go on.'

'It also makes some not so subtle references to Amy Angove.'

'Huh,' Treloar snorted, 'well that's hardly news; it became common knowledge that we'd been married, albeit briefly and a long time ago.'

'No Phil,' Tulip said softly, 'It's not that,' she hesitated, 'it's implying that you might have been involved in her death.

'Jesus!' Treloar exploded over the phone causing passers-by to stare, 'that's outrageous, that's . . . libellous!'

'No. No I don't think it is. It's clever, subtle, 'reading between the lines' stuff. It's very carefully worded, but it's there: the allegation. Basically it's putting forward the premise that you have killed three people: serial killer cop.'

'It says that?' Treloar was incredulous.

'No, no of course not. That's me . . . summarising. But you need to get some advice on how to respond and warn the powers that be.'

'Christ almighty.'

'Sorry to be the bearer of such bad news but I thought you'd want to know. I'll text you.'

'Yeah, yeah thanks Tulip,' and with that she was gone. He had wanted to ask her about her companion at the festival meeting, but now, with this. Shit.

12:37

Hey Phil, here's a couple of feed links, + follow the #s to see what people are saying.
www.uknewsnow/police/suspiciousdetective
www.newsukfeed/police/cornwallmurders
Call if I can help. Best xTx

12:39

Thanks. #'s? Phil

12:41

Luddite! On the feed pgs you'll link to you'll see hashtag (#) links, tap them to see social media comments. (If you need to sign up to see them DO IT)
Good luck Tx

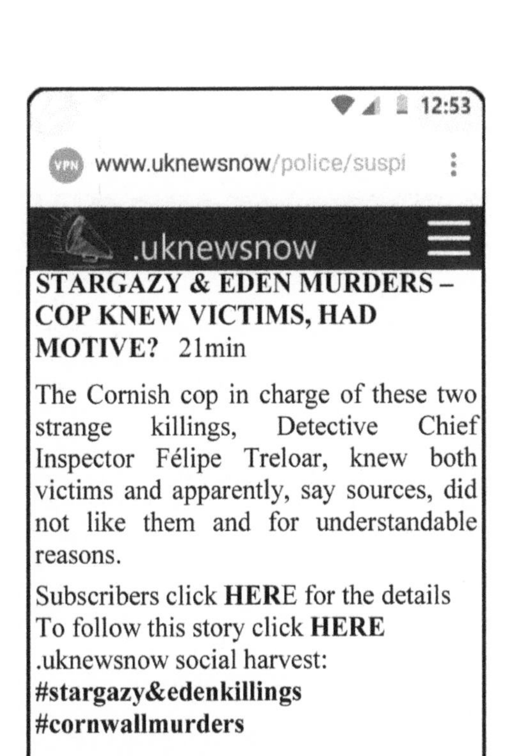

STARGAZY & EDEN MURDERS – COP KNEW VICTIMS, HAD MOTIVE? 21min

The Cornish cop in charge of these two strange killings, Detective Chief Inspector Félipe Treloar, knew both victims and apparently, say sources, did not like them and for understandable reasons.

Subscribers click **HERE** for the details
To follow this story click **HERE**
.uknewsnow social harvest:
#stargazy&edenkillings
#cornwallmurders

CORNWALL MURDERS – DETECTIVE SUSPECTED? 43min

It has been revealed that a senior detective in the Devon and Cornwall Police Force is closely connected to at least two murders in Cornwall and may be under suspicion himself.

Subscribers click **HERE** for the details

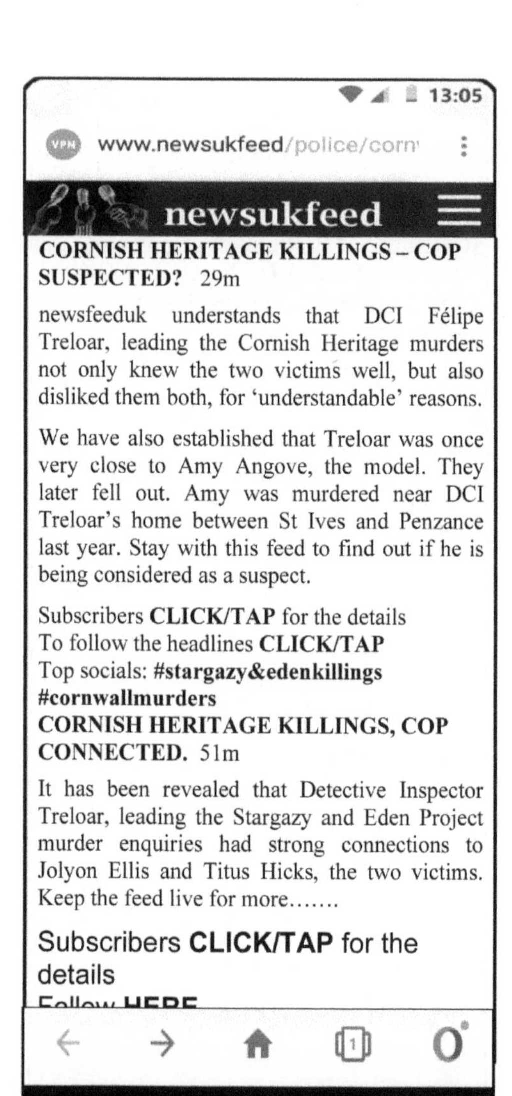
13:05
www.newsukfeed/police/corn
newsukfeed
CORNISH HERITAGE KILLINGS – COP SUSPECTED? 29m
newsfeeduk understands that DCI Félipe Treloar, leading the Cornish Heritage murders not only knew the two victims well, but also disliked them both, for 'understandable' reasons.
We have also established that Treloar was once very close to Amy Angove, the model. They later fell out. Amy was murdered near DCI Treloar's home between St Ives and Penzance last year. Stay with this feed to find out if he is being considered as a suspect.
Subscribers CLICK/TAP for the details
To follow the headlines CLICK/TAP
Top socials: #stargazy&edenkillings #cornwallmurders
CORNISH HERITAGE KILLINGS, COP CONNECTED. 51m
It has been revealed that Detective Inspector Treloar, leading the Stargazy and Eden Project murder enquiries had strong connections to Jolyon Ellis and Titus Hicks, the two victims. Keep the feed live for more.......
Subscribers CLICK/TAP for the details

Chapter Twenty-Three

Treloar's boss, Detective Chief Superintendent Nicholas 'Nicky' Chamberlain, was based at Cornwall County Police HQ in Bodmin. There was no way Treloar could get there quickly but Keast and the boys had worked miracles in The Count House and there was a fully functioning teleconferencing facility so soon the two men were face to face, virtually. Treloar brought Chamberlain up to speed and had forwarded the information Tulip Khan had texted him.

'Christ Phil, you know the game. They'll print it on the cover and then print the retraction three days later buried on the inside pages. As for the online blogs, vlogs and what-have-you . . . there's little control and less redress. Our only chance is to outmanoeuvre them.'

'But Nicky, for Christ's sake, we can't even identify them!'

'We can't, you and me, but somebody can and by Christ somebody will, I'll see to that.'

'Right. Thanks.'

'So run it past me again; how you are connected with Ellis and Hicks.'

'I didn't know either of them; never met them, never spoke to them. But there is a tenuous link to both. One of Ellis's clients in the EU funding scam was *Seafood on Stilts* the St Ives restaurant where my youngest sister chefs.

'Right well that's small beer. Half of Cornwall's businesses were clients. And Hicks?'

'Well, Elspeth Angove, my ex-wife Amy's grandmother, was a resident who died in one of his care homes.'

'Was it a suspicious death?'

'Hardly. She was a hundred and four. I think that constitutes old age in anyone's book.'

'Mmm. But Hicks did have a bad reputation. Higher than average number of deaths in his homes.'

'Agreed. But Elspeth's death was definitely natural and peaceful.'

'Yes Phil, but the connection is there for these vultures: dodgy care home and dead granny. Throw in Amy Angove, aka Lamorna Rain the tragic young supermodel, also dead before her time and . . . well, you get the drift.'

'Bastards.'

'No argument.'

'It's just a string of . . . coincidences.'

'No question. But it will get attention, you know that.'

The two men sat is quiet contemplation. Then, clearing his throat – never a good sign Treloar thought – Chamberlain smiled. Doomed.

'Look I know it's bollocks but we can't ignore it. Stand back from the Ellis and Hicks' cases and concentrate on the vandalism. Sam can run with the murders for now.'

'But Nicky, she's . . .'

'She's a Detective Inspector,' Chamberlain said in a firm voice. 'I'll support her and, well you can be there in the background, just not openly leading. I'll speak to her later. You say nothing for now. I'll be under pressure to suspend you, but I am not going to throw you to the dogs. The Police and Crime Commissioner gets nervous when the media wade in, but I will not be bullied by them and I will not be bullied by her.'

'Thanks Nicky. This is madness. I'm not involved in these deaths.'

'I know that. But answer this: did Ellis cheat your sister's boss and did your former wife's grandmother die in one of Hicks' care homes?'

'Yes, but . . .'

'Exactly. Yes isn't no. That's the problem here. Reality always falls foul of perception, you know that.'

'Yes. Yes I see it, but I hate it.'

'You and me both Chief Inspector.'

When Sam came in with supplies for their new base, she found Treloar sitting in the small garden at the rear of The Count House with the latest arrival. Luke Calloway was a valued team member, combining, as he did, exceptional IT skills and great physical strength from years of playing rugby. He had proved himself in an investigation into child abduction in St Ives, and Treloar had missed him whilst he had been on an extended vacation visiting his grandmother in Jamaica, which had turned into a temporary secondment. It was good to be working with him again.

'Luke!' Sam exclaimed, rushing to hug the large black man, 'Wonderful to see you again. How have you been? How was Jamaica, and your grandmother?'

'All good thanks and I hear you enjoyed your travels.'

'Well it's bloody good to have you here.'

Sam smiled, nodding, and sat down at the cast iron table. 'Funny name: The Count House.'

'It must have been the offices and counting house for a business or businesses', said Treloar, 'there's a Count House at Botallack near me. Used to be the mine offices.'

'Geevor?'

'No, further along the coast towards Sennen. Famous for the ruined engine houses on the cliff face. Very famous photographic site. You'd recognise it. Very Poldark.'

'Mmm . . . So that was Tulip Khan, at the meeting. I first heard about her on the Porthaven case. Smart, as I recall. Pushy, but I guess that goes with the territory. The local press boys seemed to rate her rather than resent which is unusual with the nationals.'

'Yes. She was remarkably reasonable . . . responsible even with that business in Fowey. And she got on with Colin Matthews, so she must be some sort of saint.'

'Poor Col,' Luke growled. 'Frosty really screwed him over didn't she?'

'Doc says she made him her creature,' said Sam.

'Total bitch. How the hell is she still on the force?' Luke was genuinely angry.

'You know the powers that be,' Treloar replied. 'They bury their own dead. Bad press is bad for public confidence. Police 'questionable behaviour' or corruption as we would call it, especially in senior ranks and a high profile female officer, not good at all for the new service image.'

'I would have thought better of the Chief Con.'

'Not his call. Don't worry. She'll get her due,' Treloar

spoke softly with menace.

'Who'll get her due?' asked Diggory Keast. Coming out into the bright sun, they hadn't noticed him standing in the shaded doorway.

'Frosty,' said Sam.

Treloar shot her a look. She raised her eyebrows as if to say 'what?' but he shook his head almost imperceptibly.

'Huh. Lincolnshire's welcome to that one my 'ansome,' Keast smiled at Sam.

newsukfeed @newsukfeedcallsitout 9m
BREAKING - CORNISH HERITAGE KILLINGS. Detective knew victims. Hated. V close to dead ex, didn't like her either!! #stargazy&edenkillings #cornwallmurders #suspiciousdeathscornwall #padstownews

uknewsnow@uknewsnownownownow 7m
BREAKING - Cornish cop knew both vics, didn't like them. #stargazy&edenkillings #cornwallmurders #suspiciousdeathscornwall #padstownews

Andy Sykes@dogwalkingpadstow23 5m
WTF!! Wots that got to do with anything. Stupid. Loads didn't like Hicks. Didn't know other guy. Bloody newsies stirrin things again. Dwalkers pair up. RETWEET #stargazy&edenkillings #cornwallmurders #suspiciousdeathscornwall #padstownews

. . . .

thechef@thecornishchef&artist 3m
Hi all again. Crazy times, careful dwalkers out there. Info on Eden: www@thecornishchef&artist. @bbcsouthwestnewstoday @loveDwalkingpadstow @SolihullBillingDwalker @dogwalkingpadstow23 @ #beachbody #cornishfood #padstow #padstownews @IslingtonDwlkers35 #islingtondwalkers

@thecornishchef&artist

The Cornish chef & the artist

Chef'n'artist here again. Great response to the piece on Stargazy Pie, thanks all. Crazy situation with the bodies right. Must be a lunatic at large, take care everyone,

especially dog walkers. For those of you out there (thinking mostly of friends outside UK!) we thought a bit of info about Eden might help. Over to the artist for this one.
Thanks chef. Here's a work-up of three of the bigger domes at Eden. That poor guy must have had an amazing greenhouse!

Eden is built In an old clay pit, was pioneered & developed by a Dutchman living in Cornwall! Counted 7 domes when last there (v. early, special artist permission from management, I don't get on with crowds!) One has world's largest indoor rainforest. It's a big summer rock concert venue (open air). Could fit 35 football pitches (English!) inside. Largest is 50m high, tall enough for tower of London. All linked with walkways. 7 domes, 2 main worlds. No Gulliver worlds, unless it's the tall of the Rainforest & the small of the Mediterranean! Thousands of plants, millions of visitors!!

No recipe this time. If you ask him nicely Chef might dig out something with figs or coconuts. Both grow at Eden.
Chef here, will do. Tied down? Did they take anything from his greenhouse? Poor guy. Wow!

Chapter Twenty-Four

Cecily's phone was on the breakfast bar of the kitchen in the flat above CHILL when it rang and vibrated, meandering slowly around a pale green glass chopping board. It was 11.15pm, dark outside. *Definitely Maybe,* Oasis's first album, was playing, on vinyl. Softly, through the extension speakers in the kitchen corners. It was one of the LPs she had kept in the flat after moving most of her album collection to her place in the country.

She was concentrating, preparing her favourite dish for her favourite guest, a delicious pork souvlaki, for a 'casual working supper' with Pasco Trefry the following evening. She was certain that he would take up her invitation. How could he not? Afterwards she would give him the red feather. His second. The large heavy one for his office. A great complement for the smaller one for his key ring.

But with hands and fingers sticky with almost made pita bread dough, she let the call go to voicemail. It was not long before the sound of a crowd cheering, as the phone meandered around the chopping board once again told her that the voicemail had arrived. A few seconds later a loud whooshing sound told her that a message had arrived and glancing down at the screen she could see that it was Demmy she had missed.

It wasn't long before the dough was finished and she gently rounded it and put it into a clean bowl before covering it with a tea towel.

Thinking about the fresh baked pita breads that Pasco Trefry would be amazed at tomorrow, took her back. Her mum had not really taught her much, but the little that she had, had worked, so it had stuck.

'Don't waste time learning how to cook! Just learn to do the one dish, two at the most, really well to impress the pants off

the people you want to impress, and that will see you right.' She copied her mum who had impressed the pants off Nikolaos with souvlakis, and then he had impressed the pants off her with his yacht. At the time of its first visit, one of the biggest and fastest yachts in the first phase of Eastbourne marina which he had helped build. Well, finance.

Her mum loved Queen, especially Freddie Mercury, and she told all her friends and anyone else who would listen that Nikolaos looked just like him. Even called him Freddie sometimes, which he didn't mind. He had been to their two up two down terrace, which had always been comfortable and clean and tidy, a few times. Over the last few years it had been furnished and decorated much more luxuriously.

He had clapped, tapped and danced and laughed and teared up along with everyone else every time the Live Aid video was played. And Nikolaos enjoyed having her mum on the yacht, where she helped organise parties, and no-one was surprised when she was invited to his villa on an unpronounceable Greek island which had been in his family forever. She was still there most of the time, and according to her mum in their occasional phone calls and visits back home, still having fun.

If it had not been for Nikolaos she might never have made it to Knebworth in '86 for what turned out to be the last full Queen concert. Her mum was supposed to be turning up at home for once and taking her and her mate Cindy but they didn't really want to go. Not with mum. Too much company. On the Friday her mum was at a party on Nikolaos's yacht and when she hadn't arrived home by three o'clock Saturday morning Cecily and Cindy, who was sleeping over to get an early start, decided to go, why not? On their own.

It was early August, it was warm, the weather was great and by five o'clock they had found three tickets and taken them all, just in case they bumped into someone who might be able to use the extra one. They had also found a map, fashioned a Knebworth sign out of the side of a cardboard box and the heavy use of a black felt-tip pen, taken plenty of cash from mum's just-in-case stash, and eaten cornflakes. They were both well developed for their ages and, like the experts they were, they had applied make up so they would get away with at least 3 more years if challenged by anyone. Sixteen, and more likely eighteen, as they did in the pubs, and it soon was light enough to start hitching over to Brighton.

They would then hitch a lift up the M23 towards London, then another round the South and North Circular Roads until they reached the M1. (In those days even though the M25 was a bit more than a twinkle in someone's eye, it was not fully open.) Then there would be another lift up to the Knebworth exit, then another on to the big gig at the Park. Easy.

The beeper went, telling her the 23 minutes was up for the rising of the dough, and she was back in the kitchen and on the souvlaki case. Cecily broke the dough into four equal portions and gently shaped them. She wrapped each carefully in tight fitting cling film then placed them in individual small clear plastic food bags and expelled all the air before tying them, then put them in the freezer.

Cecily's mum had a great marinade. She had said, 'Always leave the red wine vinegar till last and add an extra dash, and don't forget you need more oregano than you think!! You need loads, put half as much again as you think it needs!' So she placed the sliced pork tenderloin and other gyros ingredients into a bowl, leaving the vinegar until last, mixed it together and squeezed it all gently by hand. Sloppy, erotic, she loved this part.

'Well, let's see what Demmy and her pals have been up to,' she said to the mobile and tapped the voicemail icon.

'Hi Cecily, just me calling in. Had a good session, went on the bike with Carla and met the others there. They all went with Aleksy in the car. The new toolboxes were a good idea for all the kit, me and Carla took the smaller ones in our back packs. They all need top-ups by the way, I'll message you with a list later. That new guy Salty took care of the surf boards in both places before anyone else got a look in! Went nuts with the hammer and chisel on them. Ha, THEY won't be taking anyone out anytime soon. Best part was seeing the lawn turf at number two rolled back up and stacked in the pond. Won't go on . . . . . .', Cecily had cut Demmy off and video called her back on WhatsApp.

'Hey Demmy, thanks for calling, glad it went well. I wanted to say let's meet up after you've sent me the list and I'll give you the stuff. Meet at the flat if you want. Don't think you mentioned this Salty, where did he come from?'

'He appeared one night, seemed OK, got on with everyone. I'll say more tomorrow. No prob, I'll get the list to you when I've checked what the others need, probably need a new blade or two at least, for Salty, Ha! Got to go, see you.'

'Blades!?' The line was dead, the video now just a still image.

The tzatziki sauce would wait until tomorrow 'It should be finished half an hour before you start cooking the pork gyros, and they only take two minutes' her mum had said, 'It needs to be tasty and ready to go, but fresh'. 'Just like me and you,' they would chorus together and then fall about giggling.

Cecily glanced at her phone as it vibrated yet again, and made the whooshing sound, and saw the Gyros marinating, waiting to go in the fridge. Her mum and that night sprang into her mind again.

It was even easier than they thought it could be. Apart from the walk to the main road out of Eastbourne. It was already warming up and they weren't exactly used to exercise. Wearing T shirts and short skirts, they had already taken off their thin bomber jackets and looped them through the handles of the cargo bags which were slung over their shoulders. On the East Dean Road, just past the lane down to the tennis courts and golf course, a half-full white transit minibus pulled up. 'Well good morning ladies,' the blonde and very chunky driver had rasped when she had opened the door, 'step right up and join the party! That's exactly where we're heading!'

'This is my birthday prezzy to myself and this lot are my family, at least the ones that wanted to come to THIS party!' She told us as they were on their way to their seats,

'I've loved those boys since I saw 'em in Cornwall when I was on holiday. 'Brilliant. Love 'em, followed 'em ever since, go to see 'em whenever I can!'

'That lot' were a son and daughter and their wife and husband, with two kids each, in their late teens. They were all OK and mostly left her and Cindy to themselves. They were all from Pevensey. Queenie, who assembled PCBs, whatever they were, worked in a car park ticket machine factory in Hastings and had paid for all their tickets, the minibus hire, the food and booze, and all the petrol and the ones who were awake seemed to be looking forward to the day.

Turned out that Queenie had seen the band at their first ever gig when she was on holiday 'years ago' in Cornwall, in Truro. How spooky was that!? A few weeks later she had gone back to Cornwall 'to see the boys', for a weekend festival, to 'a funny little place' she described it as, 'called Carnon Downs', she laughed, 'when they were actually called Queen . . . not Smile, for Christ's sake where would they have got with that? There were some brothers called Knopfler on that bill . . . whatever happened to them? HA.'

'If you want a lift back, see you here after', Queenie had said as they stepped down from the minibus when it had parked up, 'have a great time, and look after yourselves eh!'.

They had walked through the cars, vans, buses, campervans and minibuses, past the merchandise tents and tables where they bought some sandwiches and two T shirts each, and on with and through the crowds down the long grassy slope to the foot of the natural bowl where they stopped. Almost at the front but not quite. Looking up at the stage.

It was hot. The openers and Status Quo were OK, then They came on and the crowd went wild, then even wilder when they started with One Vision. *It was all brilliant, even better than they were on the Live Aid video. Cecily had always loved them, especially Freddie, must have been mum's influence, and Nikolaos's, and the parties she had stayed up for when she was REALLY young.*

She had looked across to her right, as she had a few

times already, halfway through the first encore when everyone was singing along loudly or shouting to Radio Ga Ga *and saw not far away and not far back a square sign at the top of a long swaying pole saying 'Queenie's Party' as she danced along. Couldn't see Queenie.*

They came back for a second encore and just into We Are The Champions, *everyone was singing, waving their arms slowly from side to side in the air, some girls were sitting on their blokes' shoulders, and there was a tap on her shoulder. It was a big guy in a black T shirt and black jeans and he looked vaguely familiar. He smiled. 'Your mum and Nik wondered if you and your mate want to come backstage for the party', he shouted.*

'WHAT?' She shouted back.

'Your mum and Nik wondered if you and your mate want to come backstage for the party', he shouted again.

Cecily looked at Cindy and nudged her, mimed a 'let's follow him' with her head. Guy in black looked at her and shouted, 'what about them?' and pointed towards Queenie's sign. She shook her head. Not long afterwards they were looking at the stage from a VIP box in the wings close to the end of the second, final, encore. They were close and she could see everything so clearly, from the side. Could see the crowd, Queenie's party sign swayed wildly back and forth. Cindy and Cecily looked at each other and shook their heads. Everyone in the box was singing or shouting along to God Save The Queen, *blasting through speakers all around the box. It was loud. It was hot.*

Big guy in black then walked them along a long corridor and into a big room that was full of people and buzzed with noise. Straightaway she noticed it was cooler, a bit smoky. The lights seemed fuzzy with a blue haze. A massive screen at one end was split in two. One half showed people running around the stage picking up instruments and cables and mikes and stuff. The other half showed the crowd, some hanging around talking and slowly packing their bits and pieces, and others slowly meandering up the slope back to the car parks and buses and taxis to get them to the station, or wherever.

Suddenly mum was there. 'Hi darling, hi Cindy, didn't

think you guys wanted to come! Great to see you here. Come and say hello to a few people. We saw you at the front of the crowd on the screen and asked Joe to invite you in. Glad you came'. In her right hand, which she was holding out to them, mum was gripping two bottles of lager between her fingers, in the other a glass of champagne, half full. They took a bottle each.

Christ it was incredible. Cindy hadn't said a word since big guy in black had taken them from the crowd. Cecily was always good at cool, and she was playing it now like there was no tomorrow. WOW. 'Hi mum. Yeah, I've always wanted to see the boys, you know how much I like the videos, so we came anyway. Thought you'd been held up on the boat. How did you get here? Where's Nikolaos?'

'He's here somewhere, weren't they great? Hope you enjoyed it. Oh, there he is, let's go say hello, what did you like best?' Walking through the crowded buzzing room Cecily could hear guitar music, and was seeing people she knew from the TV and videos. They were like the royalty of pop, and royalty! There was some guy she didn't recognise talking to Princess Di and she did a double take. He looked very smart with a short haircut and through the crowd she saw that he had an open necked shirt. There was a guy in a black leather jacket and jeans that looked like he was probably security standing behind them. Looking around.

As she walked, she kept looking over towards the music and through a gap saw Mark Knopfler in a corner of the room leaning against the wall playing an acoustic guitar, fingers blurred, and looking around and just chatting to a guy who looked like a mental drummer Cecily was sure she had seen playing with Elton John on a video, and Paul bloody McCartney, and Eric Clapton. David Bowie was there, next to a beautiful black woman who she was sure she had seen somewhere, listening and nodding to some people who looked Chinese. She shook her head, finding it hard to believe what she was seeing, and turned to look forward again, to where mum was taking them, and saw that Nikolaos was only talking to George bloody Michael. Christ.

'Hi Cecily,' Nikolaos said, 'great to see you, glad you

made it. Hi Cindy. You might recognise this guy. Used to be with a little twosome called Wham! If my memory serves me well, I think you used to like them and I bought you a couple of their tapes.' He smiled. 'Say hi to George'. She did. And she even asked for an autograph. Stupid, she didn't have a pen. He did. She still had that serviette somewhere. Talk about embarrassing. He didn't have a problem, but she could hardly talk, and Cindy totally couldn't. The serviette was red, his pen wrote with gold ink. Amazing.

Then George looked up as a door opened and he began to clap, and was soon followed by everyone else. Brian May had walked in only followed by Freddie Mercury. They looked around slowly, took in the room, the people. They nodded at everyone and smiled and each held up a hand in a wave. They walked through the crowd slowly, shaking hands and saying hi, and nodding their heads and laughing with people.

Freddie's face was still glistening with sweat, and as he walked through the party Cecily could see mum's point. There was an amazing similarity between them. And when he walked over to them, well Nikolaos, said 'hi man, great to see you again Freddie', and he winked at mum and said, 'well, hello!', she blushed like crazy. He looked at Nikolaos and said, 'if she ever confuses us again I won't be held responsible for my actions!'

Nikolaos shook his head, laughed, clapped him on the shoulder, and said, 'Hey Fred, what an amazing show, you were fantastic, great, you were all great, thanks. It was brilliant. Thanks for the invite. Hey, this is Cecily, and her pal Cindy'. And they just chatted, like mates that had known each other for ages. Amazing. Then Nikolaos said,' Sorry man but we've got to scoot, got a meeting early tomorrow, wasn't expecting it, but you know how things are. Stay well, see you again soon. Up in London maybe, or over on the island if you like. Whenever. Feel free'.

'Right girls', said mum, 'we're off, do you want a lift? Shouldn't be long, took us less than an hour to get here, probably be the same on the way back'.

'What!?'

And twenty minutes later the helicopter was lifting off,

sending her stomach up into her mouth and swinging noisily above the M1 which was full of headlights, most streaming south just down to the right. It smelled of plush new leather and petrol, and it was noisy, very. Mum was right. Less than an hour after leaving Knebworth they landed on the golf course at Eastbourne and Cecily and Cindy got out and walked home, while mum and Nikolaos went back to the marina.

The phone made the whooshing incoming text message sound again, bringing her back. Cecily saw the pork again, waiting, and covered it with cling film before putting the bowl in the fridge where it would marinade happily away until tomorrow afternoon.

Cecily picked up the phone, looked at the messages and frowned "How am I supposed to get those?" she thought to herself, and what are they for."

Chapter Twenty-Five

The next morning, early, as Treloar was leaving Lost Farm Barn for Padstow, a few miles to the west and some hundred metres higher in altitude, Ochre Pengelly was waking in her attic room at Radgell. The early morning sunlight streaming through the window had turned the white sheets the colour of clotted cream. She climbed out of bed and crossed the bare floorboards to look out to the blue watercolour-washed horizon. Below her, a solitary rook, the blackest matt-black, soot-black of carrion birds was strutting along the far wall. Her artist's eye took in the vibrant greens of early summer field and foliage, when everything is tender, bright and fresh before the dusty late season days leach all colour, desiccating and yellowing, thickening the air.

She grabbed her dressing gown and hurried down four flights of stairs, out the back door and across to a wooden door in the granite wall. Here she entered the enchanted world of her late mother's garden. Orla Pengelly had been born and raised near Dingle in County Kerry, Eire. Unlike her husband, Talan, who loved his neat lawns and regimented rose beds, Orla had created a wild garden strewn with the plants of her native countryside: clover, foxglove, cornflower, dandelion and ox-eye daisy. It was a summer meadow sheltered within the granite walls on the barren moorlands of west Cornwall. And it was Ochre's sanctuary, scenting that morning with wild honeysuckle.

Orlando Pengelly stood by the Aga waiting for the kettle to boil. He was getting old. When he thought of those places he had intended to visit and had not, knowing he now never would, he felt a sense of relief rather than despair. When had this happened? How had he not noticed? Why was he not appalled? Was this what life was; a series of abandonings: vanity, love, ambition, sex, hope? Not that there had ever been much sex. But there was still hope: the kettle was boiling.

Barefoot, Ochre stepped carefully across the damp grass avoiding the small spiders' webs scattered in the dew like the safety nets of the most miniature of circuses. Magpies were approaching her cautiously from the east like hesitant Native American scouts checking the ground as they came. As she reached the wooden bench in the far corner she heard her brother's voice from behind. Orlando in wellington boots, ancient striped pyjama bottoms and a Cornish fisherman's smock approached with his sad smile.

'I come bearing gifts,' he handed her a large white mug of builder's strength tea.

'Thank you brother mine,' taking a sip she gazed back across the garden to the huge granite round tower at the south western extreme of Radgell.

'What's on your mind?' Orlando asked quietly.

'Something unsettled me at that . . . gathering yesterday; there's wickedness afoot.'

"Wickedness afoot'? Really sister dear you sound like one of your pirates or one of the witches from *Macbeth. "Evil is unspectacular and always human, and shares our bed and eats at our own table."'*

'Which witch said that?' asked Ochre with a grin, knowing full well it was W H Auden. 'So if evil is banal what about goodness?' Orlando was a professor of Philosophy and these were typical of the early morning discussions for the siblings.

'Ah well, goodness is rare and strange.'

'*The Tempest*?'

'What? No, that's rich and strange. Ariel's Song: '*suffer a sea-change into something rich and strange.'*

'Well there is definitely something malevolent out there. Look at what happened to Titus Hicks. And that other chap,' Ochre was sounding indignant.

'Ellis. Ellis was a grubby nonentity and we all loathed Hicks. The man was an utter shit.'

'You hardly knew him. I hear the voice of Pasco Trefry speaking'.

'Oh come on Ochre. Those two men were obnoxious, insignificant money-grubbers, hardly up there in the pantheon of evil.'

'You know full well that the wickedness was not theirs but that of their killer.' Ochre spat. 'And why did I let you talk me into this wretched festival business in the first place? For your precious pal Pasco, that's why.'

'Oh come on sweet, you're hardly hosting the event. You won't even have to attend. Your involvement is strictly limited to the design of the posters and flyers'

But Ochre was on a roll and not to be placated. 'And that's another thing. Whose idea was it to invite that awful Lacey creature?'

'Come on now,' purred Orlando, 'Dr Roz is a national treasure. And, I might add, she can't be a total cretin, she did read Natural Sciences at Christ.'

'Oh well, that forgives everything. She went to Cambridge like you and Pasco. So, oh wise one, how do you explain all that fawning, the sly, conspiratorial smiles and askance glances to camera, the false intimacy like some cheap whore. And my God the clothes! Kitten heels, Capri pants and flared skirts. And that hideous red lipstick! Queen of the three quarter length sleeve like some tawdry Princess Margaret by Cecil Beaton. What is that about? La Lacey prima donna.'

'Just image my sweet, purely branding. And you of all people can understand that.'

But Ochre was having none of it. 'Headbands and ponytails at her age. The thinking adolescent's Sandra Dee! And you! You a historian and philosopher! All that nonsense she spouts about conspiracy theories, secret societies, unexplained mystical claptrap. The nonsense . . . Dan Brownery. How can you defend her?'

'Well,' Orlando said slowly, 'actually Pasco tells me she is giving all that up for serious environmental and scientific subject matters. Hence the endorsement of, and appearance at, the Ally Ally Oh festival.'

'Huh. Time will tell. Not a lot of room for long-sleeved silk gloves and Panama hats in the scientific community. Beware, I say. Caveat emptor. She'll trivialize and popularize with that lisping, lilting voice, the oooh sooo pretty hint of

Scottish Highland and the oooh sooo elongated vowels.'

'I concede, I concede. You are not one of her multitudinous fans. Enough. What is really wrong?'

'I told you. There is evil out there, evil . . . and worse.'

'Oh come now. You know what Phil says are the motives for crime: lust, love and lucre, and in this case lucre must be the prime suspect.'

'But he's missing one: lust, love, lucre and . . . lunacy. And as you know, some people are too far out to rescue.'

And now, knowing they were venturing onto forbidden, dangerous ground, she smiled and touching his face, turned back across the grass towards the house.

Ochre's last visual memory of her mother was of her dancing barefoot in the moonlight in this very garden. The last aural memory was of her shrieking, echoing wail as she plummeted from Radgell's western round tower roof. She never discussed that day with her brother; it was just always there with them, unspoken, unexplored, unexplained.

The west tower's roof had been barely accessible since their mother's death. First their father, and latterly Orlando, with Ochre's tacit consent, had closed and locked the wooden door at the foot of the stone steps, concealing the key. But today, recollection had driven her to seek out the key, open the door, climb the filthy steps and force open the heavy door at the summit giving access onto the crenelated tower roof.

She had forgotten the magnificence of the view. A 360 degree panorama of west Cornwall. She gazed out over the crenelated towers of St Michael's Mount, the bay beyond sweeping round to Mousehole. It was this small fishing village that inspired the home port of Captain Perish Penhaligon's brig the *Torment*. This tower, where she stood at the wall's edge relishing the air, had haunted her imagination for years. Behind her was the scorched stone where a beacon had stood for centuries; a fire to be lit in celebration, to warn and, more sinisterly, to lure.

False lights had been deployed by Cornish wreckers to

lure unsuspecting shipping onto the treacherous offshore rocks and granite outcrops that lined the north Cornwall coast. The Penhaligons had ostensibly made their fortune in tin mining, but the proceeds of wrecking and smuggling had lined their coffers and helped to build Radgell.

Here she stood on the West Tower, the model for Carn Doom in Captain Perish's world. Such an ambivalent place for Ochre: the site of her mother's last action on this earth and the foundation for her own life's work and considerable fame and success. Irony of ironies.

Chapter Twenty-Six

Cecily had woken early, at around 4.30 a.m., as usual without an alarm at this time of year. It was a good job, her day was going to be busy, and timing would be everything. For this evening's 'casual working supper' with Pasco Trefry, about the Ally Ally Oh, to work as well as possible, everything else during the day needed to go to plan so that the final preparations could be made in good time. She would need to be as relaxed as possible, having achieved everything that needed to be done today.

Receiving the list from Demmy and arranging the toolbox top-up handover would ideally happen in the next couple of hours before Cecily left the flat. She knew Demmy was an early riser, unusual for a teenager she thought, but that suited their working arrangement well.

She wanted to be at a competitor's new and almost ready to open place, Camel Quarry House, for a 'walk-by', not long after the architect arrived to check the property. She knew when he would be there and that he was there for a check-up on progress. Her network kept her as up to date as it could on most things, but she wanted to have a look inside the house too and see for herself. He was from London like the owner, and she knew where he had stayed the night. He might not be on top form, she had done her best to make sure he had a good time on this visit to Cornwall.

It was by the river Camel, just a fifteen-minute walk from her place in the country, if she walked up the hill and down the narrow lane from the nearby hamlet to the South West Coast Path which ran between the boundary of Camel Quarry House and the river Camel.

She could call in at her place in the country and change into walking gear, do the 'walk-by', get back for the car and drive to Jewson to pick up those items on the top-up list she did not have to hand in the shed, get back to the flat in

Padstow and change into smarts, and be in the CHILL head office not long after Jeannie arrived to open up at eight thirty.

Then there would be a morning of admin and dealing with marketing, any problems that Jeannie needed a hand with, and there were always owners and potential owners she needed to speak to on the phone.

All before lunch with some of CHILL's keenest supporters. There was important information to pass on and exchange, and plans to be hatched if all were to continue their mutually advantageous relationships. The meeting would be at The Feathers pub, an 'inn joke' they all appreciated but never mentioned in front of one another. It had been punned to death, but Cecily still smiled and nodded and winked along with them, even though she inwardly cringed whenever one of them made a feathers' joke. Ironically, when she had first suggested they meet there, even she had seen the funny side when they had, if alone with her, made a feathers' pun.

The Feathers was at High Lanes, not far from Padstow but off the beaten track, and although no-one would be that surprised if they were to come across this particular gathering, it was better if potentially interested and otherwise nosy eyes and ears were avoided.

There was David Mortimer, an influential county councillor well connected with the planning department, Jenken (Jenks) Trevarthian, the owner of a small, high quality construction business that had a great reputation, who perpetually complained that he was always 'up to his ears' with too much to do. Yet he had found enough time and 'spare' men and materials to help considerably and at low cost, with renovating Cecily's place in the country. He was always given first opportunity to bid for renovation and building work on properties acquired and managed by CHILL.

And there was Andrew Flynn, who owned the local BMW dealership. They had all been on at least one promise with Cecily at some time, and Andrew several. She had not been disappointed when he came up with a crazy low price for her 'pre-launch' little red Zed demonstrator, a BMW Z4 3.0i Roadster that she so loved. She had not seen any problem with pointing her guests, especially those who were flying in, in the direction of Andrew's other business, an upmarket car rental company.

Jenks had been very pleased to bid for and secure lighting and other key works on the new BMW dealership building for which planning approval had been granted, despite it appearing to be in an unlikely, if not spectacular, location for such a venture.

David Mortimer had a large family, and many friends, many living up-country from Cornwall. They loved nothing more than taking a break in the luxury accommodation that CHILL could occasionally make available at remarkably low cost.

They were all pretty sure that they had been on a promise with Cecily, at least one, and that not all that had been promised had been delivered . . . yet. But they were still optimistic, and enthusiastic. None were aware of the others' promises.

Nor were any of them aware that the others were also proud owners of little red feathers. They respectively adorned a car key ring, acted as a unique bookmark, and one simply hid in an office drawer where it was fondled and admired on an almost daily basis.

After lunch, Cecily needed to get fresh instructions to Demmy and arrange the top-up handover. The details would depend partly on how the early morning 'walk-by' had gone; she could do the handover at the flat. Then she could start to relax and prepare for the evening with Pasco.

Cecily selected her walking kit for the 'walk-by' carefully. 'Jeans, light-weight walking boots, a not too conservative top and a light jacket, I think,' she said to herself as she approached the walk-in wardrobe at her place in the country. She had already carefully applied minimal make-up. Fifteen minutes later she studied her reflection in the mirrored wardrobe door. The jeans were a pair of light blue super skinny stretch jeans from Freddy, the not too conservative top was a tight fitting dark blue square cut tank top, and she had on her dark blue Hi Tec summer walking boots. Her naturally very black hair was, unusually for Cecily, in a ponytail. 'Perfect,' she said to her reflection. She picked up her coffee-au-lait coloured linen jacket and put it on, nodded at herself, and set off for the 'walk-by'.

It was already a very warm morning. The sun was bright and the sky completely blue. Cecily walked briskly down the lane, stopping just after turning left onto the coastal path and shrugged off her jacket. The tide was high but just on the ebb, and the river, just a couple of metres to her right, flowed slowly out to sea. Cecily slung the jacket casually over her shoulder; she had successfully already worked up an attractive sheen.

'Beautiful morning,' Cecily shouted to Brian Higginbottom two minutes later. The architect swung his head from the large tablet screen that he had been looking at between glances at a second storey veranda and balustrade and did a barely disguised double-take. 'When will the house be open for visitors? It's looked finished for weeks and my family would just love it here for a week or two. Are you taking bookings? I can't see a phone number, what is it?'

'Ah, hang on,' the architect said. He walked down a sandy path towards the South West Coast Path and Cecily. As he got closer, she could clearly see that he had had the late night she had hoped for and little sleep. There were bags under his eyes, which were bloodshot, and he had not shaved. 'Well, we're not quite sure yet.' He was only around forty years old, but sounded older and pompous. When he got closer Cecily could smell the alcohol still on his breath. 'Thing is the owner wants it open in a couple of weeks to catch most of the season and I know he has potential bookings . . . Oh, I'm the architect by the way, my name is Brian, Brian Higginbottom.' He held out his hand and Cecily smiled at him and shook it.

'Architect. Ah. My name is Gerry. I'm renting just over the hill,' Cecily said and pointed towards Halwyn Hill. 'So, what are you doing here? It looks ready to me, I can see curtains, and everything looks spotless. My aunt and her grandkids would love it here. They want to come down from Cheshire. What are you doing? What's the problem?'

'Well, that's just it, I can't see any, but the building inspector is saying he can't sign it off yet. The owner is well p'd off. Climbing the wall. He wanted it open months ago,

Christmas at the latest, but they've dragged their heels all along! It's taken forever to get this far. I've just checked heights, pipes, drains, boundaries . . . everything, and it's all in order just as I thought. They just needed to come and look and tick the boxes.

So, I've photographed all the details he raised and it'll all be with him in the next couple of hours. Then we'll see where we are. Why don't you come in for a look around? Don't know when you'd be able to get in but at least you'll be able to see the quality that's gone into the wonderful place. It's cost a fortune so it won't be cheap. Everything's ready. Carpets, furniture, kitchen, TVs, the owner has been paying BT for high-speed broadband for months! Beds, everything. It's been finished for weeks. Come on and have a look.'

So, she went in. It was everything the architect had made it out to be. She had expected it. Very high quality, very well finished. 'All the linen is here, even the beds are in and made, all ready to go.' 'See,' he pointed at the bed, smiling at her and raising an eyebrow, as they had looked around the master bedroom. Cecily smiled back, nudging his elbow, then walked over to the duvet and ran a hand over it.

'I see what you mean about the quality, shame you don't know when we could be in. I just want to pop outside quickly and have a look at the garden. Is there a pool?' She turned to walk back down the stairs and smiled to herself. The architect followed, looking disappointed.

There was a pool and they walked round the landscaped garden, which was not small. As they walked, the architect took a phone call, apologising to her. 'That was the owner. I've told him I've had a very good look round and that everything is as it should be. I'll send him the bloody photos too! Got to get back to town to meet him this afternoon.'

What he hadn't spotted though, was a manhole cover set at the edge of a lawn just to the right of the house that was not quite sitting properly, why would he? He was tired, hungover, and he wasn't looking for it. Underneath the manhole cover was a smashed backflow prevention valve. The drainpipe into which it had been fitted was also smashed. It fed the septic tank.

Cecily knew that the architect had not seen the page of

the inspector's report that detailed the smashed pipe and valve because it had somehow been deleted from the final version of the report file.

She also knew that these details would be resolved with a few more communications between the architect and the inspector, and a visit from the builder and his drain guy. And maybe new manhole covers all round with security features. It would not take long. And the owner had prospective guests lined up.

Chapter Twenty-Seven

Viola woke disoriented and cold. She was dirty, hands bound and tethered to a rusty iron ring in the wall of an old stone wreck of a building by a chain attached to two leather dog collars around her wrists. Her head was pounding and she was cold and sweating. She was also not alone. Sitting on an upturned barrel in an opening in the wall was Siegfried Carew.

'What's going on? Salty?' she asked. Her voice was cracked and her mouth dry and bitter. He just stared saying nothing.

At that moment a small figure dressed in black T shirt and shorts walked in pulling a bobble hat from its head. In the gloom Viola could make out the shape of a girl with long dark hair. 'So this is her,' she said.

'Salty?' she croaked. 'What the hell is going on, who is she, why am I here like this?'

'Fuck Salt what are you playing at? Why have you brought her here? Why have you brought her anywhere? We don't have time for this. We have to go.'

Here, was an abandoned feed shed just up the north coast from Polzeath.

'I found it when we were here at Easter. I like it. It's bleak and abandoned. I know how it feels'

'I don't understand' Viola said sitting with her knees up trying to get warm, 'we're friends, more than friends, why do you want to hurt me?'

'You betrayed me. Oh yes you did. My father neglected me, humiliates me but I hate him and I don't care. I loved you and you betrayed me.'

The black-clad girl shook her head. 'For fuck's sake Salt we don't have time for this and we so do not fucking need it. The Chief wants us and if the Chief finds out about this, you are in deep, deep shit. I'm going. You make your own way there. Arsehole.' She stormed out

Viola was crying softly. 'I don't understand. How did I betray you? I've done nothing wrong.'

'I couldn't let you leave. You can't leave me.'

'What are you taking about?'

'I heard Leah talking to the others. Your mother rang her. She couldn't reach you. She's heard about the murders and she wants you home now. She's going nuts. You can't go. I had to hide you.'

'I don't want to go. I am not going to go. Salty you have to let me out of here so I can call her. She will create absolute mayhem. You don't know her. I told you she's got problems but you don't know the half of it. Let me call her. Please Salty, let me sort it.'

'No! You're staying here and I have to go. I have to think.'

And with that he crossed the rock strewn floor and fastened a length of wide silver duct tape across her mouth then turned and ran through the opening in the wall. She heard his feet pounding as he ran away. Then nothing but the wind.

Chapter Twenty-Eight

Cecily had decided on Jewson, the most convenient builders' merchant and hardware store, for the top-up shopping trip as she thought she would be less likely to meet anyone she knew there than at B & Q. It was her first visit, and she was surprised when she arrived. It was seriously busy.

As she pushed her trolley round the store, eyes followed her, eyebrows were raised and there were glances and smiles between many of the other customers who were mostly men - builders, electricians, plumbers, carpenters, painters, and keen do it yourselfers, and more. They were not used to seeing attractive, flirtily clad women walking around their main supplier at any time of day, never mind before eight o'clock in the morning and Cecily drew a cat-call. She turned in its direction, waved and blew a kiss and laughed loudly. Which drew more cat-calls.

At the check-out the elderly grey-haired male assistant simply raised an eyebrow at the range of items in the basket then quickly scanned them; the two large heavy-duty bags that Cecily had pointed at first. She placed everything else into the bags as they were scanned, and as she picked up the blades she remembered the conversation with Demmy.

'Blades? Knife blades. For the box-cutters.' Demmy had explained.

'What are you talking about? What are box-cutters?' Cecily still didn't get it.

'Box-cutters. That's what Salty calls them. You know, Stanley knives. He uses them all the time.'

'Ah, right. Well, that explains that then.' The carpets had to be cut with something.

Cecily placed the now full bags back into the trolley and paid before walking the trolley to the car, attracting more cat-calls and several wolf whistles.

With the bags in the boot and the trolley back in the trolley queue, she was just getting into the car when she stopped, turned, curtsied and waved at the growing group of admirers before getting in and driving off. Looking in the rear-view mirror she shook her head and muttered angrily, 'Stupid, ridiculous. I'll wear a bag over my head next time and go to bloody B & Q. Do they deliver?'

The office was ticking along as usual when Cecily arrived, with Jeannie in complete control. There were no problems to deal with, so by 10:30 a.m. she was able to tell Jeannie that she was leaving for the day. 'I'll give you a shout if anything urgent comes out of the network meeting at lunch time, and I'll tell you ALL about the Ally Ally Oh working supper first thing in the morning.'

'All?' Jeanie asked, arching her eyebrows and smiling.

'Of course, don't I always?' Cecily replied and smiled back, then winked.

Cecily returned to her flat to pick up the four heavy duty bags of top-up kit that had been made up according to Demmy's instructions, with an addition. It was a note, a printed list. She had raised it with Demmy earlier on the phone, not long after the top-up list had been messaged through.

Cecily had pointed out to Demmy many times before, it seemed like more than fifty, that she did not want Demmy and her friends to go completely wild on whichever property they chose, and that she wanted her specific instructions followed. Otherwise the marketing support programme they were helping with would not be as beneficial to CHILL as it might be, and she would have to review the terms.

The phone discussion had been all business and that had surprised Demmy, and it had grabbed her attention. She agreed to discuss the new instructions with the others and persuade them to go along.

The addition in each bag was a list that Cecily had printed, of levels of specific activity.

Activity Level

1. Outside only. Cornish flag sprayed onto 2 windows, patio doors, fences. Pour paint over key safe numbers, superglue key safe flap shut.
2. Outside as 1 above + inside. +smash 2 windows, Cornish flag spray mirrors + wood floors.
3. As 2 above + sandpaper floor before flags, pour paint over sofa, dining table, main bed (not sheets), cut / slice carpets.
4. Your choice + outside use Steel Tarmac Tamper to smash drains. Careful of noise!

The gang needed more control and Cecily would tell Demmy the activity level needed for each property, specifically, which was especially important when she was letting them loose on CHILL properties. Cecily had already explained that sometimes there would be just one clear activity for a specific property, and that it was critical that these more basic instructions were also followed, very closely. She would tell Demmy clearly, very clearly, "If they don't do this, your friends will find themselves in serious trouble!"

Chapter Twenty-Nine

Chief Superintendent Chamberlain called The Count House and was put through to Treloar.

'An eighteen year old girl visiting from Norwich has been reported missing by her mother.'

'How long has she been gone?'

'Four hours.'

'Four hours? Are you kidding me? That's not missing, that's being eighteen.'

'I know that. You know that. But you try telling her mother that. Apparently she was ranting and raving. She thinks the girl has been taken by our guy.'

'He takes local businessmen, not holidaying students from Norfolk!'

'Phil you are on it. Sam's on the murders and you can put the vandalism on the back burner. This comes from The Chief Con and he got it from the Chief Con of Norfolk. Evidently the girl's father is some hot shot advisor to the Foreign Office and he's in Washington, and I don't mean Tyne and Wear.'

'Oh I see, another example of all equal before the law is it?

'Before you get too comfortable on that soapbox we are talking about an eighteen year old girl here who is away from her parents for the first time. I'm given to understand that the mother has psychological issues and the girl is highly responsible in calling her at scheduled times without fail. She has now missed two calls. I know it's probably nothing, but it needs sorting to get everyone off our backs, off your back. This takes priority.'

'I thought Ms Hawkins wanted the vandalism to take priority?' Romilly Hawkins was the Police and Crime Commissioner for the Devon and Cornwall Police.

'Even Rabid Romilly would concede that an abduction

takes precedence over a vandalism spree. How is that going anyway?'

'Not brilliantly. It's curious though. It's not random or mindless. Admittedly there's no pattern to the ownership; the properties have all belonged to, or are managed by, holiday letting agents, but it's not one company being targeted in particular, or any one company being spared. It doesn't look like somebody taking out the competition. And yet, the damage being done . . . well, it's as if it's to order, as if they have a checklist to follow like some demonic cleaning crew. It's definitely an organised campaign.'

'No forensics?'

'Nada. Not so far. No prints, no DNA. Nobody is running amok, masturbating on beds or pissing on floors. Some faecal matter forensics are trying to get something from. Sadly; no bloodstained broken glass or dropped mobiles. Mostly it's all very neat, given the mess they leave behind. It's deliberate, orchestrated wrecking.

'Nothing on CCTV?'

'Nope. Where there is any, either they spray paint over the lenses or they cut the wires.

'Mmm. Maybe we can set a trap?'

'Great idea, but where? We have no idea where they'll strike next. It's a nightmare. We don't have enough people to patrol the entire area. Any chance of a public appeal?'

'Nice try but Rabid has vetoed that. Bad publicity will put off the tourists.'

'Of course. The ultimate taboo.'

'Put it aside for now and focus on the missing girl.'

'Fine. What do we know?'

'I'll text you what I have. The girl's name is Viola Lawrence and she's sharing a caravan at a camping site in Polzeath with a friend called Leah Kidd. Just locate her, makes sure she's safe and tell her to call her mother. And you call me.'

Treloar saluted as Chamberlain ended the call.

'Christ,' he muttered, 'it's not even full summer season yet and the nonsense is starting.'

Treloar dialled the mobile number from Chamberlain's text

and a soft female voice answered.

'Hello. Is that Leah Kidd?'

'Who is this?' suddenly anxious and suspicious.

'I am Detective Chief Inspector Treloar of Devon and Cornwall Police. I'm calling about your friend Viola. I'd like to talk to you in person and see the caravan you and Viola are sharing.'

'I don't understand it. Vi was so happy just to be here! Her mum was dead against it. She was only allowed to come at the very last minute when my mum persuaded Mrs Lawrence. She wouldn't run off. She wouldn't.

'Where are you at the moment Leah?'

'I'm at Marilyn Monroe at Polzeath?'

'Marilyn Monroe?'

'Yeah. It's the name of the caravan, believe it or not. Actually, it's really neat.'

'And that's at The Surf Bay site?'

'Yes. It's right at the edge furthest from the road, next to the beach.'

Right. Wait there and I'll be with you as soon as. No longer than half an hour.'

'But I'm supposed to be meeting with Ravi and Joel at Strandloper.'

'We'll catch up with them.'

Treloar knew that Kitto Betties was on that side of the estuary working at the latest vandalism scene and the quickest way to reach Strandloper was to take the foot ferry from Padstow quay to Rock and get Betties to meet him on the other side of the Camel.

After Treloar had left for Polzeath, Sam gathered the troops in the dining room where the makeshift evidence boards lined the walls. In addition to Keast and Calloway she had been given four uniforms from Truro and a couple of PCSOs. She rose to address them, surprised at how nervous she felt. It was strange without Treloar.

'Right, as we all know by now, the DCI is off the murders.'

Mumbled grumblings circled the room. They all rated Treloar.

‘OK, I know, I know, and Chamberlain is fighting his corner, but for now it’s down to those of us in this room. Now for those of you who don’t know him, this is D S Luke Calloway.’

Calloway stood and nodded.

‘Right then so, let’s all get up to speed. I know Kitto Betties is not here, but Diggory, could you summarize what we know for Luke’s benefit particularly.’

‘Where’s Kitto to?’ asked Keast.

‘He’s over the river. There’s been another case of vandalism on a holiday property. A lot more damage this time apparently. It’s escalating. But that’s Phil’s problem. Let’s get on.’

Keast stood and walked to the board where the photographs of the victims were displayed.

‘Our first victim was 33 year old Jolyon Simon Ellis, a management consultant who lived in Wadebridge. He was married to Theresa Soames-Ellis, who goes by “Tipsy”. He had a reputation for cutting corners, bending the truth and cheating his clients. A particular favourite scam was milking EU funding schemes and skimming off the top. Lots of disgruntled people in his wake. Basically a minor bent player. Cause of death was a morphine overdose and the body scene was staged as a stargazy pie at St George’s Cove, Padstow. He was found on 24 June, early morning by tourists and their dog and he died sometime late the previous night or early that morning. No forensics. No useful prints, either fingerprints or footwear, and given it was a beach, and the tide had come and gone, there was nothing.’

‘So, absolutely nothing to help us?’ Luke asked.

‘Well. As I said there's no forensics for us at the scene, but ANPR - Automatic Number Plate Recognition - picks him up driving down Station Road at 21.47. He turns onto Riverside and parks in the Harbour Commissioner's car park. From there, CCTV follows him as he walks around the harbour and along North Quay Parade. We lose him as he heads up to the War Memorial and onto the coastal path. So we’ve got a rough timescale, assuming he went straight there.’

Luke and Sam nodded.

Keast continued. ‘Victim number two: Titus Hicks. Aged 51.

Another local businessman with a dodgy track record. Single, lived in St Issey near Padstow. Owned a number of care homes with questionable practices and mortality rates. Also ran 'pop-up' businesses in the summer in Padstow taking over empty shops and flogging 'tat made in China' according to Pasco Trefry, fellow Padstow resident, chair of the Ally Ally Oh festival committee and not Hicks' biggest fan.

But before anyone asks, the man has an alibi and nobody likes him for it. Anyway, Hicks was also a morphine overdose, the body pegged out like Gulliver in his own greenhouse, which is one of those solar dome affairs that looks just like an Eden Project biodome. Found day before yesterday by his gardener and he probably died late evening or early that same day.'

'Anything for us?' Luke asked.

'Not a thing,' Keast shook his head. 'Hicks lived alone in an isolated spot; no CCTV. Again, no scene forensics and if he made an assignation with his killer that night it wasn't by mobile phone or landline: no calls at all. Nothing from the door to door except the one neighbour seeing the security light in the garden. Not much liked though from the reports. Like Ellis, nobody grieving.'

'So absolutely no suspect's forensics on this one. It was a private garden after all?' asked Calloway.

'Well, we have a bunch of fingerprints with the examiner in Exeter but nothing out of place for that location: Hicks, the garden people, visiting friends and associates. Nobody 'alien to the environment'.'

'And suspects?'

'Nobody solid for it,' said Sam, 'but we're thinking it must be a local as that is their only connection.'

'Morphine not heroin?'

'Yes. Pure, medicinal and probably oral. No injection sites on the bodies. Could have come from one of Hicks' care homes. We're checking.'

'What's with the Cornish staged scenes?'

'God knows.'

'I see you guys still get the weird ones. There was a lot of noise on social media. Anything there?' asked Luke.'

'It's a shame Kitto isn't here,' said Keast, 'he spoke to

the various dog walkers and surfers who put up the posts but they had nothing more to say. Just a modern day variation on them drivers who slow down to gawp at motorway accidents. Ghouls'

'So what now?'

'More background on the victims. There has to be a reason why these two were chosen,' said Sam. 'I want everybody out there and online asking questions.'

'Same killer?'

'Oh yes. Same killer. Has to be. Same means, same staged scenes, same locale.' Sam was adamant. 'We need to be asking who didn't like these two enough to kill them, and why the staging. Then to herself, "and will Hicks be the last?"

Chapter Thirty

Marilyn Monroe was a vintage 1950s caravan in shades of peony pink. It was perched beside two others; Brigitte Bardot in azure blue and Sophia Loren in sunflower yellow. Treloar found Leah Kidd sitting in a candy-striped deckchair gazing out across Hayle Bay to Newland island.

'Leah Kidd?'

Leah looked up, shading her eyes, to see a tall, tanned blonde man in faded jeans and a white linen shirt holding out his hand with something in it. Surely this fit hunk was not a policeman?

'Inspector Treloar?' she stated in obvious disbelief, looking at his warrant card. She stood up and smiled.

'No word from Viola I presume?' Treloar asked.

'Nothing. I don't understand it. We've met some great guys and she's been really happy. She wouldn't just disappear, not of her own free will. Sorry, let me fetch another chair. Would you like a drink?'

'No, I'm fine thanks. Let's sit over here,' he indicated a bench picnic table just beyond where they stood, towards the beach. 'This is very . . .' he indicated the caravan.

'Cute?'

'I was going to say, compact.'

'Actually it's OK. I'm enjoying it more than I thought I would. We were going to camp but Mrs Lawrence wasn't having any of that: 'too insecure'. This was the compromise.

'Yeah, this is really neat.'

'You like it?' Leah asked incredulously.

'It's a little pink for my taste, but still.'

'Yes I agree. I'd have preferred Brigitte Bardot.'

'I can see that,' Treloar nodded at her cobalt blue sundress, 'azure is more your colour I imagine.'

Leah smiled. This guy was well cool.

'I understand that you haven't seen Viola at all today'.

'That's right.'

'And she regularly phones home and has missed those calls.'

'She has to call on the hour every hour. And she does. Never misses. It's part of the deal for her to be here. Actually, not quite that often, but close. Mrs Lawrence has 'issues'.'

'So in your opinion, she would call if she could. This isn't some protest.'

'No way. She would call. Vi's used to her mother. It's sad really.'

'And you've noticed nothing unusual? Nothing has changed in her behaviour since you arrived?'

'She has been a bit secretive and texting a lot. Oh, and now I think of it, she has been around less, off on her own more, but she's always been back in the evenings. Always.'

'Anything else?'

'Well, her mother phoned me yesterday to say that she wanted Vi to come home straight away. She's heard about these murders and, typically, she's panicking.'

'Why did she phone you?'

'Oh, she said she'd tried Vi but got no reply. But I didn't tell Vi. She's having such a great time and anyway, Mrs Lawrence will calm down and Vi's dad will be on Vi's side on this so it'll probably blow over.'

'Anything else?'

'Well yeah, one weird thing; she wanted to buy some hiking boots. I mean Vi's a flip-flop and ballet pump kind of girl. Hiking boots? Has to be a guy.'

'You sound very sure.'

'I've seen the signs before; in my older brother when he fell for his Italian language teaching assistant. Suddenly he was researching the Medici and making pasta, actually making it.'

Treloar smiled. He liked this girl.

'But you haven't seen her with a guy?'

'No. Nobody I don't know.'

'So. You last saw her?"

'Last night when we went to bed about midnight. I'm sorry I didn't think anything of it this morning when I woke up and she wasn't there. She often goes swimming first thing ‘cos the beach is quiet then. Anyway when I got back with the milk she still wasn’t here and so I went down to the beach food stand. That’s where I thought she’d be. At Crab & Kipper. We were supposed to have breakfast there with the boys. But she wasn’t there. We had arranged to meet. Joel and Ravi were there, said they saw her; she waved from the beach and headed past them towards the road by Ann’s Cottage, out of view.

‘Joel and Ravi?’

‘Yeah. The guys I mentioned. We met them on the first day. They’re cool.’

‘And these are the guys you arranged to meet in Strandloper?’

‘Yes, and I am well late. Can we go?’

‘Let’s go,’ he smiled and stood up, ‘you lead the way.’

Leah picked up a canvas beach bag from beside the deck chair, donned her sunglasses and hurried across to the steps to the beach.

The beach was filling up and they had to make their way through families with wind-breaks, bags and parasols and groups of youths with towels and inflatables, dodging the lone surfers striding down the sand.

‘That’s it, over there,’ Leah pointed to a long wooden one storey building fronted by a wide fenced deck with wooden tables, chairs and beer umbrellas. Large potted palms and ferns were standing between the tables and bunting in primary colours ran along the roof’s edge. He liked it on sight. They climbed a ramp to the open glass doors and stepped into a cool airy interior helped by the large ceiling fans and the open French doors that lined the sea-facing wall. Leah looked around the busy room and headed for the far window table where two young men, probably late teens, were seated with bottles of Cornish Rattler cider. As they approached the table the pair looked up smiling and waving.

‘Ravi, Joel,’ Leah indicated the two in turn, ‘this is Inspector Treloar and he is going to find Viola.’

‘Please, call me Phil. Can I get you guys anything? Leah?’

‘Fever-Tree ginger beer for me please.’

The guys lifted their bottles and nodded.

Treloar went to fetch the ginger beer, ciders, and a glass of water and a double espresso for himself. Leah moved along the bench seat to make room for him.

'Right guys, Leah tells me that Viola would not have failed to call home. I know you haven't known her for long but would you agree?'

'Sure thing,' said Joel.

'Too right,' Ravi nodded, 'she is seriously heavy about that. No excuses. It's a total pain but, hey, she loves her mum.'

'Right. And did she say anything, anything at all about going off somewhere today to either of you?'

'No,' they chimed.

'When did you see her last?'

'Last night dude,' said Joel and Ravi nodded his head, 'we were all sitting outside here on the deck, the four of us. We'd shared pizzas and then you two,' he looked at Leah, 'left about what, eleven, quarter past?'

'That's right,' Leah nodded, 'and we went straight back to Marilyn.'

'So guys, have you noticed anything unusual, anything different about Viola in the last day or so that stood out? Anybody new or odd she was with?'

The three exchanged glances and then Joel frowned.

'Well, there was that blonde beach bum.'

'What blonde beach bum?' said Leah and Ravi in unison.

'I was outside here on the phone, when was it? The day before yesterday. You'all were sitting here and I saw Vi get up, I assumed to go to the head. On her way back this scruffy guy waved to her from the door and she came out to talk to him.'

'She knew him?' Treloar asked.

'Definitely.'

'And did she seem relaxed with him?'

'Oh yeah, very. I meant to ask her who he was, but they were only together for a minute or two and I never got round to it.'

'She never mentioned him to any of you?'

The three looked glum.

'And you saw him just the once?'

'With Vi, yeah. I think I've seen him hanging around on the beach but hell, there are hundreds of dudes who look like him. But, if it is the same dude, he's always on his own, except that time with Vi.'

'And you could describe him for us?'

'Sure. He's blonde, looks kinda dirty, about our age . . . But hang on hang on!' Joel beamed. 'Ask the dude behind the bar! He's not here now but I've seen him talking to the guy and it didn't look too friendly.'

'I will. But now describe him in as much detail as you can,' Treloar set his phone to record.

'OK. Five nine, five ten, 150 pounds, scrawny, dirty blonde hair, shoulder length, wears shorts like everyone else and, yeah, yeah, whatever the weather, for some reason he always wears boots, real heavy leather boots, like for hiking.'

'No!' gasped Leah, grabbing Treloar's arm, 'it's him! It must be the one I told you about, the secret she's been keeping.'

'Right Joel,' Treloar switched off his phone, 'who do I need to speak to behind the bar?'

'Don't know his name, but he seems to be the boss man.'

'Thank you. Now anything else, anything at all that might help me find your friend?'

'You've tried her phone I s'pose,' said Ravi, 'only it's got some heavy duty GPS location shit on it she told me, what with her mum.'

'Yes. I'm afraid it's not showing.'

Chapter Thirty-One

When Cecily arrived at The Feathers she walked in through the open door and could see that Jenks had been the first to arrive. He was standing at the bar, next to a pint of what looked like bitter from an old-style beer mug. She walked up to him and rubbed his elbow with the fingers of her left hand. He had been looking the other way, at a middle-aged man and woman, in T shirts and jeans, who stood at the bar with half pint glasses of what looked like two different bitters. A few tables were occupied, but not the corner table which she had hoped would be free. The pub dart board hung on the wall a few metres away from the table, but no-one was playing.

'Hey Jenks, how are you?' He was wearing a T shirt, a pair of cargo shorts with lots of pockets, and sandals, and he turned towards her.

'Hi Cecily, can't complain thanks, drink? White wine?'

'Thanks. Please. No. No, I'll go with a cider for now, Rattler if they've got it. In a glass. It's a warm one today,' she replied as she placed her small red leather shoulder bag on the bar.

'You're not wrong, been warm since first thing. You cool enough now?' Jenks asked smiling at her and raising an eyebrow as he looked her up and down. 'You've changed.' He turned away. 'Can we have a Rattler please, a cold one, in a glass,' Jenks asked the girl behind the bar. The middle-aged couple further along the bar were following the bar-girl with their eyes as she fetched the Rattler from the fridge and poured it, then put the glass on the bar. Then they called the bar-girl over.

Cecily was wearing a large buttoned, wide strapped, orange linen dress that hung to just above the knee. Her golden dusted red feather brooch was pinned to the base of the right strap. The top button and bottom two were unfastened. She looked down at herself and then lifted a knee to reveal several inches of well-toned, well above the knee, flesh. Jenks looked at the flesh, then back up. Cecily's eyebrows were knitted in a puzzled expression, 'Yes, Jenks, I'm cool. Very. Thanks for asking.' She took a sip from the glass, 'mmmmm, great. Well, you could even say chilled, Ha!'

'Well I had to ask after this morning. What you were wearing wasn't keeping anyone cool!'

'What?'

'Well, I just happened to be at my favourite builders' merchant this morning and heard the ruckus, then saw that it was you keeping everyone well entertained. And all before eight o'clock! Most of the boys will have been late on site after that, maybe had to go home! Which reminds me, I just wanted to ask you if . . .'

'Well, hello you two, how are we today?' shouted Andrew Flynn as he strolled from the open pub door towards the bar. He was with David Mortimer and they were both looking windswept. 'Sorry we're a tad late, David wanted a spin in the new Series 2 convertible, and it took a while to get one out of the showroom. Sorry about that.' Andrew looked at Jenks' and Cecily's almost full glasses before asking David what he wanted and ordering two pints of lager from the bar-girl.

'We're fine Andrew thanks, good to see you both,' Cecily said as she straightened her shoulders and stood up straighter. 'Glad you could make it. Shall we?' Cecily replied and ushered them with her arm towards the table in the corner, catching Andrew's upper arm with her hand as she did so. She picked up her shoulder bag and followed them. She sat first, with her back to the wall, then the bar-girl arrived with Andrew and David's drinks and the meeting began.

Cecily was back in 'all business' mode, and she thanked them. 'Well, gentlemen, thanks for coming. I don't think this will take long, but I thought it would be useful to have an update on where we stand and go through anything else that might need discussing. There are one or two specifics I think it might be worth going over face to face. Firstly, I think we can be pretty sure that our progress so far has been well under the radar as we had hoped, so thanks to you all for that, and any of your staff and associates that have been involved so far.

The business CHILL has generated, especially from Cornish-owned properties has been increasing as a percentage of revenue which is just what we had hoped. Thanks David for your info and help with the planning side on out-of-county owned properties, it is much appreciated. I have to say that I'm shocked by the recent vandalism on holiday properties. We've been hit just like the others. It's a pain and I hope the police catch the people responsible very soon. I'm not sure they're taking it seriously though. David, I wondered if you could have a word with the Chief Exec at the council and ask if he can have a word with the Chief Constable? Andrew, have you been monitoring CHILL referrals?'

Before he could answer, the bar-girl arrived with a large plate of freshly made sandwiches, previously ordered by Cecily. A choice of crab, prawn, or ham, on white bread. 'Oh, thanks Billie. They look wonderful. Could we have another round of drinks please too. Same again everyone, great. Thanks. And some side plates?' The men all reached over and helped themselves. 'Andrew, the CHILL referrals for cars . . . are you monitoring them?'

'Ah. I certainly . . .' At that moment a dart clattered loudly onto the table just in front of Cecily's drink, barely missing the glass, and they all jumped. And stared at it. The dart's flights were red feathers. 'Don't say a word anyone,' Cecily prayed to herself. Then she glared at the middle-aged couple from the bar. They were now standing at the end of the rubber mat in front of the dart board and their eyes were switching from each other to the Cecily table, then to the dart board and looking as though they couldn't understand what had just happened. The lady was holding two darts.

The man looked at Cecily, who was still glaring, and then at the others. Then he held his arms out apologetically. 'Well folks, I'm so sorry about that' he drawled, 'we've never played this before. We're from N'Orleans, Louisiana, we don't have this there.'

Cecily picked up the dart, scrutinised it, and looked at

the dartboard. The angle was ridiculously acute, but she drew back her forearm and threw the dart. Straight into the bull's eye. Where it stayed.

'Well I'll be,' said the man from Louisiana, who walked to the dart board and pointed at the dart in the bull's eye, and then started to clap. He was followed by Jenks, Andrew and David, and when the others in the bar realised what had happened, them too. Cecily stood and bowed. She then reached into her shoulder bag, took out a business card and walked across to the man from Louisiana and gave it to him.

'Hi, I'm Cecily. Pleased to meet you,' she said and shook his hand. He looked surprised. 'If you're ever looking for good quality self-catering accommodation in our lovely Cornwall, give me a call. Be sure to tell your friends about us.'

He looked at her, then the top of her dress, and nodded and smiled. 'Love that brooch. Surely we will, and thank you. I might just be giving you a call.'

After sitting back casually at the table, Cecily noticed that the drinks and side plates had arrived and reached for a crab sandwich, then looked at Andrew, 'you were saying?'

Andrew shook his head, smiled, and said, 'Yep. Definitely. A very noticeable increase in revenue thanks. Well worth it. Bit of a pain having to get the cars over to Newquay airport and our drivers back to base, but it's well worth the extra costs so thanks for that.

'No problem, it's all good service for CHILL clients so that's working well. David, a big thanks for your help on the planning and approvals fronts, it's helping us keep ahead of a lot of the competition. Makes it much better for the Cornish owners too. I won't ask how the IT stuff gets done but it's working well. If you could keep me in the loop of planning applications coming through and works ongoing, that would be great. I'll keep you informed of any properties selling to owners that CHILL doesn't deal with as I hear about them. Just let me know about planning progress. Hope the outlaws had a good break last week?

'Thanks, no prob.' David replied. 'It always amazes me, the IT stuff. I just ask, no idea how it gets done! And the wife's parents had a great time thanks, much appreciated. They couldn't get over the chickens and the fresh eggs.

Brilliant idea.'

'Great. Jenks. How are you getting on with the CHILL builds and refurbs? Bringing in much extra?'

'Well, if I had enough time to do . . .'

'JENKS!' they all chorused.

'Thing is Jenks, I know that the work you're getting though CHILL is getting done. And that you've got at least fifteen more staff than last year. I should know, I borrowed your Pole not long ago.' Cecily smiled. So did Andrew and David. Jenks raised his eyebrows and nodded. 'He told me he was always getting new colleagues. Don't care whether you call them contractors or whatever . . .'

'Well yeah, OK it's all good. But I needed to replace him. No idea what happened there. You must have worn him out, he just disappeared.'

'Can't help you there. He did a good job though, thanks for that. Maybe he's gone home. Anyway, there's something else coming up that I need a bit of specialist help with, I'll catch you later about that.'

They talked for ten more minutes before the meeting broke up. Andrew gave Cecily a list of new car models and their colours and the dates that they would be arriving. Cecily gave David a list of properties she thought might be changing hands, together with their existing owners' contact details. David gave Jenks a list of properties for which change of use had been applied for, from domestic to holiday let or B & B, as well as new hotel planning applications, complete with applicants and their contact details. To conclude, Cecily updated them on events for the Ally Ally Oh, and how the festival would extend the season, and how that would benefit them all.

Cecily went to the bar to settle up and then they said goodbye and shook hands with one another warmly. David practically ran to the convertible, with Andrew trailing. As Jenks walked towards his pick-up, before they went their separate ways, Cecily caught up with him and stroked his elbow with her hand as she drew level. He stopped, looked at her, waited. She turned to him and smiled. She said, 'I'll call you. Soon. About that specialist help I need.' He looked at her and raised his eyebrows. 'Bye for now.'

Chapter Thirty-Two

One of Treloar's first actions had been to request a trace on Viola's mobile phone. Unfortunately there was nothing, and the digital forensics team concluded that it was switched off with the SIM card removed. As he talked to the students at Strandloper a thought came to him. Treloar was no techie, but he knew a man who was. He excused himself and went outside to the boardwalk to make a call.

'Jamie, an eighteen year old girl has been reported missing and my guys tell me they cannot get a fix on her phone's location, they can't see it.'

Treloar had met Jamie Deverell when investigating the Porthaven murders some years previously. The young man had gone from suspect to resource - some would say accomplice - and the two had worked together on several cases, albeit unofficially. Jamie and his partner Alasdair Frobisher ran a highly successful tech business from Jamie's home, Linton Crucis Abbey, in the New Forest. Jamie had grown up at the 13th Century abbey, which had become a private residence at the Dissolution of the Monasteries under Henry VIII, his single mother being the housekeeper to its wealthy reclusive owner. When he died and the abbey and its land were bequeathed to Jamie, there had been much speculation over the boy's paternity. Treloar could not imagine a more accomplished technical resource existed.

'What's the number? Text it to me and give me ten minutes.'

Treloar sent the text and waited on the boardwalk. In seven minutes Jamie called back.

'Whoah man who is this girl? She must have some amazing contacts. This phone has GPS tracking that is seriously sneaky US agency stuff; CIA, NSA, or some A we've probably never heard of. Wow!'

'Can you see it?'

'Oh yeah. I can give you its exact coordinates and even

its altitude. I'll text them. But from what I can see, it's on the ground floor of some small derelict building just south and west of a place called Port Quin on the cliff edge, it's stationary and has been for almost six hours.'

'Jamie you are a true star.'

Yeah, well you'd better not say you got this from me or I'll be fighting extradition.'

'No worries. I'll say it was an anonymous tip off. In fact,' he looked at a noticeboard behind him next to the entrance where he found a menu with Strandloper's address and telephone number, 'call this number from an untraceable line in five minutes and ask for me. Then when I come on the line just play along.'

'Better still, I'll call you from a public phone box near your present location.'

'I won't even ask.'

'You wouldn't understand the answer.'

As Treloar made his way back through the busy tables, a strident Australian voice boomed out from behind the bar.

'Hey guys!! Is there a Treloar in the house?? Wanted on the phone!'

Treloar diverted to the bar, identified himself to the barman and took the cordless phone.

'Hello? This is Detective Chief Inspector Treloar. Who is this calling?'

'Hi Phil,' said Jamie.

'What? Who is this? Give me that again,' he motioned writing to the barman and was handed a pad and pencil, 'repeat that last bit slowly.'

'Oh really Phil.'

'And you know this how? Give me your name! Hello?'

'I'm hanging up, bye Phil.'

'Hello? Shit, she's gone.'

He handed the phone and the pad and pencil back to the barman.

'I understand the manager isn't here right now?'

'Ruby?'

'No, a guy.'

'Oh you mean Josh. He's Ruby's son. No mate he's on

tonight. He's riding the waves all day lucky bastard.'

'Can you think of a guy about five nine, scrawny, dirty blonde hair, always wears hiking boots, doesn't get on with Josh?'

Huh! You mean Salty. Nobody gets on with Salty. Miserable creepy bastard.'

'Salty?'

'Yeah. Don't know his real name, goes by Salty. Josh would probably know. Here,' he scribbled on the pad and passed it to Treloar who read 'Josh Russell' and a mobile number.

'Thanks.'

'No worries.'

Chapter Thirty-Three

Cecily's meeting at the flat that afternoon with Demmy did not take long. It was all business, just like the earlier phone call. They talked outside. Cecily had handed Demmy a spare copy of the list which was in each of the bags and pointed out that the specific instructions on the printed notes must be followed absolutely. 'I don't know whose idea the complete trashing and shitting was the other day, but that has to stop. It was disgusting. AND it was a CHILL place so I was less than impressed! Don't let it happen again!'

Demmy was mortified. 'I didn't know until I read about it on Facebook. Honestly. I was at the other place with Carla that night. Don't know who it was. If I'd been there I'd have stopped it . . . well . . . tried, Yeuch! never had to do that sort of thing before. Sorry. I'll find out and have a word, I'll take Carla with me, she's good at judo. God, this was supposed to a bit of fun. I don't need this hassle.'

'Well, I'll leave it to you. Do what you have to. For weeks it's been going pretty well, a few over the top, but that was really too much!! Way too much!! Hey, I'm not taking it out on you though. If you need to ditch one or two of the others just do it, but don't get into trouble with them. Try to bring them round.' Cecily saw that Demmy was upset. She couldn't afford to lose her. She needed her onside. 'Aren't you gearing up for exams? What are you taking? How's the revision?'

Demmy was thrown and before she could switch track and had chance to answer, Cecily thanked Demmy for the work done at Camel Quarry House on the drain, and told her to pass on her thanks to the others who been with her. Then she held out a sheaf of money, handing to Demmy five hundred pounds in used twenty-pound notes. Before Demmy could take it, Cecily raised her hand and said, 'Don't forget, it can be taken away as well as given!'

Then she lowered her hand again. 'It's a bonus for getting that one spot on, thanks Demmy,' Cecily explained. 'Make sure you keep the biggest chunk for yourself and give the others who were on the job the extra you think they deserve. Keep some back if you like.'

After the earlier roasting, which had surprised Demmy, she had been even more surprised by the extra money. She was already earning more with Cecily than she had ever earned before. 'What? Wow, thanks. No problem,' said Demmy, 'Don't worry, I'll make sure they know what's what.'

'Great,' Cecily said, then she told Demmy that she would message the next few assignments very soon. Cecily put her hand on Demmy's shoulder as they were saying Cheerio, then Demmy made two trips to take the heavy top-up bags to a car that was parked just along the harbour-side from the CHILL office. The car then drove off along the side of the harbour towards Padstow town centre. From the flat's front first floor window, Cecily's eyes followed it and she saw that it was a dirty, white Ford Fiesta. A dark-haired male was driving. He had long scruffy hair and looked young, but she couldn't tell who he was.

Chapter Thirty-Four

Betties drove them out of Polzeath up Dunders Hill heading from the B3314 and Port Quin.

'When we get close we'll need to pull in somewhere and cut across the farmland on foot. We don't know what, or who, we'll find so let's not be obvious,' Treloar was tracking their route on his phone.

'I know the building. It's near the cliff edge. It's an old feed store, virtually a ruin, very isolated, very exposed to the elements, but still, it's on working farmland. You wouldn't want to keep somebody there for long. Too risky. Especially if there are livestock in that field at the moment.'

'It's supposedly the phone that's there Kitto, not necessarily the girl. That *would* be amazing. The phone is the prize. These kids live on their phones. It can tell us a lot about Viola Lawrence, who she's been in touch with and crucially, it should give us any new contacts. If Leah Kidd is right, and she has met somebody down here, I'd put money on him, or her, being on that phone.'

'Seem strange, Sir, you getting an anonymous call like that from this woman.'

'It's Phil Kitto, not Sir.'

'All right. But how did she know you were there? Must have seen you on TV I s'pose.'

God preserve us from bright young constables, Treloar thought, I need to distract him from that phone call 'It may well be a wind up but we need to check it out. It's not far. By the way Kitto, do you know a late teen male, hangs around Polzeath and is known as Salty?'

'You mean Siegfried Carew. I know him.'

'Great. Is he known to you on a personal basis or is he known to you as a police officer?'

'Both I s'pose. He don't have a record. He comes here

every summer with his mum; they have a holiday house in Rock. He's troubled, angry I'd say, but mostly he just seems sad. He's a loner, keeps to hisself. I feel sorry for him really.'

'So how did you come across him?'

'It were a beach party last year. Usual stuff: underage drinking, bonfire, too much noise. I took names and sent 'em 'ome. But Salty stuck in my mind, what with the name, well names really, Salty and Siegfried, and that he seemed surly and sad at the same time, and on the edge of the group, not really part of it. Why do you ask?'

'I think he's been meeting our missing girl in secret.'

'Never! I would not have put that one with a girl. No way.'

Betties pulled off the narrow road into the entrance to a field. He had been right about the isolation Treloar noted; there was not a building in sight. The two men headed uphill across the rough grass passing inquisitive, nervous sheep. The weather had turned, and the sky was now stainless steel grey, bright and pitiless. When they reached the feed store, which had indeed partially collapsed, they were assailed by the sour smell of human urine.

'Somebody's been here,' said Treloar, ducking his head to enter.

Inside, a sudden shaft of light, coming through behind him, fell on a single small ballerina pump. He coughed, fighting against the acrid smell and the motes of dust and dry straw hanging in the air. Scouring the floor, he spotted an Apple iPhone under an old metal hay feeder. Gotcha. As he donned a forensic glove to pick it up, Betties, who had followed him into the shed, spoke.

'Sir, Phil, look at this,' he pointed to a rusty iron ring secured to the wall. Attached to it by a cable tie, was a sturdy dog chain clipped to a studded dog collar, with long brown hairs caught in its buckle.

'Well,' said Treloar sombrely, 'she was here I'd say, but where the hell is she now and why bring her here only to move her on so soon?'

'Should I call in the forensics boys Sir, Phil?'

'Yeah. Thanks. But we're taking the phone.'

Viola had heard them coming. When Salty had fastened her hands and taped her mouth he had ignored her feet. Why would he not? But what Salty didn't know, was that Viola Lawrence was an ardent accomplished gymnast and she retained her flexibility. Pushing off one of her ballerina pumps, she had used her toes to force the loose tape from her mouth and her teeth to unfasten the dog collar on her right hand. Then she had wrenched the collar from her neck, and free, she had fled from the stinking ruin.

Where to go? Shit, she had forgotten the phone. She had to go back. No way. Then, horror, she heard men's voices approaching. They were coming up the hill towards her, drawing closer. No way out. Hide.

She ran to the cliff edge, losing the other shoe in the process, and frantically looked down. Yes! Just along from where she crouched, was a ledge. She would need to be careful and quick but she could do this. She crawled along to the right place, swung her legs into the void, and feeling for the ledge with her toes, lowered herself down until she was standing, pressed against the rock face, invisible from the field above.

'There's another shoe here,' came a deep voice; so close, too close.

'I see it Sir!'

'Kitto, Kitto, please call me Phil,' came the deep voice again.

'I'm sorry Sir, Phil. It's just habit and with you being a Chief Inspector and all and, well, the other ranking officers are . . .'

Chief Inspector? Rank? Officers? They were police! They had to be!

To the utter amazement of the two men on the cliff, a small face appeared from the void; a small tear-streaked face framed with tangled long brown hair, and a wide-eyed girl in a filthy blue and white striped T-shirt dress rose, as if by magic, to stand before them.

Treloar was the first to react, 'It's OK Viola. You're safe now. We are the police and we are here to help you.'

'Thank you,' Viola croaked and burst into tears.

When the news of Viola's discovery reached the team at The Count House Diggory Keast burst into the dining room.

'The boss has found the girl!'

Three uniforms ran in from the kitchen and those on the phones quickly ended their calls. There was an outburst of clapping and whooping.

'That's brilliant news,' said Sam, but deep down a nasty, petty little voice was contradicting her: *It would have to be him. Missing girl found in record time. More headlines, more TV cameras for the Chief Con's blue-eyed boy*. Whoah! This was Treloar, her beloved, what the hell?

Chapter Thirty-Five

'She's been given something I'd say, just look at her eyes and her balance is off,' Treloar and Betties were standing by the car, Viola was sitting in the back seat with the door open drinking from a bottle of water. They had called for an ambulance and Betties was to accompany her to hospital whilst Treloar took the car back to Padstow.

'You're right S . . . Phil. She's all over the place.'

And he was right. Gamma-hydroxybutyric acid: GHB. At Treliske hospital they found traces of the drug in her urine. She had been located quickly, and although the drug has a short half-life, and disappears from the system within a day, they had caught it. Treloar was back at The Count House, about to speak to Leah Kidd to give her the good news when he took a call from Betties.

'But the downside is that one of the side effects is amnesia and Viola claims that she remembers nothing of the abduction. She was sitting on the beach on her own and then she woke up alone in the feed shed.'

'Claims?' asked Treloar.

'Yeah. I'm not sure what, but I think she's hiding something. The doctor thinks she should be able to remember more about the beach, but loss of memory is not an exact science. And there is something . . . desperate about her need for us to believe her story. I don't know. Perhaps I'm reading too much into this?'

'Mmm. So she's hiding something perhaps?'

'She insists not.'

'Well, better not push too hard. Dodgy ground. We got some promising news from the forensics boys in Exeter: a nice print on the large dog collar. They're waiting for Viola's and her friends' to check the phone, but the prints look small so their thinking Viola and Leah. The collar print is different and larger.'

'I've got Viola's. She was perfectly happy to give them. I'll get them over to the lab.'

'Good. It doesn't seem like a professional job. Print left on the collar, phone left behind, albeit they thought it was untraceable; hardly a secure location and she escaped. All seems pretty amateur.'

'And if she is lying about her amnesia, what do you reckon, prank?'

'Well, it doesn't look like a kidnap for ransom or harm. Let's give it a few days and get back to her when she's more relaxed. When are they letting her out?'

'Tomorrow. She insists on going back to the caravan in Polzeath. But be warned, her mother's on her way. She's flying into The Salt Creek by private helicopter.'

Viola was now entrenched in her lie. She was caught fast by it, as trapped as she had been in that wretched ruined shed, but this time she saw no way out. She had gone too far; there was no way back. She told everyone she remembered nothing and she would stick to that. She would say nothing and there was nothing they could do to change that. She had to hold her nerve, and she would; for Salty. But at least her father had come through. She was on her way back to Polzeath not back to Norwich.

He had overruled her mother and she was allowed to stay for the rest of the holiday as long as she promised, and she had, that she would not go off on her own again and she would ring him twice a day. Viola did not feel bad for her mother. Secretly, she knew that the prospect of the helicopter flight to Cornwall would have terrified her, but she had been prepared to face the ordeal for her daughter. Love flows both ways.

Chapter Thirty-Six

'Bored? No bodies to bury?' asked Treloar answering the call from Benedict Fitzroy.

'Let me tell you a story. Once upon a time two Swedish brothers went fishing in the Skagerrak strait. The boat sank and the younger brother drowned. The elder brother was disowned by the family and fled.'

'Is there a point to this?' Treloar asked tetchily.

'Patience mate, patience. Right, where was I?'

'The surviving brother fled.'

'Thank you. So. Two years later a young Cornish maiden marries her handsome Swedish farmhand beau. Nothing unusual there. Except, the husband takes the wife's maiden name and they return to her family farm: Cove Farm. Mr and Mrs Treloar: your great grandparents.

'WHAAAAT?'

'Yes mate.'

'Fucking nonsense. Never happened. Not in my family.

'Hidden? Lost? Friendly local reverend covering up as a favour? "Brandy for the Parson, Baccy for the Clerk". You lot have been smuggling for centuries. Plus World War Two mate. Fluid times. Unquestioned boat movements; reserved occupations including farming; blind eyes turned.'

'No fucking way,' Treloar was indignant.

'Ah and that's just the half of it,' Fitzroy continued. 'Turns out the drowned brother was a Quisling or whatever the Swedish version of a Nazi collaborator was known as. After the war, widow and son also forced to flee. She remarries, well, as it happens, rich, older man who owned several local newspapers in the Home Counties. Boy joins the business, takes over from stepfather and grows it exponentially.

'No fucking way,' Treloar was starting to get an idea where this was going.

'Fucking way my friend, fucking way. Boy has kept his father's name, but Anglicized.'

'Masterson.'

'Gregory Lasse Masterson or Mårtensson as was.'

Treloar was stunned speechless. Gregory Masterson was a master of the media universe, a global media tycoon. During the course of the investigation into the Spargos trafficking ring, his son, Guy, had been killed, but not by Treloar, although Masterson had always held the police accountable for his death.

'Revenge mate, cold-served revenge: your grandfather killed his father; you killed his son. What goes around comes around. Fuck me it certainly explains those blue-eyed, blonde Nordic good looks of yours. You're a bleeding Viking!'

'So I hear you're a Viking?'

'You've been talking to Leo Benedict Julius Fitzroy, haven't you Tulip? I've warned you about him.'

'No way! Is that really his name? All those Popes! Heavy.'

Treloar smiled evilly. One up on Fitzroy.

'It is a load of bollocks Tulip. My grandpa was called Talan and he was as Cornish as my grandma Kerensa. But someone is spreading this shit and it has to be Masterson behind it.'

'Well I have checked, and Gregory Lasse Masterson is Mårtensson as was. I have a way in with his P A, Maud Fisher. She's been with him forever, totally loyal, totally besotted, but if I angle it as an attack on him I may get something out of her. She's fiercely defensive of his reputation so this Quisling stuff will so not go down well.'

'Anything you can find out Tulip. I am underwater here and the tide's coming in.'

'But that's incredible,' Sam said.

'Tell me about it.'

'Are we sure about this? We only have Fitz's account. How did he find out and how did Masterson find out if the records are so dodgy? No. No there's something fishy here.'

'When I said all that, Ben pointed out to me that

Masterson has limitless resources at his beck and call. He also pointed out that I am a 'shit magnet'.

'Sounds like Fitz,' said Sam suppressing a smile. 'So if it's true he must be . . . what . . . a cousin of some sort. You know there's absolutely no physical resemblance.'

'Yeah, well apparently his mother was a Sami from the far north; small and dark.'

'No I just do not believe it. We need to check the records. Leave it with me; I'm good at historical research. It'll be like old times,' Sam said gently.

'But the point is Sam, Masterson believes it and that is driving this media smear campaign against me,' Treloar said forlornly.

'So. We prove it's bollocks, and stop him dead.'

Chapter Thirty-Seven

Cecily's door bell rang just after 7.00 p.m. 'Freddie, darling, so good to see you. Come in. I'm not quite ready yet, it's been a hell of a day, rushed off my feet, but do come in and make yourself comfortable.' Pasco Trefry stepped into the flat and Cecily squeezed his elbow and pecked him on the cheek then directed him up the stairs. 'Just follow the music. Straight on at the top, to the kitchen,' she said. 'Do you like Fleetwood Mac?'

'I brought this, hope you like it,' Pasco said, holding up a bottle of Sauvignon Blanc, 'I've had it in the fridge so it's quite chilled, if you'll excuse the pun. Gosh what a fabulous smell, delicious, some kind of exotic bread isn't it?' He laid his brown leather portfolio on the breakfast bar and loosened his tie. Cecily was wearing a short black kimono with a red cherry and small golden dragon pattern.

'Well, it's one of my favourites actually, pita bread. It's one of my specialities,' she beamed, 'I hope you like it. It's for wrapping the pork gyros. I'm making souvlakis, it's Greek. Oh, silly, I expect you know that. Let me go and get dressed, I've only just stepped out of the shower, I won't be five minutes. Do open the wine and pour. I'd like a white, if you'd prefer a red, I've uncorked a Tempranillo, should be good to go by now. It's over there,' and she pointed to the windowsill. 'I thought we could eat and talk in here. Plenty of room for the paperwork. Do you like pork?'

Cecily walked from the kitchen, her fluffy high-heeled slippers helping her rear sway a little more than it might usually. Pasco removed his jacket and hung it over the back of a bar stool. He walked over to the window and looked out over the harbour for a couple of seconds before starting to open drawers looking for a corkscrew.

It was still very warm, and Cecily had selected linen again. Make-up had already been artfully applied. She shrugged off the kimono, nothing underneath, and took an above the knee red linen wrap dress from the wardrobe, put it on and fastened the tie so that her cleavage was not on show, and her legs could remain as hidden or revealed as she wished.

She slipped her feet into the glossy red medium-heel Jimmy Choo pumps that she had set aside earlier, stood back to look in the mirror, smiled and nodded to herself. Then she glanced at the large red feather on the dressing table before going back upstairs to the kitchen, to Pasco.

Nearing the top of the stairs she heard Pasco's phone ring.

'WHAT!?' she heard Pasco exclaim. 'How, where is she now?' . . . . 'God almighty, I'll be there as soon as I can.' . . . 'For Christ's sake! Would you believe it?' he said to himself. 'Cecily!' he shouted, 'Oh, you're there, sorry, didn't see you come back in. Sorry, but one of the girls has fallen off her bike and broken something, I've got to go, to the hospital. Sorry. Jesus. We'll catch up another time, bye. Sorry.' Pasco rushed down the stairs, leaving his portfolio on the breakfast bar.

Cecily was speechless. She aggressively turned the oven off, then glared out of the window as Pasco's Volvo disappeared rapidly on the other side of the harbour, on towards the main road out of Padstow.

Ten minutes later she was already almost one glass of red down, and she sat at the breakfast bar. Thinking and talking to herself. Angrily. Glumly. Angrily. Bewildered. 'Hell Pasco. What else have I got to try?'

Chapter Thirty-Eight

When Sam said she was good at historical research she knew of what she spoke. Her degree in History had covered the Tudor period in depth. In 1537 the Anglican church was tasked with keeping a record of baptisms, marriages and burials: the parish register was created. In 1598 the same records were required to be sent to the diocesan bishop: the Bishops' Transcripts were created. So, anybody attempting to 'doctor' the records would need to know that they were stored in two separate places. Sam also knew that the Courtney Library at the Royal Cornwall Museum held records on film up to the late 1950s thus covering the period in question. So she had news when she arrived at Lost Farm Barn.

Treloar was as ever sitting outside with his beloved cats, talking on his phone. Sam walked through to the garden and joined him at the table. He indicated the pot of coffee and pushed it towards her as she sat down.

'Her name was Angwin, his was Treloar,' he said without preamble.

'Did you get hold of your parents in Spain?'

'No, I remembered.'

'How on earth did you remember that?' she asked with genuine surprise.

'Amy. Amy always laughed about it: Angwin so close to Angove. Local names.'

'Well she . . . you were . . . are right.'

'Hah! I knew it I just knew it was bollocks! Hang on Ben's just coming back to me. Ben, Sam's here, I'll put you on speaker.'

'Samantha my beloved,' came the purring voice from the ether.

'Fitz,' Sam acknowledged with a smile as Treloar rolled his eyes.

'Well,' Fitzroy continued, 'you would be amazed at how

many databases there are out there for genealogists, professionals, amateurs and hobbyists.'

'I wouldn't,' Sam said dragging a spiral bound A4 pad from her tote bag.

'Sad bastards,' was Treloar's only comment.

'Anyway, I have checked and all those I have found all state the same: marriage of Kerensa Treloar and Sven Mårtensson,' said Sam

'It's BOLLOCKS,' Treloar shouted causing Lola the tortoiseshell cat to leap down from his lap and turn to give him a withering glare.

'It may well be bollocks Phil but it's skilled bollocks, thorough, organised bollocks to link and update all those sites, Fitzroy insisted.'

'Mmm. I'll get Jamie onto it. He'll track the bastard down.'

'Tell him to be sure to leave no traces; my guys are in there too and we don't want any . . . complications, Fitzroy warned.'

'Hah! Jamie's more than a match for your guys as you well know,' Treloar said.

'How do you know he's not one of mine?' asked Fitzroy.

'In your dreams pal, in your dreams,' Treloar scoffed.

'Boys, boys,' said Sam.'

'Sorry,' said the two men simultaneously.

'Well,' she said flicking the pages of the A4 pad, 'I can categorically state that it is officially bollocks.'

'Hah!' Treloar punched the air.

'And Fitz I also concur that it is skilled bollocks. It was very cleverly done. It's not an altered, edited entry, it's a newly created entry inserted in the Morvah record. In the Zennor record, where the marriage actually took place, it shows correctly. Whoever did this knew that you were married at Morvah and so did Masterson so he would buy it. But Morvah is Amy's family's parish not yours, The Treloars' parish is Zennor and that is where Kerensa Angwin married Talan Treloar at St Senara's.

'Beautiful and brilliant,' came the disembodied voice of Benedict Fitzroy.

'Dastardly really,' said Sam, 'if for any reason

Masterson had the original Morvah register checked it could be claimed as an omission; impossible to doctor the Zennor register so he or she bypassed it altogether. *That* is brilliant.'

'OK, OK,' said Treloar, 'I buy it that Masterson is behind it: he has the money, he owns the media and the hacks and he has a grudge about his son. But what I don't buy is why me?'

'He holds you responsible for his son Guy's death,' said Sam.

'Yeah, but why me? Why not Ben? Or even more likely why not both of us?'

There was a silence on the line and Sam looked down at her pad. Treloar waited.

'Well . . .' said Fitzroy, because you look Swedish, like a Viking. I don't.'

'Fucking Masterson doesn't and he *is* Swedish. He's half Sami, you know the small and dark people from the Arctic, but still nothing like a Viking and nothing like me!'

'No,' said Fitzroy reflectively, 'I suppose you don't look like a bugger.'

'What?' said Treloar and Sam together.

'You know, those Cornish pesky pixie things: buggers.'

'Buccas, man, B U C C A, bucca' Treloar spelled it out.

'That's the bugger! Hah! Well weren't they small and dark and hairy, a bit like trolls?'

'Jesus Sam, remind me again that this man is actually not an idiot.'

Sam smiled and addressed Fitzroy, 'Nice deflection Fitz. Very neat.'

Treloar stared at her frowning. She sighed and Fitzroy echoed her sigh down the line.

'Phil. What Fitz is trying to avoid pointing out is that the Treloars, albeit a lovely family famed in this part of Cornwall, are basically anonymous in the wider world. The Fitzroys however, well they can trace their lineage back beyond the mists of time, henchmen and mistresses to kings, famed in battle, owning large swathes of the British Isles. It's one thing to insert a false entry in the Morvah parish register it's another to hack into Debrett's, Burke's Peerage and the annals of The Tablet.'

‘Well,’ said Treloar grinning, ’if you put it like that, I take your point. Too posh to pursue.’

‘Something like that,’ she returned the grin.

‘It’s alright pal, we still love you, you blue-blooded git.’

‘Thanks mate,’ Fitzroy said, ‘I don’t know how I could go on without the knowledge that . . .’

‘Cut the crap you sarcastic bastard before I reconsider,’ Treloar interrupted, laughing.

‘Seriously though,’ Fitzroy’s tone was now sombre, ‘it’s not Masterson is it. He’s being used by somebody who is out to get you. I *am* irrelevant. The Swedish story gets him involved, gets his resources and his massive media machine rolling, but he’s just the messenger not the instigator. Somebody is using Masterson’s animosity towards you over his son’s death.

‘Who?’

‘Ah well, that is indeed the million dollar question mate, who indeed?’

Ruby is sitting at the table in the back room at Strandloper. She is sorting through a pile of records taken from a Wurlitzer jukebox looking for something that she cannot recall. What does she need? What is it? From the bar she can hear the strains of Glen Campbell. She sings along softly.

> *'and I need you more than want you, and I want you for . . .*

The door crashes open and she is ripped from the toppling chair. The door is slammed shut and she is pinned against it. Skirt wrenched up, knickers torn away, she is thrust into, gasping.

Showers of sparks pulse through her body to her fingertips and toes. It is the tall blonde man from the Padstow Hub and he is moaning. Warmth and tingling flood her body.

Bang! Bang! Bang! – somebody is hammering on the door.
Quickly, quickly, there's somebody there!
Does she speak the words?
Bang! Bang! Bang!

'Ma! Ma, I've brought your tea!'

Ruby wakes with a start, her entire body throbbing. She is in her bed at Solitaire.

Chapter Thirty-Nine

It was a cloudless, endless blue-sky morning as Treloar walked down the path at the Polzeath camp site to reach the pink caravan. He found Viola Lawrence and Leah Kidd sitting in the candy-striped deckchairs looking out over the beach and chatting quietly. Viola was wearing an enormous pair of dark-rimmed sunglasses, which she pushed onto her head as Leah called out at his approach, a broad grin spreading across her face.

'Hi Inspector! Good to see you again and well done you for finding her.

'Good morning ladies. How are you feeling today Viola?'

'Oh do call her Vi; everybody does; Viola is so . . . Shakespearean.'

Viola smiled and spoke softly, 'I'm feeling much better thank you. I don't feel sick anymore and my headache's gone completely. But I still don't remember what happened.' She added the last sentence hastily, trying to convince him.

He noticed Leah looking at her quizzically. Perhaps she had spoken to her friend?

'That's fine Vi,' Treloar reassured, 'I just need to go over what happened.'

'I don't remember what happened! I told that policeman at the hospital everything anyway.'

'Yes, but we cannot consider that as a statement, given that you were suffering the after-effects of the drug you were given; we need something for the record.'

'Of course, that makes sense,' said Leah cheerily, 'talk to the man Vi, he's very . . . friendly and not at all scary.'

'S'pose so,' Viola mumbled, sulkily.

'I'll leave you to it,' Leah jumped to her feet, 'I'm off to meet the guys at the bar. Just call me when you're done and I'll come back before you leave Inspector. Vi's not to be left alone. Strict parental orders or somebody will be sent to 'collect' her,' she added in a ghostly voice.

'Don't worry Leah,' Treloar said, 'I'll walk her over when we've finished. Strandloper?'

'The one and only. Ciao!' and with that she turned and ran to the steps down to the beach, raising her left arm to wiggle her fingers in a farewell wave, without turning.

After ten minutes of Viola repeating that she had left the caravan for the beach, walked down the steps onto the sand, and then awoke in the feed store with a raging thirst and a blinding headache, Treloar conceded defeat. He was getting nowhere and there was nothing he could do about it. The girl was adamant, consistent, and lying. But he knew that he was not going to get the truth. Clever. Keep the lie simple and stick to it. But why? He didn't understand. Why was she protecting her abductor? Fear? Shame? Complicity? He brought the interview to an end and her relief was palpable. In companionable silence they followed Leah's path across the beach.

When they reached Strandloper Treloar could see Leah sitting at an outside table on the boardwalk with Joel and Ravi. They were all laughing. As he approached with Viola the two boys leapt to their feet and rushed to meet them.

'Vi girl! You OK?' asked Joel pulling her into a hug whilst Ravi stood back smiling shyly, reaching out to brush her arm gently.

'I'm fine!' Viola smiled broadly for the first time since Treloar's arrival, 'I just hate all this fuss. I'm perfectly fine. Really I am.'

Treloar stepped back onto the sand, 'Well, I'll leave you with your friends Viola.'

'Whoah! Not so fast sheriff,' cried Leah, 'you must have a drink before you go.'

'Fever-tree ginger beer?' he asked, smiling.

'No way!' and she lifted a bottle of Cornish Rattler cider towards him. Seeing his confusion she laughed loudly. 'All perfectly legal Inspector, yesterday was my eighteenth.'

'Ah well in that case, many happy returns and let me buy you another. Guys?'

The boys lifted their cider bottles in acknowledgement of the offer and Viola asked for a Coke Zero.

'I'll give you a hand,' said Leah. She was by his side and taking his arm before he could speak.

'Thanks for your help.' he said as they crossed the boardwalk and mounted the steps to enter the cool dimness of the bar.

'Oh no Inspector, you're the one helping me. Now Vi's here they'll all start one of their endless perishing debates.' Seeing his confusion she added, 'You know the Captain Perish Penhaligon books? Those three are fanatical about them, call themselves, 'Perishers'. They go on and on about who was the better captain, Zanzibar Malone of the *Splendour* or Thrift Trevelyan of the *Mockery*. And then there's that burning issue of whether Perish and Tansy Minear actually fucked.'

Treloar laughed. She was very damning, but it did not escape him that she was completely accurate in naming the characters and the ships. He wondered if she meant to shock him with the swearing, but on balance he thought it was just her normal vocabulary. He really liked this girl. Feisty. Shades of his second, closest sister, Lucia.

When they were standing at the bar waiting to be served he turned to her.

'Tell me Leah, do you believe Vi doesn't remember anything after leaving Marilyn for the beach?'

'No way. She remembers something but she's saying squit. I don't get it. If somebody did that to me I'd want his balls on sticks.'

Treloar smiled; he believed it. Leah continued.

'But I'll tell you what's really weird; she's not scared, not at all. She's not even pissed off. She's just . . . confused and a bit sad. I don't get it.'

'You've no ideas?'

'Nah. And you're wasting your time trying to get it out of her. Unless you brought red hot needles to stick under her fingernails.'

'Budget cuts,' Treloar shook his head.

Leah laughed, 'Anyway, Vi is the most stubborn person I know; she won't budge, I promise you'

'Well if you think of anything or she says anything,

please call me.' He pulled some business cards from his pocket, and selecting one with his mobile number hand-written on the reverse, handed it to her.

'Félipe? Isn't that Spanish?'

'Yes. My mother is Spanish.'

'No way! Do you speak it, like properly?'

'Yep.'

'Oh my God how super cool.'

The drinks arrived and Treloar paid. Raising his bottle to Leah he smiled broadly.

'Feliz cumpleanõs!'

'Way! Gracias.'

Chapter Forty

For Cecily it had been an ordinary, but very busy day, running from office to office, meeting her office managers, sometimes some of the cleaners who cleaned her properties, and occasionally, guests. She was good at encouraging, motivating, thanking, and welcoming, and mostly she enjoyed it. She also dropped off CHILL newsletters and CHILL in . . . . . . T shirts. There was a version for each location. Even with an early start though she could only manage five offices.

'Hey Cecily,' Jeannie said when Cecily walked back into the Padstow office just after 5.30 p.m. 'Didn't expect to see you today.'

'Hi Jeannie, just calling in to check emails, expecting one from Germany, a holiday blogger. And maybe some Ally Ally Oh potentials. Then I'm going up for a shower and I'm going to start wrapping myself round a bottle of red and get The Old Boat to send me up a food parcel. It's been a long day. Started at Rock, finished at Gorran Haven. Still another three to go though. What about you, you OK for CHILL at Padstow Ts?'

'You're kidding right? The storeroom is all the way over there,' Jeannie said pointing towards a door on the other side of the office, 'Don't worry about me, do you want me to do the last three so you can get on with other stuff? You must have loads to be thinking about.'

'You're not wrong. I might just take you up on that, I'll let you know. Thanks'. Cecily sat at her computer to check for replies from Germany and potential Ally Ally Oh sponsors that she had been canvassing. There was nothing of interest and she closed the machine down. 'Right, that's me. I'm gone. See you Jeannie, don't be too late.'

As she looked out of the flat's kitchen window two hours later, sipping a glass of red wine, Cecily watched a fishing boat returning, listening to the *Mercury Falling* album by Sting. The vessel ran through the harbour entrance and was turning left towards South Jetty when she noticed a dark purple pick-up truck pull up. It parked at the shelter down to the right; where she had first seen the gang, which had kick-started the idea of 'business support' which Demmy was now successfully running despite her tender years.

To Cecily's surprise, Demmy herself jumped down from the cab, and her best buddy Carla closely followed. Ginger John, Carla's brother, climbed down from the driver's side, carrying a six-pack, and followed the girls into the shelter putting the six pack down on the slatted wooden bench at the back.

Cecily saw Demmy take out her mobile and tap at it. Moments after Demmy had finished tapping, Cecily's own phone sounded its whooshing incoming message alert. By then Demmy, Carla, and Ginger John had cracked three cans and were supping beer or lager, and chatting and laughing, occasionally looking up to see if any of the others were coming.

Her assumption that Demmy had sent her a message was correct. She picked up her phone and saw that Demmy was asking if Cecily was in and could she have a chat. Cecily messaged back that she was and told her to come over.

A few minutes later Demmy was also sipping red wine and they both stood at the window, watching Ginger John and Carla. 'Thing is', said Demmy, 'I wanted you to see the truck. It's wicked. I wanted you to know about it.'

'Well, I quite like purple . . . . . .'

'Oh, come on! You must be able to see it's well off the ground, and the snorkel! Demmy almost shouted.'

'OK, OK, Yep. Yep. Definitely. I can.' Cecily smiled, 'anything else I need to know?'

'Well, it's four-wheel drive with loads of modes, the floor is raised a foot more than usual and the snorkel, that's the big tube thing sticking up by the side of the bonnet, means it can drive through water. Neat eh?'

'And I need to know this because?'

'Ah, well, we can use it now, on jobs! So it means we can do more, go places Aleksy's brother's crappy Fiesta couldn't. And it starts every time. And it's faster. Thing is, it's Carla and John's Dad's, and John has been driving it for ages, around the farms helping his dad at weekends and nights. But he passed his test today!! That's what we're celebrating down there.'

'Well great. Give John my congratulations, and take a bottle of wine across. Here, take a red. That's very entrepreneurial of you Demmy, and thanks for bringing the truck over, but what does John think to the idea?'

'Well he's been out with us a few times already and likes the work, and REALLY likes the idea of being a main driver! Their dad's already said he can use it now he's passed his test, so that won't be a problem either. What do you think?'

'Well, I think that's brilliant.' Cecily said, clutching Demmy's elbow excitedly, 'I can already think of a couple of jobs coming up where the Fiesta wouldn't have worked, and I must say I do like the look of John, and the wheels. Very much.'

'Great. I'll go and tell him. Thanks Cecily'

'No problem, and thank you. Tell you what though,' Cecily said as she looked down at the shelter, 'You might want to tell John that even though the lager might look and taste like gnats p', it's still alcohol. The boys in blue wouldn't pass up a chance to stop him. If I were you I'd go tell him that he's hired as driver, and then get him the hell home to do the celebrating!'

'Good thinking. Don't want to lose them, not now. I've got an idea . . . bye for now.'

Chapter Forty-One

Sam took the call at 07.30.

'Morning Sam it's Diggory Keast.'

'Hello Dig, early for you.'

'Sam, we've had a report of a body found in suspicious circumstances.'

'Another one?'

'Yeah. It's a woman this time. Look I'm calling you because you're closest.'

'Give me the details.'

'Right you are my 'ansome. The location is called Lowenalands. Fancy new camping site near Trevose Head above Barras Bay. I've called Phil but it'll take him over an hour even at this time of day. He needs to get hisself sorted up here if this carries on.'

'What do we know?'

'A woman. That's all. The caller was a bit hysterical; young girl on her own; the site owner's away.'

'We are sure it's a death?'

'Yeah. That doctor's been out there to certify.'

'Jordan?'

'That's the bugger. And now he's buggered off to some emergency home birth or some such.'

'What is this Lowenalands?'

'Campsite of some sort from what I've been told. Posh.'

'OK text me the postcode and any details. I'm on my way.'

'Right. I'll see you there. Kit's checking the place out online. He'll fill us in with what he finds.'

Sam turned onto the B3276 towards Padstow, turning off before St Merryn to skirt Constantine Bay and the golf club before heading for Trevose Head. Lowenalands was a glamping site. The farmer had sold up and the new owner had turned two coastal fields into a select venue offering upmarket fully equipped canvas tents with en suite facilities, indoor and outdoor showers and individual hot-tubs. Sam followed the signs from the coast road driving past the entrance to the farm itself and up a granite chippings' lane towards the sea. The weather had turned again and it was a glorious still blue-sky morning with the promise of heat. The sky was bright, full of light reflecting off the Camel estuary. It was certainly a beautiful location.

Ahead she could see three widely spaced tents. They were enormous, more marquee than tent, set in a field but separated by strategically placed fencing providing privacy. At the end of the drive stood a miniature version of the tents and as Sam pulled to a stop a young woman emerged, mobile phone clutched in front of her.

'There's someone else here now . . . I don't know . . . No . . . I just don't know . . . look I have to go. I'll call you back when I have more news . . . What? . . . What now? . . . OK I'll see you then.'

She was wearing white cargo shorts and a sea blue polo shirt with the embroidered logo of a marquee and the text Lowenalands. She was a small pretty girl with a troubled expression but as Sam approached she managed a smile.

'Hi, are you with the police?'

'Yes,' Sam pulled her warrant card from her jeans' pocket. 'Inspector Samantha Scott. You?

'I'm Bry, sorry, Bryony Collins. I'm on my own this morning but that was the owner Mr Trent. He's coming down now.'

'From?'

'Oh, Manchester.'

'He's not the farmer?'

'Oh my no. There's no farmer, not anymore. Mr Trent bought the farm last year to create Lowenalands. Lowena means joy or happiness in old Cornish.'

'In Cornish I think you mean, not old Cornish; it's not an extinct language.'

'Right,' said the girl with a puzzled expression.

'Mr Trent? What is his full name?'

'Oh, sorry. I only know him as Mr Trent.'

Jeez thought Sam. In this day and age. She was beginning to take a dislike to Mr Trent before she even met him with his poncey camp site on perfectly good pasture and his authoritarian attitude to his staff. And why was this young girl in charge on her own?

'Right Bryony. So how many campers do you have?'

'Oh they're not campers, they're guests. Mr Trent insists on that.'

I bet he does thought Sam.

'Fine. How many guests do you have?'

'Oh well . . . just her.'

'Just one tent occupied.'

'Just one guest. The dead woman.'

'Really?' Sam was surprised.

'Well yes. You see it's a new venue and, well to be honest, there have been a few plumbing issues so we're not actually open yet. Mr Trent is fuming because we would have been full otherwise at this time of year. Apparently, the other two are open and fully booked.

'The other two?'

'Oh yes there's one on Ullswater in the Lake District: 'Merelands', and one up north, near Bishop Auckland on the River Wear: 'Becklands'. They're all near water you see. Anyway, I know it's not high season but we're not a 'family-oriented' venue.' Bryony raised her fingers to indicate the inverted commas.

'So no buckets and spades and swings?' asked Sam teasingly.

'Oh most definitely not.'

'So Lowenalands is aimed at adults.'

'Yes, yes! It's very upmarket, very expensive . . . oh no, not expensive . . . just . . .' Bryony blushed furiously.

'That's fine. I understand. It's not for children.'

'Exactly! It's like The Scarlet, you know the hotel in Mawgan Porth.?'

Sam nodded.

'Mr Trent loves that place. That's where he got the idea for the hot-tubs.'

'So Bryony, to be clear, there is just one guest resident at the moment.'

'Absolutely. Just Sue'.

'Sue?'

'Yes sorry. God you'll think I'm a complete moron. But that's all I know: Sue. Mr Trent handled the booking, and anyway it wasn't with Sue.'

'Sorry?' Sam was struggling to follow.

'I mean the booking. It wasn't done direct with Sue, it was all through the magazine. It was some sort of prize, so they arranged it and paid and everything, and we were to get free publicity. Mr Trent is so pissed.'

'Yes. I don't suppose this is the sort of publicity he anticipated,' said Sam.

'Fuck no!' Bryony realised what she had said and covered her mouth with her hand, aghast.

'Don't worry,' Sam chuckled. 'Right then Bryony. Can you show me?'

'Yes, yes of course. I couldn't believe it. I took her Champagne and strawberries, it was all part of the prize, and there she was . . . '

'OK let's take a look.'

'She's in the hot tub. Only . . . well it's all wrong!'

'What's all wrong?'

'You'll see.'

Bryony set off along a granite chippings' path across leading the headland. It really was a glorious morning, not a cloud in the sky, birdsong and the distant, rising engine drone of a fishing boat heading into open water from the Camel. Idyllic. They reached the back of the second marquee.

'This is it: Perranporth. The tents are named after Cornish coastal towns: Perranporth, Porthtowan, Porthcurno and the next two will be Porthleven and . . . oh, I forget the last one,' Bryony frowned.

'Never mind. It's not important,' said Sam reassuringly.

'Maenporth! The last one will be Maenporth.'

They walked up to the tent and through the open flaps Sam could make out a large bed and a cushioned two-seater wicker settee. 'Perranporth' was seared onto a piece of driftwood at the side of the path.

'She's this way,' said Bryony, skirting the tent. Ahead of

them, on the clifftop stood a raised platform supporting a hot-tub. Even from where she stood Sam could picture the stunning views the site would offer over the estuary and Barras Bay.

'It's all wrong, just all wrong,' Bryony mumbled, hesitating as they reached the raised deck

'It's OK, you stay there,' Sam said as she climbed the steps.

'Thank you, thank you,' the girl gushed in relief.

Sam could make out the back of a head and the outstretched arms resting on the tub's rim as if the woman were merely relaxing. But then something incongruous caught her eye: where she would have expected to see wooden planking or driftwood surrounding the tub in keeping with the natural look of the tents and other facilities there was a blue and white pattern. Moving closer Sam could see it was a banner somehow fixed around the circumference of the tub. Closer still, she could see that it had been hand-painted in exquisite detail and she recognised the familiar livery of a Cornish dairy.

'Oh no,' she muttered. It was another staged scene. Moving to the side of the housing she looked down into the tub. It was filled, not with water, but with a crusted, pale yellow cement. 'Clotted cream.' she whispered. Then she looked up to take in the woman's face.

She had aged in the three years since Sam had last seen her, the dark hair now heavily streaked with grey that matched the colour of the staring eyes.

'Oh no, oh no,' Sam gasped, jerking back in shock.

The body was that of Superintendent Suzanne Winters, her former boss and Treloar's greatest critic and sworn enemy.

'My Lord,' Diggory Keast had appeared silently at her side. 'Treloar said she'd get her due.'

The competition had run in a new upmarket lifestyle magazine under the hideously tortured title: 'Splendid solitude in stunning sea-cliff setting'. The idea had been promoted by a third party agency and the whole campaign had been handled by them.

There was some confusion at the magazine as to the exact process undertaken to approve the running of the competition, but all the boxes had been ticked, albeit that nobody could actually remember ticking them. Nobody recalled meeting anybody from the agency, or even speaking with them, and the agency, a reputable company, had no trace of the project and denied all knowledge.

Sam and Treloar were sitting in the kitchen at The Count House in Padstow.

'Wouldn't you have been suspicious? Sam asked.

'Christ Sam, we are talking Suzanne 'Frosty' Winters here. She was notoriously mean and never one to look a gift-horse in the mouth,' said Treloar.

'But how did they get her to enter the competition?'

'She didn't bloody enter the competition! They'll have spun her a line and she'll have swallowed it with hook and sinker. Free holiday? What's not to like?'

'But she was a senior police officer; she should have checked.'

'She was a senior administrator and book-keeper, she was no detective. And she was motivated by greed. Greed and spite. She'd have lapped it up, especially if there was to be coverage in the media. You remember how she craved the spotlight.'

'I remember how much she resented that the Chief Con always wanted you in front of the camera.'

'Yeah and what made it worse was that I didn't ask for that, I don't even like it, and she knew that. I think she was more pissed off with him than me, but obviously she couldn't target him.'

'She certainly pissed off a lot of people. Did anybody actually like her?'

'Well Col did, for a while, till he realised she was using him. If you can have a female Cronos it was Suzanne Winters.'

'Cronos?'

'You know, the Greek myth of the Titan Cronos, the one who ate his own children at birth.'

'Ah yes, that brilliant painting by Goya in the Prado.'

'So we're not short of people who won't be mourning

her.'

'But why here? Or more to the point why her, here? She lives on the other side of the country now, why not do her in over there? A lot easier and cheaper than this complicated set up. I mean I get the Cornish theme but Ellis and Hicks were local. Plus Winters was on the other side of the law. The other two were dodgy businessmen and whatever we may think of her, Frosty was a senior police officer.'

'Yeah that's what's worrying me. And everyone knew I meant it when I said she'd get what she was due.'

jonny w@surfingpadstowbeaches3 42m
Was out off Harlyn beach early am. Saw lotz polis go 2 Trevose Head nr top of cliffs. Cant see now bak on beach. Can hear sirens. Wotshappenin up there? Anythin to worry about? #padstowsurferschool #padstownews

Jonny w and 322 others follow, Joy D@loveDwalkingpadstow replied
Billyboy W@surfingpadstowbeaches 40m
Hey jonny was just along from u! In Mother Iveys bay. Back on beach now. Saw em frm board & cn hear sirens now, bt see nothing frm here either. Wotshappenin? @surfingpadstowbeaches3 #padstowsurferschool #padstownews

Joy D@loveDwalkingpadstow 37m
Hey guys, just back in Padstow with Woof, heard sirens distant on bipass. Saw O. Stay safe. @surfingpadstowbeaches @surfingpadstowbeaches3 #padstownews

Dave Constantiner@constantpadstowDwalker 33m
Standing at Trevose Head side of golf course with Charlie looking @ boys in blue. Sealed off Lowenalands glampsite. Got binocs, boys in blue staring @ hot tub outside tent. @surfingpadstowbeaches @surfingpadstowbeaches3 #padstownews

BBC @bbcsouthwestnewstoday 31m
The BBC has learned that another body has been found theatrically staged. This time near or on Trevose Head just past golf course. Death is suspicious. News still coming in so we will provide updates when we know more. If you have information do please let us know.

uknewsnow@uknewsnownownownow 28m
Suspicious!!?? Senior fmale police officer dead in cement tub looking like clotted cream!! Same female PO disliked by same detective who

disliked Hicks + Ellis. Detective suspected? #stargazy&edenkillings #cornwallmurders #suspiciousdeathscornwall #suspiciouscopscornwall

newsukfeed@newsukfeedcallsitout 27m
BREAKING. Can confirm fmale police officer dead in clotted cream cement bath @ Trevose Head glampsite. Can confirm 1 detective hated her + others killed in Cornish Heritage scenes + dead ex. #stargazy&edenkillings #cornwallmurders #suspiciouscopscornwall #padstownews

Andy Sykes@dogwalkingpadstow23 19m
FFS!!! Stunned. Can't follow that! @ least no Dwalkers. Unbelievable. So now it's a by in blu? Crazy. @SolihullBillingDwalker @IslingtonDwlkers35 #padstownews #Dwalkerspadstow

Followed by K G@manchesterfifthestate and 376 others
B Gordon@westmidsfifthestate 15m
Told you guys they're everywhere. Even Cornwall. Go there for f'ing holidays every year & can't get away from bent cops even there. Scum. Shd be lcked up. Hope he is. #stargazy&edenkillings #cornwallmurders #suspiciouscopscornwall #bentcopseverywhere #dataonbentcops

K G@manchesterfifthestate 11m
Yeah G. You did. Never know where they're gonna surface. We'll get a team on it. @westmidsfifthestate #bringdirtycopsdown #stargazy&edenkillings #cornwallmurders #suspiciouscopscornwall #bentcopseverywhere #dataonbentcops

Followed by Dreen Z@Bham@westmidsfifthestate and 294 others
Tyrone Bham@westmidsfifthestate12 8m
Everywhere man. UR so rite G. B&W. @westmidsfifthestate @manchesterfifthestate

#bringdirtycopsdown #stargazy&edenkillings #cornwallmurders #suspiciouscopscornwall #bentcopseverywhere

Dreen Z@Bham@westmidsfifthestate38 5m
Rite again Tye! More W tho. Esp in USA bt allover!! Wot shd we do. @westmidsfifthestate @manchesterfifthestate #bringdirtycopsdown #stargazy&edenkillings #cornwallmurders #suspiciouscopscornwall #bentcopseverywhere

Joy D@loveDwalkingpadstow 4m
This guy's a local. So great and straight. No way he's involved. Nice family. He's got cats. @dogwalkingpadstow23 @uknewsnownownow @newsukfeedcallsitout @westmidsfifthestate38

newsukfeed@newsukfeedcallsitout 3m
CORNISH HERITAGE KILLINGS. Are you sure? He knew all, didn't like them we've been told. Had good reasons. News still coming in. @loveDwalkingpadstow @dogwalkingpadstow23 @westmidsfifthestate @manchesterfifthestate #suspiciouscopscornwall #bentcopseverywhere #cornwallmurders

newsukfeed@newsukfeedcallsitout 1m
CORNISH HERITAGE KILLINGS. BREAKING. Cop suspension. NewsUKFeed understands there are rumours of suspension of Detective Inspector Treloar, cop who knew and hated the 3 victims of the Cornish Heritage Killer. Tap for more on our **FEED.** #cornwallmurders #bentsopseverywhere

Tulip Khan had sent Treloar the twitter thread following Suzanne Winters murder and he was incandescent. He rang her mobile.

'Who are these fifth estate bastards in Manchester and Birmingham?'

'Well, the fifth estate is the name given to media and feeds online - you know, their blogs, tweets, Facebook and web pages - the fourth estate obviously being the printed media. These particular "bastards" in The Midlands and the North West are a particularly nasty neo-fascist bunch who are anti-homosexual, anti-non-white, anti-women, anti-everything civilized and liberal as far as I can see. Oh, and they are especially anti-police who they see as a weak, powerless arm of the establishment.'

'Huh! So there not wrong about everything then. But where are they getting this crap about me being bent? Fucking Winters was the bent cop, arseholes!'

'Phil, the people that matter know that.'

'Well, they'd better keep out of my way. Thanks for the heads up though Tulip.'

'Don't mention it. If I come across anything else I'll let you have it.'

As Treloar was talking to Tulip, in the bowels of the Devon & Cornwall Police's headquarters at Middlemoor in Exeter, in a small dingy office, a member of the support staff was also sending an email. He was tasked by Romilly Hawkins, the Police and Crime Commissioner, to track the media's reporting of the police, with a special emphasis to seek out and report to her anything negative about DCI Treloar. And here was the fifth estate's thread: more grist to her mill. More ammunition for her campaign to get rid of him.

Chapter Forty-Two

Treloar was suspended. When he had arrived at The Count House there was a message to call headquarters. Chamberlain was angry but powerless.

'I'm sorry Phil.'

'Who is behind this?' Treloar demanded.

'You know the answer to that. There is no way I'll let her hang you out to dry. I recognise an agenda when I see one and I recognise a revenge ploy.'

'Romilly fucking Hawkins, our esteemed Police and Crime Commissioner.'

'Exactly. Why do you think Winters kept her job. Christ, kept out of prison after that business with the Spargos? She was bent but she was embarrassing, and she had covered her tracks well.'

'I didn't kill Winters.'

'Of course not! But you exposed her and forced her relocation to the other side of the country. This is payback from a wounded lover.'

'Winters and Hawkins?' Treloar was incredulous.

'So I hear. You knew Winters was gay or bi or whatever.'

Treloar sighed deeply.

'So I'm suspended?'

'Let's make sure it's temporary. I'll fight it from this end. You? Well . . . time to call in reinforcements I'd say. But of course, I didn't say that. Now go home.'

'I hear you Nicky. And thanks.'

Treloar placed the call.

'Hello Cornishman.'

'Hello Ben.'

'In the shit are we?'

'Yeah, you could say that.'

'Mmm. I've been following the media coverage mate.'

'You follow me?'

'There's more than one kind of 'person of interest'.'

'They're going to crucify me. Everyone knows that Winters and I hated each other.'

'Surely not everyone?'

'Well it's out there now.'

'Ah. Looks like you've got yourself a ship-sinker. Nasty little bastards. Anyway we'll deal with them later. I see our friends in the media have already linked you to Ellis and Hicks and that was bloody tenuous. Winters? More problematic.'

'I'm fucked.'

'Not at all. You just need to break the link, get away from this 'Kernow Killings – Cornish Cop Connection'. What you really need is a death with absolutely no connection to you or yours.'

'You offering?'

'Nil desperandum.'

'What's that, the Coldstream Guards' motto?'

'No that is: 'nulli secundus'. Nil desperandum is Horace as I recall. Wise fellow. He also wrote 'Caelum non animum mutant qui trans mare currunt'.

'Really.'

'Yes mate. It means roughly that you can't run away from yourself. Sound advice I've always found. But enough of the great poet. What do we have? The first two murders, well from what I've seen, the deposition sites were staged but it was fairly basic stuff: a few surfboards and sand for Ellis and some twine and pegs for Hicks. The victims were local and easily accessible. But Winters? That was different: creative, elaborate and required a lot of effort and not inconsiderable skill and resources.'

'But the Cornish themes? You thinking copycat? I won't ask how you have all the detail.'

'No, no. There's a plan here, there's a strategy and you seem to be the target. I'm thinking more than one perpetrator, and a banker.'

'Christ, I am fucked.'

'Not at all. This is going to be a challenge: I love a

challenge. They have a team so what we need mate is?'

'A team?'

'Exactly my man. A better team. Right. You go out and get the beers in.'

'Beers?'

'Oh yes indeedy. I'm coming down. I'll find a justification, don't you worry; you've got enough to be thinking about.'

And with that he was gone. As Treloar ended the call he felt a wave of relief wash over him. He exhaled deeply as if he had been holding his breath and felt himself smiling for the first time in what seemed like days. Benedict Fitzroy was trouble, impossible and uncontrollable but when the chips were down . . . well there was nobody, nobody he would sooner turn to. Ben would help him find the bastards and bring them to justice; or just kill them.

thechef@thecornishchef&artist   1m
Crazy news again! Clotted cream tub? Timing not good for recipe promo but pic of band round tub & great clotted cream recipe in blog.
@bbcsouthwestnewstoday @newsukfeedcallsitout
@SolihullBillingDwalker @IslingtonDwlkers35
#padstownews #Dwalkerspadstow #cornwallmurders
#stargazy&edenkillings

. . . .

@thecornishchef&artist

The Cornish chef
& the artist

Chef here. They've not caught the lunatic yet I see. Bodies all over the place, wow! Be careful out there!!
Someone sent us a pic from the glampsite & it looks like the breaking tweeters were right! There was indeed a painted band around the 'cream tub' that the police lady was found in. Uncanny resemblance to packaging of a well-known Cornish clotted cream! The artist cropped the pic to take out the nasty bits & cleaned up the band & here's the result:

Hope it doesn't put you off your food! You'll see loads of recipes using clotted cream - all manner of cheesecakes, fudges, buns, pancakes & on scones for an English tea - slice the scone in half, spread strawberry jam on each half then lashings of clotted cream for a proper Cornish cream tea (Devonshires put the cream on first!), tuck in my 'ansomes.

For something different though try this recipe for 2 portions of amazing mussels:

I use: Mussels, clean, 1 litre (2 pints). Cornish clotted cream 250ml - 300ml (1/2 pint). Good white wine, 1 good slug. Onion, medium, 1, peeled & chopped. Good olive oil, 2 glugs. Fresh parsley, chopped, 1 handful. French bread, 1 long stick, for dunking!

Here's how: Heat a wide pan (that has a tight-fitting lid) over medium heat, when hot add oil, then onions. Stir in, cook for 5 mins until translucent. Add mussels then wine, give vigorous stir & replace lid. After 2 minutes liquor will be bubbling hard, that's great, the steam will be cooking the mussels, add cream, stir through & put lid back on. It'll only take another 3 - 4 minutes or so. Don't wander off - you don't want to overcook. The dish is ready when mussel shells have all opened.

Discard any mussels that haven't opened, serve in deep bowls with plenty of liquor for dunking your bread, garnish with parsley & away you go. Enjoy my 'ansomes.

Anyone know what the lady cop had done? Was she bent? Other cop bent like they're saying? Cream dye for the cement? Was she dead before going into the tub? Crazy!! I like reading crime thrillers myself but this is getting a bit close to home.

Back in Middlemoor's bowels, Romilly Hawkins' gremlin was on the end of a ranting call from his master.

'Find out who the fuck leaked that photo of the clotted cream banner on that hot-tub! It must have been somebody at the fucking scene. Was Treloar there?'

'No ma'am. You had him suspended, remember?'

'Shame. I should have waited a few days, then we could have circulated the rumour that it was him. Fuck! Brilliant opportunity missed. Why didn't you point that out to me? What do I pay you for?'

The gremlin knew better than to answer that.

'Oh well, water under the bridge. But one of his team must be responsible so we can probably still link it to him, if indirectly, and get some mileage out of it.'

Not for the first time, acting and thinking without proper consideration or reflection, and jumping to judgement, Romilly Hawkins was wrong, if not completely. It had been somebody at the crime scene but in her obsession with ruining Treloar she had overlooked the obvious. The first person at the crime scene: the criminal.

Chapter Forty-Three

Treloar was reflecting on the day. It was a glorious late summer's evening and he was sitting on the deck at the rear of Lost Farm Barn with a cold Estrella Damm beer and the tortoiseshell cat Lola. There was no man on earth he would prefer to have at his side in troubled times than Benedict Fitzroy. Whilst both men had been raised in the Catholic faith, Treloar had been born and bred on a West Cornwall coastal farm in a loving family; Fitzroy had been forged and tempered by the English public school system and the British Army. Whilst Treloar could be ruthless, Fitzroy could be brutal.

The man was blessed or cursed, with an exceptional memory. For those who had slighted, crossed or injured him, or those he loved, even from childhood; well 'old sins cast long shadows'. Although a Catholic, Fitzroy held no truck with Romans 12:19: 'Vengeance is mine, I will repay, saith the Lord', and, unlike Machiavelli, he had no care for the temperature of his vengeance but he took it personally. Many a former Ampleforth College pupil or former Coldstream Guards' officer had good cause to keep a watch over his shoulder. Suddenly Lola leapt from his lap bounded onto the wall that separated the deck from the lawn and stood stock still, ears and tail raised.

'What is it gata?' Treloar murmured. But soon he too was aware of the distant incongruous noise approaching from the east. 'Thrupp, thrupp, thrupp'.

'What the hell?' he looked eastwards and there, closing fast, was the light of what was now unmistakably a helicopter. In no time it was hovering above his lawn, a spotlight beaming down. Lola, brave as she was, had disappeared.

As he shielded his eyes and gazed upwards he saw a door slide open and a rope emerge, followed by a dark figure. As it rappelled to the ground he could make out a battered leather jacket, jeans and stout boots. The rope was hauled in and a scruffy green canvas holdall was tossed down to land at the figure's feet. At a wave from the man on the ground, the helicopter rose, banked and retraced its path into the darkening sky. Leo Benedict Julius Fitzroy, named for Popes, had descended from the heavens. Despite his sombre mood Treloar smiled, and shaking his head spoke to the cat who had returned to sit at his feet.

'Showtime.'

'You really are a wanker aren't you?' Treloar said with a grin extending his hand to the approaching man. 'How the hell did you swing that?'

'Friends in high places mate, excuse the pun; useful to have a pal with access to a Wildcat who owes one a favour. And how else was I supposed to get to this Godforsaken wilderness?'

'Road, rail, Newquay airport?'

'Huh?'

'It's really good to see you,' Treloar said with feeling.

'Good to be here mate, good to be here,' and with that, he took the bottle of beer from Treloar's hand and drank it dry. 'Anymore of this gnat's piss?'

After a late supper Treloar and Fitzroy were sitting in the garden when Treloar's landline rang and he went into the kitchen. After a while he came back out with his mobile.

'That was Tulip Khan. Shit Ben, look at this,' he handed the screen over.

DEATH AT THE HANDS OF THE LAW

We are reliably informed that in his early days as a maverick detective our DCI Treloar was 'Da Law' as in 'here comes the law'. Really? The law? Well, dear reader, there have been unfortunate deaths in his last three major cases.

Admittedly, in the first nobody was brought to justice, but the second and third saw the 'unfortunate' deaths of the prime suspects before justice could run its course. No great conviction rate then for the Chief Constable's blue-eyed boy.

No wonder he stalled at the rank of Inspector for so long; though sources tell us he was held back by a superior officer who questioned his ability, suitability and even his character! And what happened to that shrewd officer?

Ah well that will be the late Superintendent Suzanne Winters now the THIRD recent murder victim connected to our dashing detective, and all three so close to home just like poor Lamorna Rain!

So Jolyon Ellis, Titus Hicks and Suzanne Winters, all crossed our hero, but it's all coincidence we are told. Where were they when the man said,'Sometimes coincidence is a plan undercover'?

'What man?' asked Fitzroy.

'Mmm?'

'Sounds like a Christmas cracker motto or one of those Chinese what-nots.'

'What are you on about man?'

'Fortune cookies! That's the bugger.'

'Christ almighty! I'm being crucified on the worldwide web and you're wittering on about Chinese restaurants!'

'It's a load of bollocks, mate.'

'Maybe, but none of it is actually untrue, technically.'

'Christ don't tell me we're resorting to the truth. Abandon hope!'

Treloar snatched the phone back and glared at Fitzroy.

'Sorry mate. It's not me in the firing line. Right. Let's apply some logic to this bullshit. Do you have an alibi for Ellis's time of death?'

'Yes as it happens.'

'Did you resent him for cheating your . . . what was it, second cousin's first wife's step-brother?'

'No. It was my sister's boss, who was one of many he cheated, it was not a lot of money and he got it back.'

'Case closed,' Fitzroy slammed his fist down on the garden table like a judge's gavel. 'Next! Do you have an alibi for the time of Hicks' death?'

'Yes again as it happens.'

'Did you resent him for killing Amy's granny?'

'No. He didn't kill her. She died peacefully in her sleep at the age of 104.'

'Case closed,' another slammed fist.

'Did you kill Frosty Winters?'

'What happened to alibi and motive?' asked Treloar in umbrage.

'Well sorry old mate. We know you have no alibi for this one and you did hate her guts. But, in your favour, you can't paint for toffee.'

Despite himself, Treloar burst out laughing and Fitzroy offered his chipped tooth grin.

'Seriously though,' Fitzroy was suddenly serious, 'this poisonous scribe is linking all three victims as are we. Did one: did all. Alibi for two: so what? They don't know that, they can't. The time of death for all three? Well how many single men with a lacklustre love life would have an alibi for early morning? They took a chance; and it was a fair bet. The truth here is not the point. This is shit-stirring, mud-slinging on an epic scale and the truly relevant point here is why? Are you paranoid mate?'

'No.'

'Mmm. Well somebody's most definitely out to get you. Listen I have one of the finest investigative minds in Europe and you, well, you have local knowledge.'

'Huh.'

'And if all else fails, there is always 'extreme prejudice'.

'We'd have to find them first.'

'That, dear boy, is why we have friends.'

It is pouring with rain. Thunder is rumbling far off to the north. He is woken by a loud banging on the kitchen door to the courtyard. Who the fuck? He hurriedly dons his jeans and barefoot, hurries downstairs and along the hallway to the kitchen.

What the hell? The banging grows more insistent. He snatches the door open.
There in the torrential rain, drenched, streaming with water, a sequined sea-green silk dress clinging to her slender body is Amy Angove. The late Lamorna Rain. The former Mrs Félipe Treloar. Dead many moons. His lost wife.

'Pippit! Pippit! I've come back!'
The dress is the bridal gown she had worn on their wedding day. But not quite. It is moving. Tiny crabs and worms are slithering across her seaweed strewn body. And something else is wrong. She is swaying. She is not standing on the cobbles but floating in the air as she would in the sea.
'NNOOO!!'

Drenched in sweat, Treloar lurches up in bed and leaps to his feet.

Chapter Forty-Four

That morning Fitzroy emerged from the hallway clad in immaculate stone cargo shorts, black tee shirt and a straw Panama hat.

'Ready,' he called out.

Treloar turned from the kitchen cupboard and looked him up and down with an expression of withering scorn.

'Christ man, it's an uphill hike not a stroll along the Champs Elysée,' he said.

'I'm wearing my boots,' Fitzroy protested in umbrage.

'You cannot wear that hat.'

'Why not? I need to maintain some sartorial standards.'

Treloar tutted and crossed to a wooden chest by the kitchen door. After rummaging inside he pulled out a faded baseball cap which he tossed to Fitzroy who caught it and lifted it to his nose with obvious distaste.

'Dear God, I can't wear this it smells of fish!'

'Give me strength,' Treloar muttered turning back to the chest. Further rummaging brought forth a navy blue Weird Fish baseball cap still in its original packaging.

'Here,' he said tossing it, 'this is brand new, unworn, pristine.'

Fitzroy caught it and grinned.

'Do you have it in black?'

They left via the kitchen door, stepping into glorious bright sunshine and a soft breeze blowing up the valley from Mount's Bay. This was Fitzroy's first visit to Lost Farm Barn and he took a moment to get his bearings. Straight ahead of him the patio ended at a low wall with steps down to grass which stretched away to a rough hedge, far in the distance, beyond which he saw trees covering the side of a small valley.

To their left there was a cultivated area and a series of raised beds with a fence beyond. To their right another hedge separated the garden from rough pasture, and it was towards that hedge that Treloar was heading. As Fitzroy followed he made out a gate hidden amongst the thorn bushes. They passed through, into the pasture, onwards and upwards.

As they headed uphill the pasture grew rougher and increasingly patchy with large stones and scrubby grass. They followed the line of a hedgerow and the transitory scent of wild honeysuckle. Ahead of them on a far brea stood a dark, looming edifice with a round tower.

'What in God's name is that?' asked Fitzroy, 'I didn't know you had an outpost of Dartmoor Prison?'

'Radgell,' Treloar replied.

'Radgell?'

'Yeah, it means foxes' lair. It's the ancestral home of the Pengelly family.'

'Poor bastards.'

They trudged on in silence. Soon the hedgerow thinned out to nothing and they were on to open moorland and the going got harder.

'Shit!' Fitzroy bent to rub his bare calf, 'what is this evil stuff?'

'Gorse, I told you not to wear shorts.'

'Ow! Fitzroy cried out in pain, slapping his arm. 'What was that bastard?'

'Probably a horse fly. Now they are nasty bastards.'

'How can you live in this hell?'

Treloar laughed. 'Is this not the man who spent his youth yomping across the North Yorkshire moors? Fitzroy had attended Ampleforth College.

'That was cross-country running and I didn't stop to admire the flora and fauna; I wanted to win. Ow!'

'Ben, for a man as hard as nails, you really can be soft as . . .'

'Careful mate,' Fitzroy interrupted, 'just because I don't have my Glock on me, doesn't mean I don't have it with me.'

Treloar did not doubt it.

Finally they reached the stones. The menhirs stood on a plateau with the only higher ground in sight the rising moorland further to the west and the brooding presence of Radgell. Scanning the horizon, Fitzroy could see the sea to his north and south and gentler farmland to the east. It was an imposing site and images of Druids and burning torches flitted through his mind and he could almost hear low droning chants. There were ten stones standing in a rough circle with one lying flat in the centre. A gentle breeze swirled around them. Treloar pulled a water canteen from his rucksack and handed to him.

'Why The Dancers?'

'Girls, dancing on the Sabbath, turned to stone.'

'Seems a little draconian.'

'More fear and belief in those times. Or, if you prefer, they were fleeing wraiths chased up from Porthmeor Cove, under a gibbous moon, by Perish Penhaligon and his crew, and petrified by his Zulu prince stowaway, Dumisani, in the *Dolphin's Smile* novel.'

'The Ochre Pengelly book?'

Yep.'

'Really? I loved that one. Wow, so these are those stones.'

'It's a book Ben, make-believe?'

'Well yes of course. So seriously, who put them here and why?'

'Early settlers making a meeting place for counsel or worship or both. A gathering place, easily identified and well known.'

'Well it's very impressive. But I still prefer the Captain Perish version.' Fitzroy moved to the side and sat on the ground, stretching out his legs and removing his baseball cap to turn his face up towards the sun.

'I used to come here with Amy, before we married,' Treloar said softly. 'Strange that I should end up living so close.'

'Ah, speaking of Amy.'

'What?'

'There's another feed circulating about you and her.'

'What?' Treloar growled.

'Well I can show you when we get back, but the gist is 'Treloar involved in another death in Cornwall and this one even closer to home, the lovely local beauty Lamorna Rain, dead on his land.'

'She lived in fucking Hampstead and it was my neighbour's land.'

'I know that, we know that, but . . .'

'Treloar looked down at his friend with troubled eyes. 'God Ben what's happening here?'

As they stood to begin the descent, Fitzroy surveyed the land below them.

'Tell me, why Lost Farm Estate? I know it's in the middle of nowhere but even so it's a curious name.'

'Ah, a sad story. It was called Last Farm Estate for centuries because it was the last estate in the parish. But in the First World War and its aftermath, the landowners, the Pitt-Townsend family, were annihilated by a combination of the war itself, the flu pandemic, murder and suicide. A tragedy: an entire family 'lost'. The locals adopted the 'Lost' title and it stuck, hence: Last Farm Estate became Lost Farm Estate.'

'Tragic indeed.'

The two men walked on in reflective silence until Treloar spoke.

'I've called for reinforcements.'

'I think we're going to need them mate. So, who's coming to the party?'

'Well Jamie Deverell, obviously. We need his special skills. If anybody can track and uncover these trolling bastards it's Jamie.'

'And he's coming here?' Fitzroy sounded incredulous.

'So he says.'

'Christ. He must think it's serious to get him to venture outside of his cave, I thought he was a virtual recluse.'

'And I've asked Tom Grigg.'

Tom Grigg was a recently retired detective sergeant of long-standing who had worked with Fitzroy in the Met before returning to his family roots in Cornwall to work with Treloar.

'Ah good man Grigg,' Fitzroy nodded, 'Solid. Thorough and reliable.'

'Yes, and he knows how we work and he lives just over the carn,' Treloar pointed back the way they had come. 'Then there's Doc Tremayne, our retired former police doctor and a family friend. He knows the pathologist, John Forbes and he'll interpret the post mortem and medical tests results without having to compromise John directly, given my new . . . standing. The how should help us narrow down the who.'

'Hopefully so.'

And lastly, Ochre.'

'Ochre Pengelly, of whom we spoke earlier? Really?'

'Absolutely. She's a neighbour, another good friend, and she understands people's souls. Motivation. The why should also narrow down the who.'

'And Sam?'

'Christ no! That would be disastrous. She's newly promoted, just back from secondment, she cannot be associated with this. It would compromise her, get her suspended too and mark her for life with the police. No, definitely not Sam.'

'She won't like it.'

'She won't know about it.'

Fitzroy looked sceptical. 'Well it looks like you've covered all the bases: cyber, police procedure, medical and psychological. Brains. And there's you and me of course: brawn.'

The return journey was downhill and easier going, though the sun was now in their eyes. As they reached the edge of the moorland they spotted a figure approaching, flickering in and out of focus like the first appearance of Omar Sharif in *Lawrence of Arabia*.

'What is that?' asked Fitzroy pulling down the brim of his cap to shield his eyes.

'Ah, neighbour approaches,' Treloar replied.

The figure took the solid form of a statuesque female swathed in shades of green and brown, her head wrapped in sub-Saharan African style.

'Well this should be interesting,' muttered Treloar under his breath.

'Who is this fair maiden?' asked Fitzroy.'

'It's one of the poor bastards,' said Treloar smiling

broadly. He raised his hand in greeting and called out 'Ochre! Hola!'

Ochre Pengelly stood and waited for the two men to reach her.

'Phil, good day to you.'

'Ochre Pengelly, this is Ben Fitzroy, Ben, Ochre Pengelly, neighbour and dear friend.' The two shook hands.

'Enchanted!' Fitzroy cried in genuine delight. 'You created Captain Perish Penhaligon! I've read all your work.'

'Really?' Ochre said in surprise. Fitzroy was some twenty five years older than her normal readership.

'Oh yes indeed. Love 'em. Bloody good yarns.'

'Well, thank you.'

'Were you looking for me?' Treloar asked.

'No, I was just out walking. Orlando is up at Exeter for a few days and I wanted to get out of the empty house. But since you're here, what time did you want me this evening?'

'Anytime after six. The others are aiming to arrive around then.'

'I shall be there.'

'Well it's been an absolute pleasure to meet you,' said Fitzroy taking her hand again.

'I'll catch you gentlemen later,' Ochre moved off uphill.

At Lost Farm Barn a small tortoiseshell cat ran across the lawn to greet Treloar as the two men stepped onto the lawn though the gate from the field.

'Hello, hello,' said Fitzroy bending to rub the cat's back, 'who have we here?'

'Ben meet Lola.'

'I thought all your cats were named for Barcelona football players?'

Treloar looked at him, eyebrows raised. 'Tortoiseshell cat? Female cat? No females in the Barça team Ben.'

'Ah of course,' Fitzroy cried in delight, scooping the purring creature up in one hand, 'Girl cat!' 'Lola?'

'Mamá is also a Kinks fan.'

As Fitzroy crossed the rear garden to the deck talking animatedly to the bemused cat in his arms Treloar smiled. Cats could instinctively recognise those they could trust: the good guys. And Fitzroy was one of the good guys.

Chapter Forty-Five

Late that afternoon Treloar and Fitzroy had headed out again walking down the wooded valley towards Mount's Bay making their way through the trees along the stream, glad of the shade, only to turn and climb back up the other bank, out onto open pasture, onwards onto the moor and back up to The Dancers. They were restless waiting for the others to arrive and both preferred walking to sitting, it felt like action. As the sun fell below the hill to their west, they descended along the hedge that separated Lost Farm fields from the empty moorland and Fitzroy broke the companionable silence that had reigned for some time.

'I can see what keeps you here, holds you here, mate. All this space it's so . . . liberating; all this . . . emptiness.'

Fitzroy, who lived in a converted warehouse on the Thames in Bermondsey in central London, relished the barren moorland. As they reached the end of the field and found themselves on open pasture their attention was drawn to vehicle noise. Looking down to the north they could see a VW campervan making its way gingerly up the track from the B3311. In its wake, forced into a slow moving stream, came a beautiful vintage Mercedes. As the two men continued down through the lush grass towards Lost Farm Barn the vehicles turned into the courtyard followed shortly after by a muddy ATV which had approached from the west paralleling their descent.

'You know what this reminds me of? The first gathering of the Fellowship of the Rings in Rivendell. Here's Boromir dismounting his trusty steed,' Fitzroy pointed at Tom Grigg climbing off the ATV. And look there's little Frodo,' he indicated a slight dark young man getting out of the VW campervan.

'That is Jamie Deverell,' said Treloar.

'Of course!'

'I'm really touched that he's come. We'd be lost without his help and he's relentless.'

'Things must be grim for him to venture out. He certainly has an impressive and valuable skill set when you're in the shit. I like him as Frodo. And Ochre is coming, a wise and magical lady: Galadriel.'

'Before you ask me why Ochre is invited, she understands people more than anyone else I know. If anyone can fathom this, Ochre can. And anyway, Galadriel wasn't there.'

'Don't be picky. And look, look!' Fitzroy cried excitedly as a small, bearded man emerged from the Mercedes' driver's seat, 'it's Gimli!'

'That is Doc Tremayne. You are confusing your stories. Think Captain Perish.'

'Christ, Tremayne! Rascal Tremayne; first mate on the *Torment*!'

Treloar nodded then smiled slowly as a tall slim woman with long dark hair slid from the Mercedes' front passenger seat.

'Whoah . . . who invited Arwen?' Fitzroy pointed, 'I thought we were going to have to toss for it, but I am now officially declaring myself Aragorn, no debate.'

'That is Lucia di Santangel Lo Verde, a champion swordswoman, and before you get excited, yes she is married,' Treloar continued looking at Fitzroy's expectant dog face, 'and of most significance to you, she is my second sister.'

'Ah,' Fitzroy's face fell.

As they arrived at the high gate from the pasture into the garden of Lost Farm Barn they could see a familiar red VW beetle pulling off the track and heading towards the courtyard.

'No fucking way,' said Treloar under his breath.

'Well now that most definitely makes you Frodo not Jamie.'

'What?' Treloar asked distractedly.

'Here is Samwise, the trusty sidekick, arriving uninvited. My God it's perfect!'

'Christ. What the hell is she doing here? How did she

find out?'

'Hell, even the names fits: Sam can be Sam!'

'Basta!'

Fitzroy looked sheepish. 'Too much?'

'Way too much.'

'Perhaps it is wearing a little thin. But it was fun while it lasted; a little light relief.'

'Leo Benedict,' Treloar growled.

'Whoah . . . now that is just below the belt mate.' Fitzroy hated his first given name. 'Right. Fine. Finito,' and with that he made a zipping motion across his lips with thumb and forefinger.

Chapter Forty-Six

The fellowship was seated around the large sitting room at Lost Farm Barn. The ceiling in this one room extended up to the beamed roof and the south facing wall was entirely glass with views over the garden and down the wooded valley to Mount's Bay. A thick solid wall between this room and the kitchen housed an enormous hearth currently occupied by two sleeping cats. A passageway ran beside it down to the kitchen from where Lucia emerged with a tray of coffee mugs which she placed on a large wooden chest beside a smaller tray bearing a jug of coffee, a bowl of sugar, a handmade terracotta jug of cream and an assortment of teaspoons.

Treloar spoke: 'Right. We know from John Forbes that the three victims were all killed with some brand of oral morphine like Oramorph, Avinza or MS Contin; effectively euthanised. Doc?'

'Well I agree with the notion of euthanasia. John confirmed that it was too pure to be heroin. It wasn't cut with anything like chloroform or fentanyl. Normally morphine is used for severe pain relief and is injected intravenously or intramuscularly but in some cases such as terminal patients with chronic long-term pain from, say, cancer, there is the option for oral ingestion. But slow-release morphine is self explanatory: crush slow-release capsules and ingest the entire dose in one go and you have a fatal overdose. You cannot buy this over the counter obviously, but you will find it in hospitals, hospices and care homes.'

'But why would one agree to take it?' asked Lucia.

'One wouldn't need to agree light of my life,' Tremayne replied, 'slip it into a strongly flavoured drink and . . . voilà.'

'OK. So, we need to check stocks in all these places locally, but I'd start with Hicks' care homes; seems too much of a coincidence. Tom, can you check that out with the guys.

They may be on it already.'

'That's in hand,' said Sam gruffly. She knew Treloar didn't want her at this gathering, she could understand his reasoning and that he was thinking of her position but she was still pissed off, if irrationally. Treloar ignored her.

'The actual deaths were simple, 'underkill'; it was about the act not the process, the process came after death. The killing was not the important thing to this killer it was the having of a dead body to stage. The staging was a grotesque form of still-life; puns excused. It is as if the killer planned the tableau and then thought of who they could find to kill to fit the picture. Am I right Ochre? You are our artist and sage.'

'I agree that the staging is important. But I don't believe the choice of victim would be entirely random. These people must share some significance, some reason to be chosen. Unless of course we are looking for a lunatic,' Ochre stared at Treloar intently but he was still glaring at Sam.

'OK, the victims must have some relevance to the killer. We need more on them. Sam, you should not be here, but as you are can you give Ochre the victim profiles?'

Sam smiled sweetly at Treloar then turned to Ochre. 'Let me have your contact details.'

Treloar spoke tersely: 'Fine. Tom, you tell us what we have so far, for everyone's benefit. We are supposed to be brain-storming here after all.'

Sam sighed as Tom Grigg stood up and moved to face the group.

'Victim number one: Jolyon Ellis. Aged 33. Local business consultant lived in Wadebridge married to . . .'

Sam tuned out. She knew all this, she had heard all this many times. What the hell was she doing here? She could have caught up with Lucia another time. She should have made her excuses and left when Tom Grigg had told her as much. Now he too was questioning her judgement. She was letting herself be compromised and it was out of character and plain stupid.

. . . three: Suzanne Winters. Well, we all know who she was. Again, a morphine overdose and the body was found in a hot-tub decked out as a clotted cream tub at Lowenalands holiday glamp camp above Mother Ivey's Bay.'

'Right,' said Lucia, 'and the connection to Phil?'

'Ellis is the most tenuous: twice removed. Ellis secured EU funding for Jowan Nancarrow's restaurants in St Ives and Phil's youngest sister Beatriz works for him.'

'And he siphoned off some of the money?' Ochre asked.

'Well, nothing was actually confirmed but there was speculation.'

'Not enough to string him up then, even given Phil's fabled familial devotion,' Ochre said.

Fitzroy and Treloar shared a grin. Fitzroy could see why Ochre had been invited.

'No Ochre, but it is a connection, albeit slight,' said Treloar, 'carry on Tom.'

'Hicks is also tenuous: twice removed. Elspeth Angove, Amy Angove's grandmother died in one of Hicks' care homes.'

'Well that's hardly a motive for Phil to kill the man. Driven to murder by the death of his dead ex-wife's granny?' Fitzroy scoffed.

'And then there's Winters.'

'Ah,' Ochre nodded.

'Winters,' Tom continued, 'only once removed. Well known established antipathy between Phil and her.'

'Yes but she's past history,' said Lucia. 'No, there's nothing here.'

Treloar nodded. 'We need to review the work at the scenes, first responses, photographs, everything. Have we missed something? Tom what have you found, anything?'

'Let's start with Ellis. Obviously it was not an easily secured scene: public beach, tide and time. Plus after the perpetrator left, you're looking at the sand collapsing, dogs, maybe foxes from the adjacent farmland, so the first of our guys on the scene had to move fast and use their phones to photograph what they could.

We have no trace of his movements on his last day alive. The wife had left early to visit her parents in St Ives, she had no idea what his plans were and we found no record of any appointments, just a number of business phone calls, all checked, all routine. But, he was known to turn up unexpected and help himself to other people's phones. We're asking around the business community. As to the deposition site? It was a risk; it is a public place. John Forbes confirmed he died late evening, early morning. Not busy then, but still. Most likely someone lured him there. Not easy to get a dead body to that site; your only access is along the coastal path, along the beach, or along or across the Camel estuary. I think we're looking at an assignation on that beach. He met his killer there.'

'Right,' said Fitzroy, 'so who would he agree to meet on a beach late at night? It's not going to be a business appointment. A woman? A man? I'm thinking sex.'

'Woman then?' said Tom Grigg. 'Past history with the ladies.'

'Could that be a motive?' asked Doc Tremayne.

'For Ellis perhaps, even Hicks, but Winters?' Sam queried.

'No. Not sex. It's too . . . contrived,' Tremayne agreed.

'Right. Hicks, Tom,' said Treloar.

'Titus Hicks died mid-evening. Massive dose of morphine, died where he was found.'

'That's right,' said Tremayne, 'livor mortis proves that. Interestingly he was a larger man than Ellis so it required a larger morphine dose but even so the amount was excessive. No signs of a struggle. Could be he would prove impossible to move but obviously the greenhouse location fitted the plan.'

Tom continued. 'Hicks was a solitary man, lived alone, few visitors other than the gardeners and a cleaning lady. Not a liked man apparently but it seems that didn't bother him. No CCTV, no telephone calls that evening. A neighbour did report seeing security lights in the rear garden coming on from about nine o'clock but thought nothing of it as there is a lot of wildlife from the woodland and Hicks himself was known to wander about the grounds after dark.'

'It was a very secluded location,' said Sam.

'It would have needed to be,' said Treloar, 'it would have taken time to truss him up like Gulliver. So we're looking at a visitor who he would have been happy to meet in the greenhouse.'

'Or somebody who surprised him in there,' said Sam.

'No. Think Sam. It had to be the greenhouse to fit the

plan like Doc said: Eden Project.'

Sam said nothing, kicking herself. Of course it had to be the bloody greenhouse. Idiot.

'Right Tom. Winters.' Treloar moved on quickly to spare Sam's blushes, she hoped.

'Winters. Well, over to Sam surely as she was first on the scene?'

'Right,' said Treloar neutrally, 'Sam?'

'Well, time of death was early that morning. Morphine overdose. When I arrived the cement was still damp beneath the crust, but it had been mixed to resemble clotted cream, not to set firm. Again, John Forbes said she died in situ.'

'Any CCTV?' asked Tom.

'Oh plenty, a comprehensive security system, but it's not up and running yet. They are planning to have everything ready for the end of July. The whole project is running late.'

'So we have the three Cornish themes. Why? Won't it scare the visitors?' asked Lucia.

'Perhaps it's a local sick of tourists. We know there are a lot of people who resent the summer influx,' said Doc Tremayne.

'Perhaps it's *Visit Devon*,' said Fitzroy earning bursts of laughter.

'There is something . . . organised, like a state-sanctioned execution by lethal injection. But the wrongdoings of these victims seem too petty, too unrelated each to the other,' said Ochre.

'Well one thing these three victims have in common mate is you,' said Fitzroy nodding towards Treloar, 'you knew all of them to a greater or lesser degree and somebody out there is very keen to keep pointing that out to the entire world.'

'Right. I was coming to that. Who is behind all this online trolling of me? Obviously, that's over to you Jamie.'

'I've already started, and I have Alasdair on it back at the abbey.'

'I have the journalist Tulip Khan working from her side,' said Treloar as Sam rolled her eyes, 'she's looking at this Viking nonsense as well.'

'Oh don't say it's nonsense mate. Look at your sister

here: a beautiful sword-wielding Valkyrie.'

'Shut it Fitzroy,' Treloar growled whilst Lucia offered her broadest smile.

As the meeting broke up Tom Grigg took Sam aside. They had worked together before his retirement and he liked and respected her, but the tension between her and Treloar had been palpable. He knew she had not been invited and was curious as to what she was doing there.

'Sam, what the hell are you playing at? You should not be here and you know it. Phil is suspended and if word ever reached Chamberlain, so would you be. I know you weren't invited. Phil would never compromise you like that.'

'I know, I know. Lucia phoned to say she was over from Barcelona and to suggest we meet up for lunch. I just thought . . . I'd surprise her. Honestly. I didn't know this soirée had been organised, obviously, and it would have been really weird just to leave. Anyway, Fitz is here.'

Tom Grigg looked sceptical.

'Sam. Think about what you've just said. Ben is . . . protected. You are exposed. You should have made your excuses and left. For Christ's sake you are a newly promoted inspector! I know you're loyal and I know you care. But you should not have come and you know it. Just don't get caught!'

Chapter Forty-Seven

By ten thirty Doc Tremayne had left for Cove Farm, Treloar's family farm on the coast west of Zennor, where he was spending the night, and Tom Grigg had left for home. Sam was long gone. Jamie Deverell had retired to his campervan with a basket of food leaving Treloar, Fitzroy and Lucia to a late supper.

'Stunning, photographic genius, expert swordswoman *and* she cooks?' Fitzroy grinned.

'What? No this is Mama's recipe: escalivada with goat's cheese and espinacas con garbanzos,' Treloar said.

'OK where's the meat?'

'There is no meat. Vegetarians remember? The escalivada has grilled vegetables: aubergines, peppers, onion, garlic and parsley with our own goats' cheese and the espinacas con garbanzos is spinach with chick peas.'

'Well it smells great,' said Fitzroy shovelling the escalivada onto his plate.

Lucia joined them at the kitchen table carrying a litre carafe of red wine and a board with bread. They ate in silence. With the plates cleared by Treloar, the three sat around the table with their wine and coffee.

'I spoke to Tulip Khan,' said Treloar.

'It is strange to me that you trust this journalist Flip after all the nonsense and meanness they have shown towards you,' Lucia looked concerned.

'Tulip's OK Lucia,' said Fitzroy. 'I admit I was highly sceptical when I met her, but she has been true to her word, and she does not scandalize or misrepresent. I think she really does seek the truth.'

'The exception that proves the rule,' said Treloar. 'Anyway, she's been tracing the stories linking me to the murders back to the beginning. There was nothing after Ellis. It was after Hicks that Ellis is first mentioned, with his link to the Nancarrows' restaurants and Beatriz alongside Hicks and Amy's grandmother. This is where my name is first mentioned. It's in some pop-up blog and then that is picked up by one of Masterson's tabloid rags and the Cornish Courier, which is also one of his titles apparently. From there, with Winters, it goes national and is picked up to a greater or lesser extent by most of the regionals and the national tabloids as we know.'

'So the question is who was behind that pop-up blog?' asked Fitzroy.

'Jamie has Alasdair looking.'

'This is all clever, not savage; cat not dog. It's like . . . a game,' said Lucia.

'Well if I was out to destroy you it's how I'd do it,' Fitzroy said. 'Slow drip, start with facts, provable facts, then embellish and embroider - but still believable and verifiable - then introduce more and more outrageous elements once the bona fides are established. This is subtle and clever. Somebody is enjoying themselves, playing with you, like a cat,' he nodded to Lucia. 'Masterson is not this clever not this . . . creative. He's used to wielding power; he doesn't manipulate, he mandates.'

'You're both right,' said Treloar glumly, 'Everything so far has been essentially true, it's the undertone, the innuendo underlying the words that is so damaging.'

By midnight Fitzroy had retired to bed.

'What are you going to do about Sam cariňo?' asked Lucia softly.

Treloar sighed heavily. 'No la amo. Nunca la amoré.'

'I know. I saw you with that witch Amy. I know you can never love Sam. There is something missing: la chispa.'

'Exactly querida. There is no spark.'

'Then you must tell her Flip. Just tell her. She's a big girl. She'll get over it. 'Tis better to have loved and lost . . .' You of all people know that. She'll move on.'

'But I like working with her. I don't want her to move on.'

'That will be for her to decide. This you know.'

Treloar sighed again and nodded sadly.

‘As ever querida, you are right. So wise. It must be all those men in your life.’

‘Basta!’ she cried and slapped him across the shoulder grinning broadly. The very Treloar grin so loved by Sam Scott.

‘Bed,’ Treloar pushed her towards the hallway from the kitchen.

Chapter Forty-Eight

The following morning a low front had crept up from the Bay of Biscay and was lurking over the Channel Islands bringing torrential rain-bursts and unseasonably strong winds to west Cornwall. Treloar and Fitzroy were forced to remain inside and chose to sit in the kitchen gazing out at the lashing rain streaming down the glass doors where Lola sat vigilant, waiting for the sun.

'Christ mate why are you such a wuss when it comes to women?'

'What do you mean?' Treloar was outraged.

'Sam. Fucking Sam. Or more to the point, not fucking Sam.'

'Oh don't you start, not this morning, I can't face all that. What exactly am I supposed to do about it? I have never said or done anything in any way, shape or form to encourage her in the belief that I feel anything other than respect and friendship. It's not bloody fair. It's not my bloody fault.'

'I know mate but ignoring it just isn't going to make it go away.'

'There's no hope,' Treloar sighed heavily, 'I just don't feel any . . . yearning for her. She's just too . . .'

'Wholesome?'

'Well, I might not have put it quite like that, but essentially, and in your inimitable fashion, you've nailed it.' They sat in silence until Treloar spoke quietly. 'I saw someone the other day at that festival meeting at the Padstow Hub.'

'Who?'

'I don't know! I need to ask Tulip Khan, she was with her. She did it, that woman. She made me think she was the only other person in the room. I haven't felt like that since . .'

'Amy?' Fitzroy asked softly.

'Yeah. Since Amy,' Treloar replied softly.

'We must track her down mate! Find her. Life's too

bloody short.' Fitzroy was gazing out the glass doors to the garden. 'I know what you mean, what you mean when you talk about women, Sam's just not like . . .'

'If you say Lucia, I will not be held responsible for my actions.'

'Would I dare? But you've got to admit some women are just so . . .'

Fitzroy was interrupted mid sentence by the door to the garden flying open and a whirl of long dripping hair, beatific smile, and stamping feet as Lucia dashed into the kitchen with two vines of cherry tomatoes. Fitzroy let out a long sigh and Treloar kicked him under the table.

'Hola! Hola gentlemen,' she dumped the tomatoes on the table and shook herself like a dog. 'Flip! Have you made coffee? Have you asked Jamie to come in for a shower? For breakfast? Vamos!'

Treloar sighed and hauled himself up from his chair snatching a hooded rain jacket from a hook by the door, he headed out into the courtyard and dashed towards the VW campervan.

'He's worried,' said Lucia sadly, 'I feel so powerless to help this time.'

'He has a lot of people on his side, and God and the truth and justice,' said Fitzroy seriously.

'You are a good friend to him, a good man I think,' Lucia smiled as she crossed to the sink with the tomatoes.

'He is a good man too.'

'You make a fine team.'

'So I keep telling him. He knows if this all goes south, I would take him on my own specialist team like a shot.'

'He knows this Ben. But this is his homeland. His home and his land. It is hard for him to leave.'

'You left.'

'I am gitana at heart.'

'A gipsy?'

'Yes, indeed. I am impressed. You know Spanish.'

'I could lie and say yes, but you'd soon find me out. No I'm afraid it was a teenage addiction to French cigarettes: Gitanes, with the gipsy on the label. '

'More a flamenco dancer I always thought,' she smiled

and twirled, an imaginary fan clutched above her head. Fitzroy groaned inwardly.

The door burst open and Treloar dashed in followed by a dripping Jamie Deverell.

'Already showered mate?' Fitzroy asked.

They sat around the kitchen table with coffee and Jamie pulled a top of the range iPad from a battered rain-splashed leather satchel. 'Alasdair's been busy looking at your victims' electronic footprints. Shall I start with Ellis?'

'Please do,' said Fitzroy stirring sugar in his black coffee.

'He's the simplest. He had a diary with business meetings, online grant and funding applications, online company searches, a little tame porn, busy accounts with Amazon and two wine companies and a penchant for Boden shirts. Nothing out of the ordinary or suspicious. No secret lovers' exchanges on email. Boring bloke.'

'Right, so the man himself gives us no clue to his killer,' said Treloar.

'I'd say not,' said Fitzroy. 'Hicks?'

'A little more interesting. He had a more adventurous taste in porn; a lot of bondage but nothing violent and all heterosexual. There are a lot of pharmaceutical and medicinal suppliers including Oramorph from two separate companies, but nothing out of line with his business requirements and no out of place drugs. There is a thread of correspondence over the inspection of one of his care homes which he has postponed twice, citing staff issues and a maintenance problem. The powers that be are now threatening a spot inspection which is not due this year. But most interesting is a slew of emails and draft letters to councils, MPs and conservation groups with the obvious, if not expressed, intention to block the 'AAO' festival.'

'The Ally Ally Oh? That's Pasco Trefry's life's mission isn't it?' said Fitzroy.

'Yes it is,' said Treloar slowly.

'And did not Sam mention this Trefry yesterday?' asked Lucia.

'Yes. She said he referred to Hicks' 'pop-up' shops

selling 'tat made in China',' said Jamie who had phenomenal recollection.

'So does this Trefry have a motive for these men's killings?' asked Lucia.

'It's not Trefry,' said Fitzroy flatly.

His three companions turned to look at him quizzically.

'He's former Home Office. I . . . made enquiries last night after his name came up.'

'Friends in high places?' asked Treloar with a wry smile.

'Friends with friends.' said Fitzroy closing the topic.

'OK fine, what about Frosty Winters?' asked Treloar using the Superintendent's old nickname.

'This is the most interesting,' Jamie scrolled through screens, 'this lady liked to spend money, a lot of money, far too much money for her earnings. Mainly on clothes and shoes and home decor. There is a great deal of research on exotic holidays which leads me to the Lowenalands trip. And here things get fascinating and very impressive.'

Jamie, normally a taciturn being, came alive when he spoke about his secret invisible world of data.

'The magazine which offered the Lowenalands prize in its competition is a genuine publication in the Masterson media empire, new and online only. It is 'home and away' themed, focusing on expensive home decoration and luxury away breaks for 'busy people'. A perfect fit for Winters.

'So they ran the competition for the weekend, she entered and won? And how would they know about this?' asked Lucia.

'Ah, well that's where the impressive bit comes in. Cuckoo code. If you look at the magazine online, the edition Winters saw, you will see no trace of the competition, but there it is in Winters's search history. The competition and the associated article have been cut into the code for Winters' eyes only. The promotional link for the new magazine takes Winters to a clone site with the competition which she entered, only she entered, and she won, as she would.'

'But what if she had not entered?' asked Lucia.

'Well, that was a risk, but then they could have said that the winner had donated the prize to her as a surprise. As it was, she did enter.'

'Ingenious,' said Fitzroy.

'Oh indeed, and excellent coding, excellent . . .' Jamie was interrupted.

'Hacking?' Fitzroy smiled.

Jamie ignored the comment. 'And of course, the same 'competition' and article were shown to Lowenalands, there was no charge to them, as it was to be a first edition promotion by the magazine, and they would benefit from the publicity. Everybody wins.'

'Fucking ingenious!' Fitzroy laughed.

'And then Ali's been looking at your nasty trolls. It's an orchestrated campaign. Alongside the genuine individual contributions there is a sophisticated bot engine churning out comment. It's very elegant actually.'

'OK Jamie,' Treloar was serious and sarcastic, 'it's good to know I have a quality adversary, so who could have done it?'

'I could. Alasdair could. Two guys I know in California, one in New Orleans, and a handful in Russia and China. But I don't see it. The job was not up for bid in the usual way. And no we don't bid for these jobs, but others do and I checked. I think it's someone new, someone new and very, very skilled.'

'Great,' said Fitzroy glumly, 'someone new, we've never come across, who is very, very skilled and ingenious.'

'Mmm,' Treloar mused, not necessarily. The soft, distant bell tolled again.

Chapter Forty-Nine

The Salt Creek

How to find us

By road:

Follow the coastal road through Rock and Polzeath on towards Port Quin and Port Isaac and on a cliff above a salty inlet (zawn), between the road and the South West Coastal Path just past Lundy Bay, you'll find The Salt Creek.

By rail:

The nearest main line station is Bodmin Parkway. Either book a taxi to bring you to The Salt Creek from there (around 40 minutes), or a car hire firm to meet you with a car. Make your way out of the station to the A38, turn left, then follow signs to A389 west. Stay on A389 turning left at Wadebridge onto B3314, then follow our 'By road' instructions.

By air:

Newquay airport is the nearest airport. Either book a taxi to bring you to The Salt Creek from there (around 25 minutes), or a car hire firm. Out of the airport turn left onto the A3059, then left onto the A39. Take 3rd exit at Wadebridge roundabout onto B3314, then follow our 'By road' instructions.

The Salt Creek has its own private helipad. Please call the hotel ahead to book a landing slot, and for GPS coordinates.

When Coco Holding was looking for a location for her most ambitious project to date, she had drawn up a shortlist of requirements, literally on the back of an envelope. It was based around treasured memories of holidays in California, and she wanted to recreate, recapture, that relaxed easy outdoor feel.

1. Coastal location
2. Large flexible grounds - pool tennis, exercise, parking!
3. Attractive original buildings
4. Orangery or Conservatory (or scope to build one)
5. Isolation / seclusion
6. Scope for spa buildings
7. Some mature garden
8. Water - stream, lake, pond . . .

She had explored Norfolk, Hampshire and West Wales but had settled on Cornwall when she found a dilapidated Georgian manor house. The key selling points for Coco, if not for the estate agent, were a ruined Orangery on the south side of the house and a rubble and rubbish strewn croquet lawn. Coco suffered the fate of many of the beautiful in that she had always been taken for a fool. But Coco was nobody's fool, certainly not the estate agent's, and she secured the property at a knockdown price.

She had fallen in love for the second time in her life and spent two years renovating, rebuilding, converting, decorating and equipping, well, supervising a large team doing so. But her pride and joy, the jewel in her crown, was still the Orangery, where the builders had discovered the original slate floor and mosaic tiled wall panels. The timbers and glass had been restored where possible or replaced sympathetically, and now the light-filled spacious room housed an 'eatery'. The many doors opened onto a slate-flagged terrace which led to an Italian garden, its central focus a lily pool with mermaid fountain. The pool had a colanaded mosaic surround and was framed with terraced beds of lavender and palms.

The croquet lawn had been revived to its original function and beyond it lay hedged tennis courts and an enclosed swimming pool. Extensive lawns had been restored or freshly sown to host pilates, yoga, and jazz aerobics classes.

The interiors throughout the lower floors were painted in matt neutral colours with names like 'clotted cream', 'summer rock pool' and 'powdered snow' and the bedrooms in the palest of pastel blues and greens tempered with white. Everything was plain and unadorned with simple modern chandeliers and wall lighting. Chairs and tables were washed wood and glass, sofas and armchairs upholstered in shades of green and amber.

Despite what Tommy had envisaged when Coco had proposed the venture, Coco had wanted to avoid the Cornish cliché of sea and sand, blues and yellows, images of fish, harbours and seahorses on every wall and sailing boats, starfish and mermaids on every surface. Not a lighthouse in sight. There was an eclectic mix of ceramics and statues collected over the years on her international travels and plundered from the Primrose Hill house. Tommy would neither notice nor care. She had toyed briefly with naming the rooms for flowers, trees, or, heaven forfend, Cornish beaches, but her better demons had prevailed. So, in the spirit of 'keep it simple stupid', it was Room One, Room Two . . . and suites: The Croquet Lawn, The Celtic Sea . . .

The only concession to colour and decorative display, other than the original mosaics and tiles, was a series of hand-painted folding screens of varying design and size to be found throughout the house according to situation. Coco could not count the occasions across the years and continents, when she had found herself in hotels taking hideous paintings from walls to stow under beds, stashing cushions and throws in wardrobes.

The individual screens in the bedrooms could be moved around the room, folded or removed altogether. Blinds were wooden and curtains were voile with lined calico or heavy plain wool depending on the season.

A small number of liveried VW campervans and VW beetles was on order. One of the worst things about Cornwall in the summer was the crowds who arrived in cars that they needed to park. Parking was a nightmare. Coco knew from her extensive travel and residence in top hotels that courtesy transport was highly valued by guests: no parking, no nominated drivers and of course additional advertising for The Salt Creek.

Now almost everything was ready to open for the first guests to coincide with the Ally Ally Oh and Coco was mightily pleased with the fruits of her imagination and others' labour. Her only concession, the only deviation from the plan, was to open for one weekend in early July for a private wedding party for the nuptials of Dr Rosamond Lacey and Bajinder Wood.

Looking back, she was not entirely sure how she had been persuaded to agree, but Tommy's agent knew Dr Roz's agent or some such and there was probably something in it for one or both of them. Coco had been around show business for too long to retain any illusions.

And so on this fine, early-July morning Coco found herself seated above the Italian garden awaiting the arrival of the bride-to-be and thinking about her brief ignominious stage career. She had no illusions about her acting ability either. Another thing Tommy had always got wrong.

Her musings were interrupted when a thirty something woman dressed, extraordinarily, in matching primrose yellow ra-ra skirt, halter-neck top, ankle socks and tennis shoes, literally skipped through an open door from the Orangery, her ponytail swinging behind her.

'Darling! You must be Coco! How utterly divine to meet you at last!' She skipped across the terrace and enfolded Coco's slender form in an awkward hug.

Recovering her senses Coco extended a hand, 'Rosamond Lacey?'

'Dr Roz! Dr Roz! *Everybody* calls me Dr Roz, you so must! I just know we are going to be the best of friends.'

Resisting the temptation to laugh out loud, Coco indicated the seat opposite hers and asked, 'Would you like something to drink?' convinced the woman would ask for Champagne.

Dr Roz lowered her voice conspiratorially, 'I don't suppose you have IRN-BRU do you? No I thought not, but do not fret, I've brought my own. I left it with that darling barman '

And to Coco's utter astonishment, Claudio emerged carrying a tray bearing a tall glass filled with ice and crushed mint, a can of IRN-BRU and a small bowl of salted almonds. He placed it on the table with a flourish and a broad grin.

'Your beverage Signorina,' he purred with a bow, turned on his heel and retraced his steps.

Rosamond Lacey lifted the glass and downed the drink in one.

'Right then darling just a few last minute details I think. Just the nosh to confirm really,' she said pulling a primrose yellow iPhone from a small rucksack. *I bet she has one to match each outfit* Coco thought. 'We had to go Spanish. Badge just adores Barcelona, well we both do. Doesn't everyone? We're off there after the knot-tying and then on to a pal's villa on Menorca, so it absolutely must be Spanish.'

Coco was astounded at the woman's ability to talk without pausing or appearing to take breath. Must be all that scuba diving for her new television series, she thought.

'Right. So to recap, the mariachi band is booked. Just the trumpeter I think for my entrance playing *La Vie en Rose*, don't you just love that song, so poignant? Well, then the vows and what have you, and then more mariachi!

'Flowers?' Coco asked figuring it best to minimise any interruption to the flow.

'Oh Mummy's sorted all that, they'll arrive first thing. It's a bone I've thrown her since I insisted on Cornwall over the 'glens',' she said slipping into broad Glaswegian.

Coco winced at the casual callousness of Rosamond's words.

'So, sixteen to stay: six couples, four singles; two nights, 'though some may want three but I have told them all absolutely no more than three as you are being so kind to let us come. Of course Badge and I are off to The Newt in Somerset in Bruton for our wedding night. Have you been there? It's just so wonderful and a total no brainer, and it's on the way to the airport of course. Not that it wouldn't have been lovely here but not with the parentals staying over. Ugh.'

'Right,' Coco nodded.

'Now, nosh time! Tapas!' she thrust the iPhone across the table tapping the screen with a long scarlet fingernail. Coco glanced down.

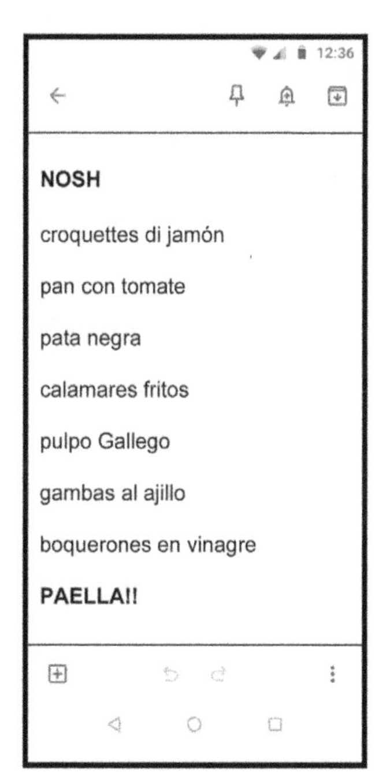

Yes, we have all this covered,' she confirmed.

'Oh and olives, oh and salted almonds,' I forgot those, Rosamond pouted.

'Olivos, alemendras fritas,' muttered Coco making a note on a post-it.

Rosamond gave her a startled look, clearly surprised that Coco should know the Spanish terms. *Misjudged again*, thought Coco, *I won't push it; guest comes first*. 'Pudding?' she asked.

'Yes! Yes, churros with hot chocolate sauce. Oh, and ice cream.' How could I forget afters?!'

'Roskilly's clotted cream vanilla?' Coco asked.

'Yummy!'

My God she actually said that, Coco thought, making another note.

'And strawberries of course and Cornish clotted cream, just has to be. You can do this sort of food can't you?' she added in alarm.

'Of course. And to drink?'

'Oh the usual stuff: Veuve Cliquot of course, Spanish wines – you choose, Estrella damm beer for the boys and . . .'

She won't say it surely, Coco thought.

'IRN-BRU!

At least she didn't say lashings and lashings.

'And the room?' Coco asked. 'The Orangery?'

'Perfect! Perfect! I don't want formal. No laid tables and place names and seating plans and all that ghastly tosh. No speeches and first dances,' she shuddered, 'just people mingling, and nibbling and mariachi. Olé!'

Chapter Fifty

The wedding day dawned, although Dr Rosamond Lacey was hard-pushed to tell: stepping out onto the balcony of the Celtic Sea suite at five o'clock that morning she was greeted by a grey blanket of warm wet air: sea fret. But never fear, Roz thought; sea fret clears with a rising temperature and the day was set to be glorious, warm and sultry.

Rosamond was to wear a sea-green silk and satin creation which was moulded to her body. The dress was artfully scattered with beadwork in the shapes of shells and strands of seaweed, the train boned and shaped like a fish's tail. On her head she wore a beaded shell comb securing a short ragged veil like a torn fishing net, dotted with tiny pearls: the mermaid bride. She carried a bunch of flowers: sea holly, white ranuncula, blue sweet pea and white roses, as if just picked from a garden and loosely bound with raffia.

As she stepped down into The Orangery a lone trumpeter from the mariachi band, hidden behind a painted screen, struck up a haunting rendition of *La Vie en Rose*.

During the ceremony there had been a short torrential downpour and that wonderful dry summer post-rain smell was drifting through the open doors and windows into The Orangery. With the formalities over, outside on the terrace Dr Roz was dancing barefoot in the puddles whilst new husband Bajinder was catching shots of sunlight on water droplets on his new iPhone camera.

Bajinder may have been a mathematical prodigy but he appeared to struggle to tell the time. Finally, he emerged down the front steps of the hotel to join a pacing Dr Roz.

'What the fuck are you wearing?' she demanded with a furious glare at her new husband.

Badge spread his arms wide and glanced down the length of his body taking in his washed-out linen shirt and battered cargo shorts down, to his ancient dusty deck-shoes, 'What babe?'

''Do not 'what babe' me. This is a fucking photo-shoot for a glamorous magazine not a bait-digging expedition. I am being paid and this is to promote my new TV series. Go and change AT ONCE!'

'Now, now,' Badge soothed, 'this is perfect my mermaid. Think of the ecological angle; too many people buying the latest fashion that they absolutely do not need; all the water wasted on producing that latest style of jeans they just must have. I am a perfect advert for world-saving economy in my old, well-worn clothes. I am a fucking star.'

'Huh!' She had to concede that he had a point. In fact it was pure genius. She herself had also eschewed the traditional 'going away' newly-wed change of clothing. Her cleverly constructed wedding dress had simply been pulled apart above the knee, separating the lower length and tail, to leave a short shift dress 'perfect for a Glyndebourne summer evening,' as her stylist had enthused.

She had donned a pair of cream canvass espadrilles and, in a nod to her publicist, her trademark Panama hat, albeit with a new band of sea-green satin ribbon. She was carrying her 'tail' in a large bag so that she could reassemble the dress for the photographs on the beach.

'Very well, I suppose you'll do,' she said grudgingly. 'But, I cannot accept that grubby shirt.'

'Worry not my pearl; I'll take it off,' Badge purred with a lascivious grin.

Despite herself Rosamond laughed loudly. Badge was young and he was very beautiful. It would do her image no harm at all for the world to admire his splendid pectorals.

'Come on,' she said grabbing his hand, 'we're really late.'

'Bride's privilege Mrs Wood.'

'That's before the ceremony you dolt,' she said pulling him towards the waiting car.

They took the Pure White Volkswagen Beetle Cabriolet through Polzeath and Trebetherick down to Daymer Bay where a vintage wooden boat was waiting to ferry them across the Camel estuary to Hawker's Cove where the celebrity magazine photographer awaited.

To Coco's not inconsiderable surprise the wedding had been a total triumph. Oh she had known that the room would be perfect, the food delicious and the wines at optimum temperature, the Champagne suitably chilled, but she had harboured grave reservations about the music. Mariachi? But she had been utterly wrong. From the lone plaintive horn playing *La vie en rose* as Rosamond finally made her appearance, to the lively dance music, it had been a memorable delight.

When the happy couple departed for Hawker's Cove The Orangery was slowly seeping guests to siestas or to the bar, and a peaceful satiated lull had fallen over The Salt Creek when the first phone bleeped.

Soon the atmosphere had changed completely as hurrying feet were heard on stairs and fiercely whispered conversations threaded through the hotel. Then, with a screech of rubber on gravel the white VW Beetle Cabriolet skidded to a halt in front of the hotel and Todd, the groundsman who had chauffeured the newlyweds, fell out of the driver's door white-faced. Coco, who had heard his arrival as she passed through the foyer, hurried to the top of the steps as the young man staggered up towards her.

'Todd! Todd what on earth . . . ?'

'She's dead! She's been shot dead at Hawker's Cove!'

Bill thebar@golfhotelstendocspadstow 51m
Dr Roz just collapsed on beach at photoshoot. Watching with binocs fm golf course hotel. Stung? Just fell, red dot on forehead, v still. Badge & photographer can't bring round. Nt looking good. Badge crying. Wots happenin @bbcsouthwestnewstoday #padstownews

James R@dogwalkingpadstow18 47m
With digger @cliffs nr G course birding with binocs. watched party? over river. Dot on fhead then fell. Not moved, others crying panicking. Was in army yrs. Looks like shot. @surfingpadstowbeaches @loveDwalkingpadstow @bbcsouthwestnewstoday #Dwalkerspadstow #padstownews

newsukfeed@newsukfeedcallsitout 44m
CORNISH HERITAGE KILLINGS. BREAKING. Correspondents have reported that Dr Roz the TV personality was shot at wedding photo shoot in Cornwall. Is suspended cop good with a gun? If you know more tell us. #padstownews #cornwallmurders #stargazy&edenkillings #suspiciouscopscornwall

BBC @bbcsouthwestnewstoday 41m
BREAKING NEWS. SHOCK. The BBC has learned that Dr Roz (Dr Rosamond Lacey), the popular TV presenter, collapsed after apparently being shot this afternoon on a Padstow beach where she and her new husband Badge (Bajinder) Wood were at a private wedding photo shoot.
BBC @bbcsouthwestnewstoday 40m
It happened at Hawker's Cove near Padstow soon after they were married at The Salt Creek hotel, across the Camel Estuary. It is being reported that Dr Roz has died. If it was a shooting this brings to four the number of recent Cornish killings. If you have info let us know.

Billyboy W@surfingpadstowbeaches 36m
@bbcsouthwestnewstoday was coming back down camel after crabbing on boat saw Dr Roz group & her collapse as went past. Got pics, dress made her look like mermaid, beautiful. Not moving, red dot on forehead. Didn't look good @newsukfeedcallsitout #padstownews

newsukfeed@newsukfeedcallsitout 32m
CORNISH HERITAGE KILLINGS. 4. Dr Roz shooting is now fourth Cornish heritage killing! At photo shoot beautiful Dr Roz was in v glamourous mermaid dress. See FEED for pic. #padstownews #suspiciouscopscornwall

Police@DevonandCornwallPolice 28m
If you have information on Dr Roz incident at Hawker's Cove contact us via **WEBSITE** or call crimestoppers ASAP. Very dangerous individual suspected. Do not take on. Report sighting. Take care. Thankyou @bbcsouthwestnewstoday @newsukfeedcallsitout @surfingpadstowbeaches #padstownews

Followed by K G@manchesterfifthestate and 437 others
B Gordon@westmidsfifthestate 23m
@DevonandCornwallPolice Well U shd know where he hangs out. Go get him if u can find him, but be careful, esp if he can shoot! BTW doc Roz ws too xxxx @bbcsouthwestnewstoday @westmidsfifthestate12 #stargazy&edenkillings #cornwallmurders #suspiciouscopscornwall #bentcopseverywhere

K G@manchesterfifthestate 16m
HA G! Good spot!! He surfaced alright. Heard hes Treloar got big place down West Cornwall nr St Ives. Doc R def too xxxx! Gd shootin @westmidsfifthestate #bringdirtycopsdown now! #stargazy&edenkillings #cornwallmurders #suspiciouscopscornwall #bentcopseverywhere #dataonbentcops

Joy D@loveDwalkingpadstow 11m
Idiots!! Some people just want to cause trouble & don't care how!! Makes me mad. He's a great guy, solid by in blu leave him alone. We loved Dr Roz!!! @bbcsouthwestnewstoday @manchesterfifthestate @westmidsfifthestate @dogwalkingpadstow23 #beachbody #padstownews

Followed by Dreen Z@westmidsfifthestate38 and 382 others
Tyrone Bham@westmidsfifthestate12 8m
Well sum people cant see it like it is. The Dr bitch is best gone even if it was a cop. @loveDwalkingpadstow @westmidsfifthestate @manchesterfifthestate #bringdirtycopsdown #stargazy&edenkillings #cornwallmurders #suspiciouscopscornwall #bentcopseverywhere

Dreen Z@Bham@westmidsfifthestate38 5m
Still rite Tye! Stupid cow. Bitch best gone. Wot about the cop, wot shd we do? @loveDwalkingpadstow @westmidsfifthestate12 @manchesterfifthestate @ #bringdirtycopsdown #stargazy&edenkillings #cornwallmurders #suspiciouscopscornwall #bentcopseverywhere

. . . .

thechef@thecornishchef&artist 2m
For the record we're shocked. Liked Dr Roz lots. See blog www@thecornishchef&artist for shooting mermaid legend info + b'fast recipe to make u smile @bbcsouthwestnewstoday @loveDwalkingpadstow @SolihullBillingDwalker @dogwalkingpadstow23 #beachbody #cornishfood #padstownews

Chapter Fifty-One

Treloar and Fitzroy were at Lost Farm Barn deep in discussion with Lucia. Treloar was in a dark mood.

'I don't know this woman. I have never met this woman. She's a television celebrity for fuck's sake; I don't even own a television!'

'Well nobody would believe that last bit.'

'Ben, please! And have you seen what those bastards are saying now . . . THEY ARE TELLING THE WORLD WHERE I LIVE!!'

'Flip querido. Calm.'

'Mate, let's face it, after that business with Amy, everybody already knows where you live!' Observed Fitzroy. 'Right. Let's look at it. Dispassionately. Dr Rosamond Lacey is a TV pundit whose latest bag is marine conservation. Now did you, or did you not, work in marine conservation back in the mists of time?'

'Yes I did. But 'A', that was back in the mists of time, 'B', she would have been in pigtails back then and 'C', this is, as you put it, her latest 'bag'. It's recent for her and prehistoric for me.'

'Right. Right that's all valid.'

'I know,' Treloar sighed,' but the media won't make those distinction will they?'

'Sorry mate.'

'And that bitch Romilly Hawkins will have the IOPC on my back.'

Lucia spoke, 'What is this IOPC?'

'The Independent Office for Police Conduct,' said Fitzroy.

'Oh,' Lucia frowned, 'I thought that was the IPCC?'

'Yeah it was,' Treloar snarled, 'but they probably had a budget surplus. Needed to spend out or lose money in the next spending round. So new name equals new branding, new website, new stationery, new signage; easy.'

'You are such a cynic mate,' Fitzroy grinned.

Lucia spoke again. 'Querido, I know you can be very annoying, but this is a lot of trouble somebody is causing you. Think. Who can this be if not Masterson?'

Fitzroy nodded, 'Lucia's right. It is a lot of trouble for you, but it's also a lot of trouble for them, a lot of effort, a campaign. And let's consider the victims. Well neither Hicks nor Ellis are major players and they evidently won't be long-mourned, if at all. But Winters, a ranking police officer, but not liked by many, and then Dr Roz? Dr Roz is a national treasure. A lot of people will be very unhappy at her demise.'

'Yeah. And baying for my blood.'

'No. that's not the point,' Fitzroy continued, 'Dr Roz is the only one who was . . . well, loved for want of a better word.

'And your point?'

'Well it doesn't fit the pattern. We have three people known to or linkable to you but disliked and effectively unknown to the rest of the world, and then BAM! Dr Roz. It just doesn't scan.'

'He speaks the truth Flip,' said Lucia.

'And,' Fitzroy was on a roll now, 'the modus operandi. The first three? Massive overdose, clean, clinical, under-kill, body staged. Dr Roz? Shot in the head for Christ's sake, from a remarkable distance, dropped on the sand. Sudden, violent . . . totally different.

'So you're saying we have two homicidal maniacs operating in Cornwall sharing a penchant for Cornish themes but using different methods?'

'No. No I'm saying again what I said earlier. Somebody has broken ranks; gone off piste. And look at the timing. The first three? Clever.'

'How so?'

'Very early morning this time of year it's light by, 04.15, but there are few people around; easy to move about and pose the bodies without being seen.'

'And two of the sites, Ellis and Winters, could have been accessed from the water,' as he spoke Treloar felt a frisson, a soft tolling in his memory like a faint, far-off, underwater bell.'

'So,' said Lucia, 'the first three could be achieved unseen, almost guaranteed.'

'Exactly,' Fitzroy smiled, 'and who the hell has an alibi for that time of day? Certainly not a solitary bachelor living in the middle of nowhere.'

'Thanks,' said Treloar with a huff, but he could see where Fitzroy was going, 'but then we come to Dr Roz and that was late afternoon, and she was shot, and I was here with you two.'

'And you have no connection with her,' said Lucia.

'And you couldn't have pulled off that shot,' Fitzroy added. 'Fuck *I* couldn't have pulled off that shot. So I say again, somebody has gone rogue.'

Sam Scott stood on the empty windswept sands of Hawker's Cove. The body had been taken away as had the stunned magazine photographer and the traumatised bridegroom, and the only other person left was the police photographer whose task was somewhat pointless as the tide had washed away any evidence at the spot where the new Mrs Bajinder Wood had dropped like a stone.

The magazine photographer had begrudgingly been persuaded to give up the camera he had been using, and a reassurance that nothing had been shared or uploaded, because of a stringent confidentiality clause insisted upon by Dr Roz's agent, who liked to control her client's image rights rigidly. Seeing nothing further could be gained from the beach, Sam turned to head over to The Salt Creek.

Back at The Salt Creek Coco had gone into overdrive to eradicate all traces of the celebration. The Orangery had been cleared, cleaned and rearranged, the layout back to that of an eatery. The flowers, plants, balloons, streamers, presents and confetti had been swept away. It was as if the wedding of Dr Rosamund Lacey and Bajinder Wood had not taken place at The Salt Creek. The guests, who had been asked to stay on to make statements to the police, were either sequestered in their rooms or gathered in small subdued groups in the bar and sitting rooms.

Coco had organised simple British and French food. No hint of tascaburras, bacalao or gambas, no pastel de almendras. Vichysoisse, cold gammon and rare roast beef, cold ratatouille, salad leaves, soft brioche rolls, Cornish cheeses, and chocolate fondant. A buffet; should anyone be hungry. Someone always was. Large potted palms and ferns were brought in, and candles scented with sea salt ozone and freshly mown grass were glowing on tables.

Sam met Coco Holding in the foyer and was momentarily confused.

'I thought the wedding took place here?'

'It did. We cleared everything. It seemed inappropriate to leave things as they were. She did not die here. The aftermath of a party is always so depressing, even at the best of times, wouldn't you agree?' Her tone would brook no contradiction.

'Absolutely,' Sam concurred, 'and most considerate. I understand Ms Lacey's parents are staying here?'

'Yes. They are in their suite.'

'And the other guests?'

'All here as . . . requested. Scattered about. I can locate them for you as required.' She handed Sam a folder with sheaves of paper. 'Here is a list of the guests who attended and a list of my people who were present.'

'Thank you. Most helpful,' Sam scanned the names.

'Can I get you anything? I have prepared the smaller private dining room for your interviews. It's just this way.'

Sam felt compelled to follow. Coco Holding was a commanding presence.

Treloar, Fitzroy and Lucia were still in the kitchen when Sam called having spoken to the wedding guests and staff at The Salt Creek to update them.

'Well that was not unexpected; nobody saw anything, nobody knows anything, everybody loved her, everybody is in total shock,' said Fitzroy.

Sam was on speaker-phone. 'Exactly. They were all at The Salt Creek, all accounted for at the time of the shooting. The boy who drove them to Daymer Bay had stayed on the

Rock side of the estuary when they rowed across to Hawker's Cove. He just saw her fall. He heard Bajinder Wood calling for help, shouting that she had been shot, and he dialled 999. He couldn't tell where the shot had come from, he didn't see anyone fleeing or acting suspiciously. He just remembered Wood crying out 'bhindi, bhindi' over and over. He fled and drove back to The Salt Creek.'

'Bhindi . . . ? That's okra isn't it? Why, why would he be shouting that?' asked Treloar, puzzled.

'No people,' Fitzroy shook his head. 'Without the aitch. A bindi is the red mark a lot of Hindu women wear in the centre of their foreheads. The entry wound was on her forehead centred between the eyes. Remarkable shot.'

'So you keep saying.'

'So nothing there to help.'

'No. Glorious place though. Coco Holding certainly has taste and style. And money. You'd love it Lucia. It's simple and elegant, light and airy, and not a wooden fish or lighthouse in sight.'

Lucia laughed and even Treloar found himself smiling.

'I tell you guys. Even Ochre Pengelly would approve. The plain walls are offset by these incredible hand-painted screens that can be moved around. Even the bedrooms have bare walls and these amazing screens. She was recommended some Canadian artist by Cecily Farrant. When this is over, before you go back to Barcelona, you should take a look Lucia. We could have lunch, the food looks brilliant too.'

'OK ladies, when you've finished planning your social diaries,' said Treloar.

Lucia kicked him under the table and pulled a face.

'So, tomorrow we go back to the beach at the same time of day,' said Fitzroy.

'No. we'll need to adjust for the tide or we'll be standing in water,' said Treloar.

'I'll check and let you know,' said Sam.

'We'll need to add about forty minutes to get the same conditions,' said Treloar.

'I bow to your superior knowledge,' Fitzroy smiled.

Chapter Fifty-Two

Treloar and Fitzroy were up on the headland below Stepper Point gazing down at the scene on the beach. Treloar pulled a copy of the shooting schematic from his pocket.

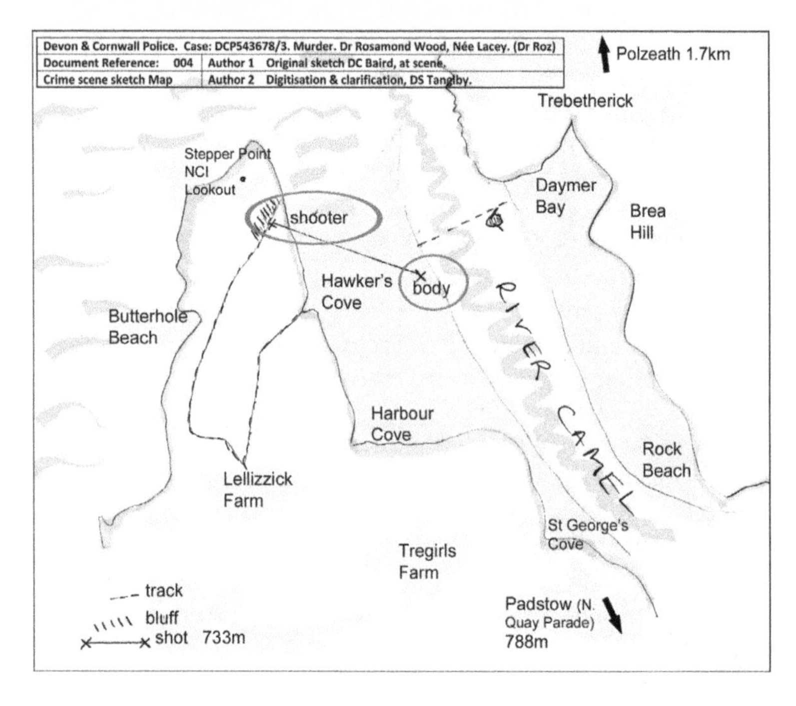

'It must have come from around here; given the trajectory, the entry point of the bullet: dead centre brow, and the exact direction in which she was facing, which we have from the magazine photographer,' said Fitzroy. 'Perhaps we could confirm that with lasers when it's dark?'

'Doubt it. Not soon anyway.'

'Why not?'

'Where she was standing won't be above water after

sunset for days. Tides'

'Yeah and the days are getting longer. No it was from here; I'm happy with that but I doubt we'll find any evidence.'

'Hell of a risk,' said Treloar.

'Hell of a shot,' Fitzroy replied with admiration. Treloar looked at him with eyebrows raised.

'What?' Credit where credit's due mate. That shot took great skill. The bullet, a.223 I'd guess, was still in her brain. That, my friend, takes some sighting, to get a dead-centre head shot like that at such a low speed? Hell of a shot.'

'Professional?'

Fitzroy pondered. 'Possibly, but certainly practised.'

Treloar had a point about the risk. They were standing on an exposed headland with no shelter and the South West Coastal Path ran past them. It was a popular walking area and after the earlier downpour the weather had turned back to warm sunshine and a gentle breeze.

'There is some cover and shelter here,' said Fitzroy. The two men were standing by a slight bluff where the coastal path crossed a rough track coming from Lellizzick. 'If you were quick you could drop, take the shot and be up and away in minutes. But there'd be little time to line up. Hell of a fucking shot mate, hell of a shot.'

'Perhaps we should look at the cousins,' said Treloar.

'Who the hell are the Couzens, local marksmen?'

'Not Couzens, cousins as in relatives. You know: Lorna Doone.'

'Are you feeling all right mate, is the stress of all this getting to you?'

The novel? R D Blackmore? Lorna Doone.'

'Not my specialist subject mate.'

'In the novel Lorna Doone is shot on her wedding day at the altar by her wicked cousin Carver Doone.'

'Is it Cornish?'

'No. Exmoor: Somerset.'

'Close.'

Treloar just stared at his companion.

'OK, OK not close enough for our man.

'No but it is our man: the Padstow mermaid. Legend has it that a local man, in Enys Tregarthen's version, he's named as Tristram Bird, with a new gun to try, went out to shoot seals and shot a mermaid by mistake. Either that or she refused his advances and he shot her, or he refused to join her under the sea, take your pick. Anyway, whichever version you choose, he definitely shot her, she cursed the spot with her dying breath and raised the Doom bar.'

'I thought that was a beer; a bitter like Bessie Stogs?'

'Betty Stogs. Yes it is, but it's named after the Doom bar. It's a sand bar that runs across the estuary from Hawker's Cove down there, to Trebetherick,' Treloar pointed across the Camel to a rocky purple and green slate outcrop between two sandy beaches. 'Over the years it's caused many a shipwreck.'

'Is it any good?'

'What as a sand bar?' Treloar asked, confused.

'No mate, not as a fucking sand bar, priorities, priorities, as a beer.'

'Yeah, but it's not as good as Betty Stogs. That's still brewed independently and Betty Stogs lived in Towednack which is a stone's throw from me. You'd have liked her: she was a dissipated drunk who left her baby to be looked after by the Buccas.'

Fitzroy's phone buzzed. He stared at the screen. 'Incoming: it's Sam,' he answered switching to speaker-phone. 'Sam! Which do you think is better, Doom Bar or Betty Stogs?'

'What?'

'Love the hat by the way, much cooler than the boring baseball cap I was fobbed off with.'

Sam was wearing an old summer striped trilby she had found on the back seat to keep her hair from blowing in her face on the exposed sand.

'Where are you two?' she demanded spinning round to survey the vantage points. Soon she focused on the two figures standing just down from the Stepper Point coastguard lookout.

'What are you doing at my crime scene?'

'Finding the point of origin for your kill shot,' he answered sternly.

'Right. Well done. Phil, Sir, you are suspended, if you

recall. Fitz you are a . . . murder tourist. Neither of you should be here. Or up there. Meet me at my place NOW!'

'One grumpy puppy,' said Fitzroy ending the call.

'Don't worry, that puppy's bark is worse than its bite.'

Fitzroy had not wanted to be reliant on Treloar for transport once the decision for him to stay temporarily in Cornwall had been made. Given the nature of the man, Treloar had not been surprised when he had hired a Triumph T100 Bonneville 865cc, helmet and full set of leathers. To be fair, it was not a bad idea, given the summer traffic on the roads, and he had even prevailed upon Treloar to get a full set of gear for himself so that the two could travel together. Given the fact that they were on the right side of the Camel to avoid the Padstow traffic, and the nature of Fitzroy's riding, they arrived at Sam's place a full twenty minutes before her.

Sam drew up alongside the Triumph where the two men were lounging against the barn's wall. *Boys and their toys* she thought as she climbed out of the car.

'What's this: the advance party of the Hell's Angels' summer tour?'

'This, I'll have you know,' said Fitzroy indicating the bike, 'is a British classic.'

'And this,' Sam indicated the VW Beetle, 'is a German classic, and what's more, they still make them!'

'Basta! It's fucking hot in all this gear. Can we please go inside?' Treloar asked grumpily.

Fitzroy and Sam exchanged a look and a shrug and Sam crossed to the door and unlocked it. They traipsed through to the kitchen and Sam went on to slide open the doors to the garden. A gentle breeze blew through, billowing the voile curtain. When she turned back, leathers, helmets, gloves and boots were strewn across the floor and the two men were barefoot, clad in tee shirts, shorts and smiles.

'Beer?' she asked.

The smiles broadened.

'Go and sit outside. I'm sure you must be hot, sticky and smelly.'

They took the Adirondack chairs at the wooden table

and Sam emerged with three moisture- glistening bottles of San Miguel which she placed on the table. They helped themselves and the two men drank deeply.

'What happened to the groom?' Treloar asked wiping his mouth with the back of his hand.

'He was in a hell of a state, understandably. One of the guys took him back to The Salt Creek and asked them to call their local doctor. He just kept repeating 'bhindi, bhindi . . . over and over again''

'OK let's get down to it,' said Treloar, 'two questions: who knew she'd be on that beach and who knew she'd be dressed as a mermaid? Oh and one more, who suggested she be dressed as a mermaid?'

Sam exhaled noisily though pursed lips.

@thecornishchef&artist

The Cornish chef & the artist

Artist here. Can't believe it - yet another one! C'mon cops!! Lots of us loved Dr Roz, but I guess someone didn't . . . big time!!

No credit for this drawing for a change, which we thought might help some of you understand more. It shows Tristram Bird and the Padstow Mermaid, not long before he shot her at Hawker's cove would you believe! W. H. C. Groome did it - for Enys Tregarthen - to illustrate *The Legend of the Padstow Doombar*, in *North Cornwall Fairies and Legends.* She was a Padstow girl, and Enys Tregarthen was a very Cornish pen name. Her actual name was Nellie Sloggett!

. . . . . In a far-away time Tristram Bird of Padstow bought a gun at a little shop in the quaint old market . . . . Do we really believe he'd buy it to shoot seals?

Tristram Bird could see over the maiden's head into the pool.

Chef here. Seals are definitely popular in Padstow when you can catch them (on camera!!), and loved on the plate in some parts of the world - maybe once even in Cornwall. Not cooked it myself yet. Using another popular Padstow sea dweller though here's an easy breakfast I cook often, Crab omelette. My favourite crab is spider crab (Cornish King Crab to some), but brown crab also fantastic.

I make omelettes individually, to keep them thinnish and make it easier to avoid overcooking. So, here is how I make **one** crab omelette. They take around 30 seconds to 1 minute to cook so doing them individually isn't that big a deal.

I use: 1 good handful of cooked white crab meat, 1 handful chopped Chervil (Fennel or Dill leaves if no Chervil. Pretty good without though too. See earlier Blog for how to grow Chervil), 2 eggs, 1 knob of butter, good pinch of salt, pepper to season.

Here's how: Whisk the eggs with the salt while a 20 - 25 cm frying pan gets hot over medium to high heat. When hot add butter, swirl around until melted, covering base of pan. Add eggs, swirling again to ensure whole pan base is covered and **straightaway** sprinkle the crab meat across the middle of the omelette, sprinkle half the Chervil onto crab. After 30 - 40 seconds use an egg slice to fold one side of the omelette over to just past the centre so it covers the crab meat, then fold the other side over the folded first side. You'll have a kind of flat oozy tube of egg filled with lovely and now warmed through white crab meat. Slide it onto a plate, add a few twists of pepper if you like, and you're good to go! Enjoy. If you don't like 'rarish' omelettes, cook them a little longer until they are as you like them.

What the hell had Dr Roz done? I'm off to raise a glass with the artist to the Doc with the hat. Hope they catch the baxxxrd soon!

Chapter Fifty-Three

With the backing of the Chief Constable, Nicky Chamberlain had reinstated Treloar despite the protestations of Romilly Hawkins, the Police and Crime Commissioner. Chamberlain had argued that Treloar had an alibi for the shooting and no connection to the latest victim and that he needed his best detective on such a high profile case. The latter had swung it, in the face of the hordes of national and international media now descending on Cornwall.

Treloar had his critics, but even they would concede that he got results. So that afternoon Treloar, Sam and Fitzroy were sitting at the dining room table in The Count House. In addition to Dr Roz having no connection to Treloar, her high national profile had allowed a quasi-official role for Fitzroy so he could now show his face on the enquiry.

Luke Calloway had organized a thorough door-to-door in Rock and Trebetherick, and the team was busy interviewing and locating any camera footage overlooking the scene of death. Luke himself had already been asked by Sam to look at social media and to trace, identify and either eliminate potential witnesses or ensure their statements were logged and leads actioned for follow up.

'Back to basics,' said Treloar,' means, motive, opportunity.'

'Well,' Fitzroy raised his eyes to the ceiling, 'let's start with the obvious: means. You are looking for somebody with great skill and access to a very nice piece of kit.'

'Right,' said Sam, 'so working on the assumption that the same people are behind all the killings, and this was not a hired-in outside contract killer, I'll get someone to look at locals with gun licences.'

'Motive?' Fitzroy continued. 'Fuck knows. Someone who resents success and celebrity? Someone jealous who loved Bajinder Wood? Someone paid to do the job? But, if we are going with the Cornish theme and the same killer or killing team as your other victims, your issue is not only who knew she'd be on that beach at that time, but also who knew she'd be dressed as a mermaid?'

'The key for the theme is the mermaid,' said Sam. 'Just shooting her on the beach wouldn't be enough to make the link obvious.'

'OK, so who would have known about the dress?' Treloar asked.

'From my brother's wedding, I recall him moaning about a whole gaggle of women, no offence Sam,' Fitzroy grinned, 'led by his beloved's mother holding secret gatherings, all men forbidden.'

'Yes,' Sam nodded, 'that would usually be organised by the bride's mother and the maid of honour, if she had one. But we're not talking ordinary people here and don't forget the magazine photo-shoot. In addition to family and close friends there would have been an entourage of her personal stylists, agent and publicists, plus the magazine's staff.'

'I thought it was all supposed to be a big secret for maximum impact?' Fitzroy asked.

'Well yes, as I said, normally but not here I think. There'd also be the dressmaker and whoever supplied her with the brief: take away the dress you take away the Padstow Doom Bar mermaid and you break the Cornish theme pattern.'

Treloar had remained silent through this exchange. He was the only one of the three who had been married and it had not ended well. But now he spoke.

'OK Sam. We need to establish who knew what and when. Start with her agent, they seem to know and control everything. The knowledge of the photo-shoot would have needed to be strictly limited to avoid a deluge of paparazzi. The magazine would have wanted exclusivity and the visuals would have been ruined by crowds of onlookers, fans and media. And let's start where she started that day: The Salt Creek. They supplied the driver to take the happy couple to Trebetherick, may have organised the boat, may have known about the dress. Talk to Coco Holding.

Sam grabbed her bag and headed for the door, 'I'll call you.' And with that she was gone.

'Of course,' said Fitzroy, 'it could have been you mate, trying to clear your name in the other cases by muddying the water with a random high profile victim?'

'Except I can't shoot, and at the time of the shooting I was at Lost Farm Barn . . . with you.'

'I know that, you know that, but don't think the media trolls will let the truth get in the way of good story.'

'Fuck Ben.'

'Just saying. Be prepared. To sort this you need to solve this. But there is something about this last killing that will help us. The Cornish theme may still follow the plan, but the M O has radically veered and, if the overall objective was to frame you, this is totally off piste.'

'Yeah, and if there is a controlling mind behind it all, they are gonna be well pissed off.'

'Love it. Divide and conquer, mate, divide and conquer.'

Chapter Fifty-Four

Sam and Treloar were back at The Count House dining table. The firearms licence check had thrown up the expected list of local farmers, a few fishermen, a random selection of citizens and two local business owners, one of whom had known Ellis, Hicks and, albeit indirectly, Dr Roz through the Ally Ally Oh festival committee: Cecily Farrant. But all had alibis. Sam had asked for Cecily Farrant's alibi to be double-checked, because she had known all the victims.

Luke's team's search in Rock and Trebetherick was continuing with little result so far. The social media trawl was also proving to be less than useful in terms of witness production. It was simply confirming the sparse details that had already appeared online. Images had been viewed but they too shed nothing new.

'Let's find out more about Cecily Farrant,' said Treloar.

'Already have her alibi details from Luke,' Sam said. 'Cecily Farrant owns several properties locally, her latest acquisition being in Church Street in central Padstow. At the time of Dr Roz's shooting, CCTV from a neighbouring property captured Cecily in a distinctive pink spotted raincoat parking her BMW at the kerb and punching in the key-code to open the gate to her garden.'

'Right.'

'There's more. Ten minutes later a call was made from the house's landline to the CHILL offices and, and here I quote, a ten minute 'rant' ensued. Not unusual apparently, and the staff member stated, "I couldn't get a word in edgeways and then she hung up on me." Also, her mobile was on and registering at the Church Street address,' Sam concluded.

'Okay.'

'So, with the other licence holders ruled out, it's not a registered local.'

'Well Ben did say the shot was exceptional.'

'Fluke?'

'He says not and he would know.'

'Well I'd have liked Cecily Farrant for it, without the alibi.'

Treloar crossed to the makeshift whiteboard where the schematic of the shooting and photographs were pinned up. The faces of the four victims smiled back at him.

'Why did someone want you dead?' he asked softly.

'Cui bono?' asked a deep voice.

Treloar turned to see Fitzroy standing in the doorway.

'Exactly. I can't see how any one person benefits from all four of these deaths. This can't be personal; it's not about love or lust, the victims are too different.'

'So it must be about lucre,' said Sam.

'But how? It makes no sense,' Treloar said.

'It makes sense to someone mate,' Fitzroy said softly.

'Well it obviously makes sense to the killer,' said Sam,' unless it's not love, lust or lucre but lunacy. We're missing something, something basic, something underlying all the . . . static.'

'Unless you're right and it is lunacy,' said Treloar, 'if that's the case we're in deep trouble.'

'That rings a bell,' said Fitzroy.

'What? Deep trouble? That must be a fucking peal!'

'No, seriously, recently, shit I can't recall. Somebody mentioned lunacy, the very word. Who was it?'

Chapter Fifty-Five

Cecily Farrant had indeed recently bought the house in Church Street, from a client of CHILL who had used it as a holiday let. In a central location opposite the wooded area adjacent to St Petroc's churchyard, when she had made her first inspection, she had known she had to have it. This was truly a matter of: location, location, location. The house was a quarter of a mile from Pasco Trefry's Rum House.

For him to reach Padstow town centre and the harbour, he would walk down St Saviour's Lane, turn left to join Cross Street, on down until this became Duke Street, and onwards to the harbour, the shops, banks and the CHILL offices. Church Street met Cross Street where it became Duke Street. Perfection. So many occasions, so many reasons to bump into Pasco, who was a predictable man of habit. He would see her, often, he would speak with her, get to know her, and he *would* love her.

For years she had hoped to acquire a property on St Saviour's Lane, but she might as well hope for eternal youth. But still, the Church Street house was perfectly serviceable, a better pied à terre than the cramped flat above the CHILL offices, and it would resell easily. After all, she would have a house in St Saviour's Lane, and it would be Rum House.

Sam, Luke Calloway and Diggory Keast had decided that the casual appearance of a few local plods out for a drink would be the best way to approach Dr Roz's agent, Tim Strathearn. So, they had engineered an accidental meeting in the bar of The Old Ship Hotel where he was staying.

'I always liked her,' said Luke.

'Thinking man's crumpet, or should I say saffron bun eh, us being in Cornwall after all?' chuckled Sgt Keast.

'Really Diggory,' Sam rolled her eyes.

'Well I wouldna kicked her oot the bed,' Keast trilled in

a dreadful cod Scottish accent.

'Diggory, you are a dreadful old relic aren't you?' said Sam.

'I always thought she sounded more West Coast than Highland,' Luke said, 'rather like the breakfast television weather lady: Carol Kirkwood.'

'Now I *really* like her,' said Keast with a leer.

'Well she is more your age at least,' Sam muttered.

'Anyway,' said Strathearn sternly, 'she wouldn't have let you in her bed.'

'Too dumb I suppose,' said Keast glumly.

'Too old pal, *much* too old.'

'Really?' said Luke, shocked.

'They've kept that very quiet,' said Sam, 'though now you mention it, her new husband must be, what, only early twenties?'

'Nineteen,' said Strathearn, 'and he's on the upper age limit for our Roz; not good for the ratings if that little gem became common knowledge.'

Keast whistled loudly and the group fell silent.

'But my God, she gleamed and shone for the camera,' said Strathearn dreamily.

'But not for you?' Sam asked quietly.

'You're very perceptive,' Strathearn snapped. 'No, not for me. She never looked at me in that way. I've always just been a member of staff. Why do you think I'm staying here rather than at The Salt Creek with the chosen ones?"

'I'm sorry. I understand, I truly do,' said Sam.

'She was a national treasure. Everybody loved her, everybody. We used to get the usual twisted hate mail, email and tweets, but mostly declarations of love and appreciation, very little nasty stuff to be fair, from my vast experience of people in the spotlight like her.'

'I was wondering about the dress,' said Sam, 'whose idea was the mermaid dress, it was so lovely and so clever with that detachable tail?'

'Oh, mine. It was rather special was it not? Well, when I say mine, I was approached by the magazine doing the photo-shoot. They had spoken to the television company who were producing her new series *The Rolling Deep* and well, obviously a mermaid look was a no-brainer. Nobody, absolutely nobody had made the connection with the legend here in Padstow. Christ, Roz would have freaked.'

'So it was the magazine's idea originally?' asked Luke.

'Well, let me think. Yes, yes it was. It was a bit of a coup for them. They're quite new, one of the Masterson stable, with offerings for yummy mummies. You know, the woman who has it all. Great for ratings for the TV show, getting in early on, that's when they make the most sales of course, the first few editions of these glossies.'

The three police officers exchanged a look. *Well, that explains that then*, thought Sam. *The magazine, Masterson again.*

Chapter Fifty-Six

'I've known all along about Ruby Russell,' Coco said nonchalantly.

Tommy said nothing. He just stared at her, stunned, speechless.

'You were so different when you got back from South Africa. And you'd hardly been discreet. She answered the phone in your room at some ungodly hour; young, female and British. Oh not her name of course, just that you were besotted with a striking, young British girl. I didn't know her name until much later.'

Tommy remained silent. He stared at the ground, head bowed.

'Perhaps it was being at the other end of the world, in another world . . . don't forget I've been to The Cape. It is a different world. Anyway, I made enquiries and I made money available for information. It didn't take much. And then when you were home, well it was an issue for you for a while. I could see that. But it faded quickly, crackled and went up in smoke.'

'You never said a word,' Tommy said quietly.

'Sleeping dogs, Tommy; sleeping dogs.'

'I don't know what to say.'

Coco smiled sadly, 'but then I discovered the boy, your son Josh.'

'How?' he cried out.

'Pure happenstance. You've always been so . . . self-focused Tommy. You've never shown any interest in this place. It would never cross your mind that I would do my research. I explored the area when I first found this place. I asked around about other hotels, other restaurants. I stayed at some, ate at others. We need to be able to recommend venues to our guests, depending on their mood and taste, like any good hotel concièrge. And so one day early on I was directed to Strandloper.'

Tommy remained silent.

'Christ Tommy it's there on The Salt Creek website under places to visit! So I went for lunch one day and I loved it. Hardly surprising it's my kind of place: different, well-run, highly rated and highly successful.'

'Yes, yes I can see that. That you'd like it I mean,' said Tommy softly.

'Well I remember the utter shock at my first sight of the boy. He was waiting tables and he was you.'

'I know, I know,' Tommy whispered.

'He was not much younger than you were when we first met. Remember?'

'I am so sorry.'

Coco looked at him, expressionless. 'Well after the shock came anger, briefly, then sadness, more lasting . . .'

Tommy interrupted, pleadingly, in total incomprehension, 'why didn't you say anything?'

'Why should I?' Coco spat. 'Anyway, after the sadness, the enduring emotion has been relief.'

'Relief?' asked Tommy, incredulous.

'Yes Tommy, flooding, all-engulfing relief. Oh I know what we said all those years ago – or more to the point what 'your people' said – all that sanctimonious posturing about our 'quiet acceptance', our 'perfect union', never needing to know the cause, the problem, never wanting to apportion blame, blah, blah, blah . . . I WANTED TO KNOW! I NEEDED TO KNOW! So I had tests. It was me. I was infertile.'

'You never said a word.'

Coco ignored him, 'all those years, it was me to blame, denying you a child, denying you an heir. So the boy – well after the eruption of anger – it was an overwhelming tsunami of relief that I could lay down the burden of guilt. The pain of that brief betrayal was nothing in comparison with the peace that knowledge brought me and still does.'

'I had no idea,' Tommy mumbled.

Coco scoffed, 'like about so much in my life Tommy. I'm glad. Truly, for you, I'm glad: about the boy.'

'I had no idea he existed,' Tommy said sadly.

'No. No I believe that. I hope you can see that it was not for me to tell you. That, you must take up with Ms Russell. But beware Tommy. It's been twenty years. He is a happy, stable fulfilled young man by all accounts and he has reached this point in his life without you. Be careful what you wish for, especially, what you wish for him. Do not act in haste.'

'You're right, as ever. I'll bide my time. I was angry but I'm not now. I don't want to upset him. I'll wait for the right moment.'

'Let sleeping dogs lie. Wasn't that one of your mantras when dealing with difficult stars and situations?'

'It was, it was. Still is for that matter.'

They sat in silence for some time.

'I love you, Coco,' he said softly, and as the words left his mouth he was suddenly struck by the truth of them. The irritations, the frustrations, his petty trivial annoyance with her over the years was snuffed out by the searing knowledge that he loved this woman.

'Yes Tommy I know,' she said softly, 'I've always known.'

Unbeknownst to Tommy Holding and Ruby Russell, their doubts and tortured self-flagellation over Josh's parentage were irrelevant. Josh knew.

Chapter Fifty-Seven

The car park on Polzeath beach had been busy that day, but still only around half full. It was late morning, and Cecily's car drew admiring glances as the Zed found a parking spot and then even more as its roof extended from behind the rear seats, tipping forward and elongating slowly before finally and almost magically enclosing the cockpit, and then locking automatically into place. Cecily noticed that she too was drawing admiring glances as she walked from the car across the sand towards the beach market.

The market was held monthly in the summer, on Saturdays when the tide was favourable, unless poor weather prevented it. The attraction it held for Cecily, to get her away from her place in the country today, was an amazing little specialist record stall she had heard about. And she was wanting to add to her vinyl collection. OK, she was also there to check out Strandloper and ensure the CHILL write-up in the 'local eatery and bar' lists for her properties was on the button, and maybe even to extend it for a newsletter article.

Wearing yellow plimsolls, a yellow and white striped sundress with the bottom two buttons unfastened, and a white linen jacket, she was dressed for Strandloper. And a walk on the beach.

The beach market was a string of stalls laid out along the base of the rocky under-hill at the top of the beach, on the other side from the car park. Ignoring the surfers, paddlers, swimmers, sandcastle builders, sunbathers, cricketers, badminton players, and slow strollers looking for somewhere to settle themselves, she focused on finding the record stall.

It wasn't hard in the end. Half-way along the string of stalls she saw, raised around two metres above a red and white striped canvas roof, what was clearly a large replica of a vinyl LP. The LP was supported by a long pole. That was what she was there for, and ignoring the slowly walking caterpillar of people making their way along the full length of the stalls, stopping and peering at almost every one, she made straight for it. There was indeed the range of vinyl that she had heard was likely to be there, and the quality was first class.

After fifteen minutes though she realised that she was running out of time if she was to secure a hoped-for seat at Strandloper, and selected her favourite from the four LPs that she found in her hand. 'I'm going to have to come back,' Cecily said, smiling, to the middle-aged man who had pointed her at the Special Edition that she had selected, paid, and left.

Strandloper was buzzing when she walked in. Busy but not heaving, there was a pleasant buzz in the air and music was playing in the background. She couldn't tell what it was. Seeing an unoccupied bar stool at the end of the bar nearest the wall she made a beeline for it and hoisted herself up as demurely as possible to take her seat, facing towards the beach. Looking around, her first impression of the décor was that it was excellent, not like a typical beach bar at all, and she realised that she may have under-egged it in the CHILL write up. Her second impression was of the cleanliness, and tidiness on the tables and bar. Definitely under-egged.

'Hi, can I get you something . . . or are you still looking?' said a young man behind the bar.

'Looking?'

'At the beers and wines. The lists. Over there,' he said pointing at a blackboard on the wall, 'and here,' he said, picking a printed plastic covered card from the bar and handing it to her. 'Daily specials are on the boards, and the list is what we always have in.'

'Ah, right. Thanks.' Cecily said taking the beer and wine list from him and scanning it. 'I'll place myself in your trusty hands and ask for a glass of Sauvignon Blanc. Is that OK?'

'It absolutely is, no problem. I'll be right back.'

'Here you go.' The young man said quite soon afterwards. 'Hope you like it. It's one of our top sellers. Bit pricey, what do you think?'

Cecily took a sip, raised her eyebrows, then another. 'Unbelievable,' she said. Bit of fizz and so fruity! Amazing.'

'Great, I'm glad. There's not many that don't have a second glass of it. It's Vergelegen. South African. Not many places have it,' he explained. Then he turned to serve a young man and woman in wet-suits who had just arrived at the bar.

'Definitely well under-egged,' Cecily said to herself as she took another sip, smiled to herself, and shook her head, looking at the glass.

Leaning into the back of the bar stool, Cecily removed the LP she had bought from its paper bag and began admiring it. It was in very good condition, as was Seal who adorned the cover and who she had always had a soft spot for. It was the second Seal album, 'the Special Edition,' the stall guy had said, 'with the fold out back cover with lyrics and photos.'

Cecily opened the back cover and began scanning the words and pictures, stopping suddenly when she saw the picture at the bottom centre. It was a small picture and she had to bring the cover to within just a few inches of her face before she could be certain. Then she looked at the young man behind the bar who had served her and then back at the picture, and then back at the young man behind the bar.

She found that she was staring at him when he turned to her and smiled. 'Are you ready for another glass already?'

'Er . . . no, but. Well, I've just bought this, on the beach. And there's a guy in this picture,' and Cecily turned the LP cover, with the back cover opened out, and placed it on the bar counter. She pointed at the picture of a group of people surrounding Seal and tapped on one of them, a man, with a fingernail, 'who looks just like you!' It could be you! Except it was taken years ago, so it isn't . . could it be an older brother?'

He looked at the picture for what seemed like a long time. 'Ah, well, no, long story.' Josh said, 'I don't have any brothers, or sisters for that matter. There's just me and mum. There's been this guy around the last few days . . . oh, excuse me, need to serve over there.'

The young man was suddenly very busy being a waitron, bringing out meals from the kitchen, cleaning tables, and pointing out to customers the specials boards for food and drinks. Cecily's second glass of wine, ordered from a bar-girl who had just arrived, was finished as she completed reading the lyrics printed on the inside of the opening back cover of her 'new' album. As she left Strandloper the buzz had become a hubbub and Cecily tried to catch the young man's eye to say thanks and Cheerio, but he was too busy.

Chapter Fifty-Eight

Treloar, Fitzroy and Sam Scott were in Padstow sitting around the kitchen table in The Count House. Luke and the rest of the team had commandeered the dining room to collate statements and update the boards.

'Weird name Count House,' mumbled Fitzroy through a mouthful of pasty.

'It was the offices, the accounting place for a business community; fishing or mining. There's one near me at the former tin and copper mine at Botallack. It's National Trust now.'

'Did you know that they mine gold and diamonds in Canada?'

'No,' said Treloar whilst Sam looked bemused.

'Yes indeedy, in Quebec; the French bit.'

'Christ!' Treloar shouted slapping his fist down hard on the kitchen table.

'Shit, Phil,' Sam jumped in her chair.

'We were thinking horses when, for once, we should have been thinking zebras.'

'What?' Sam was lost.

'He means,' said Fitzroy, 'we have been thinking the obvious when we should have been thinking the unusual. 'When you hear the sound of hooves, think horses not zebras' or something along those lines. Though what he's referring to, I have no idea.'

'She told us. Coco Holding fucking told us. Well she told you. Sam. Remember the décor at The Salt Creek?'

'She told me that a marvellous Canadian had helped with the interiors and produced the hand-painted screens I admired. She told me Cecily Farrant had introduced her.'

'Exactly! Canadian! We were thinking Joni Mitchell when we should have been thinking Céline Dion. We were thinking Anglo Canadian when we should have been thinking

French Canadian. French!'

'You have got to be kidding me,' Sam whispered.

'She's back!' Treloar groaned.

Fitzroy looked from one to the other, 'who is back?'

'Amélie. This explains it all. Sam, you asked why me not Ben, why would Masterson go after me? Ben, you asked who I had pissed off? You said it was clever, manipulative, you said it had taken skill and imagination and determination. Fuck, you even called it creative. Welcome to the world of Amélie Bonnard.'

Amélie Bonnard, a charismatic young French woman, had been suspected in the Porthaven murders that had taken place some summers earlier, including that of Oliver Osborne QC. She was also believed to be the artist responsible for the pastiche paintings in the great hall at Polgwynn, her family's former estate in the village. Treloar did not suspect her; he knew she was guilty. And she had escaped justice. But not again.

'Show me the photos of Winters,' Treloar barked.

Sam pulled the Winters' crime scene images up on her phone. Treloar grabbed it and zoomed in on the banner around the hot tub.

'It's a hand-painted copy of the dairy's livery, very good apparently,' said Fitzroy.

'Look!' Treloar pointed. 'Look at the milkmaid's buckets. One contains milk but the other . . .'

Fitzroy stared at the bucket, 'looks like flowers.'

'Fucking cornflowers. And Look. Those birds aren't Cornish Choughs, they're Pelicans!'

'So, maybe the painter had copyright fears,' Fitzroy joked.

'This painter has no fears. Sam?'

Sam took her phone and stared at the screen. 'But it can't be surely? Oh my God Phil I think you're right. They're just like those on Hugo Brookes' wall at Penmol, the Polgwynn dower house in Porthaven. I saw them in the sunroom. She painted them; they were . . . glorious. Cornflowers, daisies and poppies . . . Wait! Hicks' garden! '

'What?' said Treloar and Fitzroy simultaneously.

Sam furiously scrolled through screens muttering, 'I

should have seen it, I should have seen it.' Finally, she zoomed in on Hicks lying in the greenhouse. On either side of his body were pots of poppies. 'He didn't grow poppies. He only grew flowers in shades of white and blue: funeral flowers. We joked about it before you arrived. Funeral flowers for all the old people who died in his care homes. To save on florists. I should have seen it.'

'Whoah,' said Fitzroy slowly, 'let's calm down and think. Let's go back to the beginning: Jolyon Ellis. Was there anything there? Anything to connect this Amélie to the scene?'

'Sam?' Treloar asked as, stricken-faced, she scrolled through her phone frantically.

'The surfboard in the sand pie, one of the surfboards was blue and white. Where the hell is it? Yes, I remember Diggory laughed at the writing on it: 'BLEW IT' he thought it was appropriate for surfers. He thought it was surfer slang like wipe out or bail out. Ah here we go,' as she zoomed in her face paled.

'Christ Sam what is it?' Treloar asked, grabbing the phone. 'B L E . . . hang on that's not a W.'

'No,' Sam said softly, 'it's a U.'

Treloar continued, 'B L E U E T.'

'It's not BLEW IT it's BLEUET,' said Sam.'

Treloar, who knew enough French to recognise bleu as blue, spoke quietly.

'Let me guess. 'Bleuet' is French for cornflower?'

'Correct. And what's more 'le bleuet' is the French equivalent of the poppy in the UK; it's their flower for remembrance.

The three sat in silence until Fitzroy spoke.

'OK, OK. Dr Roz?'

'Well the obvious thing would be the wedding flowers,' said Treloar.

'Aren't they usually fancy stuff: roses, peonies, lilies?' Fitzroy asked.

'Yes,' said Sam, 'but Dr Roz would have wanted something different: natural, local, eco-friendly not forced hothouse blooms.'

'You mean something like wildflowers, field flowers,' Treloar commented.

'There must be something, somewhere on the Net. Let me do a search.'

As Fitzroy looked at his own mobile, Treloar walked over to the fridge to get beers without asking if anybody wanted one. He returned with three bottles of Estrella Damm.

'Here,' Sam pointed to a photo on her screen; a beaming Dr Roz stood by the sunken Italian garden at The Salt Creek, the fountain behind her. In her hands were a loose bunch of roses, sweet pea and ranuncula.

'Ne'er a poppy, daisy nor cornflower,' said Fitzroy.

'You were right Ben,' said Treloar, 'she wasn't part of the plan; somebody did break ranks. Amélie Bonnard is a master manipulator and controlling mind and she will indeed be exceedingly pissed off with whoever shot Rosamond Lacey.'

'It must be Coco Holding,' said Sam, 'she employed Amélie on those screens. They would have taken weeks. That would have given her time to work her poison.'

'No,' said Treloar, 'it's not Holding. Coco Holding is totally engrossed in The Salt Creek. She has money, profile, success. Where is her weakness? Where is the tiny crack Amélie would need to insert her hook? Can she shoot like our killer? This isn't Holding.'

'Well my money's on a woman. She always loved a female partner. Remember Julia Osborne? What about Ruby Russell?'

'Never!' Treloar spat with vehemence.

Sam and Fitzroy turned to him in surprise. 'Why not?' asked Sam petulantly.

'No I don't see it either,' said Fitzroy, 'she's too peripheral, she doesn't mix with these people, and like Coco, she has her own empire to run, and her lad. No I don't see it. Plus she's smoking hot.'

Sam and Treloar both glared at him, albeit for very different reasons.

'No I think Phil's right about both Coco and Ruby. They're both too established, grounded and removed from the Padstow set where it all started after all. It's somebody else, somebody closer to Ellis and Hicks with a motive to kill one or more of them as we now think it's Amélie who's out to get Phil; somebody open to manipulation and a great fucking shot!'

'And a psycho,' said Fitzroy, 'Christ how do these people find each other? There must be some hidden gravitational pull.'

'It's that bloody holiday letting agent. Has to be,' said Treloar. 'Talking of manipulation, she's a manipulator, cunning, look how she got close to us through The Count House lease, plus she introduced Amélie to Coco Holding and she obviously goes way back with Ellis and Hicks. And didn't you mention she's in a gun club?'

'But she has an alibi for the shooting,' said Sam, 'she was at one of her homes. There is CCTV of her parking her car in Church Street, entering the key code and opening the front door before disappearing inside. Then there is the telephone call from her landline to the CHILL office and her mobile didn't move from her home address.'

Treloar spoke slowly: 'Anyone who could alter those parish records could easily hack the Padstow CCTV. It's just another confirmation. We couldn't think of anyone local to all this with those skills, but we know Amélie has them in spades.'

'And what did you say about that phone call to CHILL? What did the girly say?' asked Fitzroy.

Sam scanned her phone. 'Jeannie Hicks was the 'girly',' she shot Fitzroy a look, 'and she said, "she was ranting, I couldn't get a word in edgeways."'

'Recording,' said Treloar and Fitzroy simultaneously.

'Anyone in the house could have made that call, played the recording and then hung up before Jeannie could interact. Clever,' said Sam nodding, 'Cecily Farrant.'

'But she is playing way out of her league, like Truro City taking on Barça, said Treloar. She doesn't stand a chance if she's disobeyed Amélie, she'll be livid. She is the ultimate manipulator; she demands absolute obedience and total control. She is terrifying not because she is hateful, but because she inspires total love; people, sane men and women worship her as if spellbound. It's like a cult.'

'She sounds . . . magnificent,' said Fitzroy.

'Oh she is, and totally pitiless,' said Sam.

Treloar sat silent through their exchange.

'But what does she want and why now; it's years since those Porthaven murders? Is it money?'

'Not enough of a motive for Amélie.'

'Is it revenge?'

'Not enough.'

'So what's left, It's not love.'

Treloar spoke. 'But it is. She wants what she's always wanted. For her it has always been about the Pentreath estate, her family's stolen heritage. This is about Polgwynn.'

'So you think she's involved with Masterson as well; working with him to discredit you, ruin you, asked Sam?'

Fitzroy answered, 'Something is happening at Polgwynn, something to bring her back and whilst she's waiting . . . she's keeping herself amused.'

'Absolutely,' said Treloar. 'She's manipulating him like all the others, she's using his grief and his anger. I almost beat her, I almost caught her and she was forced to flee, she lost control. If it hadn't been for your pal Brookes getting her out of the country. Why the hell did he help her?'

'He thought she might prove useful at some future time. You know these MI6 types.'

'My God You're serious! What a fool. I hope he's watching his back.'

'He thinks he'll be able to call in the debt one day,' answered Fitzroy.

'Hah!' Treloar scoffed. 'The man is truly an idiot. Amélie does not do debt. Amélie abhors debt. Debt lost her family Polgwynn. She will want to eradicate that debt which means . . .'

'Christ mate,' Fitzroy said quietly.

'But why Cecily Farrant?' Sam asked.

'I don't know, not yet, but Amélie has found a weakness, she's found a need and she's feeding it.'

'You think the Farrant woman's in trouble?' asked Fitzroy.

'Deep, deep trouble.'

‘Sam, call Coco Holding and check the name of that artist. What’s the betting it’s Bonnard?’

Sam snatched up her phone scrolled through her contacts and dialled.

‘Ms Holding? This is Inspector Scott . . . No, nothing as yet . . .One small thing, those wonderful screens? I recall you saying the artist is Canadian?’

Sam looked at her companions and nodded as she heard the reply.

‘What is her name? . . . Natalie you say,’ and with that Sam hit the speakerphone and Coco’s voice filled the void.

‘Yes, Natalie without an ‘H’. An extraordinary creature. Once she was out on the croquet lawn and I was captivated by what I saw. She was calling to the seagulls, in French. A dozen landed and formed a circle around her. She spoke to each in turn then waved her hand and the gulls flew off, each one in turn, as if dismissed. The most amazing thing. If I hadn’t seen it with my own eyes . . . brrrr . . . it was . . . unworldly.’

‘For fuck’s sake,’ Treloar whispered. Fitzroy frowned at him confused, ‘Natalie was the name she used for Julia Osborne in Porthaven, her lover.’ They were in some French nuthouse together when they were kids.

Sam was asking about a surname.

‘No. No surname. Just Natalie, like a rock star or a Brazilian footballer.’

‘Surely she must have given you a full name for you to make payment.’

‘Oh I haven’t paid yet; she hasn’t finished the work. I offered of course, but she insisted that we wait and she will invoice me when the commission is completed.’

‘And I am right that it was Cecily Farrant who recommended her?’

‘Yes. Is there a problem?’

Chapter Fifty-Nine

She was waiting, for a coffee, and a keenly awaited meeting. Mulling back, in the sun.

'Phutt' went Freddie and 'thunk' went the bullet. And Another one bites the dust *poured into her ear-buds. Queen, still amazing. She smiled as the smell of burnt cordite filled her space.*

She muted the iPod using the custom footswitch, gently shifted Freddie's business end to the right without lifting him from the bean-bag rest and shuffled slightly back and forth against the floor. Just until the crease in the dungarees that was pressing against the front of her thigh had been smoothed. 'Phutt', 'thunk', and Queen filled the buds again, and then her head. Brilliant. The play list and random shuffle were working well today. She smiled again and watched the cordite fumes drifting slowly away on the vague breath of a breeze, down the slight slope of the tunnel. Getting slowly thinner.

She muted the iPod again, gently shifted Freddie to the right a little more and settled. 'Phutt' went Freddie, 'thunk' went the bullet. And just afterwards the bullet triggered the sensors in front of the third target, two hundred metres down the slope, Killer Queen *filled the buds. Working great today. Marvellous darling! How spooky was that.*

The third target had been the centrefold of last week's Sunday Times, a full-size portrait photograph of Donald Trump, supposedly leader of the free world. 'Really! I don't think so, not my world.' she had said to friends at the pub on Sunday lunchtime. The twin sensor beams met at right angles in front of Trump's left eye. To switch on the iPod the bullet had to break both beams.

She stood, patted Freddie on the butt, smiled, unclipped the scope and laid it in the case, and holding him by the silencer leaned him gently into the corner at the bottom of the stairs to cool. She switched off the music before pocketing the buds and walked down the slope to the targets. They wafted slightly in the through-breeze of the tunnel. Still the ace shot. All good. She unpegged them, balled them up and dropped them into the bin on the floor before stepping up to the dry solid soil wall at the bottom of the slope where the bullets had joined their predecessors. She ran her hand across the surface. It was still warm in three places.

She turned and walked to the left into the recess at the bottom of the tunnel and turned off the lights before unlocking and then unbolting and opening the solid heavy door at top and bottom and stepping out to the moonlit creekside. The tide was full and it was peaceful. Water lapped against the bank just a few feet below. It flowed to the right, into the River Camel, and she could see it shimmering too, as it wound its way round and behind the hill opposite and along to Padstow.

Sitting on her favourite stone and leaning back against the rock face she shook out and lit a Dunhill International and inhaled deeply, looking into the moon shimmer on the slow flowing river. Thinking. The Lizard gun club had definitely been a smart move, as good as the golf clubs for meeting developers and owners, and those that hadn't even thought about being either yet. The Lizard Gun Club was ideal. The rifle range at the local RNAS, the only one thousand metre range west of Plymouth, was very kindly made available once a month to gun club members who were bored with the farm meets and shooting game birds. Getting out to help with the deer cull helped, she enjoyed that, not often enough though.

The Commanding Officer, Naval Captain John Culpepper, had been very understanding, he had become very keen to develop a good relationship with the local community once she had given him the chance to think about it. The Navy shooters who supervised and scored, when asked, were keen to prove their own prowess when they competed with the civvies. They had not noticed that her shots only ever just missed the bull, or that her 'just misseds' were always between two and four centimetres away from the centre of the target.

Chapter Sixty

'And this Natalie, she's still working for you?' Sam asked Coco.

'Yes she's here now. Actually she's on the terrace taking coffee with Cecily.'

Sam's eyes widened in horror, 'The Orangery terrace?'

'Yes.'

Treloar raised his hand and made a cutting motion.

'Do you want to speak to her?' Coco asked.

'No that's fine thanks. It was just a loose end. But Ms Holding please do not mention this conversation to anyone will you, it's important it remain confidential?'

'As you wish.'

'Thank you. Goodbye.'

'Goodbye Inspector.'

Treloar rushed to the sideboard and grabbed his car keys from a ceramic fish bowl.

'Don't be daft mate,' Fitzroy stood, pulling his leather jacket from the back of the chair. He grabbed two crash helmets from the floor and tossed one to Treloar.'

Treloar caught it. 'You're right Ben. Sam, follow us.'

Sam snatched her keys from the table, pocketing her phone and hurried out to hear the sound of the Triumph Bonneville roaring away.

Sam knew that it could take her over 45 minutes to reach The Salt Creek at this time of year. It was only about 5 km as the crow flies, but by road it was more than four times the distance; she had to travel the length of the estuary, almost to Wadebridge, and back across to the sea near Port Quin.

She had scarcely left Padstow when her phone rang.

'Scott.'

'Inspector Scott it's Coco Holding. Something very

strange has happened. After your call I went out to see Cecily and Natalie . . .'

'You didn't say anything?' Sam interrupted.

'No, I wouldn't have, you said not to, but I didn't get a chance anyway. Natalie had left and Cecily, well at first I thought she was asleep but she was out cold. I've called an ambulance. What could it be?"

'I shouldn't say, but it's probably an overdose.'

'What, sleeping tablets . . . surely not heroin?'

'No, well sort of: morphine.'

'I'll fetch Tommy.'

The line went dead, and with that, she was gone.

Chapter Sixty-One

Treloar and Fitzroy roared into the courtyard and skidded to a halt. Snatching their helmets from their heads they leapt up the hotel steps and burst into the foyer.

'Orangery!' Treloar yelled at the young man standing by a table against the rear wall. Open-mouthed he pointed down and the two men ran in the direction indicated, along a hallway, through a lounge, down the steps into the glass-fronted room, out the open doors and stopped dead in their tracks.

A bizarre tableau confronted them. Cecily Farrant was on the ground on her front lying in the recovery position; one leg and one arm bent. Sitting at the table next to her were Tommy and Coco Holding, Tommy on his mobile. Between them on the table were discarded coffee cups, an overturned water carafe and glass and a hypodermic needle. Tommy ended the call and stood.

'Can I help you?' he asked approaching the odd-looking pair, one in full leathers, the other in faded cargo shorts and a Weird Fish T shirt

Treloar pulled his warrant card from his shorts' pocket as Fitzroy removed his leather jacket.

'Chief Inspector Treloar of Devon & Cornwall Police and my colleague. I recognise you Mr Holding but I do not understand what has happened here.'

'You and me both Chief Inspector. I have just spoken to the ambulance and they are twenty minutes out. What I can tell you, is that my wife found Cecily unconscious after she had a disconcerting conversation with your colleague Inspector Scott. She called an ambulance and then Inspector Scott who told her this,' he indicated Cecily on the ground, 'was probably a morphine overdose. Then she fetched me.'

'Why?' asked Fitzroy.

'I carry naloxone Mr? . . .'

'Fitzroy.'

'Old habits die hard. I spent lot of time around rock stars and their entourages and I have seen many narcotic overdoses. Naloxone is an effective antidote and has few ill effects in anyone who has not overdosed. In the case of an overdose it can save a life. Cecily's breathing is still very slow but it is there. I've informed the ambulance service and they will take her straight to Intensive Care at Treliske Hospital who will be forewarned.'

'You've probably saved her life,' said Fitzroy.

'Well let's hope so, but her recovery will be uncertain.'

Coco had joined them and took her husband's arm.

'We have no idea how long ago she took the overdose. I saw the two of them about an hour before the Inspector called, but Tommy and I were . . . elsewhere in the hotel. We can ask the staff who served them how long ago they saw Cecily . . . awake.'

'Yes thank you, if you could summon the relevant staff,' said Treloar.

'Your best bet would be to ask Natalie. She may well have been the last person to see her. I have tried her number but she's not answering . . .'

'I bet she isn't,' Fitzroy muttered.

Not hearing, Coco continued, 'but there's nothing unusual in that, not if she's working.'

'Right, thank you, perhaps you could give me her number?'

Of course.'

'I don't suppose she features in any of your promotional material? Any pictures of her?'

'No nothing. We haven't finished the work so we haven't done any of that yet.'

'Can you describe her, physically?'

'Of course. She is small and slight, she has long black hair which she wears up mostly, and her most notable feature: her enormous green eyes, quite striking, green like a forest pool. She is a very attractive woman.'

'Amélie,' Treloar whispered.

Coco walked back out to the terrace accompanied by Sam, who had finally made it through the traffic.

'I'm sorry . . . Inspectors, but it was Gianni who served them and he has gone into Padstow for supplies. Natalie was seen leaving through the front door and her bike has gone. I can call you when Gianni gets back or, if you prefer, I can show you to her room, but I doubt she's there.'

The three turned to her in unison. 'She has a room?' Sam asked.

'Well, not a room as such, not a bedroom in the house. No, she has the Lundy Rooms. Would you like to see them?'

Chapter Sixty-Two

Coco Holding led Treloar, Fitzroy and Sam down the steps from the terrace and around the croquet lawn heading seawards.

'The Lundy Rooms were the first renovation on the property before I started on the main house.'

They were following a gravel path across the headland towards a long low building.

'When I first saw the building I thought the location would be perfect for a secluded romantic stay: honeymoon, Valentine's Day, wedding anniversary. Ironically, it was the original servants' quarters, from a time when the amazing sea views and isolation were not rated over shelter from the prevailing winds and distance from the main house and drive.'

As they drew closer, they could see a small walled terrace with wooden furniture and built-in barbecue shielded by bay trees in enormous terracotta pots. The building was white-washed, with small shuttered windows and a bleached wood door.

'After the conversion I stayed here whilst we worked on the main house. It's totally self-contained. Even now we have the engine house, I think I may still stay here sometimes. You'll see; it's a perfect sanctuary. Anyway, when Natalie needed somewhere to work it was ideal, and she could stay here rather than in one of Cecily's soulless holiday lets. Perfect solution.'

She opened the door and they followed her in to be met by the redolent smells of oil paint and turpentine and a wall of light. The rear of the building was entirely glass, offering panoramic views over Lundy Bay.

'Wow!' said Sam.

'It is certainly an awesome location,' said Fitzroy.

'Is that triple-glazed?' asked Treloar, ever the practical builder.

'Yes indeed, otherwise it would be raucous in here when the wind blows from the north. Let me show you round. Natalie has not moved out yet, not that she brought much with her.'

At the far westerly end of the room was an old pine kitchen table littered with artist's materials: paints, brushes, rags, bottles, splattered boards and an assortment of tools. Standing next to it, silhouetted against the glass wall, was a half-painted folding screen depicting a harbour and quayside reminiscent of Porthaven.

'There is a small kitchen, en-suite bedroom, wet-room and conservatory along there,' said Coco indicating the easterly end of the room where a corridor next to the front wall disappeared in darkness. 'Do you need me here or is it .. legal for me to leave you alone?'

'It's fine thank you,' said Treloar, 'don't let us keep you. Where will we find you when we're done?'

'Oh just ask for me in the front hall; they'll track me down.'

'And should we lock up?' asked Sam.

'Oh no. It's never locked. Natalie won't have it for some reason. Well, I'll leave you to it.'

And with that she headed back out the front door and disappeared from view across the headland towards The Salt Creek.

'They were locked up in that institution in the South of France, Amélie and Julia both, that would explain the lack of keys,' said Sam.

Fitzroy had wandered off to the other rooms and Treloar was focusing on the pine table. He had found two Clairefontaine artwork folders leaning against the legs and was opening the larger green marbled one.

'Come and see this Sam.'

Fitzroy had found very little but he was making a mental note to visit with a lady friend. It was an awesome place. The conservatory was built to the very edge of the cliff, a square glass box housing comfortable primary coloured chairs with soft cushions and contrasting tables. The wet-room, well it was a wet room with a monsoon shower and a bath against the glass wall. Neither room looked occupied in any way.

The bedroom, however, was another matter. Bags, clothing, towels, drawings, charcoal sticks, empty plates, discarded mugs and several browning apple cores were strewn about as if the result of an angry search. Or somebody having left in a hurry. But a second, closer glance around proved that there was actually very little personal here; just a few cotton shirts, shorts and a pair of flat walking sandals. Amélie Bonnard obviously travelled light; a woman after his own heart.

Fitzroy had sensed a confused, ambivalent attitude towards the woman from Treloar; a grudging admiration alongside a . . . horror. Yes, horror was the right word. He knew that she could command fierce loyalty. Hell, she had evaded the powers of law and order across Europe and he was well aware that she had had help from at least one member of the British intelligence services: Nathaniel Brookes. Dangerous game. A cursory check of the en-suite revealed L'Occitane shower oil and shampoo, an Oral B toothbrush and toothpaste, and a very expensive looking French face cream he'd never heard of. Nothing damning.

Fitzroy joined the others at the table leafing through the artwork. They were staring at a painting of a nude woman holding a towel, behind her back an unseen window lighting the right side of her body. Sam was zooming in on a screen on her phone. She showed it to the two men in turn.

'It's a copy,' said Fitzroy.

'Almost,' said Sam, raising the phone, 'this is a Pierre Bonnard painted in 1907, it's titled *In the Bathroom*. Look at the rug she's standing on: blue poppies; look at her feet, she's wearing heeled court shoes. Now look at this', she pointed to the painting on top of the small pile in the art folder. 'the rug has cornflowers, she's wearing flip-flops, she's a blonde not a brunette and . . .'

'And,' Treloar interrupted, 'the model is Julia Honor.'

'Now look at this,' Sam scrolled her phone and zoomed in on a different painting, 'this a Pierre Bonnard painted in

1926, titled *The Palm*. A ghostly female figure holding an apple stood in the foreground with palms and a garden behind her, the red-tiled roofs of a town in the distance.

'And here', Treloar turned over the first painting to the second copy beneath.

'It's the same model,' said Fitzroy, 'and she's not holding an apple,' her looked more closely and smiled, 'it's a bottle of Orangina.'

'Indeed,' said Treloar, 'they are both Julia Honor, and Julia Honor is dead.'

'Why?' Sam asked.

'Amélie would not be calling herself Natalie if Julia were still alive. She would see taking the name as an alias, and as an artist, as a tribute. When we saw her room at Penmol, remember all the paintings, there were no pastiches of Pierre Bonnard. Brookes told us that she never copied Bonnard, he was sacrosanct.'

As they were talking, Fitzroy was searching on his phone. 'Here. Look. The Times.'

DEATH NOTICE

The Honourable Julia Jocelyne Honor

died suddenly in Saintes-Maries-de-la-Mer, France on 1st March. Beloved Daughter to Lord Netherholt. Widow of Oliver Osborne QC and stepmother to Jack. Private family funeral at Netherholt, Buckinghamshire. Family flowers only please, but donations gratefully received in Julia's memory to RSPB.

'And look at this, it's from something called *Brits on the Med*.

> **Family Curse?**
>
> Poor Jack Osborne! Orphaned at 15 by the grisly murder of his daddy Oliver Osborne QC in Cornwall, doomed Jack has now lost his wicked stepmother, the Honorable Honor.
>
> And to rub salt into the wounds the lovely Julia drowned here in the Med near Sète just like Jack's birth mummy Rebecca!!
>
> Weird or What? Curse or misadventure?
>
> BoM know what we think!

'They have a point mate. No such thing as coincidence, not such a close one,' Fitzroy concluded.

'Yeah. Especially when you consider that Amélie's first connection with death; two young children when she was herself still a child,' said Sam.

'South of France?'

'Oh yes. Drowned in the Med,' confirmed Sam.

'Fuck.'

Treloar shook his head. 'No way. She would not have killed Julia. Suicide or accident. This coincidence may well be the exception that proves the rule.'

Chapter Sixty-Three

Coco and Tommy Holding were standing in the hall of The Salt Creek by the open front door when Treloar, Sam and Fitzroy, having retraced their steps from The Lundy Rooms through The Orangery, joined them.

'Ah there you are,' said Coco, 'I have Natalie's number for you.' She held up her phone.

'Would you call it please,' said Treloar.

She did so and *La Marseillaise* rang out from a phone in Fitzroy's hand. Coco cut the call.

'It was in a box of paints in The Lundy Rooms,' said Treloar. They had found it under a palette. There were two contacts: Coco and Cecily, mobile and work. Nothing more: no searches, no photos, nada. But Treloar would ask Jamie to check.

'Oh well.' said Coco despondently. She hated to disappoint.

'You say she was seen leaving on a bike?' Fitzroy asked.

Coco brightened. 'Yes, it's a bicycle, a grey and turquoise beast.'

'It's a nice bike,' said Tommy, 'Italian, Wilier Trestina Jena Hybrid, pretty new. It's an e-bike.'

'Fairly uncommon around here I would think,' said Fitzroy.

'You'd not be wrong there. New model and best part of four grand.'

'£4,000?' Sam was shocked, 'for a bicycle?'

'It's battery assisted. Only one like that I've seen around here.'

'But how did she get all her stuff here then?' Sam asked.

'Cecily brought her across.'

'Obviously,' said Treloar.

The Holdings both looked at them as if it was obvious, and it was.

Chapter Sixty-Four

Amélie was gone. Again. They had checked all the available CCTV. The only sighting was of her flying past Trebetherick Stores on her way to Rock. On her 'nice Italian bike'. As the footage rolled on, Sam could be seen driving up on her way to The Salt Creek. They had missed each other by five minutes. But as Fitzroy pointed out, had they passed, Sam would not have recognised Amélie. She was just another young body in a hooded sweatshirt and jeans; she looked like a boy.

So at 17:15, Treloar, Sam and Fitzroy let themselves into Cecily Farrant's new house in Church Street, Padstow. CHILL had provided the key-code to the gate which, luckily but strangely, had not been changed from when the house was on their books. Beyond the gate the front garden was gravel and grey stone pots of hardy Mediterranean herbs: the ultimate in low maintenance. The front door was painted in cobalt blue with shuttered windows to match.

Through the front door they found themselves in an open plan room with whitewashed walls, facing a white staircase which served to divide the space into two areas: one for cooking and dining, the other for comfortable seating. The furniture was sparse; plain wooden tables and chairs for dining, plain sofas in navy blue heavy cotton. In the living area the wooden floor was largely covered by a rug in a Greek meandros pattern in neutral tones. The entire room was dominated by an enormous photograph mounted under acrylic glass on the wall above the sofas.

'Greece,' said Sam. This whole place, from the Mediterranean garden to the whitewash and cobalt blue paintwork, it's all Greek. Her mother is Greek. And that,' she pointed to the photograph, 'that is Oia on Santorini.'

It showed a Mediterranean village of white buildings and windmills and blue-domed churches bathed in the warm light of a spectacular sunset.

'It's famous for the sunsets, how the light makes the buildings glow. It is spectacular, I've been there.'

Treloar grunted. 'You two check down here, I'll look upstairs'. He mounted the stairs two at a time.

On the first floor he found two bedrooms completely empty; not a stick of furniture, not a trace of occupancy. A large bathroom, with floor to ceiling tiling in more ultramarine and cobalt blue, a roll-top standalone bath and walk-in shower led through to a master bedroom. Here he found a brass bed with the ubiquitous white linens of holiday accommodation the world over, a hand-painted pine wardrobe and matching chest of drawers.

Again, the dominant feature was on the wall, above the bed. It was ghastly but riveting, clearly a portrait of Cecily Farrant but in the style of a Chinese woman with a green face, a print from a thousand walls. She was facing slightly to her left, unsmiling, wearing a golden kimono rather than the cheongsam of the original, her hands tucked into the sleeves. He was spellbound. It was an Amélie Bonnard.

'Phil! Phil!' Sam called.

He left the bedroom and dashed downstairs. Sam was clutching a stuffed A5 notebook, a triumphant look on her face.

'What is it?' Treloar asked.

'Cecily Farrant's journal.'

Fitzroy emerged from the kitchen. 'The fucking mother lode mate,' he said grinning widely. He was holding a prestige rifle in one hand and a sighting scope in the other.

Chapter Sixty-Five

It was late. They had collected a laptop and a gun bag embroidered with the name Freddie, together with the gun, the green-faced portrait and the journal and taken the lot back to The Count House's incident rooms. They had brought Cecily's Chanel tote bag from The Salt Creek and the list of its contents was pinned up next to a photograph of Cecily Allegra Farrant alongside those of the murder victims. Sam and Treloar had settled at the dining table and Fitzroy had joined them, bringing beers.

Cecily Allegra Farrant Tote bag contents

Found at The Salt Creek hotel 14 July

- Apple iPhone
- Hairbrush
- Tissues
- Waitrose hand-wash
- Molton Brown Fiery Pink Peppercorn hand-cream
- Chanel Rouge Coco Flash lipstick in Pulse
- Pink leather wallet containing: Barclaycard, American Express credit cards, HSBC debit card, DVLA driving licence card, all in the name of Cecily Allegra Farrant, folder of 6 1st class stamps, bank notes: 3 x £20, 4 x £10
- Pink leather purse: £4.58 In change
- Sterling silver compact mirror

- Cross propelling pencil
- A5 V&A Museum notebook – unused
- Microfibre glass cleaning cloth in pouch
- 6 red dyed feathers

The rifle and paraphernalia had been immediately sent by secure transport to the Central Hub of the National Ballistics Intelligence Service in Birmingham to join the bullet that had killed Dr Roz. But Fitzroy had asked his own people to look at the photographs.

'Are we sure this woman is who she claims to be?'

'How so?' asked Sam.

'Well, for a holiday letting agent she sure has some impressive gear. That rifle is a Czech CZ527: 26 inch barrel chambered for .223 calibre. Takes some skill to make that shot at that range with that small a calibre. Hell of a shot. And the suppressor or silencer if you must, is a Finnish Reflex T4 made by B R Tuote. Apparently, it sleeves over the barrel so it doesn't extend the length a great deal, and that maintains the weapon's balance. Clever. And the scope is a Konus F30 6-24x52. Not to get too technical, it lets in a lot of light. Italian; made in Verona. Know their glass. Very nice. So we are talking some very serious, very expensive high-end kit for a lady in the tourist industry. I didn't know your visitors caused that much trouble.'

Sam grinned despite herself. 'According to Diggory Keast, it's her only passion: shooting. No family, no friends to speak of, and she's done very well out of CHILL, so she has the funds.'

'One hell of a shot,' Fitzroy shook his head.

'I think you may have mentioned that,' said Treloar glumly.

Farrant's BMW Roadster had been secured and was still at the hotel with the forensics' team. The journal was a thick A5 notebook with a mock cream leather cover embossed with the initial C in purple and gold. Sam spread a number of loose pages across the table and picked up the notebook, opening it at the first of a number of marked pages.

'Listen to this.'

April

Well Gal, your Visit Cornwall *do wasn't the complete YAWN you'd expected was it! It was over in Polgwynn at Porthaven and you met Millie Lander again. Heavyweight now, doesn't stop eating! She told you their visitor numbers rocketed after that barmaid ran amok and they're still well up. Doing really well. People are just ghouls. You saw it again the other day when you watched Apollo 13 for the millionth time – YAWN YAWN until the shit hit the fan then the whole world was glued to their screens. What they want to bring em alive is fear, madness, mayhem, death. Weird and gory is good. Weirder and gorier is better!! Just what you need to get the numbers up for Pasco's festival!!*

> 'Christ, bloody ghoul tourism. Like rubber-neckers at motorway pile-ups!' Exclaimed Fitzroy.
>
> 'It's what Kitto and Diggory said that first day at St George's Cove where Ellis was found. But they were joking about murder being a new tourist activity. Who would have thought it would be a tourist attraction?' Sam asked.
>
> 'So it was love and lunacy. All this for Pasco Trefry, to ensure the success of his festival. Grotesque,' said Treloar.

You even met someone interesting! That lovely Canadian artist, in the galleried hall. Beautiful, stunning. Amazing green eyes. Staring at that ugly Gainsborough of Polgwynn in 1776. You couldn't get why, especially after seeing her own paintings of Porthaven Quay. Quite WONDERFUL, unusual. You'll enjoy seeing her again to talk about those seascapes for your Count House won't you? Hmmmmm?

AND you discovered that Polgwynn is on the market. The Hardcastles are selling up, retiring to Barbados!! Why was your new friend so excited about that?

Treloar spoke: 'That's it. That's the trigger. That's why she's come back. It was always about Polgwynn.'
'It's not a Gainsborough,' said Sam, 'she missed it.'

'Let me guess,' said Fitzroy, 'an original Amélie Bonnard?'

'Oh yes,' Treloar smiled, 'the flag on the flagstaff is black and white but it's not Cornish, it's the skull and crossbones; the birds in the White Lake are not herons, they're flamingos and there's a boy by the lake sitting on a surfboard. And Amélie is in it. She's sitting with the family under the cedar tree; it's unmistakeably her. Ochre believes that it fits with her sense of belonging at Polgwynn. It's the only self-portrait we know of.

Sam turned to the next marked page.

April, still
C'MON GAL!. You've got to get control over that bloody gang. If they carry on like that they're going to wreck CHILL and get you bloody well caught! Speak to Demmy, they're her mates. Find out who the idiot is, get her to get rid of him!! Or tell her to stop paying him. You just want SUPERFICIAL damage! Close enough to booking dates to force cancellations and piss off customers. REMIND HER! No major repairs unless you say so, none of the smashed toilet crap. That's going to put people off coming and mess with your own bookings. AND TOO MUCH ATTENTION. You'll have to let the pratt loose on another CHILL place or people will start to get suspicious if yours are all untouched!!

'Well Jesus, that explains the vandalism. I wonder who Demmy is, and the pratt?' Treloar looked at Sam, 'read on.'

April, still
Well Cec, your lunch with the Canadian girl at Caffè Rojano was interesting. Big eater for a tiny person - a whole Diavola Pizza, with extra chillies, saw it off before you were halfway through your tagliatelle! And she's so small!! Never thought of you as an art buff but you weren't too shabby at

all Gal, talking about the pics in the hall at Polgwynn again, and what Millie had said about the visitor numbers rocketing after the murders in the village.

Then philosophy Gal, crazy!? Thomas de something? Lived with Wordsworth in the Lake District. Good teacher, the artist. You didn't know he was obsessed with murder, only daffodils, ha. Bet you won't dig out the paper he wrote on it though – murder being one of the fine arts. Crap. He did like the opium though. Murder as art; whatever next Gal?

Fitzroy spoke: 'Eat when you can.'

'Coldstream Guards?' asked Sam.

'Jack Reacher,' he replied with a grin. 'And she's talking about Thomas de Quincey.'

Sam read on.

May
Well Cec, that Hicks has been causing grief again. Your poor Pasco, don't know how he puts up with him. You're so right. He's a shit. He can't get involved in your festival Gal. No fucking way!

Heard that you figured out bloody Soames Ellis has been on the take again. Shame for Tipsy. She's such a bimbo, but your Pasco relies on her so much Cec. Even Tipsy deserves better than that creep. She's only good for admin though!

Gal, that Canadian is just AMAZING. Not surprised you confirmed the seascapes for your COUNT HOUSE after seeing her at the seafront gallery. I know she's promised you something special. She's pretty sexy isn't she Cec! I wonder?

Three pairs of eyes turned from the dining table to a large painting hanging on the wall beside them. It was a long vista of an empty beach with the River Camel, captured from Padstow war memorial, in shades of red, vivid green and ultramarine. Strange but hypnotic and compelling. The signature in the bottom right hand corner was a stylised 'N'.

'Oh my God,' said Sam.

'Carry on,' said Treloar.

May still
Well Gal, philosophical AND helpful! Heard you talking about Polgwynn with Natalie. She said people like the macabre – it attracts like crazy – and that explains the visitor number rise. She said something weird and macabre would be a massive draw for your Pasco's festival. N said something Cornish would be really weird, an extra boost.

N said it would get the media flocking down here. When you said you didn't think you could kill anyone, N was really understanding. She got it. Said it would be different though if it was a mercy killing. Not really like killing someone straight off, cold. It'd be different, getting someone away from their struggle, out of their misery, their pain. Something gentle.

So Gal, you started. You're up and running. Went to Hicks' Bay View death camp didn't you? Lifted morphine from under his nose! He's such a waste of space, I know. EASY PEASY. No security whatsoever, I'm surprised he's not already been reported! Maybe when you're done.

June
So Gal, you and N have a plan! Love your little list. None of them will be missed. HA! THE MIKADO! You played Nanki-Poo in the school Christmas panto AND won best in show. You'll have to tell N. So, it's all Cornish themes, and you chose some each.

1 Jolyon Soames Ellis as stargazy pie

2 Titus Hicks as Gulliver visits the Eden Project

3 Suzanne Winters as a tub of clotted cream

4 TBA

5 DCI Treloar as a Cornish pasty

Sam indicated the loose drawings and notes on the table.

ELLIS NO. 1

Find suitable dune grass hiding place

- surfboards inc. Le Bleuet
- fence roll for pie crust
- spade

On the day

- morphine
- beer
- beach rug

HICKS NO. 2

- pots of poppies
- green garden twine
- tent pegs
- wicker basket

On the day

- morphine
- whisky
- tumblers

WINTERS NO. 3

- milkmaid banner for hot tub
- Cement
- sand
- cement dye
- water + heat connected
- mixer + blade
- magazine ID

On the day

- morphine
- wine + engraved glasses

TRELOAR NO. 5

- select property – clear bookings
- clear plastic sheeting for wrapper
- cement, sand, cement die
- mixer + blade
- sacks: swedes, potatoes, onions
- knives, cleaver, small chain saw, spare blades, batteries
- pots of oxeye daisies

On the day

- morphine + hypodermic

'Christ Phil looks like you've had a lucky escape!' Sam exclaimed.

'And you a vegetarian mate, that is a truly evil plan. These women have no souls.' Fitzroy grinned.

'Ha bloody ha. I told you pasties were bad news Sam. Read on.'

'OK this carries on the same entry.

Gal, do you know what N has against these Brit police? She chose these two, she wants Treloar to be last, a slow death, something special. Poor bastard, wonder what he did? Then you chose two, and you're still arguing about number four. I know you want to get Coco, Cec, but N is working for her just now. What about Demmy's pratt? He's so out of hand now, that would work, two birds with one stone. Genius!

June, still
Well Gal, you're really up and running now! Great start. Jolyon Ellis was such an idiot it was untrue. He thought he was on a promise, with you! Mad, you couldn't make it up. Piece of cake for you to get him to meet you at St George's Cove and he was never going to turn down a glass of bubbly. Good job you're fit, hardest part was piling all the bloody sand round him. Still, if you want something done properly do it yourself eh?

Cec, you've got to tell N to stop being so cryptic with the messages. Half the time even you don't get them, and you know her!

'So she acted alone,' said Treloar quietly. 'There was no moving of the body along the Coast Path or down the river, no gang of helpers sworn to secrecy. The poor bastard walked to his own death.'

Sam was turning pages in the journal, 'Listen here's Hicks.'

Well done Gal, number two done and dusted! Titus Hicks. So proud of his precious hot-house, his mini Eden. He couldn't wait to show off his latest 'baby'. It was so simple for you to fix his whisky when his back was turned. Dropped like a stone! Perhaps you overdid it with the dose. Still, worked well. But bugger! You broke a nail moving one of those bloody terracotta pots N was so insistent on. Still, another good job done. Ask a busy woman.

'Ask a busy woman what?' asked Sam.
'It's an adage,' Fitzroy explained, "If you want something doing, ask a busy woman."
'Yes,' I can see that,' Sam smiled.

Cec Gal, you got Demmy working well. No need to be worried about involving the gang after all. Demmy got that it was a special mission, that Lowenalands was a threat to CHILL, and that the grand opening needed to be screwed. No way you could have moved the cement and sand on your own. They even enjoyed mixing it. Sometimes you just do need a brutish male!

Management Skills? Way to go! Congratulate yourself Gal! Once they'd disappeared you had your own fun, dragging the dozy bint across to the hot tub from the tent. That sound as she slipped into the gloop was just great wasn't it?

'She's very proud of her achievements. Amazing how Amélie Bonnard can inspire such devotion and such willingness to follow orders, even to kill. Cecily Farrant didn't even know Suzanne Winters. Extraordinary. She must be something else. 'La belle dame sans merci, hath thee in thrall." Fitzroy said.

Treloar glared at him. 'John Keats,' said Sam tugging at a loose page.

'There's something else stuck in here with jam by the look of it . . . looks like a list. Here we go.'

Collect, need pick-up truck. Heavy.

Ordered, paid in advance. You're expected. Look older.
Need ID. Need sharp knife for cement bags.

30 bags white cement

7 bags white sand

6 tins yellow cement die

1 ~~nauf~~ cordless paddle mixer + spare battery
knauf
1 x 1 metre mixing paddle.

Take to Lowenalands, Glamping site, Nr Trevose Head.
ARRIVE 1.00 A.M.
2nd tent on left. Called Perranporth. Park by hot tub at back of Tent.
DO NOT ENTER TENT OR DO <u>ANYTHING</u> TO IT☠!!

Empty cement, sand + die into hot tub.
Fill tub to 20 cm from top with very warm water
Mix until thick + all mixed together
Take all away. SHUT GATE!
Cement + sand bags + die cartons to tip tomorrow
Return paddle mixer, paddle + battery

'Look,' Sam pointed to the note, 'she's misspelled 'dye' as 'die'.

'Very Freudian,' said Fitzroy.

Well Cec, how about that? BUGGER ALL! SOOO disappointing. Poor response by Polgwynn standards. Poor you. Perhaps everybody really did hate Ellis and Hicks, and the Winters woman wasn't local, so? Short-term WOW but fizzled out and zilch international coverage. I know you told N you needed to up the game, get someone better known but she was adamant you stick to the plan. I know it's not great that she said no to Coco Holding and THEN says she gets next dibs for No. 4. JUST NOT FAIR Gal. Sounds like she can be quite scary, and very fierce. Weird for an artist or what?

WOW Gal. Great timing or what? TRIUMPH! PERFECT! FUCKING GENIUS! Dr Roz is coming! She's going to open the festival for your lovely Pasco. Apparently she went to his college at Cambridge or some such shit, and she's getting married first at your favourite bitch Coco's new hotel! It's INSPIRED Cec! She's FAMOUS, the nation's darling and she's got a direct link to the festival! PUBLICITY CITY! Don't tell N, it'll be a brilliant surprise for her.

She's going to be so impressed by your boldness and your aim. AND it's the best fitting Cornish theme yet – the Padstow mermaid! It's fucking local! And (nobody will believe this) the tart's only going to be wearing a mermaid wedding dress. Your Jeannie's sister heard her 'people' talking about it in the bar at The Old Customs House. YOU COULD NOT MAKE IT UP. So a lovely surprise for N.

Anyway Cec Gal, she seems obsessed right now with her media campaign against this Treloar. Fuck knows what he did to her. Any ideas? Weird. He's just a local plod. V. tasty though. Perhaps he turned her down. Ha! Brave man! And she's off to Dodman Point AGAIN! What the hell is the attraction of a bloody headland on the south coast when there are plenty around here?

'Dodman Point?' Fitzroy asked.

'It's just along the coast from Polgwynn,' Treloar answered, 'OK next entry.'

WOULD YOU BELIEVE IT GAL? You saw N and she was so totally pissed off. At first she stared at you, speechless. You thought it was awe, admiration, but it turned out to be blind fucking fury. She'd heard about Dr Roz, how could she not. And asked if it was you. You said you thought she'd be thrilled. 'It was!' you told her. So what if you didn't ask? SURPRISE!!

I watched you, and her. She just glared, then walked away. If looks could kill! What was that? You think she's an ungrateful cow, you're right. Who the fuck does she think she is with her bloody cryptic texts. If she wants something doing why can't she spell it out? No wonder people get the wrong idea. She's only got herself to blame for Christ's sake. The media are descending in hordes!

They're bound to visit The Salt Creek so there'll be photos of her fucking screens and she'll get loads of free publicity and loads of work and all because of YOU! THANKLESS BITCH! It's not as if you got to make your choices in the first place remember. You were thinking about it. She came up with the names and you just agreed to her plan. They were on your list anyway. You're right Gal, IT'S NOT FAIR!

July
See Cec, all is forgiven! N's called you now, back to her normal self. Probably just jealous that your mermaid bride was the best Cornish theme and the best death! ANYWAY, enjoy your meet at the Salt Creek, maybe there'll be more than just coffee. Don't crow, you know what she's like. I'd heard she was just finishing up there, wonder if she's done yet? Maybe you could persuade her to make Coco No. 4b? All's well that ends well Gal.

July 14 11.00 COFFEE WITH N AT THE SALT CREEK

Sam closed the journal and the three sat in silence with their own thoughts. Sam spoke first.

'So who took that final dose of morphine to The Salt Creek, Cecily or Amélie?'

'We'll never know for sure, unless Cecily wakes up and tells us, but my money'd be on Cecily,' said Treloar. 'Having gone 'rogue' with the killing of Dr Roz she had nothing left to lose with 'N' so why not get rid of Coco too, who we now know she resented and wanted dead as part of the plan all along. I'd guess that Amélie saw the opportunity to be rid of a loose cannon and took it.'

'But why?' asked Sam.

'This is Amélie; why not? Being disobedient? Being tiresome? Being a witness? Being alive?'

Fitzroy was staring into space oblivious to the conversation. Finally he spoke:

'The date; today's date. It's Le Quatorze Julliet; Bastille Day, La Fête Nationale. The French equivalent of Independence Day.'

Treloar smiled, despite himself, as Fitzroy continued.

'She was totally outclassed. She had absolutely no idea who she was dealing with.'

'Nobody ever does with Amélie,' said Treloar softly.

'You do,' Sam said.

'I certainly do now.'

'Well, we've got her now. Let's put out an alert and an all ports' warning.'

The two men looked her with solemn faces.

'What? What's wrong with you two? It's her! She's named in here - all right it says Natalie and N – but it's her!'

'What you have Sam,' said Fitzroy, 'is conjecture and circumstance. You have your killer. You have the gun and the morphine. You have nothing concrete on Amélie; just the ramblings of a woman – who is in a coma – and is certainly of unsound mind. What did Ochre say?'

'Lunacy,' Treloar whispered.

'But the green-faced painting in her bedroom?' Sam pleaded.

'Commissioned? Fitzroy was exasperating Sam.

'The cornflowers, the poppies? It's her and she was there! At The Salt Creek, she tried to kill Cecily!'

'Could be suicide,' Fitzroy was adamant.

'But it's her. I know it; you know it!'

'WE HAVE NOTHING ON HER!' Treloar erupted from his seat.

The tension was broken by Fitzroy's phone sounding an incoming text. He read it, frowning.

'Sorry guys, gotta go. Phil mate I need to take the Bonneville.'

'No worries, I'll get a lift. I'll walk you out.'

'Bye Sam,' Fitzroy smiled at her and raised his hand.

'Fitz,' she said sullenly.

The two men walked out the front door and over to the Triumph Bonneville.

'We must be able to get these bastards for something,' Treloar hissed.

'Sorry to say I'm not so sure. Firstly let's take our sharpshooter. We have the gun, the bullet, the ballistics will match I'd bet, and we have the journal. But the Crown Prosecution Service will never go for it, not whilst she's in a coma: unfit to plead. If she comes round, and if she's declared mentally fit, which seems a stretch given she's killed four people out of unrequited love, well they might go for the murder of Dr Roz but the others? You know the CPS these days. The others, there's nothing but the journal. There's always the criminal damage and conspiracy but if she remains in a coma or dies . . .'

'I know, I know.'

'Then there's your enigmatic Mademoiselle Bonnard. There you're relying on Cecily Farrant waking up *and* being prepared to speak against her. Again, all you have is the journal and she uses a nickname. There is no witness to Bonnard administering the morphine; for all anyone can prove it could have been a suicide attempt through remorse using the same method as she used on her first two victims. Plausible. You might be able to track her online activity, hacking the Masterson magazine to lure Winters, but from what all the techies tell us she's too smart to leave a trail.'

'You are really making my day. And don't tell me; Masterson? Hope in hell.'

'I wouldn't be that optimistic. His hands are clean. Just because his media was used? Well he could claim to be another victim. You'll never prove facilitation. He's too rich and too well-connected for you to touch with anything you've got.'

'Fucking marvellous. So all we'll get is a few troubled teenagers who'll get community service and counselling.'

'Let it go mate.'

'So Amélie Bonnard wins again?'

'For now. Remember Ecclesiastes Chapter 3.'

"To every thing there is a season'?'

'Well, more Verse 6: 'A time to get and a time to lose'. Her time to lose will come.'

As it was, the CPS were not at all relaxed about letting Cecily Farrant slide. She was directly implicated in the murders of four people. She was a rare beast, a female serial killer, and one of her victims had been a national treasure. Whilst theoretically, all should be equal before the law, in practice, all were not equal before the media, politicians and the public. John Donne may well have written "any man's death diminishes me", but he did not live in the age of the fourth and fifth estates, with television creating personal friends, beloved by the masses of its stars.

If Cecily Farrant were to wake from her coma, she would find herself prosecuted to the full extent of the law; the CPS were preparing a solid comprehensive case against her. She was being transferred and soon she would be in the secure wing of Exmoor prison under lock and key.

Fitzroy pulled on his helmet.

'Bodies to bury?' Treloar asked with a sad smile.

'Always mate,' Fitzroy grinned, pulling the other man into a bear hug, 'You know where we are when you come to your senses.'

'I'll get the spare leathers and helmet back to the bike company and let them know you'll be in touch about the bike. Thanks again Ben. I couldn't have got through without you.'

'No worries. And of course, I got to meet Arwen! Do give the lovely Lucia my fondest regards and tell her I'm devastated that I had to leave without farewells.'

'I'll give your apologies to *my sister*.'

'Oh and mate, here's a parting gift.'

Fitzroy reached into his shirt pocket and pulled out a folded piece of paper which he handed to Treloar. Written in blue/black ink were a mobile telephone number and a name: Ruby Russell.

'What the?'

'Yeah well, you are such a wuss you needed a kick. Call her. She's interested. I spoke to Tulip. Just fucking do it.'

The two men hugged again and Fitzroy mounted his steed and sped out into the darkness.

Chapter Sixty-Six

It was growing dark as Sgt Diggory Keast drove Treloar into the courtyard of Lost Farm Barn. He climbed from the patrol car and unloaded the painting from Church Street and the two artwork folders from The Lundy Rooms.

'Thanks Diggory and goodnight.'

'Goodnight Sir.'

As the police car headed back down the lane, Treloar savoured the near silence and the cool air scented by the night flowers from his mother's pots which lined the barn's walls: night phlox, evening primrose and tuberose. Through the glass atrium which connected the two original barn structures that made up Lost Farm Barn, he could make out the glow of moonlight on the sea in Mount's Bay and the distant lights of Penzance.

A sudden burst of female laughter reached the courtyard from the rear garden. He recognised the deep throaty tone of his sister Lucia. She would be with Ochre. He carried his burden across the courtyard into the kitchen through the stable door and placed the artwork on the floor, leaning against the kitchen table. The glass doors to the garden were open wide and the two women were sitting at the outdoor table with two of the cats: Lola and Messi. A bottle of Chianti, two glasses and a pile of photographs stood between them. He smiled as they all looked content and settled. But he knew that the offerings he had brought would bring an end to their tranquillity.

'Hola!' Lucia cried, sensing him standing in the gloom of the unlit kitchen.

'Is there any left in that bottle?' he asked.

'Of course!' Lucia replied standing, 'I'll fetch a glass.'

Treloar held up his hand to stop her. 'No bring it inside please, the bottle, I have some artwork to show you both.'

They gathered around the kitchen table.

'Amélie Bonnard?' Ochre asked and Treloar nodded. 'I've never seen her work. I did think of visiting Polgwynn, but somehow it just seemed ghoulish. I have seen some of the pastiches on the website and I can appreciate the humour and the cleverness but obviously there is no . . . texture. Only in the flesh, so to speak, can you judge the skill, the execution, the quality of the work.'

Treloar lifted the heavy ornate gilt frame onto the table. 'Well I'm sure you recognise this. It was above the bed in the main bedroom.'

'Good grief. Well, obviously it's after *Chinese Girl* by Vladimir Tretchikoff, the most reproduced painting in the history of art. The subject is obviously Cecily Farrant, and the colours are skewed: the green of the face is more cadmium than viridian.'

'It's the colour of a Granny Smith's apple,' said Lucia, 'it's hideous.'

'It's the colour of envy,' said Ochre, 'it's cruel, but it's brilliantly painted.'

'Above the bed Flip?' asked Lucia.

Treloar nodded

'Well I wouldn't have it in my home. If I were this Cecily Farrant I would have hated it! She must be . . .'

'Mad?' Ochre interrupted, staring at Treloar. He put the painting on the floor and lifted the marbled Clairefontaine artwork folder onto the table, opening it to a portrait.

Ochre nodded. 'Well obviously it's Cecily again. This time, Caravaggio: *Medusa*. The shocked expression on the face of the severed head is stunning.' Ochre studied the painting closely. 'The snakes representing the hair are so vivid. Again, masterful.'

'I'm not surprised she didn't put this on the wall,' said Lucia, 'it is espantoso.'

'Yes,' said Treloar, 'it is frightful, literally so.'

'This was painted more recently I think,' said Ochre, 'it's not framed or totally finished. I would say that the artist's opinion of the subject had changed by this time. This expresses, well, contempt and hatred, real detestation.'

'Yes,' said Treloar, 'by the time this was painted, Cecily

had broken ranks, blown the plan and sealed her own fate.'

'Is everything you have brought to show me so unrelentingly grim?' asked Ochre with a sad smile.

'Oh no. Not at all. Look,' and with that he lifted the second folder onto the table and opened it to the first painting.

'Oh my,' Ochre smiled, 'now this is a very different story.' She was looking at the painting of the naked woman. 'This is after Pierre Bonnard and the subject is not Cecily Farrant. This painting expresses respect and love, fondness.'

'This is Julia Honor,' said Treloar, as is this,' he turned to *The Palm* copy.

'Another Bonnard. It is truly great work,' said Ochre. 'What will become of them, the paintings?

'I have no idea. They are not evidence. They belong to Amélie Bonnard. She may try to recover them or leave them where they were painted, at The Salt Creek. We will return them there. She may well leave them as she did with the paintings at Polgwynn. This is also Julia Honor,' Treloar turned to the last of the paintings.

It was the portrait of a woman. Her right profile was bathed in light, her head cast back, throat bared, eyes closed, lips parted. Her hands were clasped to hold her raised knees. She was dressed in a loose nightgown of the palest blue silk falling from her right shoulder.

Lucia stared at the painting in stunned silence, open-mouthed. Ochre studied the canvas for some time before clearing her throat to speak.

'*Mary Magdalene in Ecstasy* by Artemisia Gentileschi. This is a wonderful thing my friends. This should be in a national gallery. This is the finest piece here. It is in a different class from the others and they are very fine work. This is love, both physical and spiritual. It is genius.'

'This should be on a wall,' said Lucia pointing at the face, 'this woman must love this portrait.'

'This woman is dead,' said Treloar flatly.

'No!' cried Lucia, 'she is so beautiful, so adored, so . . . alive! This Amélie must be devastada.'

'One would think so,' Treloar said, 'but knowing her . . .'

Chapter Sixty-Seven

By the following morning the euphoria of her release from enchantment had worn off to be replaced by a cold, rational fury at the years she had wasted on this man. Sam had had it. Enough. Treloar had always been a maverick; it was a part of the attraction. The danger, the bravery, the non-conformity. It had thrilled her; but no more. She had moved on. She had been part of a different policing world, where the rules were essential and absolute, not for picking and choosing. Look at Jamie Deverell. OK, OK, he was brilliant, effective, and fast.

But his work was often illegal and could not support a prosecution. Fruit of the tainted tree. It was a form of cheating. His argument had always been that Jamie provided information not evidence; he was the gold prospector who found the nuggets and then Treloar would send in the miners; the digital forensics experts.

Yes, Treloar had been suspended, with no access to the proper channels, the legitimate technical resources, but she knew in her heart he would have turned to Jamie Deverell regardless. And yes, it had been personal, he had been under attack, but even so. And now he was back within the fold and still bending the rules with Ben Fitzroy. Christ, they brought out the worst in each other like some puerile game of double-dare.

Sam was what she was and she was too fixed to be anything other. She was the product of a solid, safe upbringing by sensible, responsible parents who had extolled educational holidays, piano and tennis lessons. No risk, no rebellion. Samantha Scott: hockey captain, head prefect, best in form; that hateful epithet: a nice girl. Oh she looked at Lucia and saw her glamour, her beauty; at Ochre and saw her talent, her individuality; even at poor dead Amy, and saw her fairy loveliness, her waif-like vulnerability. And here she was:

steady, attractive, reliable. Like a bloody Volvo.

And she had fucked up. She had missed things: the name on the surfboard, the poppies at Hicks', the cornflowers on the banner round the hot-tub. She had missed things and it was his fault because he distracted her. He was tarnishing her reputation, making her look . . . incompetent.

And then there had been that lunch with Lucia; that long awaited, inevitable conversation.

Chapter Sixty-Eight

Seafood on Stilts was located over two floors of a building on the quayside in St Ives. Owned by chef Jowan Nancarrow, it was now largely run by his elder son Jory and his chef girlfriend, Treloar's youngest sister, Beatriz known as Bee. The upper floor was a formal setting with white linens and distanced tables, but downstairs was more relaxed, with whitewashed tables and cotton napkins and it was here that Sam found Lucia scrolling through images on a camera.

'Querida! Look at you! A great new haircut.'

The two women embraced and kissed cheeks.

'Lucia. It is so lovely to meet up properly. I've missed our weekends in Barcelona.'

'Then come! Come! You are always welcome, just check I'll be home and come. I am to go back this weekend. The boys are coming back from their father's in Milan. They will be fat with all the bad food their Nonna has been feeding them!'

'Well that's good to know. It's been a hellish few weeks as you know, especially for your brother.'

'Yes. That's why I came. We couldn't really speak, you and I, that night at Flip's, not with all those people. But I understand it is nearly over, your hellish time, and I'm sure Flip will clear up this suspension business once and for all. I was very happy to meet Ben Fitzroy. He has Flip's back. And he has other good people on his side. Now, let's eat and then we will talk.'

That sounds ominous thought Sam as she picked up the menu.

'I have spoken to Bee this morning, although she's not here today, she's at the sister place, the *Cuttlefish Café*, and she has said that we must have the hake with lemon and bay. And to start, I shall have the grilled sardines. You?'

Sam, who hated fiddly fish and preferred all her

seafood to come in batter, had been well brought up and did not want to offend, so she also went with the hake. But, she absolutely drew the line at sardines and so chose the crab-cakes to start.

Their food came and Sam had to concede that the hake was a revelation, luckily a meaty fish with just one bone. They reminisced about happy times in Barcelona and Lyon but as they cleared their plates Lucia's expression turned from animated to serious.

'Sam. I am your friend, you know this. And as your friend, I must tell you something that you will not want to hear.'

Sam's heart sank but her brain told her what was coming.

'I know how you feel about my brother. I have known this since you and I first met. But it will never be as you hope. Never. I am sad to tell you this but Flip does not feel for you as you do for him.

Sam was silent.

'He is your good friend, he is your colleague and he trusts and values you greatly. But he does not love you and he will never love you as you want. You must accept this truth and you must move on. I know this is hard but it is the reality. I cannot stand aside and watch you continue with this hopeless dream. You are a beautiful intelligent woman and you are wasting your life. You will find someone who loves you as you want to be loved. But it will not be Félipe. I know this; I have been where you are. Trust me, this is not the end of hope it is just the end of this hope. I am sad but I had to speak.

As Sam sat facing this lovely woman, so like Treloar in many ways, hearing the words she had dreaded, but feared were coming, extraordinarily, she felt an enormous wave of relief wash over her. Enfin: liberté.

Since her return from Lyon, she had increasingly missed her work and lifestyle in France. She had actually, rationally, started to question Treloar's attitudes; his stubbornness, which she has always thought of as determination; his recklessness, which she had always seen as courage. She had been a sad, deluded fool.

'Sam? Sam are you OK?'

She was dragged from her reveries by Lucia's concerned voice.

'Lucia I am fine. I have known this truth for some time if I'm honest, but I just did not want to face the fact. My heart, and to be fair my loins, have been overruling my head. Thank you. Thank you, really, for your courage and honesty. I know this cannot have been easy for you and you are a true friend.'

'Always querida,' said Lucia sadly.

'I will move on, I want to move on, so let's speak no more of this and talk pudding!'

Lucia reached across the table and clasped her friend's hands.

As Lucia extolled the virtues of the various desserts Sam looked around her. The menu had been created by Beatriz Treloar. The enormous acrylic mermaid mural on the wall behind Lucia had been painted by Ochre Pengelly. Christ these people were an incestuous clan. What she had once found endearing was suddenly stultifying. Could she really see herself living on some far-flung farm raising three children and growing fucking herbs? This was not her world; had never been her world; could never be her world. She was made for more than this.

They made their farewells and went their separate ways with promises of Barcelona.

Sam had known for some time of course. She had seen the way he looked at that woman at the Ally Ally Oh Festival meeting at the Padstow Hub, the one with Tulip Khan. She had seen him look at Amy Angove like that, but never her; not even close. It was never going to be for her and Treloar. She had been deluding herself for too long. And what was keeping her in this tourist-infested parochial backwater anyway? She had seen the wider world; tasted its wonders. If not for him, to be with him, there was no reason to stay. Congreve's often paraphrased lines from The *Mourning Bride* burst into her mind:

> 'Heav'n has no rage, like Love to Hatred turn'd,
> Nor Hell a Fury, Like a Woman scorn'd.'

That was it; what she was feeling: rage and fury.

Enough was enough.

Time to go.

As she walked from the restaurant to her car, she pulled her phone out of her pocket, scrolled through her contacts and placed the call.

'Puis-je parler à Commissaire Sylvain Godard s'il vous plaît? . . . Samantha Scott.'

'Sam, ça va?'

'Je voudrais revenir. Est-ce possible?'

'You want to come back? Mais bien sûr, of course that is good news for us. Good news for Interpol. Have you spoken to The Chief there?'

'Not yet. But it was a condition of my return to the UK. I mean my return was conditional.'

'So there will be no problems?'

'None. I want to come back to Lyon. As soon as I can.'

'D'accord. J'attendrai votre retour. Bonne journée.'

'Bonne journée.'

Chapter Sixty-Nine

Treloar was woken from a deep, dreamless sleep by his phone's penetrating chime. At first he was disoriented as he always was when wakened suddenly and in a strange place; not his bed at Lost Farm Barn or Cove Farm. He had decided to stay overnight at The Count House. The team had spent the day clearing the property of all their paperwork, whiteboards, phones, cabinets, computers, printers, leaving the place as if untouched by their presence apart from the rubbish bags in the courtyard filled with empty pizza boxes, coffee grounds, beer bottles, Coke tins and pasty wrappers. He had felt exhausted and deflated. Better to crash out there than to crash on the way back to Lost Farm Barn. He looked at the screen as he swiped it: 04.17. What the hell?

'She's gone! She's gone!'

He recognised Leah Kidd, breathless and clearly in a state of panic.

'Leah?'

'She's gone! Oh my God she's gone!'

'Leah calm down. Leah! Quiet! Tell me what's happened . . . slowly.'

'She's gone and she's taken nothing! Nothing!'

'When?'

'I don't fucking know! I just woke up and went to get some water and she's gone. She was really pissed off last night. Tomorrow her mother is sending a helicopter to collect her from The Salt Creek. She so does not want to leave but it's the 'family holiday' in Sardinia. I s'pose it didn't help when I told her I'm staying on; my brother's coming down.'

'You're sure she's not just gone outside to the beach for a swim or to watch the sunrise or something?'

'No way. Her phone is here; she never leaves her phone. Her beach bag is here and her mermaid towel and her swimming shoes. She'd never go in the sea without them she's paranoid about those weever fish.'

He could here Leah rummaging around, moving things, a door opening and then a gasp.

'Oh no, no, no! She's taken that fucking inflatable dolphin sit-on. She knows not to go out on that on her own!'

'Go outside and look along the beach and in the surf. See if you can spot her.'

'She's gone out to sea. I know she has. She's gone out to kill herself and then her mother is going to kill me!'

'Leah! Focus! Call the guys, get out there and search the shoreline. You can do this, I know you can. I'm coming.'

'Promise?' Leah sounded for once like the girl she was, not the cocky young woman she portrayed.

''I'm coming now. Call the guys,' but before he could end the call a desolate wailing assailed him.

'No! no! no!' she sobbed.

'Leah! What is it?'

'Her turtle, she's left her turtle! She has a jade turtle on a silver chain she got in Bali. She always wears it, always. It's here by the kettle. I've always admired it and she's left it for me, here where she knew I'd find it. She's going to kill herself; she's going to die.'

This did not bode well Treloar knew.

'Leah! Call the guys. Get out there looking. Keep in touch. I'm coming.'

'Save her, please save her,' she whispered.

The roads would be quiet but even so. The best bet was to go by water. Treloar rang Kitto Betties who lived in Padstow. He would certainly know somebody with a boat. He did. A mate with a ten metre RIB – rigid inflatable boat – used to take tourists on seal and dolphin watching trips.

'Get to North Quay Sir, I'll fetch the keys and meet you there. Ten minutes.'

Treloar was running before he reached the street.

When he reached the harbour he spotted Betties, true to his word, in the large RIB, engine running. Treloar ran the length of the quay, leapt aboard and the two men headed out into the estuary at full throttle.

'I've asked around,' Betties shouted over the roar, 'and

nobody coming in has seen anything. It's all calm and quiet out there.'

They headed out along the Camel into open sea, passing Rock and Trebetherick but keeping close to the shore, following the channel. The water was high, but habit kept him following the marked channel; like others familiar with the entrance to Padstow, he knew the sands could be treacherous. As Betties steered the boat Treloar scoured the shoreline with a pair of binoculars. Nothing. Then Betties took a call.

'Something's been found at Trestram Cove. It's just coming up.'

Not another early morning dog walker Treloar thought darkly. But it was an early fishermen heading to the beach.

As they rounded the rocks at Greenaway, Treloar spotted a man with two long rods standing on the beach above the rock shelf, phone in hand. Running along the coastal path towards him was Joel, followed closely by Ravi with Leah trailing in their wake. Bouncing against the rocks of the cove was a partially deflated blue dolphin, caught by its tether. There was a still body, prone on the sand at the fisherman's feet and a small figure seated beside it rocking back and forth, arms clasped around bent knees: Viola.

'There she is Sir, that's Viola Lawrence!'

'I know Kitto,' said Treloar sombrely, 'but whose body?'

Siegfried "Salty" Carew. He had arranged to meet Viola on the beach, but she, unable to sleep, had arrived early and gone out on her inflatable. One last glorious trip. He had arrived to see her being dragged out by a freak wave. Wading in, he had reached her, lifted her from the inflatable and carried her to the shore only to make the fatal mistake of going back for her precious dolphin.

He had lost his footing and been swept off his feet and out, before being washed ashore at Trestram Cove. Viola, helpless, had run along the beach following his struggling progress only to find his dead body. Nobody had the heart to tell the girl that he couldn't swim. This time there would be no escaping the helicopter for Viola Lawrence.

Chapter Seventy

Treloar was suspended. Again. Chamberlain had called him. Again. Romilly Hawkins, the Police and Crime Commissioner, had insisted on a full investigation into the media stories about the historic cases. In a moment of rare, if misplaced humour, paraphrasing Oscar Wilde's lady Bracknell, she had apparently referred to his 'carelessness' in failing to bring murder suspects to trial. 'Carelessness, not misfortune surely, to lose so many suspects to the Grim Reaper!'

Chamberlain was furious, as was the Chief Constable, but she had friends with power and money and influence; political friends. His best chance was to wait for his allies to prove him blameless and, if all else failed, to wait for Hawkins to slip up or be voted out in the next election.

He had to admit, if only to himself, that the outcomes of that summer's cases were totally unsatisfactory. He knew Amélie Bonnard had coerced Cecily Farrant into the killing spree. He knew that Demelza Gellis and her pals had carried out the holiday property vandalism as paid agents of Cecily. He knew that Siegfried Carew had abducted Viola Lawrence, and that she was lying about her memory of what had happened.

He knew all of this, but through lies, evasions, what the CPS were calling 'plausible alternatives' - the calls and texts between Demelza and Cecily could well have been about cleaning work - and the twin facts that the main suspect was in a coma and Carew was dead; well, no prosecutions yet. And worst of all Amélie had eluded him. Again.

Chamberlain did have good news though. He had been told that Treloar had 'a powerful friend in far-flung places'. Somebody, at a 'very high level' in government, was lobbying on his behalf. And the Chief Superintendent had assured Treloar that he was not giving up on any prosecutions. He would keep pushing the CPS and reinforcing the police cases. In a bitter irony, Rabid Romilly was most keen to pursue the vandals, driven by the twin gods of property and tourism.

And then the bombshell about Sam.

She was going back to Lyon and she hadn't said a word to him! Treloar had said he would resign but Chamberlain had asked him to chill for a while. Sam's unexpected decision would play into their hands; it would leave them short-handed and whilst Hawkins might be a pain in the arse, she was a politician and self-interest would always prevail. Their success reflected on her, as did their failure. The despicable coward in Treloar just felt relief that the Sam issue was going away.

The Black Tor foot ferry ran from Padstow's North Quay across the Camel to discharge passengers on the beach near the Rock Quarry car park. It ran every 20 minutes and took 5 to 10 minutes in contrast to the 30 to 40 it would take to drive. Treloar left The Count House and strolled through the town to the quay. He had choices; he had transferrable skills.

He could work at Cove Farm with his parents and Eva, giving his parents more time to spend together to make up for the lost years. He could develop a market garden at Lost Farm Barn to supplement the family fruit and vegetable supply business. He could design and build property, Christ, he had virtually handled his barn conversion from a ruin single-handedly. He could go back into marine conservation.

And there was always Ben. Fitzroy had been after him for years to join forces in his secret specialist spook squad. So on reflection, it wouldn't be Ben lobbying on his behalf; he wanted him out of the police. No, it had to be Viola Lawrence's father, grateful for his daughter's deliverance. That was the only thing that made sense.

No panic.

He stepped off the ferry onto the damp sand of Daymer Bay and looked back across the river to where Dr Roz had fallen, and up at the bluff from where Cecily Farrant had fired. Then he turned left to head along the beach to Trebetherick.

It was a glorious summer's afternoon and the beach

was busy with laughing children, but he turned his back on the crowds and headed up onto the coastal path. As he passed Broadagogue Cove on his left, a line from the John Betjeman poem *Trebetherick* drifted into his mind from childhood. Not the more famous, "Sand in the sandwiches, wasp in the tea" but his preferred rhyming line, "Squelch of the bladder-wrack waiting for the sea". Squelch: an irresistible word for a boy.

He followed the path round towards Hayle Bay and ahead of him lay Polzeath Beach and at the top of the sands, Strandloper and Ruby Russell.

Chapter Seventy-One

On the cliff edge west of Porthaven quay stands Penmol. The house takes its name from the Cornish meaning 'bare end'. It is well-named, standing at the edge of the cliff, at the end of a gated road leading seawards from the main Polgwynn drive, at the end of the road for Hugo Brookes. Formerly part of the Polgwynn estate, the looming former dower house with its crenelated towers and mullioned windows, was lost by David Pentreath, Amélie's great grandfather, to Brookes' grandfather in a card game in Paris in the 1930s.

The telephone rang and Hugo Brookes walked the length of the hall from the sunroom at the rear of the house to answer.

'Brookes.'

'Dr Hugo Brookes?' asked a pleasant female voice.

'Yes, this is Dr Hugo Brookes. To whom am I speaking?'

'This is Inspector Samantha Scott of Devon & Cornwall Police. I don't know if you remember me? We met after the murder of Oliver Osborne?'

'Of course I remember you. And congratulations on your promotion, you were a sergeant then as I recall.'

'Thank you, yes.'

'To what do I owe the pleasure this morning?'

'I'm calling to ask whether you have heard or seen anything of Amélie Bonnard recently?'

'My. That is a name from the past Inspector. No, no I have had no contact with Amélie since that murderous summer. I think it highly unlikely she would return to these parts. What would bring her back?'

'Polgwynn is on the market Dr Brookes.'

'Indeed it is. But where would she find the money? I do not imagine that she has the capital for such a purchase.'

'Perhaps not, but friends perhaps?'

'Perhaps, but I do not count myself amongst them, and certainly do not possess the funds to buy Polgwynn.'

'So you have had no contact?'

'None whatsoever.'

Sam sighed. 'Ah well, thank you for your time Dr Brookes.' She said, completing her final task of the investigation.

'My pleasure Inspector,' and with that he hung up and strolled back along the hallway into the bright light of the sunroom with its panoramic views across to Dodman Point.

'That was that female police officer, Samantha Scott.'

'Oh yes, I remember her. Pretty thing obviously doting on her boss Treloar.'

Brookes took his seat at the old wicker table and smiled at the small woman opposite him.

'I was so sorry to read of the death of your friend Julia in The Times.'

'Yes that was sad. But towards the end she had become very . . . nécessiteuse, you say, needy?'

Hugo Brookes physically felt the temperature drop around him. Surely not? But he continued, if shaken.

'Well my dear, it is a total delight to see you, as ever. And of course you may stay as long as you wish.'

'Thank you Hugo. I always wanted to finish that wall,' she said pointing to the former outside wall of the house, now the backdrop to the sunroom, 'the balance is not quite right: too many cornflowers, I think.'

As he watched, she turned and crossed the sunroom to the open door to the garden. She raised her arm and let something fall from her hand. Caught by the breeze, it drifted away across the lawn towards the sea: a red feather.

Epilogue

**ALLY ALLY OH FESTIVAL
TO STEAM AHEAD**

THE CAMEL COURIER can report that after much soul-searching and consultation with families the ALLY ALLY OH festival is to go ahead on 26 September as planned. It is understood that the Chair of the festival committee, Pasco Trefry, was intending to cancel out of respect for the victims of this summer's murder spree, but an intervention from Bajinder Wood, widower of Dr Rosamond Lacey Wood, and reassurances from the local community have persuaded him that the event should proceed.

Mr Wood, speaking to THE CAMEL COURIER said, "Roz would have wanted this event to take place as it is promoting marine conservation, an issue very dear to her." Cornish artist and author, Ochre Pengelly, has agreed to open the festival in Dr Roz's place. Tim Strathearn, Dr Roz's agent has also spoken to THE CAMEL COURIER. "Dr Roz would be delighted that this event will proceed, dedicated to her legacy as an ecological warrior."

THE
ALLY ALLY OH
FESTIVAL
26TH - 30TH SEPTEMBER
MARINE CONSERVATION EXPOSITION
BEACH COMBER STALLS
GIG RACES
DRIFTWOOD & SEAGLASS DEMONSTRATIONS
DRAGON BOAT RACING
RNLI RESCUE DEMO
SEAFOOD STALLS
PIRATES' PARADE
ART EXHIBITION
FISH COOKERY MASTERCLASSES
OCHRE PENGELLY TO OPEN 10.00 26TH
PADSTOW, ROCK & CAMEL ESTUARY

About the author

A story crafting wordsmith met a psychologist and L A Kent was born.

L A Kent is the pen name of Louise Harrington and Andy Sinden. Having lived in Cornwall for 20 years L A Kent writes not only about the dark, evil, obsessed, and sometimes plain mad and bad characters appearing on the dark side of their books, but also empathetically about the county, its people and their lifestyle. And bring to life Cornwall and the visitors that descend from the UK, mainland Europe and further afield, even as the villains put people to death.

Prior to writing, both travelled extensively in their corporate lives, spending time in the USA, Canada, Australia, Brazil, Hong Kong, Malaysia, Taiwan and Singapore to name but a few, as well as frequently spending time in most Western European countries.

They lived and worked in South Africa for two years, also visiting Namibia and Zimbabwe and bring these world experiences to overseas scenes in the DI Treloar crime thrillers.

Credits

Thanks and credits are due to Laura Smith and Aune Head Arts, photoeverywhere.co.uk, and Harryarts for the use and reworking of the Stargazy Pie, Eden Project biodomes and microphone images in Sad Pelican. All other drawings and images are the work of L A Kent.

More DI Treloar Crime Thrillers

ROGUE FLAMINGO

Cornwall: set in Porthaven (Could it be Gorran Haven?)

Also in The Camargue in the south of France.

BROKEN DOVE

Cornwall: set in St Ives & Penzance.

Also in Amsterdam & London.

SILENT GULL

Cornwall: set in Fowey & Polruan.

Also in Brighton.

Lightning Source UK Ltd.
Milton Keynes UK
UKHW010629260821
389510UK00001B/146

9 780957 510975